Rhea Hawke: Galactic Enforcer

Outer Diverse

Splintered Universe Trilogy

By

Nina Munteanu

Starfire World Syndicate

Outer Diverse

Cover Design and Typography: Costi Gurgu
Interior Design: Nina Munteanu

Published in United States by:

Starfire World Syndicate
2132 Cherokee Pkwy
Suite 2
Louisville, 40204, KY, United States
www.thepassionatewriter.com

ISBN 978-0-9823783-3-5 Trade paperback (alk. paper)
ISBN 978-0-9823783-4-2 Digital

Library of Congress Control Number: 2011937045

Printed in the United States of America on acid-free paper

For Kevin

Acknowledgements

I consulted the wisdom and science of many authorities in the areas of space exploration and habitable zones, AI, biotechnology, sleep biology, neurobiology, and ecology. The most notable source was NASA. Any mistakes are mine, not theirs. My sincere gratitude goes to Clelie Rich for impeccable editing. I especially thank Craig and Vanessa for their inciteful comments on the manuscript and fun discussions on story, character, fractals, and multi-dimensional travel. I owe you six cappuccinos now, Vanessa? And Craig, we're up to a dinner and a case of your favorite? Thank you, Costi and Vali, for creating a cover that LIVES! Vali, you really are Rhea! Karen, as always, you have my heartfelt thanks for all matters relating to making dreams come true. I'm honored to be aboard.

Praise for *Outer Diverse*:

"Nina Munteanu is ... a master of metaphor ... a creator of fantastic worlds and cultures. She combines her biological background with the infinite possibilities of the cosmos and turns an adventure story into a wonderland of alien rabbit holes. When the action starts it goes into hyper-drive ... Rhea Hawke, is a fresh and multi-faceted heroine."
> — **Craig H. Bowlsby**, author of *Horth in Killing Reach* and creator of *Commander's Log*

"...A rollicking science fiction plot with all the trappings...Hawke is a maverick in the Wild West tradition, up against the world ... a genetic mystery with lethal powers."
> — **Lynda Williams**, author of the *Okal Rel Series*

Praise for Munteanu's previous works:

"*Angel of Chaos* is a gripping blend of big scientific ideas, cutthroat politics and complex yet sympathetic characters that will engage readers from its thrilling opening to its surprising and satisfying conclusion."
> — **Hayden Trenholm**, Aurora-winning author of *The Steele Chronicles*

Darwin's Paradox is "a thill ride that makes us think and tugs the heart."
> — **Robert J. Sawyer**, Hugo-Award authot of *Wake*

Angel's Promises is "a stunning example of good storytelling with an excellent setting and cast of characters."
> — **Tangent Online**

Collision with Paradise is" a very intelligent story, with fantastic world-building."
> — **Romantic Times**

"Munteanu asserts her mastery of the sensual SF romantic thriller. [*Collision with Paradise* is] an unforgettable read that's immensely alluring, surprising, and heart-throbbing."
> — **Yet Another Book Review**

"Whatever has black sounds has *duende*."

Manuel Torres

"Black sounds: behind which there abide, in tenderest intimacy, the volcanoes, the ants, the zephyrs, and the enormous night straining its waist against the Milky Way."

Frederico Garcia Lorca

I'm a human. Despite my human mother having tecked *me for baldie traits earlier than I can even remember, I still* look *human, still feel human ... most of the time ...*

The psychology books claim that by age five most of us are sufficiently formed emotionally, socially and cognitively to define our remaining lives from our experiences and actions. I defined mine with violence.

Perhaps I was born to it. I can't blame my mother, though I did for much of my life. She couldn't help being what she was anymore than I could help being what I was. I am my mother's daughter. Passion was our ruin. I do *blame the Vos. If that brutal alien race had not attacked Earth, the baldies wouldn't have come to save us, and I would not have stumbled one night in confused alarm, thick from a broken slumber, into my mother's bedroom and found her there in an unnatural coupling with one—and done the unthinkable. I would not have later enslaved myself on a career of killing for a baldie elite guard, executing criminals for them, while imagining a baldie face each time I pulled the trigger. I'm my mother's daughter; she gave away her body and I gave away my soul.*

The spiritual books claim that we are driven by our soul's yearning to be whole and cleansed of that deep wound—the original sin—we all carry inside us. Perhaps we are all no more than difference engines, fuelled by the desires and longings for redemption that steer us to the occasional and fatal collision of the heart.

I knew nothing of this when I was five—and killed an innocent man with my eyes; nor did I think of it today, as I was about to kill another ...

ONE

My heart pounded up my throat. I gazed past the long barrel of the Q-gun drilled into my face to V'mer's menacing grin. The shapeshifter bent over me like a vulture as I lay on my back in the mud. My chest heaved with pain and acid rain stung my eyes, forcing me to blink.

"Now whose fear do you smell, bitch?" V'mer snarled. He shoved the gun further up my nose. The sour smell of congealing blood cloyed in my nostrils. I gulped in sobbing breaths, tasting blood. V'mer sneered down at me out of yet another alien face he'd taken on. He'd assumed the giant form of a hairless purple-skinned Eosian. He'd literally torn out of his clothes. Rain sluiced down the smooth muscular flesh of his naked body, and his bald head shone in the amber street light. "I heard about you," he went on. "Rhea Hawke, the only human Galactic Enforcer. She loved baldies so much she *tecked* herself into one—"

I squirmed up in sudden rage, but he slammed his boot hard on my torn shoulder and laughed sharply. I seized in an agonized breath and let my head fall back. White spots strobed in front of my eyes.

"You're one to talk," I hissed out between wheezing breaths and fought against passing out.

"You mean the form I've taken on? I did it so you could feast on my magnificent body and use your baldie *tecks* to smell all of me." He barked out a stuttering laugh. "Wanna kiss me, Officer Hawke?" He went into a mock sing-song: "*Rhea, scare-ya, wouldn't you cry? She kissed the baldies and made them die ...*"

Alarm seized my heart. How did V'mer know about that malicious tease at the precinct?

V'mer let his laugh die down to a frown of concentration and stroked his face, mock-philosopher style. "Or is it more that you hate your own kind so much ...?"

My eyelids involuntarily fluttered shut, and I felt myself slide into darkness. How did it come to this? It was only minutes ago that I was the one in control ...

Θ

I found myself absently curling a lock of my hair around one finger and resting my leg on the console as Benny eased into a large circle of Del City. I peered down into the darkness and barely made out the AI city sprawled on a large island surrounded by a rough sea. The dark sea occupied 98 percent of this bleak water planet.

"Mar Delena's ocean is toxic with a pH of less than two," Benny informed me. My ship's voice was a calm tenor. I dropped my leg to lean forward and gazed down at the lights of the city. I made adjustments to the primary controls as Benny descended. Sheets of rain veiled the sentient city in shifting curtains of a shimmering skyscape. "That's because the sulphurous rain has a pH of three," Benny went on. "The caustic rain is a maintenance chore for the AIs that run the city's infrastructure. They're always repairing. That's why all the streets are just left as dirt. The dirt lets the acid rain percolate into the ground. Of course it makes for a muddy place, but the Delenians don't seem to mind."

"Wonderful," I muttered, gazing at the towering buildings, whose rounded roofs encouraged the corrosive rain to sheer off harmlessly to the ground. "Remind me to come here for my summer vacation ..."

Understanding my sarcasm for what it was, Benny

ignored my remark and nattered on, "The indigenous people have evolved thick hides of oily fur that protect them against the acid rain. They also have a digestive system that enables them to drink the water."

"Ugh!" I groaned. "Like a lemon juice cocktail."

"There it is, Rhea," Benny said.

"I see it." I peered out my portside window through the rain and recognized V'mer's small *scythe-wing* below. The ship resembled a bird of prey with a head-like cockpit flanked by crescent-shaped wings that flared out to the bow in a point. By analyzing its heat signature, Benny confirmed that the *scythe-wing* had only set down moments ago.

We'd just jacked the particle-wave stream thousands of light-years to this ancient dusty solar system. I chased V'mer here from a mining colony on Nexus, where the Badowin ran the largest illicit manufacture of Dust in the galaxy for Dark Sun— all cleverly under cover of a mining operation for Spice, a less dangerous narcotic. A little Dust showed you 'God'; but in larger quantities it threw you convulsing over the precipice straight to chaos. I'd pursued V'mer to the planet Nexus in the M103 star cluster on the Perseus Arm and shadowed him into a crowded bar that smelled like a cross between a garbage can and a distillery. He was too busy making a deal with another Badowin to notice me initially. But he managed to slip away when my own appearance caused a stir. He ducked out through a rear exit, and I sprinted after him, leaving a wake of confused relief behind me. He stole a Badowin *scythe-wing* and escaped with five kilos of Dust. The logical choice for him was to come here, to Del City, home of one of the largest Dust-addict populations this side of the galaxy. Originally built by the Badowins, Del City was run entirely by AIs with the help of a native slave population. The sentient city produced the best AI parts in the galaxy. Machines making more machines and quietly doing business with yet other machines.

"I'll take us in." I took the controls and aggressively swung the ship for a swift landing. Benny was perfectly capable of doing it, but I enjoyed the thrill of landing and taking off too much.

As the ship touched down, I congratulated myself. Yet again, I'd anticipated V'mer's move. He'd be unloading his Dust on these poor addicts for a choice payment. Dust was in great demand; the galaxy's most dangerous and addictive but most euphoric narcotic on the slipstream market. Fortunately, it was rare, not easily produced, and very expensive, as a result. The payment V'mer would receive for this load alone would fuel his ship for a whole year. And keep a whole community in euphoric intoxication for a month. That wasn't his concern. It wasn't mine either: *he* was. Taking him in was my prime directive. V'mer was a member of the largest crime syndicate, Eclipse, and guilty of murder and major Dust smuggling. It was his dubious connection with the Uma 1 massacre and the Vos, the hostile alien race that had almost destroyed my own planet, which made him valuable to the Guardians just now. And had me chasing him through the galaxy to bring him back for interrogation.

Which brought me here, to this gloomy planet orbiting Fomalhaut, a bright isolated star below the galactic plane about twenty-five light-years from Earth.

The Badowin race originally came to Mar Delena looking for profit. They found a semi-intelligent furry species with six appendages and large orange eyes. They lured the Delenians with Dust and inducted them as slave labor to create the machine city. The Badowin then abandoned them to their fate. All Dust addicts by then, Delenians lived for illicit shipments from smuggling rangers like V'mer. Luckily for the Delenians, the sentient city needed them to help run its machine shops and therefore kept them housed and nourished and with sufficient currency to pay for their expensive habit. Otherwise, the city paid no mind to biological intelligence when it chanced to make its way here, which was mostly in the form of Dust smugglers.

And those who chased them, I thought with a faint smile as I shrugged into my Great Coat and pulled my hair out from under the collar. I hastened out of the cockpit, closing the coat with a press of my hand. I then opened the starboard hatch and hauled myself out of the *ray* class ship into the rain. As I climbed down the retractable ladder, the wind sent the rain sideways, lashing my hair across my face. A strong sulphur smell stung my nostrils. The whole planet stank like a swamp.

I leapt down lightly from the ladder and pulled away the curls of wet hair plastered to my face then hastily tied it back with an elastic I'd fished out of my Great Coat pocket. I commanded Benny through my internal mouth com to lock down and scramble the *scythe-wing*'s signals, trapping V'mer's vehicle here. *You're not getting away from me this time.* I dug into another pocket for my soyka gum, threw a stick into my mouth and started chewing, as I picked my way through the litter. I slid occasionally over soaked discarded wrappers. The pungency of urine, cheap drug, and vomit cut through the sulfur odor: the typical smells of an AI city unconcerned with biological ergonomics and hygiene. And a community intoxicated with Dust.

Several barefoot Delenians in tattered rags appeared as if out of nowhere and swarmed me, begging for Dust. Even in their alien eyes, I recognized the telltale pigment glow that betrayed long-term users of Dust. Vermin. *I'm helping you …* Not that they'd see it that way. In fact, if they knew I was here to take away their Dust supplier, *I* might be the one in trouble—except for the fact that I was an Enforcer. They knew my ebony Great Coat concealed an arsenal of maiming and killing weapons. The Delenians rightly feared us; but they worshipped Dust.

I swiped at them like flies and glared at them. Hardly worth saving, I thought. They scattered but continued to follow me as I walked briskly toward the dark city streets.

A particularly intense-eyed youth lunged forward and snagged the hem of my calf-length Great Coat with four groping hands. "Are you a Guardian?"

I snatched the coat out of his multiple hands and strode on, ignoring him.

"Save us!" cried another. "Give us Dust!"

Head right, Benny instructed through my com implant. *V'mer's signature is still warm. You can't be more than a hundred meters away. He's heading for the seedy part of town.*

"Like this isn't?" I murmured, rolling the gum in my mouth with my tongue. I jogged into a narrow dirt street and left the murmuring Delenians behind. I turned a corner and halted, drawing in my breath. My quarry stood barely twenty meters ahead, watching me with a smirk, as if waiting for me. He was still in the hunched form of a Badowin miner. The miner's dull yellow overalls were plastered against his hairy skin. I snatched the MEC holstered to my thigh and aimed in a two-handed grip, but V'mer dashed around another corner.

I pelted after him.

I halted again at yet another junction and realized I'd lost him as quickly as I'd found him. I could only hear my own racing breaths and the hissing of the rain.

I threw impatient glances left and right and tongued my com: "Where, Benny?"

I'm sorry. I can't detect a clear signature anymore.

Damn the creon! He'd probably changed form again. I re-evaluated my three choices and drew in a long inhale. The sharp odor of rotting garbage and old solvents cut the undercurrent of cheap smoke and unwashed bodies. Then I caught it: confusion and fear. My lips curled into a feral smile as I turned right, in the direction of the scent: it was a dead end. Even better. And it explained the rancid spike I'd inhaled. A dim street light cast my lurching shadow ahead of me as I ditched silence for speed and pounded down the dark alley.

I'd been tailing V'mer for close to a month. But even considering my unique intuitive abilities to detect shapeshifting Borrs, I'd begun to feel that he was playing with me, baiting me: every time I closed in, he eluded me, but never managed to get so far that I couldn't sniff him out again. This time I finally had him, though. He was caught in a dead-end alley on a forgotten planet in the wasteland of the outer galactic North Pole. Changing shape wasn't going to do him any good this time.

"I've got you, creon," I whispered smugly, slowing to a walk and raising my MEC pistol. The sour odor of garbage and waste-chemicals grew overpowering. The alley opened to a small courtyard with no other exit. I spotted the Borr after a quick scan: a very tall naked shape scrambling along the top of the garbage piles that crept up the edge of the courtyard. Damn! He'd shifted into an Eosian.

When he saw me, V'mer halted and stood up to full height, splendidly and completely naked, except for his boots. With the exception of Ennos, my boss, who sat behind a desk all day, most Eosians were extremely fit with bodies of corded muscle. V'mer stood in defiant challenge at the far end of the courtyard, as if daring me to close the distance between us. I didn't have to: my MEC would do the job. I had set it to knock out the sturdiest Borr. If I was lucky, he'd tumble to the ground and I wouldn't have to haul him out of the garbage pile. I would have preferred to drag back a small Badowin than this large Eosian, though.

Snarling in a predatory smile, I blew out a bubble and popped it with my teeth. *"When you go up to the mountain often, you will eventually encounter the tiger* ... Chinese proverb," I said. "Where's the thorn on your rose now, V'mer?" I said with a sneer. Last month Bas in cryptology had passed me a decrypted message between two Eclipse agents. He wasn't supposed to, but I knew he was sweet on me, although I never let on. The message alluded to an elite assassin who was part of a group called the Nihilists and went simply by the code name of The Rose. My subsequent stealth work had since revealed a coded, as yet to-be-decrypted hit list that was specifically meant for The Rose. I was certain V'mer was The Rose. I stepped forward and took aim—

The ground gave way.

I yelped in shock and inhaled my gum. The MEC flew out of my hand with a clatter. I smashed my right shoulder against something sharp and plummeted through blackness until I hit bottom, left leg collapsing under me with a white flash of pain and a bone-wrenching crunch. I heard V'mer's laughter through a febrile daze and made out his black silhouette against the rainy sky above. Damn my hubris! I'd misinterpreted his spike of excitement—the smell of burnt toast—as I'd stepped forward and into his trap.

I sucked in shallow raw breaths, certain that I'd broken my leg and a few ribs. I had a good idea of what my shoulder, which pulsed with pain, looked like. I'd fallen into the waste crusher. The soft garbage and the shielding fabric of my Great Coat had saved me from a worse fate. Then again, I was trapped here, immobilized by my wounds. Would V'mer solicit the Delenians to turn on the crusher? It might have been better to have died quickly.

I heard the whirring of a motor and panicked. But the walls didn't move. Within moments a mechanical arm maneuvered down. It gruffly scooped me up and lifted me out of the garbage chute then dropped me painfully to the ground beside the gaping hole. Several Delenians crowded around to watch and murmured among themselves. Someone whispered "Guardian."

Before I had a chance to even think of moving, V'mer tore off my Great Coat with its arsenal of weapons. He discarded it behind him and laughed, swinging his slim Q-gun toward my face. Then, as if reading my mind, he stepped hard on my gun-hand, immobilizing it with a 'tsk tsk'.

I glanced longingly past the MEC to my Great Coat and felt naked. Millions of thixtropic nano-sensors incorporated into its durable yet flexible fabric let it respond to any number of internal and external stresses, providing me with a shield from the cold or from a weapon's discharge. But it had to be on me to work.

He sneered. "That coat saved your life. Just enough for me to kill you the way I want. Nice to have friends, eh?" He pointed to the mechanical arm with the long barrel of the gun and threw a cursory glance at the small crowd of Delenians. "But, then again, you wouldn't know about that, would you? Guardians don't have friends. Especially *you*. And why should you? You're such a pathetic human, Hawke. Living a lie. Keeping secrets. Bad secrets." He drilled the cold muzzle of the Q-gun into my nostril, tearing skin. It made my eyes water.

I wheezed out sobbing breaths, realizing that everything

14

V'mer said disturbed me viscerally. It resonated with personal hatred and made my heart pound with unreasonable fear. I'd only met him once, briefly on the *Ulysses*, then caught glimpses of him during the course of my pursuit. Why had he taken such a macabre interest in my life?

What did it matter? I was headed for chaos. My MEC lay in the dirt, beyond my reach. The pistol hidden in my boot was equally unreachable and the hidden weapon embedded in my arm was immobilized beneath the crushing weight of his foot. I was supposed to bring him in alive anyway — not kill him. As for my ultimate weapon of insanity — that's exactly what I'd have to be to use it on him.

The metalloid muzzle of his Q-gun tore into the soft flesh of my nose, trigger poised to turn my face to mush. As I fought to stay conscious, I wondered why V'mer hadn't killed me already.

Ө

"I know!" V'mer barked with sudden macabre inspiration, pulling the Q-gun from my nostril and stroking my cheek with its barrel like a cruel lover's hand. "It's *you* you hate!" He cackled with laughter and heaved a solid kick into my ribs. I cried out and saw stars, unable to move.

He dropped the Q-gun and scooped up my MEC then squatted gleefully down beside me, keeping my arms pinned.

"Ah, the MEC." He ran the thick gun barrel through my wet hair and leaned closer. "Operates like a sophisticated Q-gun."

He couldn't have been more wrong. The Magnetic-Electro Concussion pistol was the best—and worst—thing I'd ever made. The image of Officer Asphalios's face melting in front of me came back to haunt me. Out of hubristic genius, I'd tailored the MEC to behave uniquely by species, based on their DNA structure. I could sweep my MEC in a crowded room and melt all the shapeshifters, only knock out Eosians and leave humans totally unscathed. But Asphalios hadn't been what I'd thought

15

he was. He wasn't what *anyone* thought he was. And I was still paying for that.

"The specs on the info-pod you gave T'lem were wrong," V'mer went on. "I know this weapon. What it can do. I saw evidence of your handiwork on Omicron 12. This weapon does everything you said it did—you just gave T'lem the wrong instructions. If that stray Q-shot hadn't killed him, T'lem would've been really ripped that you jagged him." V'mer deftly fingered the weapon's control network. "Let's see ..." He glanced from the MEC to my shivering face. "It's set to stun a shapeshifter. Well, let's change that to a Delenian." He played with the settings.

He aimed recklessly at one of the Delenians, and shot him. The young man promptly crumpled to the ground. Two friends scrambled to him, and he stirred with a soft moan but remained unconscious.

"He's alive!" one of the more lucid Delenians announced.

"Good," said V'mer. "I wouldn't want to kill a customer." He turned back to me with a nasty grin. "Of course, it's set to leave a human totally unscathed." The grin turned malevolent. I saw him change the setting on the MEC and knew what he'd done before he said it: "Let's set it to kill a human ..."

The smile curled into something vicious and he pressed the gun against my forehead. "Imagine," he said as a spike of sick pain surged up my gut, "getting killed by the weapon of your own design. Doomed by your own Doomsday device."

"If you kill me you won't ever get the design," I got out between panicked breaths.

"I don't need the design," he shot back, evil smile taking over his entire face. "I've got the MEC. So—"

"You're wrong!" I panted, straining my weapon-arm from underneath the weight of his knee. "You can't build another one by taking it apart. I built a failsafe mechanism into it. The MEC'll be incomplete and useless. The parts won't match the whole—"

"Well, I don't really give a jag," he drawled, lips curling with pure hatred. "Everybody wants your MEC to destroy some race. But I just want *you* dead. So ..."

Before I had a chance to inhale sharply and do the unthinkable, he pressed the trigger—

Nothing happened. My heart slammed as I barked out a hysterical laugh of relief. I'd only felt a brief vibration. I was still alive. Incomprehensibly.

V'mer flung the MEC away in anger.

"What the jag!" He spat out. "Of course you made it so it would never kill a human."

I hadn't, although it was a very good idea.

"But I have something better," he said with new inspiration. "It'll make you happy," he continued cheerfully. "More happy than you've ever been in your pathetic Galactic Enforcer life. So happy you'll die from it."

He leaned over to pull out a soggy package stuffed into the soaked overalls that he'd discarded on the ground when he'd changed shape. Then he brandished a dispenser. Dust. I couldn't believe it. He was going to overdose me with Dust!

I gasped out a sharp laugh of disbelief. "You're going to waste it on … *me*?"

"It won't be a waste, Hawke," he said venomously, closing in on me. "I'm going to have a good time watching you convulse to death."

Why didn't he just shoot me with the Q-gun? He was being totally illogical! Wasting precious Dust in front of these Delenians, who desperately coveted it. I'd never tried Dust, but I'd read enough about it to know that I'd rather be shot in the face by a quintle particle gun than suffer the effects of Dust overdose. The dark energy quintle particles would resonate with my tissue and mush my face into nothing. But it was fast and it beat the torture of Dust. In quantities meant for commercial use, the potent drug acted as a nerve stimulant and created a state of euphoria, inducing the release of chemicals that resembled those produced during orgasm—dopamine, endorphins, oxytocin. Side-effects—excess salivation; a runny or bleeding nose; with prolonged use leading to eventual blindness—seemed worthwhile to its clients, mostly Gnostics looking to experience God first hand. I would bypass all that. An overdose would send me screaming over the edge, hemorrhaging in painful death spasms.

V'mer applied the dispenser to the container of Dust, then turned to me. "What good did it do to *teck* yourself, eh? None of those baldie skills can help you now, Hawke." Dispenser full, he squatted over me. I shivered from more than the cold. "Like the ability to smell emotions." He sneered. "By the time I'm done with you, you'll be able to smell your own death wish."

He leaned closer. "So this is what fear smells like, eh?" He inhaled deeply, savoring it, as if for the first time. I knew better. His confidence and stature told me that he'd shaped as an Eosian often enough; he'd said that purely for my benefit. Not only could I distinguish a shapeshifter from the original article, but I could tell by the smell if a shifter had worn a form long enough to become comfortable in it. It wasn't often that I'd encountered a shifter who was. V'mer came awfully close. If he had shifted as an Eosian rather than a Xhix on the space station, I might not have smelled him out.

"Fear smells a little sour, doesn't it?" He stood up. "At least *yours* does!" he cackled menacingly, stepping firmly down on my hand. "Can you smell my amusement?" He barked out a startled, titillated laugh and straightened to glance down at himself. "Chaos, what they say about these baldies is true, eh?" He was obviously referring to the Eosian's heightened libido. "I'm getting a hard-on just thinking about what's going to happen to you!"

I looked up from his erect penis to his leering face and sobbed, "Why are you doing this?"

He laughed malevolently. "Because you're the gate to my nightmares. You're a menace, Hawke. To yourself and to others. To all of us. You're a jagging disease."

God! He was insane. He didn't make any sense. I forced my screaming muscles to move.

Annoyed, V'mer kicked me. I grunted, sucking in my agony through burning lungs.

"That's better," he muttered. "Tasting your fear is so delicious. I can't wait to devour your death convulsions."

Shapeshifters had a peculiar vernacular, I thought with bizarre objectivity: everything exciting and thrilling, particularly if it was sexual in nature, was often related in metaphors of food and eating—

I felt a sharp prick as he drilled the dispenser against my thigh. Instantly, a surge of heat flamed out in all directions and my heart raced. A tingling numbness rippled through me, then lanced me like a million razor blades. My vision exploded into sharp focus, colors brightened, and images fluoresced into garish contrast: the first step to Dust blindness. Oh, God! I had a few minutes left before I went into convulsions and lost my ability to breathe or fell comatose and bled to death as my systems spasmed offline one by one.

Then, as if he was handing a dead person a chance to live, V'mer stepped off my hand and laughed like a mad man.

My arm was free! In a sudden adrenalin rush, saliva pouring into my mouth, I stretched out my arm, aimed, and fired my implanted explosive dart by digging my fingers into my palm. I barely noticed the smart of torn flesh. V'mer's eyes widened and gaped at the bloody tear in my arm through which the projectile had issued. He stumbled back and looked down at deep purple blood already weeping out of the hole in his chest. He lunged for his Q-gun and picked it up, shouting, "You little fucker—"

Something snapped inside me at his words and triggered a buried reflex, one I dreaded as much as dying. Rage flared up and lit me on fire. An insane energy blazed up and poured out of my eyes.

I saw V'mer's terrified face as he recognized his fate—an instant before I wiped his face right off with a melting stare. My mouth fell open, and I released an open-throated roar of anguished hatred, willing V'mer's flesh off him.

I might have shrilled out words of fury, I wasn't sure. I vaguely heard Benny, as if in the back of my mind: *You killed him, Rhea! STOP!*

I couldn't. It was as though something in my brain had snapped. I couldn't stop until there was nothing left of V'mer, except a steaming pile of bubbling flesh and viscera. Only then could I stop screaming.

I collapsed and felt the sudden urge to vomit. God! What had I done? I retched out my dinner in convulsive coughs. Oh, God! It was like the time before. What had I done? Oh, God! Oh—

The first violent spasm shook me, and I tasted salt as my nose, already running from the drug, began to bleed again. Dust was kicking in hard. My ears popped and I felt something wet trickle down my face. Blood. I was already hemorrhaging! I glimpsed the Delenians, scrambling around the discarded Dust and dispenser. Dust happily in hand, they turned their attention on me again. They didn't look friendly. In fact their hostile intention was obvious. I'd killed their Dust supplier, after all. Once he'd wasted a pile of it on me. Three of them courageously advanced on me, brandishing pieces of metalloid piping. They recognized my pathetic condition.

I crawled to my Great Coat, dragging my useless leg behind me until the excruciating pain in my chest knocked me flat to the ground. I craned and aggressively pushed out my face with a menacing grunt and glared at the advancing Delenians. They backed off momentarily. Then, seeing that no incandescent glow formed in my eyes, they crept forward again. Gasping for breath, I stretched out with a trembling hand to my Great Coat, just out of reach. In response to my forceful thought, the sentient coat jerked into my groping hand, and I shakily pulled it on. I instantly felt its attempts to help my body cope with the shocking onslaught of the drug overdose, pumping me with atropine, pralidoxine chloride, and benzodiazepines. Apart from stopping my nosebleed and letting me breathe a little more easily, nothing else changed: I still felt my body violently shutting down.

The Delenians backed off, recognizing the power of the Great Coat. They peered at me with dull curiosity as I retrieved my MEC and holstered it with a shaking hand. Knowing I was safe from them now, I concentrated on dragging myself down the alley. I had a few precious minutes to get back to Benny before the drug took me. It wouldn't be enough. After several attempts, I managed to tongue on my com.

"Benny!" I stuttered out between halting breaths. "I'm not going to make it!"

Hang on, Rhea! Benny responded in my ear. *Maybe I can get to you, if you could only get out of the alley. It's too narrow for me to get into.*

"I can't!" I sobbed. It was like asking me to fly. The Delenians mutely watched me drag myself, sucking in air that burned my lungs. Everything broke up like a pointillist painting. Then, in a flash, it all winked out to pitch dark. I scrambled by feel …

… A violent seizure sent me into agonizing pain … I felt a sudden warmth between my legs that I knew was blood … then my bladder and bowels emptied. *Oh, God! Not already!* … Ghoulish images struck me like hot coals … I smelled my own fear … It stank like a bog … Now scrabbling blindly, not sure what direction … Wheezing in painful breaths … Suddenly unable to breathe, throat squeezing shut … Heart seizing … Dizzy in a haze of … was it thunder …? Must be … I was lying face up with the rain pelting my face and a thunderous roar that sounded a little like mad laughter … then the darkness was taking me and I knew I was falling into a death coma …

TWO

I wake out of a febrile dream to catch the rancid smell of something disturbing and unfamiliar. A feverish ache that flares with the cloying smell of a sudden spike of pain. I do not question how I can smell the pain that is not mine, but I know it's real and that it belongs to my mother. This is confirmed as I hear my mother's plaintive wail—

I pelt to my mother's room and halt, stiff with fear. My mother lies naked with her face buried in the pillows of her bed, hands tied to the bed posts like a prisoner, and a naked baldie hunches over her. He gropes her buttock cheek with one hand, while holding a round device over her in the other hand, and rocks himself over her as she moans in pain then plaintively grunts out: "No, please!—Oh, YES—"

I scream, "Stop hurting my mom!"

Both my mother and the baldie turn abruptly to face me. My mother looks shocked. The baldie trades surprise for amusement and jeers, "You little fucker—"

I scream in terror and rage. What happens next is even more terrifying. A glowing energy flares up inside me. It concentrates behind my eyes into a seething flame and bursts through my eyes at the alien. He barely has a chance to utter a guttural cry before his body melts like putty.

I stare in shock at what I have done. I see the horror in my mother's eyes. Then she screams. This time the agony is unquestionable. They are the screams of one who has lost something precious—

Θ

I bolted awake with a scream. I snapped my eyes open and through a murky film saw that I was lying in a bed in a room that was unmistakably in Neon City's Med-Facility on Iota Hor-2. I'd been here a few times already to repair wounds I'd received from previous missions. My precinct was located in Neon City. So was home. If one could call it that. Iota Hor-2 was the nearest thing I had to home, since I'd left Earth as a kid to wander the galaxy with my itinerant mother.

The sheets and my nightgown were soaked, and I was tacky with sweat. I pulled my arm from beneath the covers to pull the wet hair out of my eyes, and tried to focus; I couldn't and realized that my hand was trembling. I breathed deeply and curled into a ball. My whole body began to shake violently and I felt my breaths grow shallow and uneven.

I hadn't had that nightmare for a while and wondered if it would haunt me again like it did when I was a child. I'd managed as a teenager to lock away those horrific events of when, at age five, I murdered a man with my eyes. But my recent act of rage on Mar Delena must have nudged it all back.

It was many years later that I came to fully recognize what I'd sensed through my newly *tecked* powers and then witnessed with my eyes: my mother had a particular penchant for bondage and sodomy. And alien men; baldies especially. It had been an excruciatingly pleasurable pain that my mother had been experiencing, which I had sensed through my sleep. So strong that it woke me up. The poor baldie I'd killed with my eyes had only been obediently serving my mother's perverse sexual wishes. His sexual prowess had been his undoing. Had he not been so successful in arousing my mother, I might not have been jolted awake and acted out my tragic misunderstanding. I'd thought I was saving my mother; instead I'd killed an innocent man.

As if it were yesterday the vision remained irrevocably clear: my mother's smooth alabaster body, writhing in tortured ecstasy as her purple-skinned lover moved in synchrony over her. Then the horror on my mother's face as I killed the man I thought was hurting her.

The room began to spin relentlessly out of focus and made me feel ill. I ducked back under the covers and clamped my eyes shut. Disturbing memories persisted, demanding my attention:

We stole off the planet in the middle of the night, leaving a wet slimy puddle where my mother's lover had once been. We took the first off-planet transport available. It didn't matter where it went. My mother never talked of the incident with me, except that one time when we stole into the night and left Earth forever. Once safely aboard the transport my mother hastily explained that she'd had me *tecked* when I was only three and it had just then come into force when I was physiologically ready. But my powers were obviously too strong and uncontrolled, my mother explained as we'd settled in our cramped berth aboard the galaxy transport.

I remembered how my mother had knelt down to face me and had taken me by the shoulders. She'd gazed at me with fearful eyes and commanded me to exercise self-restraint. Which was terribly ironic—though I wasn't old enough at the time to recognize the irony—considering that my mother was the last person in the galaxy to recognize self-restraint. We drifted from system to system, running away from too many questions. Eventually my mother fell back into her old habit of sleeping with every Eosian she ran across. I fled at thirteen and never saw my mother again.

My teeth were chattering and I moaned out my misery—

Someone touched my shoulder and I flinched.

"It's okay, Officer Hawke," a soft female voice assured me. "It's natural to have the shakes after a Dust overdose. You just had another Dust dream."

Nightmare, she meant. I pulled down the covers from my face and blinked up at the swimming image of a matronly Med-attendant standing beside the bed.

"You're just releasing the Dust toxins," she said kindly. "You've been in a drug-induced coma for ten days. We had you in a healing-tank for your ribs, shoulder, and leg. They're pretty well healed but they'll be tender for a while yet. You'll be fine in a few days. Now that you're out of the coma, I'm afraid you'll have Dust dreams for a while, but they'll fade eventually. The nausea and dizziness will go very soon too, followed by loss of the shakes."

"I can't … see," I stuttered through chattering teeth.

"Dust blindness. Not permanent, according to the doctor," she comforted, patting me on my shoulder. "He told me that your vision will return to normal in a few days. You're a very fit and resilient young woman, Officer Hawke. You heal like a Scandi. Your body is doing a great job, sweating it all out."

"Thanks," I said, feeling somewhat comforted.

Θ

I drenched the sheets nightly, shivering in fitful nightmare-ridden sleeps that promised the return of the same déjà vu nightmare that used to plague me as a teenager … it always began as a wet dream: a delirious encounter with a strange yet familiar man who smelled of a deciduous forest. I would be staring out at the Kitsilano coastline from my tower apartment window before lying in bed. Then he came to me, magnificently naked and muscular with his face in shadow, long hands caressing me with reverence, gently removing my nightgown. We made tender love. Then, as many dreams did, my lover disappeared and I found myself alone, dressed in a flowing gown, wandering a familiar hallway. I knew that when I turned the corner into the art studio — *my* art studio — a different man who smelled quite similar but uniquely different, would rush me with a knife. Violently slashing out, he maneuvered me to the open window — I always bolted awake, drenched in sweat, before he had a chance to do more. It always felt so real, but I knew it was all a dream — the Vancouver of my youth no longer existed; the Eosians had altered my world.

Θ

As the nurse had assured me, I recovered quickly. In two days, the shakes had dissipated to sporadic trembles, which could remain with me indefinitely, according to the doctor. He'd solemnly informed me on the afternoon of the second day that the trembles could disappear completely within a month or stay with me exactly as they were for the rest of my life. He had no way of telling how my body would react to the Dust onslaught. Because Dust affected receptors in several parts of the brain and operated on both the central and peripheral nervous systems, no nano-treatment or neuro-surgery was capable of completely eradicating its effects. It was next to impossible to find, let alone tell the difference between nerve or receptor damage that would repair itself and that which was irreparable. Only time would tell if the AI-meds had caught everything and my body healed itself completely.

Spooked, I fished for my clothes in the dresser as soon as I had a chance and flung them on. As I pulled my clothes out of the dresser drawer, I caught my face in the small mirror and briskly raked back my chaotic hair, tucking it behind my ears. My gaze settled on my eyes. They blazed like emeralds on fire;

Dust pigment. Dust had intensified my dull hazel eyes to an electrifying intensity. I was lucky I still had my eyesight, I decided with a shiver. As I dressed, disconcerting thoughts of what spastic trembles would do to my Enforcer position plagued me. Did it mean a desk job? Was my career over? Chaos, maybe that was a moot point. I was already in trouble for frying V'mer instead of bringing him in. It was just the tail end of a series of bad hits that Ennos would, no doubt, point out.

Letting out a long exhale, I found my Great Coat and took a deep inhale of its sentient fabric. As I smoothed it out reverently, I felt a warm glow of comfort. This was all I had in the world. And Benny, my ship. Finding my utility belt and MEC in the folds of the coat, I pulled the belt on and tucked my MEC in its holster, then shrugged into the coat. I checked the coat for my Enforcer badge and hidden weapons, then, finding my package of soyka gum, fished out a piece and popped it into my mouth, chewing languidly and turning the gum in my mouth with my tongue. I closed my eyes and breathed in its fresh narcotic then strode out of the med-facility, eager to leave the antiseptic smells behind me.

A warm blast of fragrant air hit my face as I entered the afternoon din of Neon City's surging crowd. Before plunging into the crowd, I took in a deep breath. Iota Hor-2 smelled like Earth. I inhaled the sweet aroma of gadpie and chokecherry flowers and glowed in the comforting warmth that bathed my face from Iota Horologii's brilliance. I glanced up at the orange-streaked face of Iota Hor b, the ringed giant that occupied a large part of the azure sky. It dominated Neon City's sky as it orbited the yellow-orange main sequence dwarf star, Iota Horologii.

Neon City was built on the planet's Earth-sized and tidally influenced moon, which the Eosians had bio-geo-engineered to resemble Earth. With a wildly eccentric orbit around the gas giant and seasonal swings from Siberian winters to tropical summers, the moon had initially been less than hospitable to all but the most hardy microbes. Once the Eosians were finished with it, Iota Hor-2 looked and smelled like Earth, right down to the seeded plants and animals and its twenty-four-hour diurnal cycle. A perfect place for all of Earth's displaced humans, looking for new homes.

I shouldered my way through the milling crowd of humans and aliens from as far as Cygnus Arm. Seeing my Enforcer Great Coat, they gave me a wide berth and I effortlessly sailed through with arrogant steps.

Neon City supported the largest single population of humans in the galaxy. For the very reason that the Eosians had intended: to provide them with a new home resembling the one they'd left. In the meantime, the baldies had transformed my home planet into a lush jungle. I'd heard that they'd introduced their own trees, the *vishna* that supposedly made them immortal, and had coaxed Earth to revert to what it had been prior to the agricultural revolution thousands of Sol years ago. The Eosians had made Earth their home, living a symbiotic-organic life through their superior bio-technology. Why they'd gone to such trouble to rehabilitate my largely urbanized and polluted former home, I couldn't fathom. Especially considering their bio-technical abilities. They could have chosen any number of more pristine planets and customized them, like they'd done with this moon. Of course, I knew why: the baldies had nostalgically claimed Earth as their ancient homeland and had felt no regret in displacing humanity to remake their home.

I stiffly climbed the stairs of the Galaxy Guardian's Iota Horologii Precinct, gazing up at the huge solid doors of the towering building, and took in a deep breath.

Θ

I entered the Great Hall of the precinct with brash steps. I looked the picture of haughty confidence. No one could tell I was sweating nervously under my Great Coat as it billowed out behind me like the sails of a ship. I'd always kept to myself, which had earned me a reputation as a loner, and although most of the Guardians—all baldies—normally avoided me, I noticed them giving me more room than usual today. Even the concierge was unusually curt with me. News of the incident had obviously preceded me.

"Cold bitch," I overheard someone mutter in the shadows, and knew it had been directed at me. I'd been called worse. Today I felt like one, though, as baldie eyes flamed into me with contempt or fear. I was sure everyone knew what I'd done. I rounded a corner and there they were: my nemesis and his thugs loitered in the hallway. Eight or so Guardians, a fair bit older than me, leaned casually against the wall like greasers looking for action.

"Look what the tappin dragged in!" Euaimon drawled as I walked past, trying to ignore them. "Laura's brat is back!"

Euaimon had been one in a long string of my mother's lovers.

"Lucky for the kid, her creon of a ship rescued her—*again!*"

My lips tightened, hearing the barrage of laughter. I didn't bother to acknowledge Euaimon by turning my head, but I blew out a casual bubble with my gum then brought it back lazily into my mouth.

"You two belong together, Hawke!" Euaimon jeered. "You jag up and that hunk of junk saves your sorry blenoid ass!"

I passed the mob and tried to hasten my steps without making it obvious.

"You're nothing like your mother, Hawke," Euaimon ended contemptuously.

Euaimon was one of the older baldies who'd strongly protested my becoming a Guardian Enforcer. I suspected that he hated humans at least as much as I hated baldies. Except for my mother, that is. It seemed that *everyone* loved *her*.

"Watch out, guys," Euaimon went on, "There's only one kind of Eosian that Hawke loves and that's a dead one."

I winced at the reference to my tragic mistake last month and nearly swallowed my gum. I almost broke my stride and forced myself to continue. Then stiffened at the distorted nursery-rhyme I thought I heard sung in the crowd, the same one V'mer had mocked me with: *Rhea, scare ya, wouldn't you cry…? She kissed the baldies and made them die …*

I thought I'd heard the last of that churlish taunt. Euaimon confirmed that I'd heard right; he called out in a jeering voice, *"But now she'll melt you with her eye! ...* Well, now you're the one who's going to fry, Hawke. You've gone too far this time!"

I picked up my pace and didn't care if they noticed. When I rounded a corner I sighed. The Eosians were purported to be a gentle pacifist species. For thousands of years they'd pursued an isolated life style of incredible self-restraint on the jungle planet of Eos in the Pleiades, living like naked savages in symbiosis with nature. It was a simple existence where no violence had been recorded for millennia. I saw little evidence of that gentle, wise, and self-restrained spirit in these Guardians. I found most of them narrow-minded, arrogant and derisive, making lusty demands to fulfill their licentious and greedy appetites. If they'd ever been the peace-loving nation I'd read about, I wondered at the price they'd since paid to join the galaxy —

"Hey, Hawkeye! Wait up!"

I slowed down. I didn't feel like talking to anyone right now but Basileus was one of the few friendly Eosians in the precinct. Maybe the only one. He was also the only Eosian I knew who sported hair on his head, which made him an oddity. Something I could identify with. He'd gotten himself *tecked* for hair and I had to admit I liked it, even though I wondered why he'd done it. Basileus would have been a very attractive man from his features alone. But the wavy brown hair that fell to his shoulders balanced his chiseled masculine features with a unique softness that was more than pleasant.

He filed in beside me, a full head taller than I was. I was tall for a human female at just six feet, but Eosians were giants. In fact, humans were generally considered small beings in the galaxy.

"You look like shit," he said cheerfully.

"Thanks." I threw him a withering look. "With compliments like that who needs an insult."

"It wasn't meant as a compliment." Basileus chuckled softly.

I blew out a breath of exasperation. "Listen, Bas," I bit out,

"I don't have time for any of your jag today."

He looked slightly hurt, liquid eyes shining like dark pools in a forest. "Hey, I'm on your side, Hawkeye—"

"I told you not to call me that," I snapped and picked up my pace, hoping he'd take the hint and fall behind.

"Come on, Hawke," he said, stubbornly keeping up with me. "Everyone needs a friend. Even you."

"Well, I'll be sure to look for one when I have a moment," I retorted. "But I don't see any around just now."

"You wouldn't know a friend if you stepped on him," he shot back, stunning me into jerking my head round to stare at him. He looked suddenly conciliatory, as if he wished he could take it back. "Look, we're off to a bad start again." He looked awkward. "I just wanted to say that ... eh ... I'm sorry about what happened, Rhea. I had no idea ... about ... eh ... well ... that you ... eh ..." His voice trailed off.

He was obviously uncomfortable with my newly discovered ability and what I'd done. Who wouldn't be? But I wasn't in the mood to talk about it with anyone. Especially a baldie. And despite his *tecked* hair, Basileus was definitely still a baldie.

"Well, yeah ... *that*," I said with a sarcastic smile. The unspeakable. "*The afternoon knows what the morning never suspected*: old Swedish proverb. See you around, Bas."

He nodded, looking deflated. "Sure. Good luck with the old man," he added, falling back to leave me alone. "He's mad as chaos."

As if that was news. "Thanks for the heads up," I said over my shoulder. I threw the gum into a dispenser and picked up my pace. My chest tightened as I drew near to Ennos's office. I halted at the door and took in a long breath, raking back my hair in a feeble attempt to look more presentable. I knocked.

"Come!" His basso voice rumbled, like a coming storm.

I exhaled, straightened my Great Coat, and opened the door.

THREE

"You know, Hawke, I sometimes think you belong to another world," Ennos said in a calm voice that simmered with anger. "You haven't a clue how this one works."

I met my Eosian boss's stern gaze with a pained expression. I'd often thought that myself.

"What in chaos happened?" Ennos growled from behind his large gadpie desk at me, seated in front of him. "What in the Sacred Universe were you thinking?" His eyes were dark with fury as he leaned forward, huge hands flat on the desk. I couldn't hold his gaze. My eyes kept flickering from his face to the desk. "I want to know, Hawke," he railed on. "*What were you thinking?*"

"I wasn't, sir," I said glumly, studying the floor now.

"Damn right!" he shouted, commanding me to look up. He pointed a sausage-thick finger at my face. "You weren't. You just killed our prime suspect."

"What'd you expect me to do?" Frustrated anger flushed into my face as I gripped the chair's arm rests. "Take his hand and ask him to surrender nicely? He's a member of the deadliest crime syndicate, one of their top assassins, and directly responsible for one of the worst massacres in the galaxy—"

"You're one to talk about massacres, Hawke!" I winced at his reference to my tragic blunder almost a year ago. Surely he understood the difference between the unprovoked slaughter of innocent people and my execution of murdering terrorists. "I asked you to bring him back, not put him in a coffin!" he railed.

I felt a spike of defensive anger tug my chest tight. "He Dusted me and would have splattered me all over the alley if I hadn't—"

"You melted him, Hawke!" he bit out. "There was nothing left of him when you were finished. Chaos, why didn't you tell me you were *tecked* with that illegal trait?"

"It wasn't illegal when my mother had me *tecked*," I said

in a strangled voice and tucked my legs under my chair. My mother wouldn't have given me a *teck* trait that was illegal.

He rubbed his bald head and frowned. "Well, it's illegal now, and both your mother and the doctor who *tecked* you ought to have had their heads examined."

I had to agree with him. I never understood why my mother had selected that particular trait. The best I could come up with was that she wanted me to be able to fend for myself. My mother had obviously anticipated that I would be alone quite young; perhaps she'd even planned it.

"Blessed Epoptes, why didn't you tell me you had it?"

I stuttered, "I—eh—forgot about it." My face heated. Thanks to my other baldie *teck* I could smell his rising anger and cringed at what he was inhaling of my thoughts. "I've always kept it in check—but something just happened—"

"Don't give me that blenoid-shit, girl. You *chose* to use it. You enjoyed disintegrating him into mush." Ennos stabbed at me with his stubby finger. "Didn't you?" I avoided his glare. I wasn't sure what I'd felt and swallowed several times to keep the anxiety that rose in my throat down. He raised a brow ridge where a brow should have been—except that Eosians didn't have brows; they had no hair at all. "We have witnesses, Hawke."

I dropped my gaze to examine the floor tiles but could still feel his sharp stare cut through me.

"Even in that remote sector, news gets out. Especially that kind of news. The city AIs gave Galaxy News excellent footage, Hawke. Guardians don't chase down criminals then kill them in cold blood by melting them with their eyes, shouting 'Die, freaking baldie!'"

The room fell into a long silence and I felt my insides churn. I had no idea I'd shouted actual words at V'mer when I'd melted him. I finally glanced up furtively to find Ennos leaning back with a deep scowl, thick arms folded over his barrel chest, and studying me with narrowed eyes. They were the color of the ocean during a storm.

"You're a menace, Hawke. To yourself and to others."

God! Those were the same words V'mer had used.

Ennos shook his bald head at me. "I ought to dismiss you with a dishonorable discharge for misusing a questionable *teck*." He let that sink in as I squirmed in silence. I'm not sure what expression I wore but it infuriated him: "Don't you think I can smell what you're thinking?" He leaned forward with his elbows on the desk. "Damn it! *I'm* a baldie!" He slammed his hand down.

I flinched. I used the derogatory term a lot, though never in an Eosian's presence ... until now, that is, when I'd shouted it to the world on Galaxy News.

"You seem to hate anything non-human. But you appear to reserve a special hatred for us, Hawke," he growled. "Maybe it's because we took your planet away from you. Or you're resentful that we saved you from the Vos. Makes you feel inferior." He studied me for a long moment. "You can't stand being in the same room with one of us. Universe knows why you joined up with the Guardians." He pushed his large face close to mine. "As for me, I only hired you because of ... well, as a favor to your mother ..."

He'd hesitated only briefly, obviously noticing my distress. Did my mother know *every* Eosian? And did they *all* owe her a favor? Ennos had been kind to me. Like a stern father. I owed him a great deal. He'd pulled me off the streets of Ogium 9, provided me with lodgings and regular schooling while I trained as an Enforcer. I swallowed hard, clutching the arms of my chair, but kept my face even, tacitly inviting him to continue.

"... Chaos, you're still the most intuitive Enforcer I have in the Guardians: the only one who can sniff out shapeshifters every time. That's why I put you on the Uma-1 massacre case in the first place," he rambled. "That's why I sent you in to infiltrate Eclipse and get on the *Ulysses* to find The Rose. It still amazes me how you do it, piecing together all the subtleties like vernacular, smell, body language. I've relied on it so many times—"

"It was my mother who got me *tecked*," I cut in. "Wasn't my idea. I don't even remember getting *tecked*. She had to tell me to explain, well ..." All my Eosian-like abilities. I shrugged.

"Chaos!" He pounded the desk with his fist, making me flinch again. "I don't give a quintle whose idea it was." He shook his head ruefully. "I must be the biggest jagging creon to have hired you. I don't know what I was thinking ..." He kept shaking his head and looked away for a moment, eyes focused on the past. "I thought I was doing us all a favor: your mother, who wanted you off the streets; a legitimate job for you instead of a jail term for illicit weapon sales and me ... well ..." He let it hang then turned back to me with blazing eyes. "I convinced myself that you would mellow out with age. Mature and settle down. Find yourself. But you haven't, Rhea." He tossed the info-pad down on the desk. "This last outburst shows me that."

I swallowed convulsively: I knew I was in trouble when he addressed me by my first name. Where was this leading? He appeared to be circling like a vulture around some topic.

Ennos expelled a long breath. "You're still an angry young woman. A dangerous one. We're here to protect the galaxy, not intimidate it. Your entire career with the Guardians has been dominated by bad choices. Heartless choices."

I thought him cruel to say that, but I knew he was thinking of Officer Asphalios's death. I thought it unfair of him to accuse me of cold-heartedness when I'd witnessed it in virtually all my Eosian colleagues, much of it directed at me. I knew it wasn't so much my lack of heart that he found fault with as my constant bungling. If only I'd done what I was supposed to do, he wouldn't have cared how many people I'd put away. Ennos had personally overseen my training in the arts of stealth tracking and dispatch. No, it wasn't my cruelty he rued; it was my ineptitude. I was an embarrassment to his precinct. Feeling cornered, I squared my shoulders and grew stiff with anger. "But I'm a g-good Enforcer," I stammered, not believing it as I said it. "I get the job done—"

"Too well," Ennos cut in. "I say monitor a native uprising on Omicron 12 and you exterminate a whole insurgent army singlehandedly with that genocidal weapon of yours."

Not even Ennos believed me about mistakenly setting my

MEC to kill instead of stun those Rills; my reputation for anti-alienism had preceded me. Despite repeatedly telling myself that they were just vulgar Rills and murdering terrorists, I suffered guilty nightmares of the incident and had secretly wondered why the Guardians hadn't thrown me into Sekmet for it. Finally, I'd rightfully come to the conclusion that the insane cruelty of the incident had not bothered Ennos, so long as I hadn't embarrassed him in front of the Legess with whom the Guardians had a relationship; Ennos didn't care about the Rills anymore than the rest of the Galaxy did.

"I say investigate the link of a criminal syndicate to a chain of killings," Ennos went on, "and you bring back a crazy wound-up tale of a Vos conspiracy and a dead Guardian." I inhaled sharply, wanting to interject, but he wouldn't let me. "I say find the main suspect and bring him in and you melt him and bring me his pieces instead. Now we'll never know if he was The Rose." If V'mer was their elite assassin, I thought, then at least I'd slowed them down; but I didn't dare voice my thought. Ennos waved his hands in exasperation. "How can one person be both my best and my worst operative at the same time?" He shook his head. "Do I have to remind you what you had to do to get that piece of information on V'mer? Was it worth it? We needed V'mer alive for questioning. You've set us back months, possibly years in the Uma-1 investigation and related hit list," he growled. "And too many people are dead."

Ennos seemed determined to bring up my entire litany of transgressions. I balled my hands at my sides and surged to my feet. "That's not fair! How many crimes and disasters have I prevented because of my intuition? It's saved a lot more lives than it cost ..." I trailed, noticing his changed stance.

He'd steepled his thick fingers against his mouth and stretched back in his chair, balancing it on two legs with his foot. His distended belly rose up like a little mountain. Ennos had replaced anger with thoughtfulness as though he'd just surrendered to a decision.

He waved me down. "Sit, sit," he said. As I did, he lifted one eyebrow ridge and studied me for a few moments. His lips puckered and he sucked in a whistling breath through his teeth. It was a habit I found annoying. And I didn't care for the way he was looking at me either. "How long have you been with us, Hawke?"

"Eight Galactic standard years." I didn't like where this was leading. "Two as a full Enforcer."

"It's no life for a pretty young girl like you. How old are you now? Twenty?"

I straightened in the chair and flung my head back, gazing briefly up at the ceiling and expelling a long breath. "Twenty-three," I said.

Ennos chose to ignore my frustration and went on. "With human life expectancy now at about 200 years, you're just beginning yours. You humans are popular in the galaxy right now. This is a dead-end job, Hawke. You've been injured a couple of times already. This last brush with Dust overdose might have taken you out. If it hadn't been for your ship, you'd be dead. You should be looking for a decent job and settle down. Get a family. You know the galaxy well, you're handy with mechanical tools and virtual materials, and you have a good investigative background. Galaxy News needs talented people. You'd make a great roving reporter."

I kept my expression dead calm but my heart was slamming. I gave him a long hard look. "Are you firing me?"

"No," he answered. A tremor of a self-conscious smile flickered on his purple face. He tried to look casual but his blue-gray eyes gave him away. "Just putting you on indefinite leave."

I felt suddenly giddy with dismay. This was the topic he'd been circling.

"I'm doing you a favor, Hawke. In your present condition, you'd have to take a desk job, and I don't think the precinct would take too kindly to that." So the doctor had spoken to him. And Ennos was right: they'd make it miserable for me. "It'll be your choice. Get your life in order, Hawke. Make amends with whatever is firing you up and settle it. When you do, you're welcome back."

I stood and leaned forward on the desk with both hands,

pushing my face up to his with imploring eyes. "You can't do this." I heard the shrill of panic creep into my voice. "It's my *life*. This is all I have—"

Ennos let the chair drop to all fours again and leaned forward on the desk with his elbows. He met my gaze dead-on. "That's my point." He leaned back again, dead calm. It scared me more than his anger. "Find a man, Rhea. Settle down. Visit your mother. When's the last time you saw her?"

I couldn't answer and glanced away.

"I thought so," he said. Then he added, almost tenderly, "She came to see you, you know. When you were in the med-tank." He braided his sausage fingers together and rested his clasped hands firmly on the table. Sure, my mother came to see me, along with all her old boyfriends in the precinct. "No one had to tell her," he went on even though I was trying not to listen. "She knew you were hurt—she always does."

I slammed my hand on the desk, immediately regretted my angry outburst, but found my voice: "I might have toasted our best lead, but you can't take me off the case now. I'm the one who flushed V'mer out in the first place when Asphalios and I intercepted that Eclipse hit list and I got V'mer's connection not only to the Uma-1 massacre—"

"He's not the only connection to those religious killings."

"But his direct connection to the Vos—"

"Still speculation, Hawke. *Your* speculation, to be more precise. I still can't buy it. The Borrs had their homeland destroyed by the Vos, for quintle's sake; why would the Borrs turn around and side with the Vos?"

We'd been down this path before. Perhaps the Borrs were intimidated, or just plain mercenary and the Vos had made them an offer they couldn't refuse. I remained convinced that the extra-galactic Vos were using Eclipse—which I'd learned was full of shapeshifting Borrs—to re-invade and had bought every shapeshifter they could get their hands on. I'd never trusted shapeshifters; they always seemed to be in disguise. And for sale. I was convinced that this latest rash of murders by Eclipse was related to the Vos. I continued, undeterred, "I know all his contacts, both in and out of Eclipse—"

He raised his great hands up in exasperation. "I can't afford you, Hawke. We're still handling the flack on this one. There's talk of Enforcers having too much power. The local planetary governments are angry enough as it is about previous transgressions, of which you've had more than your share. This stuff flares up every time someone like you does what you just did."

"But I'm still—"

"You don't get it, Hawke," he cut me off, smacking the table with his large hand. "I'm not just taking you off the case; I'm closing it. You're the only proponent of a Vos link and you keep killing your witnesses. We'll pursue the spiritual killings some other way, with other—less controversial—operatives, but we're not chasing some Vos-related fantasy. You're the only one who believes that the Vos have something to do with Eclipse's Uma-1 massacre and The Rose's hit list. There's nothing here to show me that the Vos have returned or intend to. It's over, Hawke." He snapped the dossier shut with a finality that made me flinch.

With that final move, he'd nullified my last two months of work: the countless hours of research; dogging subversives and terrorists across the galaxy to dark alleys and smoky back rooms of seedy bars on nameless planets; the needless sacrifices made by colleagues, not to mention my own blunders. With the case shut, Asphalios, even V'mer, had died for nothing.

"I went along with your crazy hunch," Ennos continued savagely. "Now I'm cutting it loose. This investigation is over. You've done enough damage. I want your gun, your badge, and your Great Coat. We've impounded Benny."

He was leading to this but it hit me like a MEC concussion wave anyway. I swallowed the saliva collecting in my mouth and kept swallowing down the ache that rose in my throat. A sudden tremble shook me. Tears stung the backs of my eyes and threatened to close my throat. He *was* firing me. Only, Ennos couldn't do it outright. He was too soft on me. Because of my mother. He was trying to ease me out by convincing me it was my idea. Mouth compressing to a thin line, I commanded myself not to cry in front of him; I'd never cried in front of anyone. But I couldn't say what I wanted to say or the dam would break and the tears would flow. I could only stare at him with the eyes of a wounded animal, pleading and glaring at the same time.

"Hand them over," Ennos said, taking advantage of my silence. He motioned to me impatiently with his hand, eyes shifting away.

I fumbled shakily for the sobek wallet that held my Enforcer badge and slammed it a little harder than I'd intended on the desk. Then I pulled out my slim *pocket* pistol from an inside fold of my Great Coat and placed it on the desk beside the badge.

"The MEC too," Ennos said. "You know the rules," he reminded me. "It's non-regulation. No civilian is permitted to have a non-regulation weapon or to carry anything higher than a Class D."

I sucked in a long breath then snapped open the holster on my thigh and surrendered my MEC alongside the *pocket*.

Ennos scowled at the gun. My weapon of senseless destruction, he'd called it. Yet he'd pleaded for the design earlier, then bullied me with threats of confiscation after I'd demonstrated the MEC's capability for devastation.

"Just so you know, sir," I said, hand resting on the weapon and eyes pinning his, "if anyone tries to design this MEC from its parts, they'll never succeed, because I rigged a failsafe mechanism based on an algorithm only I know. It'll be useless."

Then I slowly let go. Ennos's face remained stony cold but I thought I noticed it twitch and his eyes briefly falter.

"The coat," he said.

After another moment of hesitation, I shrugged out of my Great Coat, the Enforcer's real badge. My shield. I folded it carefully and slowly, stroking the smooth sentient fabric with trembling hands, then placed it on top of the badge and weapons. I stood rigid in my black sleeveless top and trousers, arms hanging stiff at my sides and fighting off shivers. I felt naked.

"That's all, Hawke," Ennos muttered. He avoided my eyes and waved a dismissive hand while finding some files to study. "Get your personal things in Stores. Take a holiday in the Rec-Center. Find your life again," he ended, not bothering to look up, and I knew I'd been dismissed. And fired.

Θ

Bundle of personals under my arm, I reached the main hall that led out of the precinct and saw a crowd of Eosian Guardians loitering by the door. Terrific. They were the regular crowd that gave me a hard time. The ones who didn't think I deserved to be a Guardian. The same ones who'd advised Ennos not to make me one. Some of them, perhaps all of them, had been my mother's lovers at one time. Euaimon led the pack, smiling like a man enjoying his dinner.

Without turning my head I glanced fleetingly at their leering faces, feeling vulnerable without my Great Coat. I set out to ignore them and kept my eyes on the exit as I passed. When I made it to the door, face heating with the knowledge of their eyes drilling into my back, they began to applaud.

"And stay out!" Euaimon's shrill voice followed me as I fled down the stairs.

FOUR

I listlessly waved my bare arm, exposing the IDR embedded in the underside of my lower arm, to unlock the door to my decrepit apartment in Neon City's eastside. The door slid open and I shuffled inside. Sensing my presence, the house lights spattered on, and the door shut itself behind me as I tripped over something. I did a wild dance to keep from falling and heard Jasper's ferocious meow of resentment.

"Well, it's your fault for getting in the way," I snarled at my tappin. "Why do you always do that?" I let the exasperation of the day enter my voice. "Dumb animal."

Jasper rubbed against my legs, purring loudly like a motor. The tappin resembled Earth's extinct cat in temperament if not in looks. Cats didn't have ferocious five-centimeter long incisors and three tails. "Come here, you big goof." I pulled him into my arms and squeezed. "You glad to see me?"

I dropped into a soft chair, stroking the tappin who was purring on my lap, and stared vacantly into space as my thoughts focused inward. *Find a man and settle down*, Ennos had suggested. Yeah. With who? Who'd want a bitch like me? I grabbed Jasper's face and buried my nose in his hair, inhaling the freshness of outdoors. Jasper smelled like the forest, organic and sweet, with the complex aromas of flowers and moss. He was a local stray who'd decided to adopt me as part of his harem. We had this arrangement: when I was home I fed him and he slept over; when I wasn't home he had lots of other places he went to keep warm, fed and safe. It worked well, considering my extensive and odd hours as an enforcer. Jasper started licking my nose with his raspy tongue, breathing out his familiar fishy smell. He always seemed to know when I needed affection. "You're it, Jazzy. You're my man. I don't mind sharing you with all your tappy girlfriends—"

My home-manager chimed: "Welcome home, Rhea. You have two messages," the AI said. "Would you like to see them?"

"Sure," I said, as I kicked off my gravity boots then slouched lazily back, cross-legged in the chair. No one ever called me. I half-expected, half-hoped, it was Ennos, rescinding his decision to let me go.

The first message holo flickered in front of me and I jerked upright—

V'mer's face sneered at me. "Yeah, it's me, bitch. And seems that you got away from me if you're watching this now. I might even be dead too. You're an Enforcer, after all. Did you kill me with your eyes? Yeah, I knew about them, bitch. So, let's say I'm dead. Yeah, that would be my destiny." He paused, eyes burning with hatred. "I might be dead but this isn't over yet. I can reach you from the dead. Because I'm not alone, unlike you. I have *family* ...And, by the way, you know, I'm not The Rose—I was code-named The Lily. The Rose is still alive and you'll find its lethal thorn soon enough, Hawke," he trailed menacingly. Then he gave me a chilling smile that sent me into a spasm of shivers.

I jolted as the message spontaneously destroyed itself.

V'mer's menacing image disappeared and the room went silent, except for my heart beating hard. Of course he'd rigged good evidence to self-destruct.

I knew he'd told the truth, recalling the pieces of a half-destroyed message Bas had secretly played for me a month ago: *"Lily failed ... The Rose is our best assassin ... to retrieve a message on Ulysses."* They'd brought in The Rose to finish off what V'mer had not completed. The question was, what had he failed to complete? I was sure the answer lay in the still encrypted hit list that Asphalios and I had intercepted. I shook my head and swore out loud. I felt my body shake as though a dead man was touching me. Ignoring the second message,

I hastily found a flight jacket, pulled on my boots and opened the door to leave the apartment.

"Would you like to see your second message?" my home-manager reminded me.

"No," I said. "Store it for later." I was in no mood for more bad news—the only kind of news I was getting lately.

As I dug my trembling hands into the jacket pockets, I wished that I still had my Great Coat.

I walked briskly through my neighborhood, bathed in the warm colors of a blushing evening sky. I forced V'mer, The Rose, and the Uma-1 case from my mind. I'd been fired, I reminded myself. I threw cursory glances at the decrepit sidewalks, the worn apartment facades, and the empty faces of the people, mostly non-human, in the streets. They brushed past me like I was no one of consequence. I was just another Neon City eastside urbanite now, indistinguishable from the hygiene technician next door or waste-disposal mechanic across the hall.

Θ

Night shadows crept in and kept me company as I wandered aimlessly. Iota Hor b glowed orange in the night sky, bathing Neon City with its warm light like a harvest moon. I stopped for a moment and let my gaze drift away from the luminescent planet toward the night sky. I could just make out the brightest Southern Hemisphere stars, Betelgeuse and Rigel, shining in the east and Achemar and Al Nair to the west. And high in the sky, Ankaa twinkled brightly. I felt the tug of their aching beauty and longed for a different set of constellations. The ones I'd grown up with.

My hands dove deep into the pockets of my flight jacket as I recalled the first time I'd seen the Milky Way on Earth. I remembered the night my mother had sat with me on Ambleside Beach and first pointed it out. She'd explained that it was a huge spiral galaxy of billions of stars about fourteen billion years old. Fascinated, I dreamed of travelling to the farthest arms of the Milky Way.

When I'd joined up as an Enforcer, the Guardians gave me my own starship, a rare *ray*-class retro Earth/alien design that no one else wanted. It didn't matter to me. Benny was *mine*. Thanks to Benny's plasma shields, we'd weathered treacherous ionic storms, gamma-ray bursts, and the high-velocity clouds of the breathing galaxy. We jacked the Magellanic Stream and travelled to the farthest arms of the spiral galaxy, surfing scalar fields into thrilling particle stream shortcuts. We'd even slingshot our way around the black hole in the galactic core using its immense gravitational field and high-energy emissions. I'd witnessed many galactic wonders like the terrifying beauty of nebulas: tangled filaments of dust and ionized gas that poured out in jets and waves from the stellar corpse of a neutron star. Pulsing electromagnetic energy, the shock wave of material flung from the supernova created a spectacular lightshow that shredded anything in its path, drawing me into breathless wonder ...

And now the adventure was over, I concluded and

dropped my gaze from the stars to the dimly lit street. I was grounded. Benny wasn't mine anymore. I was only twenty-three and I was already a has-been.

I found myself wandering into a public land-transport station. A car sidled up just then. I stepped into it and let it take me to the Hive, Neon City's posh residential section in the old refurbished industrial part of town. It was a retro-artsy section of the city where the trendies lived.

The car eventually stopped and let me out. I wandered the Hive, casting my gaze past the line of oak trees brought in from Earth, immaculately kept gardens and apartment buildings that still resembled the old factories from which they'd been converted. The fully equipped flats inside, however, were spacious multi-level residences. Many Hive dwellers were holo artists, vid-creators, and info-providers. And most were human. I could never afford to live in the Hive. A lot of the trendies who lived here couldn't either. But they did anyway.

I stopped in front of a local rec-facility and thought of my shakes. The walk had done me good, but the spasms remained. A workout might help, I convinced myself, mildly intrigued by what a facility in this part of town would provide. I was going to miss the gym at the precinct. I entered the trendy art-deco building and made my way to the front desk.

"I'd like to try the gym out," I said to a large Xhix hunched over the holo-vid that showed a Xhix woman stretching in a yoga pose. "Then maybe I'll join."

"No try outs. Gotta join." The Xhix sniffed, glancing up with just one of his wave-sensitive eyes, leaving the other five fixed on the holo. His skin was the color of mud and indicated a general contentment. I could smell it: honey and cinnamon.

"I'm not joining until I know I like it," I insisted, eying the rates posted above. "It's a major commitment of funds and time."

"Look, lady," he said brusquely, skin flaring into a ruddy color and now glaring impatiently at me with all six eyes. They shifted color even as I looked at him. "You can see the facilities from here. Choose. Join or leave."

I gazed past him inside the facility and saw a diverse setup that might challenge me sufficiently. It was nothing like the gym at the precinct. But I couldn't expect a community facility to be that well equipped, even if it was in the Hive. Several men and women about my age were using the weights, bars, and holo-chambers. It looked good. But I didn't like this alien's attitude. He was rude and unreasonable and grated on me.

Channeling my frustrated anger of the day, I leaned over the counter as if to share a secret, something the gossiping Xhix couldn't pass up, and drew him to mirror my action. He flared pink, eyes deepening to scarlet with curiosity, and leaned close. Within an instant I had his arm in a *vizion* vice grip. The alien yelped, turned blue, and emitted a sour smell. He caved into a heap under the pressure of my painful grip, all six eyes flickering in different directions.

"The Jewish have a proverb," I growled in his ear, hearing him whimper as my grip tightened. *"Don't open a shop unless you know how to smile.* Now, I need to check it out before I fork over five hundred credits to be a member. Do you understand? Just nod if you do."

He nodded.

"Good," I said, smiling tartly at him, then let him go.

He scrambled back, knocked down his chair, and flinched, spooked. "Go ahead, lady," he stammered. "Stay as long as you like."

"Thanks," I said, not looking back. I had already made my way in.

I noticed an attractive dark-haired human about my age ignoring me with such intensity I knew he was doing the opposite. I tried out some of the equipment and found myself studying him furtively as he worked on the weight machines. I let my eyes drift approvingly over his lean body, following the fluid movements of his glistening muscles, taut and straining in exertion. I noted intelligent eyes the color of a thunderstorm, a long slim nose, and perfectly shaped mouth, held in a kind of grimace as he pulled on the weights. Tousled steely brown hair and the stubble of a young beard suggested boyish abandon; but the arch of his dark brows and the set of his firm jaw suggested masterful control. Despite being dressed in casual gym shorts and a gray T-shirt, his features were decidedly aristocratic, and he wore his face like a French nobleman. He was probably as arrogant as one too, I decided, looking away.

Still, I found myself covertly glancing back and advancing close enough to inhale his emotions over the sweat; the enticing scent of strawberries and musk. His face was a paradox: powerfully composed features softened by a dark smear of day-old stubble and uncombed hair. He looked familiar somehow, stirring up a complex mixture of excitement, arousal and curiosity counterpoint with an undercurrent of dark dread. I was certain that I'd never met him—I'd have remembered that face, that body. And yet … why did I know that intoxicating smell and how delicious he would feel pressed up against me?

On my way out, I stopped to fill in the holo-work for a membership.

Ɵ

Fresh out of the shower, I ruffled my hands through my wet hair to help it dry, and stood in front of the bathroom mirror, enjoying the dryer's warm wind as I inspected myself. The workout had done me good. I was satisfied with how my body had performed. My lungs and ribs were fit; they could handle the cardiovascular exercise, and my right shoulder and left leg were only marginally stiff. The med-facility had healed me nicely, I reflected, turning to gaze over my shoulder at my reconstructed scapula in the mirror and rubbing the top of the synthplast with my hand. Except for a mild ache there was no physical sign of the dreadful wound, which had apparently exposed my bone. Nuyu treatments and synthplast surgery had taken care of that.

I twisted my body a little more, stretching my left leg forward, and ran my hand along the firm roundness of my buttocks to a five-centimeter long jagged scar on my lower left cheek. It had been the first major injury I'd received as an Enforcer. I'd gotten it from the slash of a dool blade in a skirmish with some Venik slave traders who'd ambushed me on EpsEri 2. It happened before nuyu had become routine in every part of the Galactic Order and before I'd learned how to handle my Great Coat. I hadn't since bothered to have the scar removed. Perhaps it reminded me of my chosen mission in life and the fine balance between dedication and consequence that I needed to walk daily as an Enforcer. I let my gaze drift to a set of puncture marks along my right thigh from a blenoid attack. Another souvenir. I'd been a Guardian Enforcer since I was fifteen. First as an Enforcer-in-training, then the last two years as a full Galactic Enforcer. It was the only thing I knew. I bowed my head and closed my eyes.

I took in several deep inhales and opened my eyes with a stretch of my neck to critically study my face. I wasn't a beauty. My face was dominated by strong features for a woman: a long, almost aquiline nose and a full mouth, framed by well defined cheek bones and a firm jaw. I did little to enhance my attractiveness. In fact I usually couldn't be bothered to do more than brush my dark hair, often tying it back in a loose utilitarian ponytail. When I finally met my own gaze full on, the challenge in my still bright hazel-green eyes forced my brows into a plaintive furrow and I set my lips into a tight purse. What was I going to do now?

I abruptly turned away, pulled on a short bathrobe, and shuffled barefoot out of the bathroom, hands ruffling through my hair to help it dry. Jasper rubbed against my bare leg, purring loudly. The tappin had obviously elected to stick around for a while. I bent down to stroke his fur. "You really did miss me, didn't you, Jaz? How many girlfriends are you standing up to spend some time with your old lady, huh?"

I wandered to the holo portrait of my father, Colonel Mark Hawke, and reached out with a trembling hand. He smiled back at me with the confidence of a hero who never expected to die and honest eyes that dared to prove him right. My father was a handsome man. He cut a dashing figure in his black uniform and short jet-black hair in air force brush-cut style. I had no memories of him. He'd been killed in the Vos invasion before I was even born. My mother was six months pregnant with me when a Vos shot my father down. He died just as the Eosians came to rescue Earth from annihilation. I let my trembling hand fall to my side.

Lucky for Earth, the reclusive Eosians, who'd sworn to protect the galaxy, had taken themselves out of self-imposed seclusion seventy years prior, to form the Galactic Guardians. At the time, the galaxy was a chaotic tapestry of disparate and bickering alien worlds. The baldies had initially created a loose alliance that served the purpose of achieving communication and ensuring fair trade while promoting order. Eosians found themselves excellent arbitrators in disputes, feuds, and misunderstandings and naturally fell into their current 'policing' role. Strange, I reflected, how a race of professed pacifists had formed one of the most disciplined military powers in the Galaxy. All in the name of justice and peace. Yet they often resorted to violence to keep it.

Many Eosians had left their home planet in the Pleiades, and intervened with their superior bio-technology. The Eosians eventually overpowered the Vos, who retreated out of the galaxy, leaving Earth mildly ravaged but intact. The Eosians' only condition in helping the humans was that Earth now belonged to them. They claimed that it had been their original homeland many thousands of years ago before their forced emigration to Eos. Several humans suggested that this had been the intention of the baldies all along, that they'd waited in the self-imposed bliss of ignorance for an opportunity to come to Earth and take over, accepting the cost of losing their peaceful nature—unleashing their arrogance and violent nature—to join the rest of the galaxy. Violence and war had been a hallmark of their ancient history, apparently the reason why they'd supposedly been evicted from ancient Earth in the first place.

The baldies soon made good on their contract and colonized the planet. In return, they provided humans with incredible bio-technology, such as *tecking*, and bio-technically superior sentient ships along with an inviting eviction package. Most humans took it and left to search the galaxy for a new home. The Eosians had mapped the entire galaxy and could provide human refugees with good places to start a new life. Many refuges came here, to Iota Hor-2, because it resembled Earth so much, thanks to the Eosians' clever bio-geo-engineering.

My mother was one of the few who'd remained behind, content to live in disgrace amidst this arrogant race. Drifting among them like a pet looking for love. How far she'd fallen from grace. Skidded down from being the wife of a genuine hero to a baldie's whore. My mother had her own version, of course: the Eosians had rescued her from a terrifying fate and she was forever grateful to them. Love, especially sexual love, was her only gift.

Like most humans, my mother had firmly believed that the Vos were the incarnation of Evil. The Vos weren't even from this galaxy. Neither were the Epoptes, the phantom 'gods' the Eosians supposedly consulted through their dreams in order to police the galaxy. According to the baldies, the Epoptes had commanded them a hundred years ago to end their reclusive existence to form the Galactic Guardians and to fight the Vos seventy years later. Luckily they did or Earth would have been destroyed and humanity rendered extinct.

Rumors of what the Vos looked like and the treacherous things they did to their victims were just that: rumors. No one had ever lived to tell. I was familiar with most of the rumors: depending on who you talked to, the Vos were anything from giant god-like humanoids to massive reptilian-like creatures with glowing red eyes or huge fluorescent blobs of amoebic protoplasm. They also ate their victims. Of course, the obvious question was: if no one had ever survived a Vos encounter, how could anyone possibly know this? Galaxy News spread as much fantasy as it did real news, I thought with a cynical and humorless smile.

Out of sudden macabre curiosity, I instructed the house to find the Galaxy News vid of my transgression on Mar Delena

49

and sat down to watch. It had aired while I was in the med-tank and—for better or worse—I'd missed it.

The holo of the Xhix newscaster appeared. "I have Jay Montana reporting on an incident in the northpole outer regions." The vid switched to Montana, a sallow-faced human with sandy hair, who faced the camera with a simpering smile.

"Thanks, Steve," Montana said in a nasal voice. "What I'm about to show you is one of the latest, perhaps the worst, acts of atrocity recently perpetrated by the Galaxy Guardians in the name of peace."

The holo shimmered into focus with a lurid scene of the rainy planet, and I abruptly shivered. The view looked past V'mer's naked back and caught me sprawled on the ground. Facing the camera, my mud-spattered and acid-burned face was plastered with tangles of wet hair. Blood streamed out of my nose.

"God," I whispered. I felt my stomach clench. "Is that what I looked like?"

The anguish in my eyes suddenly glowed with a reddish light, and I opened my mouth in a roar. Then an incandescent flash burst out of my eyes. It flamed V'mer, who melted into mush as I yelled those insane words.

I felt a sudden wave of nausea and fled to the bathroom where I lost my dinner in violent convulsions.

The holo vid continued as I recovered in the bathroom, and I heard Montana's recriminating whine: "This deadly woman, the Guardians' only human, had herself *tecked* with baldie traits, like super-smelling capability and this deadly melting power. Is she the prototype of a new super-Guardian? Are these self-appointed lawgivers using *tecks* to create a super-police to dispense their own version of justice? What will be next in their tyrannous plan to control our Galactic Order?"

I left the bathroom and shakily dropped into one of my plush chairs. I instructed the home manager to stop the vid. In the sudden silence, I felt my heart pulse. No wonder Ennos was upset with me. I'd driven a chink in the crumbling galactic safety net the Guardians had worked so hard to create. This new wave of cynicism against Guardian law and order played into the hands of Eclipse and the Vos plans for attack. Of course the media didn't understand. They didn't know what I knew.

Although V'mer had failed to kill me, he'd done the next best thing: ruined my life. I realized that V'mer was right. He was still calling the shots, even from the grave. By goading me to kill him with my eyes, V'mer had simultaneously removed the last known connection to the Vos conspiracy—*himself*—and succeeded in slandering the opinion of the only person who knew—*me*.

Ennos had played right into V'mer's ploy. He didn't understand the danger we were all in. He thought I was a creon, blowing *hedon*. By dismissing me and closing the case, he'd just condemned the galaxy to a Vos attack. Somehow, Eclipse's Uma-1 massacre and The Rose's hit list were connected to an impending Vos attack. And I appeared to be the only one who recognized it: an ex-Enforcer with no gun, no Great Coat, no ship, and no backup.

"Terrific," I muttered, pulling the tappin, who'd been rubbing against my leg, into my arms. "I've had worse odds, I suppose, but I can't remember when, Jaz."

FIVE

"Cube 9, Officer Hawke," the librarian said in a simpering voice.

"Thank you," I responded with cool authority.

Although I no longer had my badge, the librarian—who knew I was an Enforcer and who had no reason to think that had changed—permitted me access to the restricted holos, which included a fairly robust database of local PD files from most sectors of the Galaxy. These obscure files often held gems of information mostly overlooked by the Guardians who had little time to scour through millions of files. I, on the other hand, had lots of time.

Settling into a comfortable chair facing a data-retriever, I spent the entire morning researching and looking for any connections among the Schiss spiritual sect, shapeshifters, and the Vos. I found V'mer's prescience and his inordinate personal hatred for me—not to mention his creepy holo-message—particularly disturbing. I could never admit the thought to Ennos, but I had the distinct impression, illogical though it was, that V'mer had baited me not only to follow him to Mar Delena, but also to kill him with my eyes. He'd giddily taunted me, despite his knowledge of my melting *teck*. As though he'd wanted the world to know and didn't care if he was killed in the process. In his message, he'd predicted his own death, as though he'd planned it. Who were those others he'd mentioned? Colleagues in league with the Vos? Perhaps the Vos themselves? Had the Vos targeted me? That was unlikely; no one else knew about my accusation except Ennos, who didn't believe me anyway, and Bas. Not even V'mer knew that I'd made the connection between him and the Vos. V'mer had definitely exposed me and would have succeeded in killing me if it hadn't been for Benny. As for who The Rose was and who was next in line on his or her hit list, I had no idea.

If I could substantiate my intuition that V'mer along with a small enclave of the Eclipse—the Nihilists in the message that came with the encrypted hit list—were really working with the Vos in some insidious plan to subjugate the galaxy, Ennos would feel bound to reinstate me and re-open my case.

Overcoming my reluctance, I raked back the hair from my face with my fingers and reviewed the files on Eclipse. Feeling personally drawn back in to the dark nefarious world of shapeshifters and Eclipse—a world I'd have preferred not to enter again—I forced myself to read. And to think back to a month ago when I killed another innocent man …

Θ

A month ago…

"How do I know you're green about this, slave?" T'lem's multi-timbral chorus boomed and gurgled. I quelled the impulse to recoil under his hot putrid breath and found myself staring with revulsion at the mucus-colored saliva dripping from his several mouths. The shapeshifter had taken on the form of a Venik, a large reptilian race from the HD177830 system with indolent eyes gray as steel and six poison-clawed razor arms. I suspected that he'd chosen that form to intimidate me or at least unsettle me. T'lem tapped on the table between us with a claw, stroked my MEC that lay on the table with another, and played with the info-pod I'd placed on the table earlier with a third hand. A fourth hand was stuffing a barbecued blenoid leg into one of his slurping mouths. Seeing my interest, he said, "Go ahead, slave. These legs are the best. We get them fresh from Zeas Corporation straight from Upsilon 3."

I lifted my hand and shook my head with a smile. We sat at a corner table in the *Blitz Blazé*, a smoke-filled bar on *Ulysses*, the largest orbiting space station in the galaxy. This was my first visit aboard the 30-km^2 space station. I was admittedly impressed by the self-sufficient O'Neill-style agrarian colony. The station housed immense rotating cylinders with huge gimbaled mirrors and maintained a circular motion of 1 rpm to create artificial gravity. Built by the enterprising galactic corporation ZetaCorp Aeronautics and cleanly powered by ancient Atlantean crystal bio-technology that trapped spectral energy, *Ulysses* was hailed as a great scientific achievement. I knew better. ZetaCorp had served as a front for Eclipse for many years, and *Ulysses* was nothing more than a goon's luxury headquarters. Specifically, A'ler, one of Eclipse's highest in command. I knew very little about A'ler, except that she ran *Ulysses* and that she was very interested in my MEC. When Zec, my gangster 'friend,' offered to set me up to deal with one of A'ler's cronies aboard *Ulysses*, I couldn't say no. It was an ideal opportunity to investigate Eclipse's connection with the Uma-1 massacre.

The bar stank of cheap drug and the odor of intoxicated

aliens and their questionable secretions. The colony, and this place particularly, attracted a dubious mixture of travelers, looking for business. I kept a peripheral eye on the entrance, throwing furtive glances through the pungent yellow fog of *hedon*. I briefly registered the various alien forms—several of them Eclipse shapeshifters, by their smell—hunched over dark tables in the blissful contentment of their vacant minds or waving their hands in animated discussion. The incoherent noise of drugged conversation provided me with the opportunity to have an intimate conversation with T'lem.

"I'm telling you I'm green," I assured him, sliding into the Venik vernacular. I pulled out a stick of soyka, placed it in my mouth, and chewed slowly. Then I leaned back and sipped on my Plock Nectar. I could smell T'lem's indecision. He wanted to believe me because it meant incredible power for him and his boss, A'ler. My unique species-specific weapon would revolutionize terrorism and warfare, and I was only asking a million up front for it. I played the gum in my mouth with my tongue and then said, "So, why aren't I talking to A'ler if she's the one buying?"

"No one's buying yet, slave. Besides, you're lucky to be talking to me." He was apparently her secretary and the man I really wanted to keep occupied. "How do I know you're green and not feeding me some jagging shit."

I ran my tongue along my purple lips and smiled, hands arranging my long robes—I was unaccustomed to wearing anything like a dress. "Talk to Zek," I suggested casually. "He knows me from way back, when I shifted as a human. We did some real black on Ogium 9. You can trust me and the merchandise."

"I know Zek. Good guy. Already talked to him." T'lem grinned out of one of his many mouths, or at least that's what I thought it was. He had several orifices on his face with which he ate, spoke, and did a number of other things all at the same time. "It's because of Zek that you're here now, slave." He inhaled greedily on a smoldering mash of poi root. Tendrils of brown smoke curled up from two of his mouths as he blew out a stream directly at me.

The smoke caught me unguarded and made me cough. Its cloying smell of burning compost turned my stomach but I didn't show it. "Then you know that I always deal in good faith—"

"Not with Eclipse, you don't," he cut in, shifting his considerable reptilian mass to lean forward. The chair creaked. "You've never dealt with us before."

I firmed my lips and swallowed hard. "The price was never right before," I lied. Zek had tried for years to get me involved with Eclipse but I'd steered away, knowing their history. It was bad enough that I was dealing with low-life. Eclipse were evil and dangerous.

T'lem folded a pair of arms across his massive chest plate and leaned back with what looked to me like a frown. "I think that you've chosen your customers unwisely in the past, R'lan," he said, settling in to study me carefully. He was obviously referring to the sale of my *pocket* pistol design to the Guardians. It had since become the standard weapon of an Enforcer.

I eyed him calmly, chewing my gum with an open mouth and manipulating it between my teeth, and straightened my dress. In the guise of a shapeshifter, I resembled an Eosian, purple and hairless, thanks to Doctor Rava's illicit temporary *teck*. No one, save Ennos, knew that Rhea Hawke had designed the *pocket*. The rest of the galaxy had no idea, so when I took credit as R'lan, an Eosian arms dealer—supported by Zec Zeballion, a legitimate arms dealer and my previous slumming partner—my alias and legitimacy were assured. Regardless, I kept one hand near my slim *pocket*, hidden in the folds of my robes.

I'd already discovered through my smelling *teck* and heightened intuition that more than ninety per cent of Eclipse's higher membership were shapeshifters. About thirty Galactic standard years ago, when the Vos had destroyed Borrias, the shapeshifting refugees infiltrated the rest of the galaxy. Many of the Borrs had become associated with Eclipse and had swiftly gained important positions in the crime organization, supplanting Humans, Xhix, and Veniks. What this meant for Eclipse and its criminal activities, I could only guess. But, while that discovery was certainly diverting, I reminded myself that I was here to investigate Eclipse's connection to the recent Uma-1 massacre and to flush out the identity of The Rose and his intentions. The message Bas had decrypted suggested that The Rose was coming here, to the *Ulysses*. This sale of my MEC was my ticket. T'lem would never pay me the credits. But he badly wanted the MEC design. How badly, I was hoping to find out soon.

I let a smile cross my lips. "The *pocket*'s just a toy to your Q-gun," I said. "Its only interesting trait is its ability to track a mark once you've targeted them. It still shoots like a regular pulse weapon." That sale to the Guardians had been my last and had effectively taken me off the arms design and supply market. I'd half suspected then and still suspected now that Ennos had offered me a job with the Guardians more to prevent my continuation of illicit arms design and sales than for my actual skills as an Enforcer. This present ruse made him very nervous. I was certain that the prevention of this very scenario was why he'd hired me in the first place.

"What I'm offering you now is exactly what you need," I continued coolly. "A discerning weapon of mass destruction. The power to be a one-man army of precision assassins."

I boldly snatched up the MEC from the table, deftly playing the controls, and aimed directly at T'lem's face. "Let's say you want to kill all the Borrs in this room and knock out the Eosians without touching the Xhix, Horlians, Humans, or Veniks." I faked a trigger press at T'lem's face and had the satisfaction of seeing him flinch. Then I casually swept the room with the MEC. "Done." I placed the MEC carefully on the table. "Now," I leaned forward, eyeing him with cold precision. "Like I said before, I provide you with half the information now for a million Galactic Credits." I tapped the info-pod to life. A holo of my MEC sprang from it along with diagnostic instructions for using the DNA controls. "The rest of the design and prototype MEC come later for another million." I tapped the info-pod again and the holo vanished.

T'lem stroked his face with one hand, steely eyes narrowing. Then he suddenly cocked his head to the side and looked vacant, as if listening to something. I concluded that he was carrying an ear-com, like me, and was receiving an incoming call. Judging from the way his eyes flickered to me and the expression on his face, I had the distinct impression that it was about me. And that wasn't good. No one was supposed to know who I was or that I was here.

After a long pause in which one of his side mouths muttered under his breath, he refocused cold eyes on me and said, "You are very presumptuous, R'lan."

I remained silent and leaned back, eyes fixed on his with stubborn resolution amid a show of mild indignation. T'lem shifted under my steady gaze and cast his eyes past me, searching the bar. He shouted, "V'mer! Over here!"

I flinched at his shout but swiftly recovered and glimpsed a Xhix, who'd just entered the bar, sauntering over to us. I could smell that he was another shapeshifter. Eclipse seemed to be full of them, I concluded.

"This is V'mer, just returned from Uma 1."

I clamped my mouth shut. It must have gaped open for an instant. Good God! T'lem had just handed me what I was after. Was V'mer The Rose? This was too easy. Unless they weren't going to let me walk away with it. My hand slid down and hovered over the *pocket* strapped on my thigh under my loose robe.

"I could have used your MEC on Uma 1." V'mer sneered, looking me up and down with cold eyes. "I heard what you did on Omicron 12." A dirty smile slid across his face and he nodded. "Impressive."

My heart slammed and I stopped chewing my gum. How in chaos had he heard about that? That meant he also knew I was Rhea Hawke, not R'lan. Had Zek sold me out? My mind raced with options as I covertly checked out the exit points.

"Is that so?" I said and resumed chewing my gum in forced casualness. I didn't like the way he looked at me. It made me feel indecent. "I wonder how you came by that knowledge," I said crisply. "I should kill you now for it. I was paid a lot by the Legess to impersonate a human Enforcer and rid them of native terrorist insurgents who were blowing up their factories and murdering Legess—"

"You *are* a human Enforcer." V'mer scowled, pushing his face close to mine and showing an intense hatred I couldn't understand.

"I'm a *shapeshifter*, creon," I hissed back and let my hand wander to my MEC on the table.

"Not one of *ours*—"

"Enough bickering," T'lem said crisply, trapping my hand beneath a crushing press of his reptilian paws.

I abruptly swallowed my gum and suppressed a painful cry. My face tightened but I forced it to remain calm.

"V'mer, apologize to the lady," T'lem continued in an icy calm voice. "We don't want to scare her away."

"You don't know *what* you are." V'mer scowled.

T'lem picked up my MEC with one of his other hands and fiddled with some of the controls. "We are very interested in this weapon, after all, aren't we, V'mer?"

Now it was his turn to point the MEC at my face. I fought from recoiling and tried very hard to maintain my composure. I stared defiantly at T'lem and pushed out my lower jaw. All show. All bluster now. V'mer had called my bluff. Hand trapped under the crushing embrace of the Venik's paw, I felt like a cornered animal about to be slaughtered. My free hand slithered down to my hidden *pocket* gun.

Just when I thought things couldn't get any worse, my peripheral vision—always aimed at the entrance door—spotted Officer Asphalios entering the bar. He was escorted by two Eclipse shapeshifters in the form of large Xhix, followed by an eight-foot tall massive bird-like alien. Although a biped with human-like torso, legs and arms, the black-feathered alien's head resembled that of a raptor, and his long robe failed to completely hide the great wings attached to his arms. A Khonsus!

"For the love of Creos," I muttered under my breath and

noticed Asphalios's eyes roaming the place, probably for me. Terrific: my undercover partner—obviously no longer undercover—was going to expose me as well. The Khonsus—no doubt a renegade—hovered over Asphalios, huge yellow eyes clamped like talons on the young Eosian. The Khonsus were a strange species. Usually content to remain on their planet, Horus, this normally introspective race boasted incredible mind-probing powers that were somehow connected to their planet's life-force. It was said that once a Khonsus left his home planet, his mind-probing ability diminished only slightly, but the wisdom that accompanied it vanished completely. Although it was said that they were incapable of physical violence and could not kill you, they only needed eye contact to rob you of your mind. While they would sagely never consider this abhorrent practice on Horus, here on *Ulysses*, anything was in season. The Khonsus had obviously made eye contact with Asphalios earlier. I kept my gaze off the Khonsus, even as his magnificent liquid eyes acted like a magnet.

T'lem nodded at the door. "Ah, here's the man who shared all your secrets with us. Like what you did on Omicron 12 ... *Officer Hawke.*"

So they knew everything. I felt my universe slide into chaos. I watched Asphalios search the smoke-filled bar and we soon made eye contact. The Eosian's dark eyes looked drugged. I knew that they'd tortured the truth out of him and probed his mind against his will. What else had he involuntarily given away about our mission besides my identity? Up to now I had always worked alone. Although I'd strongly objected, Ennos had assigned me a partner for this case. Ennos had assured me that Asphalios was the very best systems hacker he knew—even better than Basileus. Asphalios had also once worked for ZetaCorp and was very familiar with the crystal matrices used in A'ler's com systems. I doubted that even Asphalios could break into A'ler's coms, but my opinion didn't count for anything, and he came with me whether I liked it or not. As per Ennos's orders, I'd reluctantly given Asphalios the task of breaking through T'lem's office into A'ler's inner office for communications while I kept T'lem distracted in the bar with my MEC deal. Now Asphalios had blown my cover and was going to get us both killed.

His eyes lit up with recognition and Asphalios addressed me directly, confirming that he knew me. *"After victory, tighten your helmet chord,"* he'd spoken the Japanese proverb that was our code to indicate successful data upload lucidly enough, but his next words were spoken like a maniac: "All these shapeshifters are Nihilists, Hawke." Chaos! He even addressed me by name. "They're using Eclipse. The Vos are—"

"We need a demonstration of your impressive weapon," T'lem cut in, pointing the MEC at Asphalios and effectively silencing him. T'lem surprised me by releasing my hand and giving me the MEC. "Perhaps you'd like to dispose of this Guardian spy yourself before he reveals more of your Guardian secrets. Unlike us, he won't keep your secrets, Hawke. He told us all about you, after all." T'lem grinned like a malicious boy.

I stared confused at T'lem, but only for an instant. Within a heartbeat, I confirmed that T'lem had not tampered with the MEC controls since I'd set them: they were still set to kill a Borr and stun an Eosian. I pushed out my lower jaw, aimed the MEC at Asphalios, saw his brief look of terror and shot without hesitation.

Asphalios's cry startled the bar to silence.

He didn't just crumple unconscious to the floor. His chest and side of his face disintegrated and caved into a mass of gaping flesh and bone. He was dead before he hit the ground. Blood spurted out of what was left of his chest and neck, forming a large dark purple pool.

I heard T'lem's victorious bark of laughter as I clamped a hand to my gaping mouth in horrified disbelief. What had I done?

"Chaos! You were right, V'mer!" T'lem shouted gleefully. "The jagging MEC works. She did it again! We have everything we need now. Kill her and get the gun!"

I recovered swiftly as others stirred into action. T'lem lunged for me. I jerked left and ducked into a battle crouch, just avoiding a shot from a Xhix. The quintle wave meant for me caught T'lem in the chest. He grunted and slumped forward on the table in a splattered mess. I dropped to one knee and clenched my lips, MEC tracking the bar in a rapid sweep. I killed several Eclipse shapeshifters in various alien guises as they moved aggressively toward me, shooting.

I caught a glimpse of V'mer, snatching the info-pod then dodging to safety through a back exit, the only shifter who'd managed to elude my MEC attack.

The giant Khonsus quickly advanced. He wasn't a particularly agile creature; but he didn't need to be. With eyes for weapons, he made a formidable foe. He raised his arms at his sides, unfurling massive feathered wings that ripped through his robe, and his huge body lifted off the ground. As he glided toward me, he opened his massive beak-mouth and sang a strangely enticing melody, notes floating out to me like petals of a scented flower. I avoided the instinct to look at him. I would have liked to bolt out the same exit as V'mer, but I had some unfinished business with Asphalios. Besides, the Khonsus was too close and nearly upon me. He had no weapon but he was massive and could break my neck easily. They say that the Khonsus are unable to inflict physical pain; but he was a renegade, after all. I fumbled with the MEC controls, trying not to meet the alien's magnetic gaze. I felt my eyes stray to his as he floated toward me, singing like an angel.

In a weak moment I met his gaze and instantly felt the icy grip of his probe, like talons closing. I inhaled sharply. The brute smiled through his large open beak, fluting his mellifluous dirge, as I felt the stirrings of pain clawing out my resistance. Eyes locked, my hands clambered blindly for the code from memory. Hoping desperately that I'd found it, I aimed with shaking hands and shot the bird-alien from less than a meter away. The MEC wave caught him in the chest. He jerked back in abrupt silence then recoiled forward. Panting in relief, I leapt out of the way as he toppled, face forward, with a loud thud.

In the brief silence from the shocked patrons, I sprinted to Asphalios's dead body, bent over him like a vulture, took his bloody face in my hands and kissed his mouth, then fled the bar.

I could hear the bar come back to life as I ran. No one pursued me as I pelted down the empty corridor of the huge space station, dizzy with shock and heart pounding in my head like a MEC concussion wave. I focused only on the immediate need at hand: escape. While I remained an Eosian, I was an open target. Too many people had seen me, and the station might well be broadcasting my image on its local vids. Eclipse agents were bound to catch up with me within a short time. My temporary *teck* would last another four hours before it wore off and I reverted to my human self. I ducked off the Central Axis corridor toward one of the mammoth agricultural areas and found a small wooded area to hide in until the *teck* wore off.

I squatted down on a bed of soft moss among some Tilia trees and gazed down in a daze at the still bloody info-pod I'd removed from my mouth and held in my hand. What had just occurred sank in: T'lem knew Asphalios was a shapeshifter and had tricked me into killing him with my own weapon. In that initial act of violence, I'd provided them with the means to retaliate with force. I'd be dead; they'd have the MEC and the design. Only T'lem hadn't counted on my swift recovery. It was both my savior and my downfall: I ended up confirming the status of assassin that he'd only intended to establish.

After four long hours, I confirmed that I'd reverted to my human shape and color. I swiftly disrobed to a tight bodysuit and discarded my robes in the bushes. I put the info-pod back in my mouth and swallowed it down before leaving my hiding place to the vehicle hangar. No one questioned me and I made it through the security gate without mishap. I found Benny waiting for me, unscathed. No one had boarded him and we managed to ship off the space-station with ridiculous ease.

Θ

I gazed down at my shaking hands on the library table. They were clammy and reminded me of how I'd clutched Benny's controls with sweat-covered hands until I'd gained enough distance from the *Ulysses*. It was only then that I'd relinquished the controls to the sentient ship and washed Asphalios's dried blood off my hands.

I slumped in my seat and stuffed my trembling hands in my trouser pockets. No one at the precinct understood. As far as they were concerned, I'd killed my Eosian partner in cold blood to save myself in a single act of brutality. No one believed my story that he was a shapeshifter. I had to admit, it didn't make sense to me either. Asphalios was too innocent, too nice, to be a shapeshifter.

The info-pod I'd pried loose from his back tooth when I'd 'kissed' him had yielded a prize that might have made his sacrifice meaningful—if Ennos had done something with it. The messages Asphalios had successfully uploaded from T'lem's office com contained, among other things, the message to A'ler, commander of the *Ulysses,* with instructions for the Rose:

A'ler: Our elite agent, the Rose, *will pick up the enclosed command message, which contains a specific hit list, by using an encrypted code access. Please destroy once the code indicates successful access. I am counting on your discretion and cooperation, as usual.*

—The Ancient One

We could only guess what individuals or groups were next on Eclipse's list for annihilation. Alas, even Bas's skill in cryptology hadn't cracked the attached encrypted hit list. He'd even passed the hit list to me, unaware that I'd already surreptitiously made a copy for myself; I'd been known to decipher a few codes. With Bas's help I discerned that the unique signature of the message identified it as being an extra-galactic message from the Vos. We'd run across missives from the Ancient One before, and I was sure he or she was some ancient Vos being. But when I presented Ennos with my ideas, he vehemently disagreed and thought me reckless to make such an inflammatory conclusion. He'd asserted that it was a political bomb. It was bad enough that Eclipse had obliterated the Schiss for no known reason. If word got out that even hinted at what I was suggesting, there would be panic in the entire galaxy, particularly in sectors inhabited mainly by humans, the principal targets of the Vos. But Ennos had given me a chance to prove my case by finding V'mer and bringing him back. A chance I'd messed up.

I rose from my chair, feeling the spasms of Dust trembles at a thought that refused to leave. Could I bring myself to do it? I was no longer an Enforcer. I had no starship. Without the sanction of the Guardians or the protection of my Great Coat I'd be more vulnerable and alone than I'd ever been.

"Chaos," I muttered to myself. I wanted my life back. I seized my jacket from the back of the chair and, throwing it over one shoulder, left the library with determined steps.

SIX

As I made my way down a narrow litter-strewn alley, I wondered why *teck* doctors holed up in the seediest part of town. I had to convince myself that this was the right thing to do. I knew I was one of the best at subterfuge. On my own, I had managed to infiltrate Eclipse undetected for a week before my fellow operative gave us both away. Ennos still blamed me for it. Maybe he was right.

I hesitated at the entrance of the old commercial building and noted that Doctor Rava didn't appear on the registry. Had the clinic moved?

I pulled in a long breath and forced myself to open the door. It creaked open and I entered. The hallway stank of garbage and body odor. I covered my nose with my hand and made my way down the dingy corridor to where Doctor Rava's clinic used to be. It was no longer there. I read the sign: "Nuyu Treatments: Define the New You!" I stood in a daze for a moment, disheartened. I was about to back away when the door opened and an old man shuffled past with a nervous glance at me. I decided to go in and inquire.

A middle-aged human receptionist eyed me with some

curiosity, and I stepped toward the desk with a small smile of greeting.

"Do you know where Doctor Rava's clinic has moved to?" I asked.

The woman scowled. "That awful man's in jail," she said scornfully. "They arrested him for all those illegal *tecks*."

"Who? Guardians?"

"No."

"Well, thank you." I turned to leave.

"He was awful," the woman repeated.

I left quickly and shut the door with a sigh. I decided to look Rava up in the community database, and struck for the nearest local library. I found him quickly and not exactly where I expected: in a local jail. Terrific. I frowned at the holo. Rava was holed up in the local PD because—

"For the love of Creos," I hissed out. He'd killed someone.

The database was restricted and would not provide more. Heaving a long sigh of resignation, I flicked off the holo, slung my jacket over my shoulder, and left the library.

Θ

"I'm Officer Hawke, Enforcer with the Galactic Guardians," I said brusquely to the young human officer at reception. "I need to see Doctor Rava." I flashed my ID at him. I was counting on him to respond to my authoritative posture — he couldn't be more than twenty—and that he wouldn't ask for my badge, which I'd surrendered to Ennos. Would he confirm my status on the database? I hoped that the holo-work on my Enforcer status was taking its normal sluggish time and that I still appeared on their database.

The young officer blinked several times and stuttered, "Yes, Sir—I mean Ms ... eh, *Officer*, I mean."

I fought down a smile. I hadn't counted on being recognized, but it was obvious that he had seen me on the Galaxy News vid and was terribly intimidated by my presence in the flesh.

Desperately trying to maintain his cool, he swallowed without even checking anything and said, "Down the right corridor, first hall to your left. Cell 09, Officer Hawke. I'll open the door for you when you get there."

I nodded to him without smiling and headed down the corridor he'd pointed out. When I reached Cell 09, I peered inside the small window in the door for a moment before it creaked open. After a glance up at the surveillance camera, I entered the cell and suppressed a flinch as the door clanked shut behind me.

The cell was more like a small apartment. I wandered through the living room, past the small kitchen and bedroom, and eventually entered a tiny lab cramped with bottles of chemicals, beakers, and arcane equipment. I found Rava there, tinkering with some vials. Hearing me, he turned and stared.

"Officer Hawke! A wonderful surprise!" Doctor Rava's greenish leather-like face creased with a million wrinkles in a genuine smile of pleasure. If he was wondering whether his illicit *tecks* had caused a problem and I'd come back for my currency, he didn't look or smell too worried. Considering where he was, perhaps he had other things to worry about.

"Doctor Rava." I nodded and approached the nine-foot tall Sporian, giving him a faint smile.

"Well, well," he said, tilting his elongated head to one side and giving me a good look with his large disarming eyes. The old Sporian emitted a mixed aroma of peaches and brandy, which suggested that his sexual gland was putting out. He hugged me against his bulbous pear-shaped body by wrapping his two very long arms around me. Some things never changed, I thought, feeling wry amusement tug at my lips. "You look well, Officer Hawke. I trust my *tecks* served you well?"

"They did," I said, holding back a bitter smile. The *tecks* worked. It was everything else that went wrong.

"No complications, then?"

"Just a headache," I said. "And some discomfort during the transition." Temporary *tecks* were considered volatile and unreliable at best. Most didn't work. They were illicit partially because of their varied and generally unsubstantiated side effects. There had also been the odd case of a temporary *teck* causing permanent damage to a subject.

"Ah, understandable," he nodded. "Expected with so fast a transition."

"They say you killed a man," I said, deciding on bluntness.

"That's what they say," he repeated methodically. "Died of complications from a temporary *teck*."

My stomach clenched. "How is that possible?"

"Happens."

I studied the pear-shaped Sporian in silence, rethinking my plan.

"Alas, you're the only person my *tecks* ever worked on," he volunteered.

"What?" I gaped at him. Was that true? The *only* person?

"So, why are you here?" he asked bluntly.

"I need another treatment," I said bluntly back and wished I could retract it. What *was* I doing here?

"Eosian again? You do them well," he said eagerly, his gland spiking its emissions.

I nodded, firming my lips to keep calm. Yes, I did Eosian well. Thanks to the *tecks* I already had.

"Makes sense," he reasoned. "Your races share very similar DNA, after all. You both spring from a common ancestor, eh?" He didn't wait for me to respond. "So, when do you need it?"

I hesitated. "But I thought—I mean—can you make it here?" I stammered, gazing around me at the tiny facility. He was in a prison cell, for God's sake!

"Of course I can!" he said with a scornful chuckle. "The PD are idiots. They think they're humoring me when I ask for supplies. But they have no idea what I'm doing." He found a data pad and scrawled madly on it with a pen. "Just bring me these materials from the pharmacy along with a sample of your DNA—I'm afraid they confiscated all my files, including yours. I can have the infusions ready in a week or so for your initial treatment."

He handed me the data pad and I glanced at the hardly legible writing. I felt committed now. And terrified.

Θ

Hands in my pockets, I strode languidly from the local PD office, along the dark wooded path toward the public land-transport station. I bowed my head, lost in thought. This escapade I was planning was as liable to get me into more trouble as it was to get me out of the trouble I was already in. With my track record, it was a certainty. I snorted. "I should give up before I even begin," I muttered to myself. "But I've already begun," I sighed then felt my breath hitch. I'd said that before—

It was the trigger of a déjà vu and the sudden portent of danger. I felt sudden regret for taking the woods. I'd travelled this path many times as a predator. Now, without my Great Coat or MEC, I was easy prey for the thugs who lurked in the urban forest. I wished I'd taken the *pocket* I kept under my pillow.

Feeling like a puppet in a dream, I knew they were coming before they appeared: three Xhix sprang at me from behind the trees. They laughed as they drew out their Q-guns. This would have been easy with my Great Coat and MEC. But I didn't even have my *pocket* now.

Then, like enacting a choreographed dance, I knew I would carve out a swift swing-kick, and down two of them; I knew I'd dive into the thick forest as the third Xhix opened fire. I knew that I'd succumb to a massive shudder and stumble on something in the dark then fall.

I forced my convulsing body to crawl into some low shrubs as the remaining Xhix crashed blindly in the dark after me. He suddenly slowed, and I couldn't place his quiet rustling beyond the thunder of my own heartbeat. Yet I had a clear image of exactly where the Xhix would emerge. He would walk right past me without seeing me. I heard him close in, still not seeing anything. Then at precisely the right moment, I kicked out with a loud grunt and caught the Xhix hard in the arm. The Q-gun flew out of his hand, right into my waiting hand. He lunged and I fired. He fell right beside me.

I stumbled back, breathing hard for several moments. I forced myself to my feet, thinking of V'mer's ominous words. This could easily have been a random park mugging—they were unfortunately fairly common in these parts. Or was this part of V'mer's posthumous plan unfolding? Was I on The Rose's hit list?

SEVEN

After spending a good part of the day trying to crack The Rose's encrypted hit list, I entered the gym in the late afternoon, nodding with a curt smile to Tom at the front desk. He grinned at me, skin darkening to a deep ebony. I wasn't sure what that color signified and couldn't tell from the smell, though I had a good idea that it was friendly: he emitted a pleasing fragrance, like fresh exotic fruit.

"Hey, lady!"

Tom knew my name but for some reason he had decided to keep calling me *lady*. I didn't mind. I liked the anonymity his strange endearment carried. He'd turned out to be very friendly to me since that first day and I'd warmed up to him.

"Hi, Tom! How's Mini today?" I said, referring to the pretty female Xhix who worked out daily and who always managed to be within focus of Tom's roaming security camera.

Tom grinned. "She's in the holo-chamber doing laps. Working up a sweat."

I let a mischievous smile show on my face. "So are you."

The Xhix laughed and opened the security door for me.

After stripping down to a short one-piece bodysuit and removing my boots in the dressing room, I strode to the mats, barefoot. In the four days I had been coming here, I'd developed a routine that took me through the exercise mat, weights, then bars, and finally to the holo-chambers, where most members spent their time. Hardly anyone else bothered with the mundane equipment. I preferred it. Raw and real, it kept me focused on why I was here.

I completed the first leg of my exercise routine and stopped to wipe the sweat that ran down, when I spotted that same dark-haired man, and realized that I'd been covertly searching the gym for him. I'd spotted him each time I came to the gym this past week. I just now caught him watching me, when he thought I wasn't looking.

I toweled off the sweat from my face, arms and legs with an amused smile. Aware that he was surveying me as I hung the damp towel around my neck, I strode to the small cafeteria, conscious of the swing of my hips and exposed cheeks of my behind. I slid into a chair and contemplated getting a drink but gave way instead to the warm glow of exhaustion and leaned my head back, shutting my eyes for a moment.

"Mind if I join you?"

I jerked forward and my eyes snapped open. The man I'd been stealing glances at all week stood before me with a maverick smile and eyes like a sudden thunderstorm. The dusting of dark stubble on his face signified at least a day of growth. He held two cups of steaming soyka and offered me one, flashing a lightning grin.

He smelled of trouble and any other day I'd have brushed him off with a sardonic remark. But today I didn't. Realizing that I ached for some human company, I took the cup with a faint self-conscious smile and nodded my assent.

He took my cue and sat across from me. "I'm Serge."

"Rhea," I responded, not offering my last name and keeping it conveniently on a first-name basis.

He brought the cup to his mouth but didn't take a sip. Instead he boldly studied me in silence over the mist rising off the hot soyka until I blushed with frustration. Had I caught recognition in his expression?

"I've noticed you coming here, alone, for a while now," he explained with a wide smile. "And I just wondered if you'd go out with me sometime."

What bold cheek! My initial reaction was one of affronted defiance, but I controlled it and ran my tongue over my upper lip in mock seductiveness. "Is this where you regularly pick up your chicks?"

He laughed. A little nervously, I thought. Was he blushing? "I don't normally do this," he said, stroking his stubbled cheek with a clean well-manicured hand. "I just thought you'd like some company, being new to the neighborhood."

It was a logical conclusion, to assume I'd just moved there. He had no way of knowing that the gym I normally frequented was in the Guardian precinct. And that I lived clear across town in the cheap section of Neon City.

Then he stunned me with his next remark. "You're an Enforcer, aren't you?"

I tensed, then quickly recovered with a smirk and brushed the hair off my face. Leaning back in my chair, I crossed my arms and asked, "What makes you think that?"

"Well," he said with a disarming smile, "you provide lots of clues."

I eyed him skeptically. "Such as?"

"For starters, the way you always sit with your back to the wall."

I gave him a mocking smile. "I could just be from Nigel 7."

"I'm betting you aren't," he said. "Besides, there's more overwhelming evidence." He opened his smile to show his teeth in a boyish grin.

"Oh?" I tilted my head and found myself enjoying this game, although the Enforcer in me wondered where it was leading. I lifted a brow of inquiry, inviting him to go on.

"For instance, you keep to yourself, no friendly chats with the other ladies. And you carry yourself with command," he answered easily. "I saw how you handled that Xhix at the front desk a few days ago. What *was* that hold you put him in?"

"You've just described a mean bitch," I said, flashing him a sharp-edged smile.

He raised a finger at me, taking up the gauntlet with enthusiasm. "Ah, there are additional clues to suggest you're more than just a mean bitch," he said. I wasn't sure I liked how he'd phrased that. "And did you know that Xhix can see through anything?" he added pointedly. "That's why your friend Tom works here, to satisfy his voyeuristic tendencies. He's got the hots for you: when he goes black it means he's sexually aroused, you know. He's looking through your clothes drinking in your naked butt."

"Like I'm wearing an awful lot to cover it right now." My tongue brushed my upper lip again, and I tossed my hair back in mock seduction. "Besides, how do you know he isn't eyeing *your* butt?"

He laughed sharply, then recovered and launched back into his argument: "Then there's the way you relentlessly attack your routine. You have remarkable self-control ..."

Yeah, I'd had many years to get that one right, I thought grimly.

"... You're strong and really fit ..." He'd been watching me on the bars. "But you're nursing some tender areas ..." He'd been watching me closely. "Injuries incurred on a mission, perhaps?" He raised a knowing brow. I smiled coyly back and raised my brow in response. "By the way," he added, leaning forward. "I'm really good at Opsis massage." He gave me a bold crooked smile. "There's also your penchant for black, the Enforcer's color," he continued cheerfully. Now he was really fishing. "Plus you've got the right build for an Enforcer." He was repeating himself now. Perhaps to give himself an excuse to brashly look me over again. "You're quite tall for a human female." He grew pensive, eyeing me contemplatively and reaching out for my face as if to touch it, then stopping himself. "And a glimmer of sadness—maybe regret for some botched assignment in the past—in those beautiful green eyes."

I swallowed and felt my face heat. Luckily it was already flushed from my workout. "Hazel," I corrected. "They're hazel. And Enforcers are virtually all Eosian," I argued, ignoring his flattering tease.

"I heard they have a human. It's you, isn't it? Come on, admit it," he persisted with a smug grin. He knew he was right and I was just being elusive.

I studied his face, searching, smelling for trust and compassion. I found a provocative sweetness. In his dimpled smile and stormy eyes. In the curls of dark hair that swept recklessly over his brow. In the spicy dark smell of his sexual attraction for me. I had to admit I was impressed with his assessment. Too impressed. My brows came together in suspicion. "You're blenoid-shitting me, aren't you?"

"Okay," he confessed, smiling like a boy caught stealing at a candy store. "You got me: I made it all up. I recognized you from the news vids. You're the one who smoked that shapeshifter on—"

I surged to my feet, knocking over my cup, and spilling it on the table. Wiping madly with some table napkins, I blurted, "I really have to go. Thanks for the soyka."

He stood up with me, ignoring the mess and my flustered response. "So, how about it? Will you go out to dinner with me?"

I forced a smile—it might have been more of a grimace—and said in a rush of words, "I don't think so. Nice to meet you, Serge." I left him standing at the table and retrieved my flight jacket and gym bag then left without looking back.

Θ

I shivered and drew my jacket tight over me, knowing full well that it wasn't because of the cold. Hands in my pockets, I strode languidly toward the public land-transport station and let my thoughts wander back to Serge. I'd really wanted to say yes. I was lonely and desperate for human company. And Serge was sweet, attractive, and powerfully alluring. The thought of his scent alone stirred my body with the desire to press against him and kiss his mouth ... that delicious mouth that smiled with genuine mirth and made me want to grin and hang onto his words. And those eyes of thunder and lightning that gazed right

73

through me as if he'd known me all his life. In truth, I felt the same way—as though I knew him—when he held me in the embrace of his intense gaze; I bathed in a mantle of otherworldly familiarity, though my heart fluttered like a teenage girl's on a first date. But enough ruminating. I had things to do, my career to salvage. And possibly a world to save ... if my hunch was right. I couldn't afford distractions ... or more disappointments. And Serge was likely both of those.

I waited only moments in the twilight of evening before a car sped into the station in response to my presence. The door swung open and I boarded the empty car.

"Stanley Station," I instructed. The car responded by shutting its door and accelerating on the multi-tracked Urail. I settled into a comfortable seat and stretched my head back to relax, running my fingers through my hair to sweep it off my face.

"Let's face it, Rhea," I muttered to myself with a wry smile, "you're not very good in that department. Rhea and love aren't like hand and glove—"

Wait! I'd said that before too. Irrational despair crept up my back, stiffening my neck muscles. I felt the tremors of a dark foreboding swell inside with a feeling that everything was accelerating with the car. A vision of the whole world on a careening path for disaster with me at its helm shook me. Then another sudden sensation of déjà vu overwhelmed me, and I felt like I'd entered a dream—no, a nightmare—

—The car abruptly accelerated and jagged off the line to my home station. It was heading for the industrial side of town and picking up speed.

"What are you doing?" I knew I'd say ... did say ... "I order you to slow down and return to the Stanley line!" I lurched to the emergency panel on the wall beside the seat. I knew what was going to happen next, felt the jar of realization in my stomach. I pressed the emergency stop button ... to no avail. Knew that. The car continued to accelerate, throwing me off balance as it careened around corners at a speed the track wasn't built to accommodate.

I knew I'd say it: "Oh, God!" Knew I'd try to pop open the emergency hatch and escape before I couldn't anymore. I puppeted my actions as though I wasn't part of it, looking on. I knew the hatch was jammed. I knew a sharp corner was coming up, even though I'd never been in this part of town before—

A hard collision threw me onto the seat and out of the nightmare. I saw another car in front of mine. I'd caught up to another car and rammed it. Its occupant seemed to understand that my car had gone renegade and I heard the squeal of its emergency brakes. Just in time: we hurled around the sharp corner at a still uncomfortable speed but the cars didn't fly off the track.

Both cars skidded into the next station and stopped. I forced the car door open and stumbled out, wishing to thank my rescuer. But the other car was empty. Its occupant had already left. They must have run away, I thought, eyes sweeping the station. Feeling very unsteady on my feet, I sat myself on the platform and hugged my knees, bewildered.

I waited a few moments to let my breathing return to its normal rhythm and the shakes to subside before getting up. What was happening to me? Why did I keep having these strange premonitions? Who was trying to kill me? And who had intervened?

Θ

I stripped and pulled on a pair of men's briefs and a loose sleeveless T-shirt, then got into bed. I lay on my back under the covers and absently studied the ceiling of my bedroom, trying to quiet my unruly mind. I didn't sleep very well, despite my heavy workouts. Before the incident with V'mer and getting Dusted, I could fall asleep anytime and anywhere, I'd often relied on that ability during long and tortuous stakeouts. Now sleep came fitfully and at a cost. Among feverish psychedelic nightmares, V'mer's malicious face haunted me nightly. V'mer was right: he might be dead but he was still tormenting me. Why had he been so interested in torturing me? And did that have anything to do with his dubious connections with the Vos? Who were the accomplices he'd referred to and were they trying to kill me? Was The Rose one of them, I wondered, thinking of V'mer's reference to me finding The Rose's lethal thorn soon enough. Was The Rose a Vos? I shivered at the thought of that vile alien species that took no prisoners. They'd killed my father and millions of humans.

I sighed and crossed my hands behind my head. Thinking of Serge, I closed my eyes and turned onto my side then brought my legs up against my body. It had been a long time since I'd wrapped my arms around a man and touched him with my lips. The first and last time: I was eighteen and he was twenty-two, a boy I'd met in school. He didn't know I was an Enforcer but when we made love in the back of his *viper* he thought I was spooky. He found an excuse to drop me off right after and never called. I tried to reach him after that and he never answered. I knew he'd dumped me. From then on I never went anywhere without my Great Coat. From then on, there was no mistaking me for an Enforcer, and men simply avoided me. It was easier that way.

Serge appeared to be an exception. He knew I was an Enforcer, one who held devastating powers. Yet I didn't intimidate him and he wanted to see me. I knew he was attracted to me; I'd smelled it on him. I abruptly convulsed in a sudden violent shake. Uttering a moan of despair, I curled up into a tight ball and trembled to sleep.

... It always began with a stranger coming to my bed. He crept over the foot of my bed like a lion, naked and smelling like a forest in spring. His face was veiled in shadow but it didn't matter; I recognized his muscular body—he was my noble lover. I let him pull off my nightdress. He caressed my thighs with gentle hands and I opened to him, body aching for his like a muse for a long forgotten poem. Then he lay upon me like a Great Coat, warm skin molded over my yearning body, and his lips touched mine. It coaxed me to stir and join him ... but I already mourned what would follow when he disappeared and my heart throbbed with dread ... already alone ... alone with another man brandishing a knife ...

EIGHT

Back at the library, I navigated through the holo database, hoping to find some motive for the Vos to order Eclipse to massacre ninety-two Schiss priests, among hundreds of initiates and acolytes. They'd effectively eradicated the order. If I discovered why they'd targeted the Schiss for obliteration, I'd likely know what they were planning to do next. And who was on that damned hit list I couldn't crack.

I reread the files: the Schiss were just one of the millions of spiritual and religious sects searching for God that littered the galaxy. They were Gnostics, a common philosophy in the galaxy. What set the Schiss apart was that their membership was almost exclusively human. Originally only allowing humans from Earth, they had recently permitted a few non-humans to join. Humans still made up over ninety percent of the order when V'lem murdered them all by introducing a poison gas in the airway system during one of their gatherings.

The peaceful Schiss had devoted themselves to the use of dream-meditation, particularly lucid dreaming, to achieve transcendence and evolve closer to God and what they called the universal consciousness. Several of its older founders had experienced the Gate Hallucination a hundred years ago.

I leaned back and pulled at my hair with both hands as if to tie it then let go and ruffled it brusquely. I had read about, and marveled at, this bizarre Earth phenomenon. A hundred or so human spiritual leaders had simultaneously and independently dreamt of a huge cone-shaped gateway on an alien landscape. In their dream, thousands of alien beings emerged naked through the gateway and morphed into human shape then proceeded to massacre another race of furry alien quadrupeds. Some scientists suggested that it might have been some random extra-galactic phenomenon. Some religious types decided that this mass dream was a revelation of great significance, a mass hypnosis by a higher being. They concluded that the mystics who had shared the dream had witnessed a portal into another dimension. A gateway to the land of the gods. But what did the massacre signify? That humanity would annihilate alien beings? A deluge of speculation followed, some of it more bizarre than the phenomenon itself.

Discussion focused on what brought about the vision as well as its significance. Agnostics tried to explain it with science: a possible synchronous magnetic phenomenon permitting society to behave like an autopoietic system. Like the independent formulation of calculus by Newton and Leibniz or the theory of the evolution of species by Charles Darwin and Alfred Russel Wallace. Or McFadden and Pocket independently but at the same time promoting that electromagnetic fields were the seat of humanity's consciousness. Multiple independent discoveries had increased on Earth a thousand-fold since the nineteenth century. The reason was obvious to some scientists who declared that the fabric of humanity's society was acting like a neural network, learning, interacting, and sharing toward the achievement of a common zeitgeist. Though loopy, the theory of spontaneous and persistent synchrony was based on some reality, I considered, and as a result couldn't be totally discounted.

Followers of certain occult groups claimed that these human mystics had been chosen by the higher consciousness of the universe to see the portal. Linked to the thought consciousness of the universe, the portal was a physical manifestation of a geometric blueprint that occultists called 'Sacred Geometry' and that the time had come for everyone to 'see.' This tied into the Gnostic beliefs about 'experiencing God' and the recent prophecy by Raphael Martinez, the eccentric leader of the Hermetic Order, who claimed the coming of a violent End of an Age, the *Suntelia Aeon*. His dire prediction might yet prove prophetic, I decided, thinking of the Vos. There was otherwise nothing new or remarkable about it, given that the ancient Greeks had predicted this cataclysmic End of Age several thousand years ago. The second part of Martinez's prophecy, an arcane reference to twin souls linked to the *Suntelia Aeon* was too weird for me to recall.

I thought about the Gate Hallucination again. Fascist groups took advantage of the image to suggest that this was a clear message from a sentient universe of humanity's ultimate destiny to rule the universe. This sparked a renewal of anti-alien prejudice.

The mystics were hounded for details of the portal, the alien people they'd seen exit the portal, and those they'd massacred, and the alien landscape: dimensions, designs, colors, shapes, numbers. It was found that their dreams were exactly the same in every detail. Which was really creepy, I decided. And probably a hoax. Ironically, amidst the hubbub of interpretation by both the secular and non-secular community, those who'd experienced the shared dream remained silent about its meaning. Most of them went into seclusion and many disappeared altogether, never to be seen again. The blessing of sight had turned into a curse of burden.

Suddenly curious, I did a search and narrowed my eyes when I saw the result: over eighty percent of those who'd experienced the Gate Hallucination were either dead or missing within twenty years of the shared dream. None had died of old age. Many of the deaths or disappearances alluded to strange circumstances. Several had been murdered. Others had suffered bizarre accidents. The only human mystics left who'd experienced the Gate Hallucination were Schiss priests. About twenty of them. And they were all dead now, thanks to V'mer.

I sat up straight, wondering if I'd stumbled on something important. Why were the Vos interested in murdering these eccentrics along with the rest of the sect? Was there a connection between the Gate Hallucination and the Vos's envisioned alien massacre?

I pushed back from the desk in frustration and tersely waved my arm through the holo to extinguish it. I pulled my hair back and lashed it into a ponytail with an elastic from my pocket, then stood up and stretched. This was still getting me nowhere. All I had was more questions.

Θ

"You sure you don't know who *tecked* you?" Doctor Rava murmured as he took another skin swab off my arm.

He never stopped asking me, I thought, growing annoyed, and shifted in the reclining patient chair. "I told you, my mother never told me who the doctor was. We lived in Vancouver, British Columbia. We actually never spoke about it."

Doctor Rava shook his head. "Pity," he said. "It's the best damn *teck* I've ever seen. Almost as though ..." He trailed off, suddenly lost in thought. I welcomed his silence, glad that he'd finally shut up. But not for long: "These temporary *nano-tecks* are nothing like real *tecks*, permanent *tecks*," he went on. At least he'd forgotten about mine in his generic rhetoric. "Remember, once I give you the initial treatment next week, you can create the effect within a few hours with one infusion," he said. "You need to continue the infusion every seven hours. Otherwise, the pigmentation and hairlessness will start to wear off in ten hours and you'll be your beautiful pink hairy self again within a standard solar day." He smiled. I grimaced back with a purposeful toss of my brown mane. One thing I liked about Doctor Rava: except for my original *tecks*, he never asked questions. He never once asked me why I was temporarily *tecking* as an Eosian.

Θ

I strode into the gym with brash steps. After a nod to Tom at the front desk, I continued inside, feeling my heart beating hard. I'd decided to accept Serge's offer to have dinner together. But after a cursory scan of the regular clientele, I realized he wasn't there. I searched more closely, checking all the possible places. I hung out near the men's room for a while. I even considered stealing inside for a look, then reconsidered. I'd only been in a men's washroom once—to kill a man. After a short but hard workout, I left for home, disappointed.

Serge wasn't there the next day or the day after that. I fought the emptiness inside me. Then I got angry with myself for letting a man dictate my emotions. Someone I didn't even know. Chaos, I had work to do, things to prepare, my life to get back into order. Why was I bothering with this guy?

I kept myself busy at home trying to crack the encrypted hit list, then in the library, studying public holo-records and collecting everything I could about the *Ulysses*. When I found my mind drift of its own accord to Serge for the tenth time, I abandoned my research, left the library and marched to the PLT. I made a detour to the Hive and, finding Serge still not at the gym, sidled over to Tom at the front desk. I easily pulled out the information I needed: Serge's last name. At that point I could have done a full info scan on him but refused to play cop this time. I set aside my cynical cop-reflex and decided to let things unfold naturally.

I'd barely gotten inside the door of my apartment, when I instructed the holo-com, "Put me in touch with Serge Bastion." I waited nervously for the image to appear.

Within seconds, Serge's shadow-stubbled face materialized. "Hey, Rhea!" He looked genuinely pleased to see me, and I felt a flush of pleasure heat my face.

"Eh ... I haven't seen you at the gym for a while," I said, feeling my face flame with self-conscious awkwardness.

"Your timing's impeccable; I was out of town and I just got back moments ago," he said. He did look tired, I conceded.

I gave him an awkward smile and practically stammered, "If your offer's still on, I'd like to take you up on it." Then I added, "Dinner, that is." Now I was definitely blushing. Then I added forcefully, "But it's not a date."

He looked amused, lips curling faintly in a half smile. "Then, what is it?"

"Call it a ... meeting." I suddenly found his sideways smile infectious and burst into a snorting laugh at my ridiculous remark.

He grinned like a boy. "How about I pick you up in an

hour for our … meeting?"

"How about I meet you there," I said.

"Okay," he agreed. "I suggest Vinny's Potty."

That was a high class—and expensive—restaurant in the Hive. I should be saving my credits; I wasn't sure where or when I'd be getting any more.

"He makes the best Pot-stickies this side of the galaxy," Serge added with an irresistible smile.

I suddenly decided it was worth it and felt a broad smile crease my own face. One of the hidden perks of my line of work was that I was always away and had no time to spend what I earned. As a result, I'd accrued a good sum in my savings account with the Galaxy Bank. I could afford to spend some now. With my decision, I felt a sudden warm glow. A light-headed, happy kind of warmth. Something I hadn't let myself feel since I was five.

Θ

As Serge had promised, Vinny's Pot-stickies were excellent, I decided, finishing the last of mine. But the décor was a little passé: early twenty-second-century Earth art deco with liberal use of primitive nature art on the walls. Perhaps that's what made the place charming to the trendies who frequented it, I thought as I glanced around the table at the locals, who were mostly human. I could tell from the funky clothes—mostly natural weaves—Old-Age jewelry, their generally long, braided hair, retro make-up, and languid body movements that most of Vinny's clients lived here in the Hive. I suspected that Serge lived here also. His aristocratic bohemian appearance fit rather well with this eclectic crowd. I stood out in my flight clothes and felt some relief that I'd at least taken a brush to my hair and bound it back.

"So, what brought you to Iota Hor-2?" I asked, turning inquisitive eyes back on Serge, seated across from me. "Do you have family here?" I played with my after-dinner soyka as he finished his last bite and leaned back.

"No family," he said simply. "I came here because it reminds me of home. How about you?"

"The precinct's here," I answered flatly, offering no other reason.

"Where did you live before you became a Guardian, then?"

He was pretty good with the questions, I thought, feeling a little defensive. *He* was the one who was supposed to be answering *my* questions. "Lots of places," I answered cagily, sipping the soyka. "Did you leave family back on Earth?"

He shook his head and stroked his stubbled face. "I have no family. They're all dead. The war ..." His voice trailed off.

I nodded solemnly and dropped my gaze to my cup, thinking of my father. "Yeah."

"So, why did you become a Guardian? I mean, you're pretty unconventional for one. Galaxy News described you as a loner who drives a non-regulation ship."

I looked up sharply. "I didn't choose the Fauche ship," I said defensively, glad of the chance to respond to his added comment and avoid the difficult question. "No one else wanted Benny, so I took him."

"Benny?" He smiled with amused curiosity.

I returned him a wry smile. "After the brother I never had."

He nodded, looking confused. Perhaps he was slowly coming to realize the consequence of asking me too many questions. I came to my conclusion too quickly, for he seemed to take what I'd said to heart and regarded me with bemused sympathy. He pressed with the question I hadn't answered: "Forgive me for saying so, but the Guardians—Eosians—aren't generally known as being warm and kind. More like cold logic machines. But *you* ..." He blinked several times. "*You're* not—" He broke off, almost choking on the words he wouldn't speak as if it hurt him to think of what I was. As though he had a personal stake in it.

Cold-hearted? Was that what he meant to say? He had no right to judge me, I thought sullenly. He didn't know me.

Then he pinned me with an intense gaze. And something passed between us. I can't say what, but it felt as real and as strong as the heat burning my cheeks. Like liquid fire his eyes burned, lighting a way deep inside me to where my dark soul ached. To where the child in me still wailed from that awful thing I'd done with my eyes—and he saw it all. Must have.

Before I could stop it, a sob tore out of me, part of that wail that I strove to disguise with stumbling words. I'm not sure what I said, but he blinked and released me to focus past me.

When his gaze returned, it was harmless. But his words weren't. "What about that unconventional weapon you carry?" he persisted. I forced my face to stay calm, but felt my eyes narrow slightly. "They call it a disaster weapon," he added.

Damn Galaxy News! Had they really told the world about my MEC? "I carry it because I made it," I said proudly, then was instantly annoyed with myself for admitting that to a stranger.

"Really?" He looked both impressed and horrified at the same time. Had I finally shocked him? "Why in chaos would you invent such a thing?"

"I made it to save as many lives as I could," I snapped defensively.

He blinked but recovered with a sheepish smile. "Sorry, if I offended you, but I was just curious and I think I know what you meant about saving as many lives as you could. But speaking of curious ..." He inclined toward me, leaning his crossed arms on the table, and studied me with a crooked smile that I couldn't read. "Why would you join an organization that naturally excluded you because you were the only human? The Eosians are a self-professed supreme race. They're not known for their humility or unconditional acceptance. They must have made it hard for you."

I shrugged and forced a casual smile. "It doesn't bother me," I lied, then added crisply, "I didn't join to make friends. I became a Guardian to help make things right." I swallowed in sudden misgiving and hoped he wouldn't bring up all my misdeeds—at least the ones he knew about. This whole conversation was going to chaos.

Serge continued as though he hadn't heard my rebuttal, "Maybe you did it to prove that you were as good as an Eosian." His eyes lit up suddenly with inspiration. "Maybe even on a dare—"

"I told you," I cut in, flashing him a withering look. "I joined to make things right."

"Is that why you chose baldie traits when you *tecked* yourself?" he asked boldly. At his mention of my *tecks,* my throat tightened, and I started to feel like a cornered animal. This was the last thing I wanted to discuss. "Was it to be more like them? Galaxy News documented how you could smell out your prey," he explained. "And that eye-melting thing is a rare baldie trait, isn't it?"

Interesting how he knew that. It wasn't something the Eosians advertised.

"You could have chosen any number of alien abilities," he went on. "Hearing from 45 to 80,000 hertz frequencies like the Fauche, for instance. Or wave-sensitive sight, like the Xhix. Or the Scandic rapid healing. Why'd you choose baldie ones?"

"It wasn't *me,*" I said sharply, trying but failing to remain cavalier about it. "My mother chose them. She got me *tecked* when I was really young. I don't even remember it." I'd long ago guessed why my mother had chosen baldie traits: Laura Hawke obviously had a weakness for baldies, especially in the horizontal position. God, my mother should have had a baldie for a daughter instead of me, I thought sourly. I drew my brows together and set my mouth into a tight line.

"Hey, I'm sorry," Serge said, suddenly tender. His eyes softened into dark sparkling pools as he offered a conciliatory smile. "I didn't mean to make you uncomfortable. It's just that everything about you interests me. You're just so ..." he trailed off, with a self-conscious laugh. He reached out for my hand and covered it with his. I felt its warmth spread up through me like a balm.

I blinked away my discomfort and let the gates of vulnerability open—something about his face invited it—to give him my first genuine smile. "That's okay. I ... well ..." I trailed off as well, deciding mid-speech against revealing more of myself, and instead let my smile open to a grin.

His eyes went darker and he tilted his head a little to one side, studying me. "That's the first real smile I've seen on you. It lights up your whole face … God, it lights up the whole room," he added, eyes sparkling like galaxies. I knew my mouth was big and my smile bigger, which I didn't consider an asset. He seemed to disagree. "Did you know that you get little dimples on the corners of your mouth when you do that?" he said, reaching out as if to touch my face, then quickly retracting it when he caught my instinctive recoil, slight though it was.

I dropped my gaze to the table, suddenly shy, and let my grin falter to a guarded smile. "I didn't think anyone would like an Enforcer."

"You don't scare me if that's what you mean," he said.

My head jerked up and I snapped my hand out from under his, to stare at him. Again, he'd surprised me with his remark. But somehow he hadn't delivered it aggressively.

"I could see you intimidating a lot of people," he added calmly, eyes probing deep into mine as though he knew me. "But I'm not one of them."

I raised a brow and crossed my arms over my breasts. "Oh, really?"

"Yeah, really," he responded, now grinning like a rogue. "So, what do you say? Will you come home with me?"

I felt my heart race. I wanted desperately to say yes. "I don't think so," I said, taking a last long sip of soyka and getting up from my chair. "Thanks for dinner. I better go. It's getting late. You don't need to leave—I'll pay my share at the till."

He stood up with me. "My place is just around the corner, on your way home. I promised you a wonderful massage," he said with a slanted smile. "You could use one. For that shoulder. I can tell it's stiff." He moved closer and I could smell his attraction to me: like a forest after a rain-storm with a sharp undercurrent of musk and a sweet hint of strawberry. "And I make a delightful soyka," he added, teeth showing in a broad grin. "I add a little cinnamon and nutmeg and the richest, most sinful sheyling cream. And, just to add a little fire, a pinch of chili imported from Earth. You'll adore it." This time he reached out for my hand and between his rakish smile, heady scent, and the warm touch of his hand, I felt my resolve cave.

"Okay. Just for a massage and that delightful soyka."

NINE

It was already dark when we left the restaurant. As I had guessed, Serge owned a loft in the Hive. We walked side by side, careful not to touch, along a path through a large park to his apartment complex. It was an old converted vehicle manufacturing factory. We had to climb a tall set of metal stairs on the outside of the building to his door on the fifth floor. When he let me in, the overhead lights came on, revealing a spacious two-tiered living room, complete with expensive furniture, an indoor stream, holo-wall, full bar, and funky art from all over the galaxy.

I stood in fascinated awe, circling around and gazing at the artwork. I'd passionately studied art as a young girl. In another life, perhaps, I might have been an artist myself. Things didn't work out that way, I reflected, mind casting back to my never-ending safari with my itinerant mother then slumming with Zec's nasty crowd. Art school and a career in the arts was abandoned for survival.

I recognized several styles and artists from Ursae Majoris, Ceti, Gliese, and a few other systems—Chaos! He even had an original Hapaan! I had a replica of the exact same Fauche statue at home that had cost me a cool two thousand credits. I hated to think what this original had cost him.

Serge excused himself, leaving me to roam about, satisfying my curiosity, and I soon heard the buzz of his soyka machine in his small kitchen. A strange piece on one far wall that looked out of place caught my eye. It was a thermal fluid rendition of—it couldn't be! I stood my ground, hesitant to approach, but leaned forward and felt my eyes narrow with concentration, awe, and disgust. The piece was part of a series of controversial renditions of the Vos. It depicted them as noble gods, suffering undue cruelty in their banishment from the galaxy. The thermal art work must have been very sensitive to any change in temperature because it was already shifting slightly in tone, movement, and background in response to the proximity of my warm body. In this depiction, a Vos, portrayed as a giant humanoid, lay naked and half-reclined on the ground beneath the long blade of a menacing Eosian. The muscular baldie stood over the Vos like a vulture, his engorged penis erect and his mouth drawn back in malicious ecstasy. A large Epoptes, a stunningly beautiful dark angel with gossamer translucent wings, floated behind the Eosian, with one arm draped over the baldie's shoulder like a lover. He peered with cruel satisfaction at the suffering Vos. The Vos's face expressed noble anguish as his bloody hand reached out in supplication to the murderous Eosian. It was a cruelly beautiful and disturbingly erotic rendition.

Compelled to get a closer look, I was about to approach when Serge reappeared with two mugs of steaming soyka. I caught myself and turned to accept my cup. We stood in awkward silence, regarding each other, for a moment. I pointed to the Hapaan: a tall wiry sculpture of a Fauche, standing like a hunter poised and listening with its large ears, in the swirling pool of a bedar swamp. The material, a polysynth fiber, created the effect of subtle movement embedded within a classic 3-D design of swirling holo imagery. The pool was cleverly created to reflect the atmospheric movements of the large gas giant, Bedar 9, the home system of the Fauche. "Is it an original Hapaan?" I queried.

He smiled, rather smugly. "Yes."

"From Moner 7, right?"

He nodded, impressed with my knowledge. "Moner 7 attracts the best artists in the galaxy," he said. "You guessed correctly. That piece is one of Binder Hapaan's best from his

Moner-7 days. He's rightly one of the best in fluid art today."

I nodded. "I really like his elegant tones and subtle but clever use of metaphor. He doesn't overstate, which is so easy to do with that medium. There's a simple logic to his work, like how he's captured the pool." I pointed. "The rapid turbulence feeds into a larger methodical fluidity. Chaos drifts into order."

"You certainly know something about it," he said, looking very pleased. He grinned like a boy at me. "I was lucky to get it before the prices blasted through the ceiling."

I nodded and took a sip of the hot drink, almost burning my tongue. "Is that what you do?" I fished, realizing that for all our conversation, I knew very little about him. "Collect and sell art?"

"You could say that," he answered cagily. He was quietly studying me again.

Slightly uncomfortable under his stare, I waved pointedly to the thermal artwork and tossed him a grim half-smile, eyebrow hiking up. "Why do you have one of those? It's offensive."

"It's art," he said simply.

"But it portrays the Vos as mythic hero. Not as the vicious killers they really are. They almost destroyed your home."

He shrugged, unaffected. "I'm an art collector. The series is actually gaining popularity, if only for its shock value." He smiled wryly and gave me a knowing look. "Art is about emotion."

I felt my mouth shift with a turbulent current of emotions, proving him right. "Popular only among a group of perverse people who, if they lived in twenty-first-century Earth, would all be devil worshippers," I said grimly.

"Maybe Satan just got a bad rep." Serge shrugged. "Like the Vos."

I gave him a hard look, searching for what lay beneath his enigmatic eyes. Was he mocking me? I felt my lips curl in a half-grimace. I couldn't help staring at the thermal art.

"What are you talking about?" I said, feeling the edge in my voice. "Who in their right mind would feel sorry for the Vos?

They killed your family. And millions of others. As for portraying them as gods ..." I snorted in disgust. "Nothing they've done has shown them to be godlike; quite the opposite. It's not only morally illogical but implausible to think of them that way. Besides, it's all myth. Gods are a myth. Vos. Epoptes. I don't believe any of it."

He regarded me quietly for a moment. "What do you believe in, then?"

"In me."

I watched him curb an amused laugh. I hadn't meant it hubristically but he'd obviously taken it that way. So be it, I thought; if he wanted to misinterpret, I'd let him. He didn't know me very well. And why should he? He didn't know my history, how I'd had to rely on my own powers of discipline and control since I was five to ensure I didn't needlessly hurt anyone again ...

"Well, you sure put them all in their place, didn't you?" he said with a wry smile. What in chaos did he mean by that? I was about to retort some response and leave, when he abruptly put his drink down and reached for mine. "Time for your massage," he announced.

Put off balance by his move, I relinquished the cup as he took my hand and led me to his bedroom. I barely had time to note the starkness of the room when Serge said, "Take off your clothes and lie face down." I blinked at him in hesitation. He insisted. "It's the only way I'm going to do a decent job." Then in a challenging tone, "You're not a prude, are you?" He touched a pad by the door and the lighting softened into swirling mauves, pinks, and lavenders. Soft ethereal music filtered in.

I realized that he wasn't about to turn around as I undressed. What was I doing here? I should have left. With a swallow I began to disrobe. Jacket first. I laid it on the chair by the bed then pulled off my black sleeveless top over my head. I found his eyes smiling appreciatively at my naked breasts as the top came off my face. He continued to watch as I bent down to remove my boots then my trousers. He raised a brow at the last article of clothing. I pulled off my briefs, let them drop to the floor, and stood tall and defiant, unashamed of my body, though feeling terribly vulnerable.

He motioned for me to lie on the bed. I lay face down on the soft downy cover, inhaling his wonderful scent on the covers, and waited for something to happen.

He gathered my long hair in his hand and pulled off the elastic that bound it. After first fanning it out over my back, he moved it aside, tracing my shoulder and neck in a gentle caress. He began slowly, massaging my back and injured shoulder with his fingers in light circular strokes, then with the palms of his hands using alternate pressure points. My eyes fluttered shut at the painful ecstasy. He was definitely skilled in Opsis massage: he knew where all the critical primary and secondary pressure points were and how to manipulate them. Serge moved down my back to my buttocks, along my thighs—lingering slightly along the set of puncture marks left from blenoid teeth—then legs and finally to my feet, caressing, kneading, softly scraping with his fingernails. As he massaged the soles of my feet I started to relax and let my mind wander. I might have even drifted off.

At some point, I realized that he was using more than his hands: he alternatively brushed his lips and drew his teeth along the soles of my feet, whiskers trailing up my legs. I started to tremble and wasn't sure if it was the usual Dust aftereffects or excited anticipation. I didn't care. It was exquisite and electrifying.

His whiskered face travelled to my inner thighs, lingering briefly over my puncture scars, and drawing out an involuntary shiver from me. Stubble and tongue teased into the crease of my buttocks, deep to where my legs met. I sucked in a silent moan with heaving shallow breaths and smelled his sex, a sharp pungency in a turbulent mixture of wet forest bog and sweet wild fruit.

He coaxed me around to face him. I saw that he'd removed his clothes and stood naked, eyes dark with lust. They blazed with intense yearning, but fixed on mine, asking permission. Overwhelmed by his tender overture, I gave him a tremulous smile of invitation. He climbed with his knees on the bed to straddle my thighs then brought his face close to mine and brushed his lips over my mouth. My eyelids fluttered shut at his touch, sweet like a summer rain, and with the promise of a burgeoning day. He kissed me, slow and deep. His kiss was sweet and bracing. In a flush of heat I felt a sudden burst of moisture between my legs.

Serge kissed the valley between my spread breasts, whiskers and lips trailing to my belly. Then he parted my legs with his hands and, with a groan of rapture, buried his face between my legs to caress me with his tongue.

I bit back a gasp and quivered, feeling each stroke like the shaft of an arrow, sharp and tantalizingly penetrating. I bit down hard on my lower lip to keep from moaning as he teased out exquisite tendrils of painful and vulnerable longing.

Just as I thought that I might collapse into wild sobs, he released me and moved back up my body, defining every slope and curve with his tongue and lips. Drawing out silent sighs. My breaths stuttered as I felt his manhood swell hard against my pelvis. Overcome by urgency, I arched into him, mouth snapping open in delirious desire. Knowing exactly what I wanted, his lips seized mine, tongue lashing in like a wild fire and tasting me. Then his phallus plunged deep into me with long rhythmic thrusts. I seized in a soundless gasp and undulated with him, feeling his excitement coil around me in a tightening embrace of infinite devotion. For an eternal instant, I let him envelop me in his white light and lost myself completely inside his universe—

Then a spasm of released tension welled up. I wanted to cry it out but instead bit down hard on my lower lip and felt the explosion pound up and snap my head back with the intensity.

He shuddered out his ejaculation with a hoarse shout, then slid off and collapsed beside me uttering a satisfied moan. After some moments of silence, he propped himself up on an elbow and regarded me with a shy smile. "Did you like it? I mean ... did you come?"

I smiled sideways and nodded. To my amazement I'd felt

with this stranger as if I'd come home.

He still looked uncomfortable. "I just expected you—It's just that I've never made love with a woman who didn't ... well ... make a sound." He laughed sharply, nervously. "I mean, don't get me wrong—I enjoyed it. It was just ..." His voice trailed off.

I mimicked his grimace. "Creepy?"

"Well, yeah." Then he quickly amended, obviously catching my expression. "Well, not creepy. Just strange. I didn't expect it to be like ..." Serge sighed, bringing his hand tentatively close to my breast to stroke me, then pulled back, and left it by his side. His face hardened. "So, you get off on being the strong and silent type or something? Is that some stealth thing they taught you at Guardian school or did you have your first screws in your parents' house?"

Now *I* was getting uncomfortable. I abruptly drew the sheet over me and sat up, hugging my knees to my breasts. I avoided looking at him and swallowed convulsively as I focused on the swirling colors of the room's lighting. I hadn't been very successful with my previous lover, my first and only lover, at eighteen. Why should this be any different?

"Hey," Serge said, suddenly tender. He leaned closer and touched my knee. "I still like you, Rhea. I don't care about the silence. I just wasn't ready for it, that's all."

I turned to give him a searching look. His face glowed with genuine feeling and he was still emitting his delightful strawberry and musk fragrance. I sighed, opening to a vulnerability I had not dared to show since I was five. "You can touch me again ... if you want to," I said almost imploringly. "I really like it ..."

Serge gave me a rakish grin and pulled the sheet from me. Then he gently cupped my breasts in his hands and brought his lips to mine in a tender kiss.

TEN

It was early morning as I sighed awake, finding myself alone in Serge's bed and sprawled amid his sheets. I inhaled the tantalizing aroma of frying butter and onions. I could hear Serge in the kitchen, singing, dreadfully, in Italian. I smiled.

I realized that it was the first time since I'd been Dusted that I'd slept through the night and not awoken to a violent shudder. I didn't think I'd ever slept so soundly in my life.

I swung my legs over the side of the bed and looked around for something to put on. My clothes had disappeared. I found a deep blue silk pajama top and slipped it over my head, pulling out my tousled hair. I glanced down and noted with satisfaction that the pajama top covered enough of me to make me decent. Then I shuffled to the kitchen where Serge stood with his back turned to me, dressed in the other half of the silk pajamas. He was frying up some peeka eggs with tofu strips and singing some Italian song with the gusto, if not the musical acumen, of an Italian.

Serge turned with a bright smile, eying me appreciatively from top to bottom. "Ah, the princess awakens. And you found my top. Your clothes are getting cleaned; they'll be in the cleaning chute ready for you once we finish breakfast. You can set the table while I entertain you with my woeful stories of mishap and mayhem," he said, turning back to the eggs.

I smiled lopsidedly and found some plates and cutlery for the table. Although I listened attentively to his amusing tales of encounters with crazy artists and greedy buyers, I found myself absorbed by Serge's physicality. Unaware of my preoccupation, he continued his monologue, laughing at his own jokes. I realized that I was listening not so much to what he was saying as how he was saying it. I observed the cadence and laughter of his voice, his mannerisms and gestures, how he moved his sinewy body. When his whole body erupted in laughter, it warmed me like the glowing summer sun.

I thought about reaching past him to retrieve some fresh fruit from the counter, but instead I followed his sensuous movement as I would an alluring piece of fluid art. He turned this way and that, adding ingredients and stirring. Butter. Spices. Herbs. My eyes danced over the toned muscle of his back and arms, the firm slope of his rounded buttocks exposed above his low-riding pajamas—

He turned sudden eyes on me, pulling my gaze into his like a moth is drawn to a fire. Overwhelmed by naked desire, I lost myself in his eyes like an insect in a storm, and leaned into him, hands gliding over the silky material barely covering his rump. His eyes flamed into mine and his scent surrounded me. Grinning like a boy with a slingshot, he slid his hands under the pajama top and embraced me. I vaguely heard the sizzling of frying food as we kissed. Our arms entwined. He tasted of summer dreams and the molten glow of Vancouver Harbor at sunset. When we finally broke off, both gasping, his eyes dove into mine with incredible devotion. Then he expressed surprised bewilderment. What had he expected?

Uncomfortable, I released a husky laugh. It broke the tension, and he followed suit. He pulled me close and we kissed again. Keeping me in a tight grip with one arm, he tended the eggs and roamed freely beneath my pajama top in tandem with his other hand. Between gropes and giggles, I helped, or rather hindered our breakfast preparation.

We finally sat across from each other at his cozy dining-room table to eat breakfast. With his elbow on the table, he leaned head in his hand and stared at me with a silly absent smile. His look reminded me of a boy who'd just found a lost treasure and was admiring it with a kind of incredulous wonder. It made me feel anxious and wonderful at the same time.

I pointed at his untouched plate with my fork.

"You're not eating," I said with a self-conscious laugh.

"Yes, I am," he responded with a self-pleased chuckle. "I'm feasting on you, the girl of my dreams."

Suddenly uncomfortable again, I looked down and smiled

coyly. "The way you look at me sometimes, as though—"

"—I knew you from before?" he finished for me. I jerked my gaze up and found him evaluating me with a maudlin look. "You just remind me of ... *someone*," he explained with an enigmatic smile. His face moved with complex emotion as he contemplated the wall beyond me. "She's so much like you ... and yet ... you're different in so many ways ... it's uncanny ..."

I found that curious. He'd also looked familiar when I'd first seen him. But I knew I'd never met him. "Someone special?" I fished.

"Yes." He didn't offer more.

I searched his face for unspoken answers and couldn't gauge his expression. I felt suspicion cloud me and decided to be blunt. "Are you married?"

He looked amused. "No."

"Is she still alive?" I asked in macabre curiosity.

He sighed and I caught a shadow of pain in his face. "Not exactly."

I hadn't expected that. How could someone *not exactly* be alive? Either they were or they weren't.

In the silence that followed, Serge bolted down a huge portion of eggs. Then, mouth still full, he caught me with an intense stare. "Rhea, have you ever had a dream so real that when you woke up you thought for a moment that it actually happened?"

"Yes." I nodded with a crooked smile and bit into a pulpy gadpie fruit. "Lots of times, actually." I was still mulling over the woman who was *not exactly* still alive.

"Tell me about one."

"You first," I said coyly, elbow on the table and leaning my face on my hand.

"Okay." He grinned, happy to accommodate me. He leaned back, muscular chest stretching into taut lines. "But, it's not a nice one. More like a recurring nightmare."

My lips grew taut and I nodded half-frowning. "I get those too."

"And it isn't mine. It was my girlfriend's. You still want to hear it?"

I knit my brows and gave him a withering look. "Maybe not, if you keep stalling." She was his jagging *girlfriend*?

"Okay, well, she kept dreaming about getting into a PLT car that jags offline on her, speeds up and careers off the regular route. In her dream she knows what's going to happen because she's had a déjà vu. The car speeds too fast toward a critical corner."

I felt my heart race. He was describing my experience of a few days ago.

"Isn't that creepy?" he asked.

"What happened?"

"Nothing. She always woke up." He shrugged. "Of course."

"Of course," I repeated. Then I gave Serge a hard searching look. "Does she still get that nightmare?"

"I told you, she's ... well ..." He trailed off.

I pursed my lips. "Right," I said sharply. "She's not exactly alive." I mimicked his tone. "And what exactly does that mean, 'not exactly alive' ...? Not exactly dead?" I persisted in an edgy voice.

His face clouded with genuine heartbreak, and I felt immediate regret for my snide remark. He expelled a long breath and leaned forward, clasping his hands together on the table. "She's been in a coma for a year," he said, then broke from my gaze to look away. He blinked several times in obvious grief. "She's never coming out of it."

I swallowed down my regret at being so recklessly callous. I wanted to lean forward to cover his hand with mine in comfort, but restrained the urge. "I'm so sorry. I was just—" I broke off, swallowing again, and thinking how odd it was that his girlfriend's dream and my déjà vu experience appeared so similar. I realized that most of my bad-tempered reaction was on account of his attachment.

He seemed to read my mind and took my hand. "Rhea, she's not my girlfriend anymore. She's with God now."

I should have felt relieved. But somehow I couldn't help a

stirring pity for the other girl. Sliding my hand out from under his, I challenged, "You mean you abandoned her?"

He blinked several times in obvious frustration and ran his hands briskly over his stubble. "No, of course not. We're just parted; she's no longer of this Earth. We loved each other. In fact, it was love at first sight," he said, gazing straight at me. Then he blinked and noticed the time. He stood up. "Speaking of parting, I must go. I'll be late for my appointment."

Serge disappeared into the bathroom to shave and clean up. I returned to the bedroom to retrieve my clothes from the cleaning chute and got dressed. I then slid past him into the bathroom to brush my hair as he made his way to the utility room to change. It took all my control not to stroke his clean-shaven face and detain him yet again, but I respected his need to leave for his appointment even though I had nothing planned for the day. I soon caught a glimpse of him through the bathroom door and suspended my brushing to stare at his reflection in the mirror.

He looked like a monarch, transformed in an expensive immaculately fitting charcoal tocanai suit with his hair combed and face clean-shaven. I'd only seen him sweaty and unruly in casual gym clothes. This suit, spun from the rare tocan melded with AI nanos, appeared much more in element with his dignified mannerisms: he exuded the confident image of a man of power and motion. I felt a slight twinge at being outclassed.

Serge appeared a little preoccupied as he straightened his jacket. But when he caught me gazing at him through the mirror, he gave me a warm smile and sauntered over.

"I have lots to do today," he said, standing behind me and looking at my reflection in the mirror. "But I'd love to meet you at the gym at the usual time and we can go for supper then come back here." He grasped a handful of my hair and brought it up to his nose. "I love your hair," he breathed out in a rapt voice. "It's much nicer long like this than short like ..." He trailed off with a crooked grin. I wondered at his choice of words. As if he'd ever seen it short? I hadn't worn it short since I was twelve. He brushed my hair to one side with his hands to kiss the back of my neck. My eyes fluttered shut briefly at the touch of his lips and the surprising erotic exhilaration of his smooth cool skin, faintly scented with aftershave. "My treat," he added between kisses.

"I'd love to," I said, pressing my hand over his and turning to face him. "I've got lots to do too," I lied. What did an ex-Enforcer do? I'd been loafing around since I'd returned from Mar Delena. Since meeting Serge, I'd procrastinated on my Eclipse/shapeshifter research and code-cracking. I'd found my resolve to carry out my crazy mission melting away. Doctor Rava wouldn't have my treatment *tecks* ready until next week in any case. I didn't have to make my decision until then.

"Rhea, stay with me, here," Serge whispered into my hair with sudden excitement. "Move in. Stay." I smelled his enticing fragrance of strawberries and musk and knew what I wanted to say.

"I'll think about it."

Θ

I returned to my flat, my mind already made up. I entered the empty apartment with a sigh at my familiar surroundings. The place felt safe, but lonely. I wandered to my workroom, sat at my workbench and absently handled my weapon-making equipment. I'd spent many hours here with a cup of soyka and Jaz parked on my sketches as I worked on my holo design unit. To what end? I was looking at a new career now. I stood up and entered my bedroom. I peeled off my clothes and threw them into the cleaning chute then changed into a fresh pair of black trousers and gray sleeveless top. With a growing smile, I tossed some extra clothes and toiletries into my backpack.

I was about to leave the bedroom when, thinking of the close calls I'd had in the park and land-transport, I turned to the bed. After a moment of hesitation, I slid my hand under my pillow, finding the cool metal handle of my second *pocket*, the one Ennos didn't know I had. I'd also made a second MEC, but it was stranded on Benny. I threw the *pocket* into my bag and went to my kitchen to feed Jasper.

As if he'd heard the tingling of food cubes in his dish, the tappin entered through my open window and purred.

"There you are, Jaz," I said, seizing the animal and giving him a big hug. "Miss me?" He wanted down, so I let him drop to the floor, and he went straight for the dish. "Better pace yourself, Jazzy, that's going to have to last you for a while. Don't know when I'll be back." I smiled, with spicy thoughts of Serge.

Watching Jasper eat prompted me to check my cupboard. I found it mostly bare, but discovered a bit of chocolate. I slid some into my mouth, savoring the rich sweet cocoa.

Back in my living-room, I checked my messages and noted, without surprise, that only one new call had been left on the holo-com: it was from my landlord—no doubt a reminder to pay my rent. My gaze drifted to my father's holo image on the wall, and I lingered on his heroic face. Then I closed my eyes and breathed in deeply, centering myself for my Tai Chi form.

I focused inward. When I opened my eyes with a long exhale, I stepped in fluid movements to the meditative exercise. I performed my graceful slow-motion dance, limbs coiling to an inner rhythm and seeking that place inside me that was calm and at peace.

As my body poised and turned in choreographed postures of the dragon, the tiger, and the crane, I found my mind drifting back to Earth where at the tender age of four I'd first learned Tai Chi in Stanley Park with my mother. Every morning the two of us performed the graceful dance in unison. We'd stepped through the eighty-three postures in synchrony, mind and body united with nature and the universe, mother and daughter linked in spirit and soul.

Until I'd killed that baldie and our universe shattered and collapsed on us.

I found myself sighing into space and gazing again at my father's holo on the far wall. The Eosians had saved Earth, but not for me. Or the rest of humanity, as it turned out.

I recalled viewing that momentous first greeting of 215 standard galactic years ago when Azaes's purple face became an instant icon to humanity as his transmission found its way into every form of communication on Earth. It was humanity's first contact with an alien race and, though humbling at best, was considered of such significance that humanity's calendars were marked from that day. I sat down and instructed my home manager to replay the historic vid:

"I am Azaes," said the attractive Eosian in acceptable English. He stood in front of an intriguing background of towering dark blue crystals that glinted inside a glass-like building. Azaes wore a deep purple robe that was provocatively open, displaying his muscular and hairless chest. "I'm spokesperson for the peoples of Eos, a small planet in the system you call the Pleiades. I bring tidings of peace and prosperity in cooperation with humanity. I bear gifts of knowledge far superior to yours: the ability to quell disease, poverty, pollution, even death as you know it. Yes, the gift of eternity. We will share these wonderful things with you when you are ready to receive them." Then came the bludgeon: "You are not ready yet. You still wield hostilities and wage war upon one another; you covet power and greedily lust after your neighbor's treasures. Your disrespect for your environment is testimony to your disrespect for yourselves." Then, as suddenly as he'd appeared on the worldwide vids, Azaes disappeared, his two-minute speech stirring up more calamity than a year's worth of war.

I leaned back and absently ran my hand through my hair, appraising the supercilious Eosian more closely. I recalled that what followed were ten televids—his 'ten commandments'—each outlining an Eosian virtue to which humans could strive and an arcane reference to humanity's eventual Awakening. The vids had been humiliating. They cemented in most human's minds that Eosians were not so much interested in sharing as dominating. It would take years to eventually mollify the hysteria caused by Azaes's threatening intellectual arrogance, and anti-alien feelings would remain for the most part among the masses. I thought it no surprise that he was murdered when he came to Earth fifteen years later, supposedly the first alien to set foot on Earth. Azaes had allegedly forsaken his immortality to accompany his beloved, Genevieve Dubois, to Earth. He had no idea, I reflected, how much he had forsaken for his love of a human woman. Already disliked and feared, Azaes ensured his own demise when he displayed an awesome power. The two of them vanished soon after, fodder for rumors and myth.

Earth would be free of baldies for another hundred years, until Eosians decided to end their isolation, create the Galactic Guardians, research the galaxy, and terraform. They only came in great numbers when the Vos attacked, thirty years ago. Not soon enough, I thought, staring longingly at my father's image. I seized my backpack and left my apartment.

As I stepped outside to go to the library for a few hours to while away some time before meeting Serge at the gym, I spotted a familiar figure lurking in a side street across from me. I squashed the urge to lean forward for a better look. But it was obvious that it was Bas. What the chaos was he doing in this part of town? He was trying too hard to look casual. He was *not* watching me with such effort it was obvious that he *was*. Had Ennos sent him to spy on me? I crossed the street and pretended that I hadn't seen him.

ELEVEN

The day had been sultry and hot and the night provided little in the way of reprieve. It was still thirty degrees as we returned from supper to Serge's place. I flopped into one of his plush chairs and brought up the bottom of my blouse to wipe the perspiration off my face. I felt a refreshing coolness where the air wicked away the sweat that sluiced down between my breasts. For all its expensive furniture and art and other décor, the place had lousy air-conditioning.

Serge whistled lightly and I jerked my blouse down to cover my bared breasts. He smirked at me, eyes flashing with appreciation. I responded with a mock glare.

"Close your eyes," Serge commanded me. I gave him a

puzzled look. "Go on," he said, grinning sideways. I gave him a warning smile then did as he told. "Now open your mouth."

I giggled, a little nervous. "What is it?" When he didn't answer, I dutifully opened my mouth, half convinced he was going to offer me a piece of himself. I listened for him to unzip his trousers but heard nothing. In the silence I suddenly felt something cold and juicy on my lips and tongue. Then I smelled the intoxicating fragrance of strawberries. Real strawberries. My eyes snapped open as I bit down and tasted a burst of flavor.

"Did you get these from Earth?" I said with a full mouth. He beamed at me. "They must have cost a freighter-load!"

"They grow them right here, Rhea." He laughed. "But they were still expensive." From behind his back he pulled out two bowls filled with cut strawberries and fresh cream. He winked. "Let's go up to the roof. It's cooler. There's a breeze outside."

He led me up a corner staircase to a trapdoor, which he opened, after giving me his bowl. Once he lifted himself up, he crouched down to retrieve both bowls and let me haul myself up to the roof onto my knees. I felt a slight breeze on my face as I rose to my feet and gazed at the stars. Serge's building was one of the highest in the neighborhood and commanded a good view of both the city and the night sky. I cast an appreciative glance around me before following Serge to a large bed that occupied the middle of the roof.

I barked out a delighted laugh. "You're prepared!"

"I like to sleep under the stars, especially on hot days like this," he responded, pulling off the protective cover then stripping to just his trousers and sitting on the bed to eat his strawberries. "One of the perks of living on the top floor."

"Sure is," I agreed. I sat next to him and spooned some strawberries into my mouth, closing my eyes and savoring the taste of hot summer days and children laughing.

Serge caressed my arm then pulled at my clammy top. Keeping my eyes closed, I laid down the bowl and raised my arms to let him pull it off me. Then I reclined on the bed and let him slide off the rest of my clothes. I heard him remove his trousers then felt the bed give way under his weight as he lay beside me. He didn't touch me and I finally realized that he was gazing up at the stars and at Iota Hor b, luminescent in the northern sky.

I turned to face him as he lay on his back. His face was moist with sweat from the heat and he was emitting a different kind of aroma, not the one he usually did when he was aroused. He smelled of an alpine meadow in spring, fresh and alive with a complex fragrance of sweet and spicy perfumes.

"It's a beautiful night to watch the stars," Serge said in a gentle voice, balancing his bowl of strawberries on his chest. He pointed to Betelgeuse, a red super giant star and one of the brightest in the night sky. "The name, *Betelgeuse*, means mysterious woman in Arabic. Your star, perhaps …?"

I caught him grinning at me for a moment then he turned back to look up. I followed his gaze, and reclined on my back to enjoy the view of the night sky above. "Along with that one," I pointed to Rigel, "it forms part of the Orion Constellation on Earth." I found it gratifying that I could still see them here, on an alien moon orbiting a gas giant in a solar system over fifty light-years from home.

"It's a mysterious universe," he said, still contemplating the night sky. He'd put his bowl of strawberries down and placed his hands behind his head. "Filled with strange and bizarre astrophysical creatures. Black holes, bursters and pulsars, quasars, magnetars and dark energy."

"A lot of which we now understand," I conceded, spooning a huge portion of the berries into my mouth and savoring their fresh wet flavor. "Thanks to the Eosians."

"Ah, yes, the Eosians and their gods … But have they given us the whole story?"

I leaned over the bed to place my empty bowl on the floor then turned to face him again, propping myself up on my elbow. He met my eyes with a strange look and drew himself up, mirroring my action and propping himself up.

"Okay," I prompted. "Tell me a story."

"Here's one: what if everything exists as part of a fractal

continuum?" he said. "No beginning and no end."

It sounded intriguing. "You mean no singularities? No Big Bang?"

He gave me a sly smile and gently traced the curves of my body from breast to hip, rousing my flesh with quiet desire.

I brushed my tongue across my upper teeth seductively then returned him a slanted smile of invitation. "Go on."

"Okay, what if every conscious being, every soul, was a gateway along that fractal continuum …? But, for each soul, there was a part of that continuing whole that they never consciously perceived and a whole time continuum they weren't aware of." His fingers roamed then lingered, tracing the shape of the slightly raised scar tissue on my buttock. Serge knew all my scars by now—the outside ones, that is—and caressed them with special feeling. "They could only look outward and in one direction, to the outer universe, never recognizing that a whole inner universe existed inside them, full of people like you and me, and that together, these two divergent universes, these *diverses*, formed a *metaverse* of all that was, is, and will be."

I smiled, amused, and grabbed his hand to direct it down between my thighs. "Diverse? Metaverse? You're making this up as you go along, aren't you?"

His hand bounced up from where I'd moved it and he ignored my jibe and continued, fingers idly brushing along the blenoid-tooth punctures on my thigh, "So, somewhere between the infinities of inner and outer universe, these diverses would meet. And at this violent interface you would experience the clash of two worlds boiling with grotesque unimaginable phenomena and seething with paradox: black holes, quasars; intuition, *déjà vu*, clairvoyance … order in chaos … darkness at the heart of all beauty … a mathematician with faith … the strength of surrender … dying to live … loving your enemy … hurting someone you love …"

He was staring deep into my eyes and I found myself caught by some hidden meaning in his alarming intensity. At some point this had ceased to be conjecture, and I wondered what he was really trying to say to me. In the growing darkness, his stare pierced my heart like the hot blade of a knife. I inhaled sharply with a vision of my nightmare and felt the sudden heat of blood rushing up into my face.

Then his penetrating gaze vanished like vapor and his eyes crinkled with pleasant whimsical thoughts. "Okay," he continued, his voice returning to its casual tone as he drew circles with his fingers on my abdomen, "So, if time was a circular, never-ending loop, then the past of one diverse would be the future of the other."

"And where they met ...?" I prompted just for the fun of it, feeling amusement tug the right corner of my mouth up.

"In dreams, Rhea," he responded enthusiastically. "Or lucid moments of open-mindedness ... Trances. Precognition. *Déjà vu* ... all the paranormal stuff for which science has absolutely no explanation in this limited dimensional world. *A mysterious power that all may feel and no philosophy can explain*, as Goethe once said."

I couldn't help a smirk. "So, you're suggesting that when someone experiences a *déjà vu* they're actually tapping into their own 'past' in this other parallel universe."

He pushed out his lips thoughtfully and rubbed his well-manicured hand over his mouth and bristly cheeks. "It's more complicated than that; not quite parallel in the way you'd think, but, yes, you've got the gist of it."

"And when I follow a hunch to find a criminal, I'm tapping into that same thing," I went on.

He smiled appreciatively. "Yeah. Some mystics call it mining 'the collective unconscious' ..." He frowned slightly. "It may seem that way but that's not it at all. It's more like *duende*, I suppose."

"Oh," I said smoothly. "You sure thought a lot about this."

"I have," Serge confirmed, eyes sparkling like jewels.

"Some old Spaniard came up with that word."

"A poet."

"Doesn't it mean a demon or some evil spirit or ghost?"

Serge smiled like a magician. "Not quite. It's better

described as a compelling earth-force, an inner spirit that fires the heart and connects the soul to the essence of life … in all its forms and dimensions."

I shifted on the bed. "Okay, let me get this straight: when I have a hunch or a déjà vu, I've just glimpsed this other universe, the inner diverse through this earth-force."

"Not necessarily. In certain dreams you enter the portal that joins the two and because the inner diverse is your past, you get a subconscious glimpse of your future in the outer diverse, moments or years from when you entered so when you actually experience it, it's as though it already happened. Think of it as though you were a stone, skipping along the water, diving in briefly along your trajectory to see where you are and where you're going."

I studied his face for some sign that he was teasing me with all this and found nothing. "You said, not necessarily. Meaning sometimes you're looking into this other—eh—diverse, this inner diverse?"

"Yeah," he said, rolling onto his back to view the dark sky overhead. "But only mystics can achieve that kind of penetration."

"Like the Schiss?"

"Perfect example," he said smugly, closing his eyes with a lazy smile and clasping his hands behind his head again.

Involuntarily tightening my lips, I thought of something my mother said. "According to my mother," I said, "the Epoptes have this phenomenon called *joining*, which supposedly links a person to the entire fractal network of the universe through some ritual with their sacred tree, the *vishna*. But from what I can figure, it's just a fancy word for kinky sex," I scoffed, snorting out my disgust.

"Ah, sex," he said, rolling back on his side to face me with a wry smile. His hand stroked my breasts, teased my nipples hard then he cupped my left breast. "Another beautiful interface. The most potent and divine avenue between the diverses."

"Oh, right!" I laughed and slapped his buttock cheek. "Spoken like a man obsessed with sex!"

He grinned back and seized my waist then pulled me gruffly on top of him as he emitted a flush of strawberry scent. The sudden contact with his warm body drew out a sharp inhale of anticipation from me and I felt a burst of wetness where I stirred for him, hot and impatient for his love. He chuckled and grabbed my wrists then rolled us over onto my back, pinning me beneath him. "Like sex isn't constantly on *your* mind, my beautiful *chérie* with the gorgeous smile," he breathed, lips hovering over mine, almost touching. Certainly teasing. I felt him hard against me and flushed with heat.

"You mean like some Gnosis thing? Experience God through orgasm?" I stared up at him with an inviting smile.

He grinned. "Something like that." I felt his breath on my face, his warm flesh against mine. My own breaths escalated as his face drew closer. But his lips only brushed mine and he drew back. I smelled his ardor melt to contemplation as he searched deep into my eyes.

"Do you believe in destiny, Rhea?" he asked, rising up onto his knees and straddling me. I drank in his naked magnificence and sighed with impatience. "… That destiny brought us together …? What about fate?" I didn't respond but my eyes must have told him. He looked disappointed but not surprised. "No, I didn't think so. That's truly ironic."

I wondered what he was thinking as he sighed and gazed past me into the night sky with a wistful look. Where was the irony in my disbelief?

When he returned his gaze to me, he seemed to search deep into my eyes. "What about God, then?"

Was it a plea? What could I say? I didn't believe in God.

"I don't know," I offered, beginning to feel uncomfortable again. My mother believed in all that. Laura Hawke's hero was Genevieve Dubois, after all, who had experienced an Epoptes first hand. The 'god' had supposedly provided a revelation to Dubois about the universe through a *vishna* tree. How she'd done that I didn't even want to know. In any case, from all the things my mother had related and the historic vids I'd seen, I had found no evidence that Dubois had brought back any great wisdom — just an Eosian lover who'd gotten her pregnant.

"The baldies believe in the Epoptes," Serge said, leaning over me and playing with my hair. "They claim these gods guide them through their dreams to be the watchdogs of the galaxy. That's quite a responsibility they've taken on."

"Well," I said, stirring restlessly beneath him. "I haven't seen evidence of these Epoptes yet." It was all unverified myth. The story of how the Eosians were created from the irresponsible and flagrant sexual relations of these so-called gods with primitive humans back in the stone age, was mildly farfetched ... except for the indisputable fact of Eosian DNA being so similar to human DNA. I acknowledged that Eosians and humans shared a common ancestry. But I didn't have to swallow that blenoid-shit story of how they were divinely created.

Serge gazed intensely into my eyes. "What if the Epoptes do exist, Rhea? And the Eosians are getting their instructions from them."

I gave him a hard look and slithered out from under him to sit up and cross my legs. "You don't believe that, really ... do you?"

He studied my face for a moment. "What if they exist but they're wrong?"

TWELVE

Slouched in front of a library holo-file, hand tucked between my legs, I jerked awake. I'd first lapsed into a daydream about Serge, eyes gazing but not focused at the holo in front of me. Then I must have dropped off into a doze. I'd been imagining his muscular chest pressed against my aching breasts and hands on my buttocks pressing me against him.

I pulled my trembling hand from my crotch and stretched my neck back to sit up straight. Sex with Serge had cured me of my Dust shakes. I wondered if it had resulted from all those orgasms. But the cure had come at a cost: I slept a great deal. I seemed to need ten hours each night when five hours used to suffice. I supposed it was all the sex and that I wasn't used to it. He was very energetic and enduring. Was he running me ragged? I didn't care. We were behaving like a couple of Rills, I thought with a self-mocking smirk. I didn't mind.

The thought of sex with him, often frantic, passionate, and just beyond control, drove me to distraction. I'd become obsessed with it, probably making up for all the years I'd abstained. I felt a tender ache and a moist fever flow between my legs at the thought of him and the enticing smell he gave off. I began to wonder where he went all day and realized that I was starting to feel possessive.

I surged to my feet and paced around the research cubicle, raking my hands through my uncombed hair. I smoothed it back and lashed it with an elastic. I was a mess and found my thoughts feverishly returning to Serge. I still didn't know him. Was he really an art dealer? If he approached his art with even half the passion he gave me during sex, he was a hot commodity. Was he telling me the truth about not having any family?

I leaned over the holo-console, toying with the urge to research him, then at the last minute recoiled. I had decided from early on to respect him and let him open up at his own pace. Like me. There were secrets in every household, I conceded. And I wasn't a cop anymore, I reminded myself.

"C'mon, girl," I mumbled to myself. "Do something useful."

I'd been researching the shapeshifter community and focused my attention on the holo file again:

While several organisms could change their shape in some way, including some Eosians, records indicated that true shapeshifters were originally from Borrias, a small planet in the Perseus Arm, about six thousand light-years from Earth. Borrs actually had no home planet. They'd scattered throughout the galaxy in the last several decades since evacuating their destroyed planet. No one knew what they really looked like, because when the Vos destroyed their homeland, the Borrs adopted the forms of the indigenous peoples of the planets they colonized. Much like the reclusive Eosians, Borrs had kept to themselves in the galaxy prior to the destruction of their planet and their forced emigration. Shapeshifters weren't generally trusted in the galaxy. Their gypsy ways and tendencies for off-color behavior gave them a stigma. Several had turned to criminal activities to get by. Many were rangers, smugglers, general scoundrels. And, as I'd discovered, shifters now ran the most notorious crime organization in the galaxy.

Aside from Earth, Borrias was supposedly the only other planet attacked by the Vos, which was itself an interesting oddity. I'd often wondered what the two planets held in common for the Vos. Borrs and Humans didn't seem similar as people, except that Borrs appeared to prefer the human form.

I continued to review V'mer's colorful history of malicious and treacherous acts. After skimming several years worth, I lost all trace of his existence, as though he'd appeared from nowhere. I continued my search well back into my own childhood, hoping to find him again. And I did. I found an imageless text record on Helsig 2 for the multi-planetary corporation, MedTOX, a company that specialized in inter-species genetic engineering and useful viruses. The record described its employees, among whom were U'clid and M'leez, both genetic manipulators and virologists there. They were described as being Eosian. I wasn't surprised: while the human form was the shapeshifter's preferred shape — something about most compatible physiology and temperament — the Eosians, who shared a similar ancestry with humanity, were the next most popular shape assumed by shapeshifters. Their eldest of three children, V'mer, was included because he was already on the payroll.

The files included some grizzly data from the local PD: V'mer's mother died of a suicide shortly after his father died—no, wait, the father had disappeared. U'clid, had vanished without a trace when he was visiting Earth on business eighteen years ago. All three children disappeared and the mother was posthumously accused of destroying them, out of insanity. But that had obviously not happened, I reflected, because V'mer re-emerged years later. As for the other two children, I had no way of tracking them; their names hadn't been given.

According to the records, V'mer would have been twelve years old when he lost his father. His siblings were obviously younger—there was no record of them. I did the math: I would have been five ...

There was something creepy about all this. A warning flag in my mind sent a chill through me. I checked the date and place of U'clid's reported disappearance. My heart slammed. He was last seen in Vancouver, Canada, and his reported disappearance was the day after I'd nuked my mother's Eosian boyfriend. I swallowed down the bile rising in my throat and found my mind racing: Was U'clid my mother's dead boyfriend? He would have been cheating on his wife to be with my mother. And it would certainly explain V'mer's personal hatred of me. If V'mer was indeed U'clid's surviving son, then I was partially responsible for the criminal V'mer had become.

I raked back rogue strands of my hair, sweeping them into the elastic, then rested my head in my hands. Was I systematically wiping out a whole family with my eyes? Who were those others V'mer had referred to? He had two siblings. A younger brother and sister. Were they the ones V'mer had mentioned in his threats? Was one of them The Rose? Was I destined to kill his whole family?

I closed my eyes and tried to concentrate on my breathing as my mind raced with horrible thoughts. I'd convinced myself that joining the Galactic Guardians was my true path to righteousness. Protecting and maintaining order and freedom in the galaxy was an honorable pursuit. The discipline and high ideals of the Guardians was exactly what I'd needed to keep my awful melting power in check and redeem my earlier transgression. But a string of failures seemed to plague my career. More innocent blood was spilled on account of my ambition for justice. Even V'mer had said it: I was dangerous to everyone and everything.

Ennos was right. My life had been a string of blunders ever since I'd committed the greatest blunder of them all, thanks to my mother's 'gift.' Why was it that every time I tried to do the right thing, I created an atrocity instead? As though God had it in for me ... Yeah, like there *was* a God. There were no gods. No Epoptes. The Vos, who'd fashioned themselves as gods didn't even come close. Beings of superior capabilities. Tyrants, even. But not gods. That was too easy. And nothing was easy in this universe, I concluded.

ϴ

Serge sat across from me at the Homestead Restaurant, known for its Earth-style dishes. He quietly enjoyed his supper of chili, Caesar salad, and garlic bread as I, feeling restive and slightly nauseous, picked at my sushi with my chopsticks.

Serge had attempted to engage me in light conversation at first and then abandoned the effort after a few laconic responses from me. He'd tried monologue for a while then finally lapsed into silence, throwing concerned glances between my down-turned face and my untouched plate.

He broke the silence with a question: "So, this MEC of yours ... did you design it all by yourself?"

I raised my head and eyed him warily. "Why do you ask?"

"I just thought it was an interesting sideline for a Guardian Enforcer, that's all. So, are they complicated and do you do it in your head or on some holo design program?"

My eyes narrowed with distrust. "Everything's up here." I tapped my head with my finger. "I make it a point not to keep records."

He firmed his lips and nodded as I looked down again, picking at my food.

We'd been quiet at the table for some time when, struck by a sudden macabre curiosity, I raised my gaze and asked, not too politely, "So, this critically ill girlfriend of yours ... how did she get that way?"

He looked up at me, mouth full of food, slightly startled and obviously unwilling to discuss the topic. "You don't really want to know," he said through all the food.

"Sure, I do," I persisted coolly. "I'm an Enforcer."

He sighed in resignation and leaned forward, challenging me with his eyes. "OK. After making glorious love with me, she left me sleeping in the early morning and went upstairs to her art studio, probably to create some new work—she often got inspired after making love with me." He wasn't pulling any stops with me, I thought, stiffening. "Someone was waiting for her," he went on. "He brutally attacked her with a knife and she fell out of her twenty-story-high apartment window onto a deck three floors down. She broke her back and suffered severe brain damage and massive internal injuries from her knife wounds. I wish to God I had woken with her ... maybe I could have done something to intervene. But I slept in and the bastard got her. She's been on a life-machine for a year and isn't about to come off. That detailed enough for you?"

I swallowed. "Yeah."

I gazed back down at the table and felt a nauseous shame for bringing up a topic that obviously made Serge uncomfortable. It was obvious to me that he blamed himself for his girlfriend's state. Was that why Serge woke so early every morning? I considered that this poor woman's fate closely reflected my recurring nightmare. Oddly enough it compelled me to press on and I returned an intense gaze on Serge. "What's she look like?"

This time he responded with a wry humorless smile. Then he frowned darkly, eyes piercing into mine. "Dead," he said. "She looks dead, pale and lifeless with tubes coming out of her." He pointed on his own body. "Here and here." He stabbed his thorax and left side with his finger.

I inhaled sharply. "Oh." I felt an abrupt sympathetic pulse of pain in my thorax and left side.

Then his eyes focused through me as he allowed himself to travel to the past and I saw his face transform. It made my throat swell and I swallowed down roiling emotions of misgiving. What in chaos was I doing, torturing him?

"She was remarkable looking," Serge said almost dreamily. "The most beautiful woman I've ever met. Very feminine. She had poise and grace, honest eyes, a warm heart and an innocent spirit. Almost naïve in her trust of the world. She was an incredibly creative and successful artist and a book trader and I used to love watching her dance ..."

In short, everything I wasn't, I concluded, examining the table again. Ironic how this woman had even taken my abandoned dreams and realized them. The closest I came to dancing was in my martial arts form.

Serge added, "She looked just like you."

I jerked my head up to find his eyes refocused on me with an appreciative smile. His eyes sparkled like a sunlit field covered in morning dew. He'd traded darkness for lightness and seized my hand. "You're her spitting image." He then laughed with genuine amusement and let go of my hand. "But it's uncanny how different you are ..."

I squirmed in my seat as he paid the bill by waving his arm with embedded IDR over the pay-holo on the table. A green message floated above his arm, indicating completion of his transaction with the Galactic Bank.

"She wasn't tough like you." Serge turned back to me with an easy smile, blithely unaware of my discomfort. "She had none of your fury. She wasn't a fighter. She was a peaceful soul." Then he tightened his lips, eyes studying me with a hardened stare. I felt myself recoil in my chair. "If she'd had your warrior spirit, she might still be alive and well right now."

I laughed sharply, releasing a nervous tension, and heard an uneasy edge in my sardonic voice, "So, what are you saying? That she's an angel and I'm the Devil?"

His eyes flashed at my challenge. "That's good," he said with a nod, evaluating my metaphor. "No, I'm not saying that. But you have to admit you're not an open book, Rhea. Chaos, what woman sleeps with a killing weapon of her own design under her pillow? You're a very complex woman, motivated, no doubt, by your unique life experiences on this world." Then he gave me a rakish smile and said, "And I'm enjoying the adventure of finding out who you are."

Slightly disarmed by his guileless charm, I felt a smile

creep over my intended glower. "You got out of that one rather eloquently," I said.

"So did you," he replied, winking at me and rising to his feet. "Let's go home and celebrate our achievements."

"Okay," I obliged and, hooking my arm in his offered one, let him steer me out of the restaurant. Why did I still feel so terrible?

We walked in silence and I felt the warm breeze of the night caress my face as I listened to the murmurs of the city. I glanced up at the night sky. It was clear and unveiled a heavenly bounty of twinkling stars. The enormous fiery ball of Iota Hor b shone to my left, and at the sight of it I felt my breath almost hitch with strong emotion. An inexplicable sadness and a deep yearning for home weighed me down. I missed the heady aroma of freshly cut grass and honeysuckle blooms … the exhilaration of watching red maple leaves vault on the wings of an October wind … the sweet sound of my mother singing me to sleep at night and the promising sunrise of an innocent girl's new day.

As we neared the park close to his building, Serge squeezed my arm and quipped with a casual smile, "Almost home … Hey, 'Boadicea,' what do you say to a duel? My pistol against yours." He laughed, wiggling his pelvis and obviously thinking he was being cute.

"No," I bit out, suddenly very cross. "I'm going home. *My* home." I broke from him to cut through the park.

"Hey!" He seized my arm forcefully, reacting to my dark mood. "No, you aren't."

"Jag you," I snarled, struggling free. "I have to feed my tappin."

"Sure. But not now. In the morning." He grabbed my arm.

"Let me go!" I twitched out of his grip and struck him in the face. He stumbled back, cheek blistering red, but lunged out to seize my arm again, swinging me around so I collided against him. "Leave me alone! Jag off!" I yelled, losing control.

"Not like this," he said in a rough voice. Then his voice softened, "You've been looking for an argument since we met for supper. And I finally pissed you off. I was just trying to cheer you up. I'm sorry, Rhea. If I've offended you in any way, believe me I didn't mean to. Please come home with me." His eyes pleaded with me.

I suddenly felt very tired and let my shoulders sag. It was all I could do to keep from collapsing into tears. He seemed to realize this and folded his arms around me. I willingly sank into his embrace and let him lead me back to his place.

Once inside, he took me by the hand and gently led me to his bedroom. I let him undress me and maneuver me to the bed. He coaxed me to lie face down on the bed, then he loosened my hair and began to give me an Opsis massage.

I closed my eyes, feeling my tight muscles relax one by one.

"Something happened today," he said, breaking the long silence. "Where were you?"

I remained silent.

"Rhea?" he prompted.

"Mmm," I murmured, face buried in the pillow.

He stopped for a moment and set his hands on my shoulders. "I know this has nothing to do with my old girlfriend. You were looking for a fight and that was just an excuse. What happened today that got you so upset …? Talk to me, Rhea."

I sighed, turned my head just enough to be able to see him, and pulled some stray hairs away from my eyes. After a long sigh of resignation, I forced myself to speak: "Do you remember asking me about whether I believed in destiny?"

He resumed his massage. "You didn't exactly, if I recall."

"What about you? Do you believe that we're fated to play out a particular life-path no matter what we do? Or do you think we have some control over our future?"

"Hmm," he murmured, now stroking my arm. "I think it's a combination of the two."

"I knew you'd say that," I responded glumly.

We remained quiet for a moment as he continued his massage, patiently waiting for me to continue. When I didn't, he offered in a low soothing voice, "Well, here's my thought on the matter: what if our perception of destiny is nothing more than

117

our inner-mind recognizing the many dimensional pathways already followed by our soul in that other diverse ...?"

I smiled wryly at him for bringing up his farfetched theory again. "I almost like that one, Serge," I said. Emotion welled up my throat, shaking my voice, "I sometimes feel like my whole life is a dream defined by a few pivotal moments of lucid action and thought."

He stopped his caress. "What happened today?"

After a long moment of silence, I turned over onto my back. "I defined my life when I was five years old."

He half-smiled. "That's what the psychologists say. You're usually everything you'll be by age five."

"Then I'm a natural born killer."

I saw him frown with concern and lean back to study me.

I sat up, eyes gripping his in terrified determination. "I murdered an innocent man with my eyes when I was five years old."

To his credit Serge didn't say anything. But his face creased further with concern as he waited for me to expound.

I heaved a sigh. "My mother never told me she'd *tecked* me until after ... she ... they ... I caught them together, doing ... and I thought he was hurting her." My breaths grew shallow as I fought from letting the tears spill out. I finished in gasps. "He ... shouted something at me ... I melted him ... I didn't even know what I was doing."

I had no idea how I'd gotten there but found myself scooped up in Serge's arms, wailing out convulsive tears. He stroked my hair and murmured, "It's okay to cry ..." as great tearing sobs racked me. "There ... there ... *chérie ... ma petite ...*" he murmured. "It's the first time you've cried since it happened, isn't it?"

How did he know?

Much later, when my weeping had subsided and we sat in quiet solace as Serge stroked my hair, he said tenderly, "I don't believe in that kind of destiny, Rhea. You are master of your own life." He kissed my wet eyelids then pulled me down with him on the bed and held me for a long time. Then he made gentle love to me and I almost keened my climax aloud.

Θ

I sighed awake and let my eyes open slowly. I stretched like a lazy cat and thought briefly of Jasper. I hadn't been home in a while but Jasper knew how to look after himself; I'd been gone on longer trips as an Enforcer. I felt my leg brush against Serge's. A glance at the clock told me it was seven in the morning local time. Turning to face Serge, I observed that he was still asleep next to me. A smile crossed my lips as I realized that for the first time since I'd shared his bed, I'd woken up before him. Was it possible that for once I'd tired *him* out?

I studied him, relaxed in the bliss of sleep. His face was a complex and paradoxical tapestry of noble god and ruffian. Tousled hair and rough stubble laid siege to strong, noble, and stern features that included a long straight nose and confident jaw. His smile, boyish and vulnerable, opened a universe that I gladly fell into and his trusting mouth was made for kissing. His eyes were the color of a thundercloud, intelligent and soul-piercing. They seemed to effortlessly draw the truth from me. But they were closed now as he sighed in sleep. And with those closed lids, the potency of his face melted to a delicious vulnerability, and I wanted nothing better than to be his helpmate, to protect him and listen to all his jokes, genuine belly laugh, and crazy stories.

Serge was a mystery, I decided as I leaned my head on my hand and watched his body rise and fall with each soft breath he took. When he'd first swept into my world like a summer storm, he'd totally unbalanced me and irrevocably changed the focus of my life. He'd torn down my barriers in one easy sweep of his wild charm and seduced me completely with humor, banter, and genuine warmth. Yet, for someone who'd shared so much about his philosophy and beliefs, I knew next to nothing about Serge's personal life.

His complexity was nowhere more apparent than in his touch. Whenever he touched me I felt unfathomable exhilaration and the thrill of being on the edge of control. It was as though he'd both known me for eternity and was discovering me for the first time. There was a certain familiarity and tenderness that came only from the devotion of a long-time lover in the way he held me, ran his hands through my hair or stroked my face. Yet the way he looked at me, kissed my body, or seized me in a sexual embrace, surged with the electricity of new passion. Serge embodied paradox.

Who was he?

Θ

"I have to go out of town on business for a few days starting tomorrow," Serge said, propping himself up on an elbow in bed. It was 23:00 Local Time, and we'd just made love. I'd learned that asking Serge for details got me nowhere and resigned myself to silence. He must have sensed the disappointment on my face, as I stretched out lazily beside him, body still betraying the languor of spent passion. He leaned over to kiss me on the cheek and offered in a tender voice: "I've got some clients on Opus 9 I have to talk to. I'll be back to eat you from head to foot in a few days."

"You'll eat me *now!*" I commanded, diving under the covers with the confidence that he could. Serge had shown immense sexual endurance. I intended to test his limits. I hooked a slender leg over his muscular thigh and drew him snug against me, then had my mouth on his chest, running my teeth playfully across his rising nipples.

He growled his arousal then winced as I bit playfully. He yelped. "Ow, woman!" And dove under the covers to glare at me.

I smiled tartly.

"Is that the way you want it, eh?" he smirked, eyes gleaming with mischievous cruelty. He seized me in a painful grip and kissed me hard on the lips, tongue probing deep, claiming his territory. I clawed him passionately, felt him wince. Then I bit him hard on the shoulder. He flinched and let go of me for a moment, shouting his objection. I broke from his hold and leapt out of bed, hesitating only long enough to ensure that he was giving chase.

He chased me all around the house, pouncing on me as I shrieked like a girl, and made his conquest in every room. Other times I chased him, kicking obstacles aside. Chairs crashed into walls. Tables scraped across the floor. We made love all night like feral Rills.

THIRTEEN

When I awoke in Serge's bed, I stretched like a cat, felt my body ache in several places, and sighed. Serge was gone. I gazed dreamily around his stark bedroom. There was nothing personal of him in here. It was a cold room. I stretched over to his side of the bed and pushed my face into his pillow, breathing him in. I already missed him. He seemed to fill me with warmth and purpose. He exuded such incredible sexual energy. Now, without him next to me, touching me, I was tired. Empty. And cold.

And I remembered what I was: a has-been Enforcer. What in chaos did a has-been Guardian Enforcer do? I still hadn't figured that one out. My plan to save the galaxy on my own had all but dissolved. I'd begun to conclude that my hunch was crazy, like Ennos said. I'd made it all up in my head out of a desperate angst, to feel important and useful; there was no Vos conspiracy, no shapeshifter involvement, no imminent collapse of galactic order. V'mer had probably been The Rose and had just steered me wrong. And those supposed attempts on my life were the self-concocted paranoia of a lost woman. I needed to relax and forget about it all. Settle down and look for something else to fill my life other than being a Guardian Enforcer. For now, feeding Serge's unfathomable appetite for sex was enough for me. My brain was presently coasting in a numb kind of hedonistic euphoria. I'd shared his bed for close to two weeks and felt no urge to change the arrangement. If only he didn't keep leaving on these mysterious business trips!

I rubbed the sleep out of my eyes and checked the time. Good chaos! I'd slept in until noon. I wasn't normally an early riser but this was ridiculous. What was wrong with me? Then I remembered last night's marathon.

I swung my legs over the bed and groggily rose to shower off. Instead of going straight to the bathroom, I restlessly wandered Serge's spacious apartment, following our passionate love-trail of the previous night . . . and well into the morning. We'd copulated like fierce animals in every room; on the dining table, in the living-room stream, then wet and sliding on the kitchen floor.

We'd grown more frantic as night slid into morning: carelessly knocking over furniture, even a few of his art pieces. Serge didn't seem to care, I considered in sad bewilderment, as I surveyed the wreckage that he hadn't bothered to mop up before he had left this morning. I bent to pick up a piece of Hapaan's ruined sculpture and shook my head, baffled. The hundred-thousand credit sculpture was totally destroyed.

Serge had been so flagrant and rough, practically attacking me, I reflected, still feeling the bruises. On the edge of being cruel and out of control.

Then after, he'd been so gentle with me, drawing my curled body into his and licking the blood off my lips from biting hard during my climax. Sitting on the kitchen floor and leaning against the wall, he'd regarded me with a curious almost plaintive expression on his beautiful face.

"Why?" He had breathed it out. "Why *are* you silent?"

I had to look away and bent my head to lean against his muscled shoulder, closing my eyes. That silence encompassed so much. How could I tell him? I knew that if I opened my mouth all the hurt and guilt would flood out and drown me in it. Sometimes it was all I could do to stop it.

Serge gently took my face in his hands and lifted it until I felt his warm breath on me and trembled. His lips brushed mine as if to kiss it all better. It almost did, and I held back a gasp as he drew away. Compassion was always my undoing.

"Oh, Rhea ... Rhea ..." he whispered hoarsely as I opened my eyes to gaze into his. They sparkled like galaxies. He wiped teardrops off my lashes, tears that I hadn't realized had flowed, and smiled in sad acceptance. "You can trust me, you know. You don't have to hold back with me—"

I stopped him with a kiss. He pulled me closer in a tender embrace. We sat, entwined, as he'd stroked and kissed my hair, murmuring, "You're my destiny." He'd pulled back a rogue strand of hair from my face and gave me one of his careless smiles. "When you first gave me your dimpled smile on Virgil 9, it took my breath literally away. Your smile always does that—"

I smiled sideways and let my brows come together in puzzlement. "I first smiled at you at the gym in the Hive, right here in Neon City. We never met on Virgil 9." I'd never been there. Virgil 9 was an inhabited moon of 70 Virginis-b, a gas giant orbiting a G5 yellow-orange main sequence star, fifty-nine light-years from Earth.

"It was after I knocked you down in the hall outside Shlsh's—" He cut himself off and grimaced.

"What? Who?" I said with a puzzled smile.

His face flushed and he smiled carelessly. "I must have dreamt it," he said, emitting a burst of confusing aromas, a complex mixture of sweet meadow flowers, fishy smell of a lake, and the musk of bog and cottonwoods.

"In that other diverse, of course," I teased.

His eyes widened and he stared at me briefly. Then he seized my face and kissed me. When he drew away to gaze at me, he said, "I believe that when two souls are meant to be together, no matter where or when they're travelling in our infinite wrinkled universe, they'll find each other. Each time, in each life. Forever."

"You mean reincarnation?" I asked.

He sighed out. "I mean that these two souls will know ... they'll recognize each other somehow every time."

"Like Lorenz's 'strange attractors,' star-crossed lovers

colliding in the vast reaches of empty space," I murmured with a goofy smile, half asleep, and rubbing my face against his chest.

He responded more seriously than I'd expected, "More like soul mates, twin fires." Then he cupped my face with his hands and was kissing me again, whispering, "*Vrai … vrai …*"

That was French for true, I realized. "*Oui,*" I added with a crooked smile, "*C'est vrai.*"

He looked at me, startled. Then, suddenly enlightened, Serge grinned. "*Oui, oui, ma chérie …*"

It had been five in the morning when he scooped me in his arms and carried me back to his bed, whispering, "You're my universe, Rhea." He laughed softly, lips brushing over my face. "No matter what happens, believe that … *ma chérie …*"

His reverent voice soothed me and, already succumbing to a half-dream state, I'd let him lay me gently on the bed. Then he lay down beside me, drawing the covers over us and, spooning me, folding his arms over me. I'd fallen into a deep sleep almost instantly.

My eye caught the tiny bleep of my portable com, propped upright on Serge's entranceway desk. Thinking it might be Serge, I scrambled to the com and flicked it on—

Bas's startled and amused face lit the small screen. "You look like shit, Rhea," he said cheerfully, then glanced down my body, pupils dilating. "But your breasts are lovely."

I instantly covered them with my hands and squatted down to hide the rest of me from the com-cam. "What do you want, Bas?" I asked in a clipped voice.

He kept craning in a searching stare of curiosity. "Where are you?"

"None of your business."

"Well, you haven't been home, obviously."

My first thought was Jasper. "Get to the point."

"Well, my friend Jake at the local PD recognized you from the … eh … News vid. He handles B'n Es mostly. He just mentioned to me in passing, because he knows that I'm your … well … eh," he blushed a little, "I work with you."

"And?"

"Your place was trashed last night."

"What?" I stiffened.

"It was done by a professional, Rhea. Only your place got hit and whoever it was knew what they were looking for. They were methodical. The sweepers couldn't find traces of anything. No identifiers—"

"Thanks, Bas. I'll be in touch." I cut off before he had a chance to react and rushed to the bedroom to get my clothes.

Θ

I entered my place for the second time that day at 23:00 Local Time. This time it was after visiting the local PD to follow up on the break-in. The officer, Jake Nahamera, had been quite friendly and reasonable. I managed to be a little amused by how he treated me. He seemed a little scared of me. No doubt my fancy show on Mar Delena had impressed him.

When I'd first entered my apartment, it had felt a little disconcerting to find my place violated and everything in a mess. I'd flinched in a nervous start when Jasper leapt inside through the window I kept open for him. Gathering the purring tappin into my arms, I laughed at myself and slowly wandered from room to room, searching for anything missing. I found nothing. My workshop was particularly in disarray. My sketches were thrown on the floor, the holo obviously tampered with, and some of my tools destroyed. What were they looking for? The MEC I'd surrendered to Ennos? Or notes on its design that only resided in my head? Or the copy I'd made of The Rose's hit list from the info-pod I'd smuggled off the *Ulysses*? Even Ennos didn't know that I'd made a copy, I thought as my groping fingers found the small pod case tucked safely under the fabric of my worn couch.

I pulled it out and as I turned it in my hand, I closed my eyes and inhaled deeply. My breath faltered as I recognized the smell. Bas was right: professionals had done this and left no ID. No ID an ordinary person could detect, that is. But I was no ordinary person. And it was unmistakable: a shapeshifter had been here. I could smell him—no, *her*. And a trace of something very familiar, just out of reach, that triggered surprising and disturbing images that surged like a tidal wave: the delicious heat of Serge's kiss—receiving an excruciating kick in the ribs from V'mer—Serge's warm flesh pressed on mine—V'mer drilling my MEC against my head—

The onslaught made me stagger back and break out into a sweat. *What the chaos was that?*

I dropped into a chair and looked down at the pod container. Without warning, my heart pounded, and I knew the container was empty. I snapped it open. The pod was gone! They had their prize. Now only Ennos had the information, and he wasn't doing anything with it.

I found myself staring at my holo-com. The stored message light was winking. I never had watched that second message I'd received the day I'd come home from Mar Delena, the one I'd refused to watch. It couldn't have been Serge because I hadn't met him yet. It was unlikely to provide a clue to what had happened here, but it was another unanswered question, and I didn't like too many of them at the same time. Taking the remote, I scrolled through several messages from my landlord—to that second message I'd refused to watch and instructed the home com to open it for viewing:

V'mer! He was smirking. "Oh, by the way, your mother tastes great. She isn't anything like you."

Heart slamming, I sprang to my feet and raced out of my apartment.

Θ

I rushed to the nearest PLT station and gruffly instructed the car that responded to take me to the Westside, to Elysian, where most of the Eosians lived. It was a well-established, very upscale part of town, with old graystone buildings constructed like Earth's New England. Within a short time I stood in front of the iron gate of an old apartment complex, impatiently waiting for the holo to alight. It soon did with the disheveled and annoyed face of Basileus.

"Who—" His eyes grew wide and he leaned forward to get a better look as if he didn't believe what he saw. "Rhea?"

"No, it's her evil twin," I responded sourly. "Let me in, Bas."

He frowned at me, returning to his casual facade. "What are you doing here, Hawke?" He glanced away briefly, then looked back at me. "It's even past *your* bedtime."

"Damn it, Bas!" I said. "Let me in and I'll tell you."

He nodded and I heard the lock give way. I entered and pelted up the stairs to his flat.

"Does this have to do with the break-in?" he said as I rushed into his living room. "What's up, Hawke?"

"I need Benny," I said. "You have to help me get him."

"What?" he exclaimed. "But your ship's impounded. You haven't been re-instated, have you?" he asked hesitantly.

"No." I fixed him an intense, pleading look. "It's my mother, Bas. She might be in danger. I've got to find her and warn her." I didn't even want to think that it might be too late; V'mer's message was two weeks old, after all.

FOURTEEN

"Listen, Hawke," Bas said, showing his fear as we approached the security door of the precinct impoundment hangar bay. "This is a major offence. Stealing Guardian property, especially an armed sentient ship. You realize that this will put you in a very bad position with the Guardians. And me, too, if anyone finds out I helped you. They'll hunt you down, and you'll be lucky if all they do is send you to work the penal colony on Sekmet."

Bas was always so dramatic, I thought with a wry smile. "They don't send you to Sekmet for stealing a piece of junk, Bas." Sekmet was reserved for lifers, mad senseless killers.

"So, before we go in," Bas continued in a low hushed voice, ignoring my remark, "you have to explain it all to me."

Peering through the door's window, my gaze swept the hangar, and I spotted what I was looking for. Benny stood at the far end, unscathed but decidedly lonely. My beautiful ship, my brown-green camouflage two-man interstellar craft with his elegant and practical design took my breath away. His long snub-ended snout was flanked on either side by narrow concave triangular fuel-scoops. Foil wings at his stern folded up over his fuel scoops. They'd left the pilot's canopy shield up to give the inside of the AI-ship some air.

Benny was a rare retro/state-of-the-art Fauche design, which used old-fashioned Earth sleep technology along with a sophisticated Fauche kappa particle fuel system. Two hundred years ago, harvesting dream-time theta waves was considered an innovative use of required hibernation during long space voyages. Now, with new particle-stream travel, hibernation was no longer necessary. But the innovative Fauche had improved the archaic bio-technology for short-time use. The *ray* was the smallest ship capable of long distance star travel along the 'stream,' thanks to the Fauches' inventive fuel technology. Benny was the first—and almost last—of his kind. There were only four others that I knew of in existence. But Tangent Shipping could find no interested buyers, which was why I got Benny.

"Explain to me why I'm doing this for you, Hawke," Bas insisted in a voice that I thought was approaching a whine. "I'm risking my own reputation to blacken yours. You have to tell me what's going on."

"I can't, Bas," I said, turning to him with an apologetic look. "I don't even know myself. Something crazy is going on and I think my mother's involved." It wasn't quite a lie, but it wasn't quite the truth either. It was all I could divulge for now. I wasn't prepared to tell him about my former transgression.

Bas firmed his mouth then exhaled loudly through his nose with obvious frustration. "Why do I keep doing these things for you?" he mumbled to himself and opened the door with his hand ID.

"Because you hate me?" I smiled, then returned my gaze to Benny in the hangar.

"Maybe," Bas snorted. Then, following my gaze, he added, "They have him on the list for decommissioning, you know."

"What?" I snapped my head round to face him.

He nodded with a knowing smile of regret. "No one else wants him, Rhea. He's too small. He's old. He has a weird setup that no one likes, and he doesn't suit the Guardian protocol."

My lips tightened. The Guardian protocol of two Guardians travelling together at all times. Or using ships built by ZetaCorp rather than Tangent Shippers. Although Benny was classified a two-man ship, he turned out to be quite cramped during long-distance travel, which suited me just fine. It provided me with an excuse to travel alone.

"Ennos can't even give him away," Bas added.

I felt my throat close. Ennos had already given up on me—and on Benny. He obviously didn't expect me to return. He was giving my ship away for parts.

"I've got to rescue him from the scrappers, Bas," I said with new conviction, pushing past the emotion choking my voice.

Bas met my pained gaze with an understanding one. Then he looked at me sternly. "Hawke, you're going to owe me big time for this."

"I know," I said, then impulsively leaned forward and kissed him on the cheek.

He stared at me. I grinned at him, pulled out a stick of gum, shoved it in my mouth and entered the hangar, running stealthily along the wall toward my ship. Knowing I'd already activated the intruder alarm, I pelted toward Benny. I had a minute—two tops—to get away before security figured out what was going on and sealed off the hangar.

Bas strolled with loud steps toward the security guard room and entered the room. I saw him chatting animatedly with the excited young security guard as I entered my ship. Benny was in deep sleep. As I fired up the engines, I saw the guard bolt out of the guard room and dash toward me with his rifle.

"Rhea? Is that you?" Benny piped up.

"It's me, Benny," I said, chewing madly and seizing the controls. "I've come to rescue you from the scrap yard."

"I'm so glad to see you!"

"I missed you too, Benny. But there's no time to chat now. You have to let me get us out of here."

"Done."

I swung Benny around and shot out of the hangar bay as the guard fired on us.

"Yeah, I owe you for that one, Bas," I murmured with a grateful but sad smile as Benny sailed into the upper atmosphere of Iota Hor-2. "Big time, buddy."

"I guess we're both fugitives now," Benny said as we shot past the *Athena*, Iota Hor-2's orbiting defense/research station, without incident.

I blinked. "Yeah," I agreed solemnly, gazing at the long solar panels that surrounded the station. I didn't have the heart to tell Benny that no one was likely to be chasing us on his account. Even the scrappers had better metalloid to chase.

FIFTEEN

Iota Hor-2 had attracted many Eosians because of its Guardian precinct but also because it had been bio-geo-formed to resemble Earth. It was one of only a few other colonies the baldies had established that were as large or larger than Earth itself. One was Gliese 876-12, where another Guardian precinct was located. Chances were good that my mother lived there. Wherever there were a lot of baldies, Laura Hawke couldn't be too far away. Of course, that in itself presented me with a particular challenge right now.

I leaned back in my pilot's chair and ran my hand through my tangled mop. I scraped it back into a tight ponytail with an elastic from my pocket as the machine-gun stutter of heavy metal guitar boomed in my cabin. I glanced with a crooked smile at Benny's audio readout and recognized "Whiplash" by Metallica. Benny knew how to satisfy my particular penchant for early twenty-first-century Earth rock. God, it was good to be flying again, I thought, then lost my smile as I thought of my mother. I couldn't quite understand her obsession with Eosians. I conceded that they were a generally good-looking species, with an incredible libido and slightly exaggerated extremities, which my mother would appreciate. They were reported to be extremely sensual, sexually alluring, and highly appreciative of natural beauty, of which my mother had plenty. Was it all just a sex thing with her? *Face it, girl,* I thought to myself, *your mother's a slut, pure and simple.* And Eosians were natural gigolos. They made a great pair.

My mother had fantasized that one day she would see Eos. Her hero was Genevieve Dubois, the space explorer who'd flown the last of a series of ill-fated ZetaCorp flights to Eos some two hundred years ago when it took years to travel anywhere in the galaxy. Dubois was the first—and only—human to have set foot on the mythical planet of Eos, secluded in the giant blue nebula of the Pleiades. After apparently experiencing an epiphany of universal proportions, when she encountered one of the god-like Epoptes, Dubois returned, pregnant, to Florida with her Eosian lover, Azaes. They mysteriously disappeared after being taken into captivity by the American government and ZetaCorp for questioning. Rumors abounded that Azaes had unleashed a tremendous and fearful weapon out of his head on a human—the melting look, I figured—which condemned him as a dangerous monstrosity. Humans rallied to have him imprisoned or banished. Even killed.

The historical records suggested that Dubois and Azaes were murdered soon after. My mother, however, agreed with popular lore that they'd escaped to live a simple secluded life, and that Dubois's baby by Azaes was born and its descendants were living to this day. The most popular story — and therefore the least likely—was that only Dubois got away, travelled north to Canada and returned to her native Quebec where she stoically gave birth alone to her child in some abandoned barn in the country. The whole thing smelled of mythos.

Despite the rampant anti-alienism, many humans strongly believed that Dubois bore this child, making her the first human to give birth to a human-alien. A fanatical cult, *L'Ordre de l'Arbre Sacré*—Order of the Sacred Tree, sprang up in Quebec, and its mostly human members devoted themselves to the notion that Dubois's child was a kind of messiah who walked secretly among humans and was linked to the tree of life and knowledge, the *vishna*. They regarded the *vishna* an ancient soul that carried infinite wisdom and the answer to achieving the 'balance of all things'.

The Order of the Sacred Tree claimed that all the ills plaguing life in the galaxy were due to a misalignment of forces, an imbalance that the now-extinct Hopi Native Indians called *koyaanisquatsi*. They claimed that this messiah—Dubois's child—would provide the balance needed to begin a new age of enlightenment and peace. They spread wild stories of how the child was consummated not through her lover Azaes but somehow through Dubois's interaction with an Eosian *vishna* tree, which had godly powers and came to be known as one of the sacred trees, along with the migratory trees of Horus, which were also thought to be ancient souls.

According to the Order Genevieve Dubois had, in fact, perished in a giant *igapo* that flooded Eos's great forest as she saved the natives from the evils of her mad crew. The legend claims that Dubois was swept up by the *igapo*, battered and dying, to the top of the highest *vishna* tree and there joined with an Epoptes. When she died, the Epoptes took her form, and it was she who returned to Earth with Azaes. Their child was the first Epoptes to live among humans ... as a human, bringing the message of the ancient souls for achieving sacred balance and eternal existence.

Members of the Tree Cult swelled to the thousands, spreading the word of enlightenment through sacred trees, such as the native oak, the extraterrestrial *vishna*, and the mythical migratory trees of Horus. Yet their membership and much of their practices remained veiled in mystery. I couldn't understand their popularity in a world of rampant anti-alien sentiment. Perhaps this was why the Tree Cult remained a secret society. The Tree Cult continued to petition for Earth to acquire the sacred *vishna* tree of enlightenment. Well, Earth had them now aplenty, I thought with a sour smile. Only there were hardly any humans left there to enjoy them.

"Take us to Gliese 876-12, Benny," I instructed. "We'll want to take port in Phoenix City." It was the largest of the domed cities on the moon of Gliese 876-b, a gas giant that orbited the white dwarf star, Gliese 876. And where the Guardian precinct was located. If my mother was on the moon, that was where she'd be.

"Okay, Rhea. We'll be low on kappa particle fuel, but the gas giant there will serve us well."

"Our next gas station."

"It'll take us about eight standard galactic hours to get to Gliese 876-b."

"That'll get us to Gliese 876-12 about noon Local Time," I said after checking the readout on the small moon It had a diurnal cycle considerably shorter than that of Iota Hor-2. It was a long time to wait for a shower. Normally Benny was equipped with all the amenities of long-distance travel. But I had stolen him during stasis-maintenance. He was dangerously low in water, so I didn't dare use it for something as unnecessary as personal hygiene. That could wait until after I found my mother.

"Time enough for a snooze, Rhea. I suggest you get some rest." Benny cut the heavy metal music.

"Good idea, Benny," I agreed, yawning as if by suggestion in the sudden quiet. "A good opportunity to fuel up on my dreams."

"Do you need a prompt?"

"I think I'm okay," I said, preferring to choose my own dreams, and pulled on the nano headset that would retrieve my theta waves from REM sleep for Benny's long-term fuel store. It was ancient Earth technology from over 200 years ago. In a strange but brilliant move, Tangent Shippers, ZetaCorp's main competing ship builder, had incorporated this retro trait as part of its state-of-the-art kappa particle energy fuel system in the *ray* class ship. A kind of modern anachronism that appealed to my appreciation for quirky bygone things.

I settled back in my seat and closed my eyes. It took a while for me to fall asleep, but my exhaustion finally subdued my active mind, and I drifted off.

Θ

Benny nudged me awake with his auto-pilot arm. Feeling somewhat refreshed, I blinked my eyes open with a long stretch and saw that we'd achieved orbit status on Gliese 876-12. I glanced at our fuel status. Benny must have already dived into the gas giant's upper atmosphere to scoop his kappa particle reserve before orbiting the moon.

Gliese 876-12's ecosystem wasn't as friendly to its inhabitants as Iota Hor-2, I thought, gazing with a yawn down at the rich yellow-ochre tones that veiled the hazy moon of Gliese 876-b. Bathed in warm shades of a constant sunset, Phoenix City had been built under a giant energy-shield dome to protect its inhabitants from the incessant incoming stellar debris. As a result, we required special clearance to make port. Playing it safe, Benny had provided us both with an alias, in case the Iota Hor-2 Guardian precinct's APB on my theft had already reached the Gliese precinct through the Galactic Net.

"I've already established contact with Phoenix Ground Control. We're cued for entry. Unfortunately, there aren't too many *ray* class ships around, so we'll stand out a bit," Benny announced. "However, you're in luck. I just determined that the Galactic net went down soon after we left the precinct, so there's little chance the Iota Hor b Guardians got word out."

That sounded a little too convenient, and I wondered if Bas had something to do with it. He was an expert in galactic communications. Another favor I owed him.

"They won't know about your little transgression yet,"

Benny went on. "Plus I've given myself a new look. I'm yellow and I've added some bulk to my aft section."

"Good, Benny. What are you calling yourself?"

"Benjamin."

I laughed. "That's bound to send them astray."

"And you're Jane Raptor."

I raked back my thick hair and tucked it behind my ears. "Good," I muttered. We were going to get caught. Benny hadn't considered one thing. "However, it's all moot once I pass through the RADs."

There was a moment of silence before Benny answered. "I could surgically remove the IDR from your arm, Rhea."

"And pay the surcharge of a non-Galactic member? Besides, I don't have any cash to pay the port-fee in the first place. I'll need to pay direct through the bank. We'll just have to risk it. When I'm in Phoenix City, I'll liquidate my funds. Then we can go anonymous."

"Pardon my asking, Rhea, but can't the Guardians simply put a stop order on your funds? Freeze them?"

I shifted in my seat. "I'd have to be a Code-1 Priority for them to exercise that kind of authority over the bank. I'm probably a Priority 4 or 3 at best for stealing you. Money's still God in the galaxy and bankers still have all the power." Benny had a few lessons to go in cynicism, I thought.

Benny was, however, an expert in administrative communications and handled most of it for me. I only had to identify myself, once Benny had made all the arrangements for the timing window and trajectory specifications, then I took us in.

Once secure in our allotted hangar bay, I released my hair from its elastic and brushed it nervously. Then I rebound it, annoyed that I was concerned about my appearance. I pulled on my flight jacket and stuffed a few items in the pockets. "See you soon, Benny. I don't expect to be staying there for dinner. The shorter our stay, the better off we are. The galactic net is bound to reinstate soon." We were fugitives, after all.

"But you haven't seen your mother since . . . well, since a

long time."

Even Benny hesitated, I thought with a half-smile. "That's okay, Benny. I'm not sure I'll get a warm welcome. And even if I do, I don't want one. Besides, I'm just here to make sure she's okay. Not spend time with her."

"Whatever you say, Rhea. I've got things to do. I'm already in contact with the Ground Control AI Service to refuel and get supplies."

"Like water," I added, desperate for a shower.

"Right."

Θ

I strode with forced casual steps out of the Phoenix Sky Port and pulled out a stick of gum. I glanced at the security men and women as I passed the RADs unnoticed, chewing slowly to the rhythm of my steps, then emerged with a smug smile under a permanently blushing sky into the heat and sweet mesquite smell of Phoenix City.

Generally hotter, redder and louder than Neon City, the town was densely populated with towering buildings that rippled in the heat and glowed like burning embers under the fire of Gliese 876. Many of the tallest buildings were capped with glass-domed promenades, gardens, restaurants, and landing platforms. Their orange reflections glinted like exotic lanky mushrooms.

The city bustled with the thrum of commerce; air vehicles of all sizes zinged overhead in a constant rush. Phoenix City was a major banking centre. Even the Galactic Bank, my bank, had their head office here. All of the tallest towers were banking facilities. Save one, the Guardian precinct.

I headed straight for it. If anyone knew where Laura Hawke lived on this planet, they'd know. And if she was in trouble they'd be the first ones to know as well. My challenge was to find out without getting myself caught. I was counting on Benny's report about the Galactic net being down and that these local Guardians didn't know about me yet.

A loud spark and booming pop above sent me flinching into a combat crouch. My head snapped up just in time to see the fireworks display of some large interstellar debris being zapped by the radiation screen surrounding the city. Smelling the sharp burst of burning matches, I laughed quietly to myself and realized from the general apathy of the crowd that one could easily single out the visitors from the locals from this reaction alone. I'd forgotten about the debris-filled system and the need for the shield, the reason we had had to wait several hours for clearance to take port in Phoenix City. Benny had told me earlier that waits of as much as a day occurred for visitors wishing to penetrate the shield during a fairly dense debris shower. The Gliesians took pride in the well-publicized statistic that only two incidents of debris penetration had occurred since the shield had been built a hundred years ago.

I took the local transport to the centre of the bustling town.

As I stepped off the transport car at the downtown station, I glanced up at the sun, whose bright halo through the burning sky resembled a ring of smoke. Even though it was mid-morning, the nearby star constantly blazed with fiery sunset shades from the fine particles in the atmosphere. Gliese 876-b hung like a colorful baseball in the sky just over the skyscrapers of the densely built city. It resembled Iota Horologii, but much smaller.

I shouldered my way through the jostling crowd toward the large monolith, with its GG holo above shining like a bright yellow sun.

It turned out that I didn't need to go any further than the concierge. He knew Laura Hawke very well and directed me to my mother's place, just five blocks away. My intuition had paid off again, I thought, hurrying out of the building with a sigh of relief. Luck was on my side ... for once.

I took my time walking the five blocks. According to the concierge my mother was all right. He'd seen her only three days ago at the precinct, looking radiant with her arm hooked around a smug Kratos, the head of the precinct. It figured that my mother was okay, I realized, with mixed emotions and shoved my hands in the pockets of my flight jacket. What was I doing here, then? At the very least, perhaps I could secure some information from her on V'mer, I thought, fingering the info-pod in my jacket pocket.

When I reached the apartment building, I inhaled deeply and felt my heart slam. Why was I so nervous? I stood for several moments, rolling the gum in my mouth with my tongue, finger poised on the holo board. Then, with a swallow, I smoothed back my hair and sounded my presence.

Within a few heartbeats, Laura Hawke's beautiful face appeared, and I stopped chewing. Aside from a few more wrinkles around the eyes, she hadn't changed since I had last seen her nine years ago. Her beauty was still obvious. Age had only deepened it. She studied my face for a puzzled instant before recognizing me with widening eyes and showing delighted surprise.

"Rhea? Darling, is that you?"

I swallowed down the saliva that had gathered in my mouth and nodded. "It's me."

"Come in! Come in!" my mother exclaimed and I heard the security lock unlatch. I entered the graystone art deco building and took the lift to the third floor. The place was pretty upscale, built like some of the old-fashioned buildings in Vancouver, where I'd grown up. Laura's lovers were providing for her nicely, I thought cynically. Or maybe her art was finally selling. Then I was rounding the corner of the hall and saw my mother standing expectantly at the open doorway in a low-cut long dark green flowing dress. She looked genuinely pleased to see me as I approached and felt my heart pound with mixed emotions. My mother seized me in an exuberant embrace, exclaiming, "It's been so long, darling!"

I stiffened and kept my arms at my sides. My mother let go, and I saw the disappointment and confusion in her face.

"Come in, come in," she said, motioning me inside and closing the door behind us. It was obvious from her puzzled expression that she was wondering why I had come. I was beginning to wonder the same thing.

She watched me nervously as I roamed the living-room, glancing at the holo-art on the walls, absorbing the decor. She spoke first. "Would you like something to drink? A soyka, perhaps?"

"No thanks," I said, inspecting a holo-version of a Monet-style watercolor. It was obviously a Laura Hawke. My mother had always had a passion for old Earth Impressionistic art.

"I started to think I'd never see you," she said. "Then I saw you on Galaxy News. I saw you melt that Eosian—"

"Shapeshifter," I cut in sharply.

"Yes ..." she agreed in a vague tone. Was she thinking of the insane words I had shrilled out as I melted him? Did it bring back guilty or recriminating memories?

She cleared her throat. "Did Ennos tell you I visited at the Med-Facility?"

"Yeah." I continued to wander the room restlessly, unwilling to sit down, and chewed my gum even though it had gone stale.

"Is ... that why you came?" she asked almost meekly.

"No," I said flatly, finally turning to face her with a stern expression. "I came ... because I ... need some information," I lied. It seemed that my mother wasn't in any obvious danger. And I wasn't about to admit that I'd come to ensure that she was all right. "Where's your holo-com?" I asked, pulling out the info-pod from my jacket pocket. She pointed to an alcove where a console sat then followed me to it. I pushed the thumb-sized pod into the slot of the holo-com as my mother sat down in front of the console. Lips tight with emotion, I leaned over her shoulder and stabbed a code into the keypad. A holo of a human materialized. The human features morphed into several other aliens, displaying some features in common, until settling into an Eosian. They were all the various manifestations of V'mer that I had encountered throughout my month-long pursuit of the shapeshifter. Eosian was the most likely form my mother would have seen V'mer in.

"The shapeshifter I melted was this man." I paused for a

moment to gain my composure. "So, is he familiar?" I peered over my mother's shoulder. "Did you …?" I trailed off, unable to say the words.

"Sleep with him?" my mother finished for me. She twisted her neck to throw a pointed glance at me. "You came clear across the galaxy, after avoiding me for nine years, to ask me if I slept with someone? A criminal?"

"That's right," I said coldly, returning her wide-eyed look of bewilderment with a steady hard gaze. "Did you?"

"Why would you think that?" she asked, obviously offended at the inference.

Good, I thought with cruel satisfaction. I wouldn't mind making my mother angry. "Just look at him and tell me," I responded evenly, ignoring her affronted reaction.

If she was wounded by my lack of compassion or sensitivity, she decided to bury it. She turned back to the holo with a sigh and tilted her head in contemplation, studying the shapeshifter's Eosian form. "I'm not sure," she finally said.

"You're not sure!" I shrilled, jerking up from my bent position. I paced the room, releasing a frantic energy, and tossed my gum into a dispenser. Reining in my anger, I finally turned back to my mother and folded my arms across my breasts with a long exhale of tired frustration. I pointed to the holo. "Look carefully. It's important. Did you sleep with him?"

She considered for a while, placing her slender fingers to her lips and tapping. Then she nodded. "Yes, I think so. Fairly recent, too." Now she was smiling with a fond memory. "Yes, I remember now. It's his eyes. Something tragic in them. He talked a lot about his mother who'd died and about some weird universe and something called a diverse … He reminded me of …" Her eyes flickered away suddenly with dark thoughts.

"U'clid?"

My mother looked up, startled. "Why, yes! How did you know? And his name … you know his name …"

"V'mer was his son."

"And you … melted him? Just like his … Oh, my God—"

"He Dusted me, Mother," I cut in. My heart pounded in

my ears. "He also belongs to the most treacherous crime syndicate in the galaxy. He's personally responsible for wiping out an entire religious sect. And his father's no slouch either. He was an active member of Eclipse."

"Oh, dear." My mother was fascinated. "I never would have thought ..."

"No, you wouldn't have," I said brusquely, wandering the room again. "You were too busy satisfying your libido to even take an interest in the guy fucking you. Or did you choose your favorite sexual position, in which case you'd never have seen his face anyway—"

"Rhea, stop!" my mother said. "That's so unfair. You make it sound like I'm some kind of ... floozy pervert." She looked away, eyes focusing on the past. "That time with U'clid was the first time I'd ever done that. In fact, it was U'clid's idea. But I like to experiment; I like adventure, like Genevieve Dubois."

My mother's hero. I looked up at the ceiling in disgust. And how in chaos would she know Genevieve Dubois' favorite sexual position?

"So I went along." My mother continued in a dreamy voice, "I had no idea. The experience was so ... well, out of this world."

Until I had nuked the bastard.

"So I kept trying that position with other Eosians after ..."

God! Did I need to hear this?

"... but it was never even close to—to—" My mother's face puckered and she wept, hiding her face in her hands.

"I can't believe this!" I burst out. "You're crying over some disgusting sex thing!" Then I wondered if my mother's sadness was really for the man himself. Perhaps he had been tender and my mother was really weeping for his soul. She'd told me nothing of him, whether it had been a typical one-nighter or they'd been seeing each other for longer, like a week. Had she known that he had a wife and family on Helsig 2?

"You're so cold-hearted," she said, sniffing in her sobs.

I swerved round to face her and glared at her. "Look at

141

me." I seized my mother by the shoulders and shook her violently. She looked away, almost frightened. "I said, *look at me!*" I screamed, losing all self-control. My mother stiffened and fixed startled eyes on me. "I'm what I am because of *you*. Yeah, I'm a cold, mean bitch ... I'm a product of your flagrant unrestrained and irresponsible behavior. *Tecking* me at three with ... with *that*." I let go of my mother. Tears of rage were building up. "*You made me.*"

My mother let her shoulders sag and seemed to collapse into a husk of her former self. She looked suddenly very old. "Yes," she admitted. "I was irresponsible and I did make you. But not the way you think." She was silent for a while, looking down at her hands. When she looked up directly into my eyes, her eyes were full of tears, and I felt my stomach shift. "Rhea, I never *tecked* you."

I jerked back as if she'd struck me. The implications were—"*Who*, then?" I demanded in a shrill tone.

"No one, Rhea," my mother answered meekly. "You were never *tecked*."

"What?" My stomach heaved.

"Those Eosian traits you have are your own. You were born with them. You're part Eosian."

NO! It felt like I'd been knifed in the gut. I couldn't stop my voice shaking. "But how is that possible. My dad is—"

"Not Mark Hawke. I made him up, found him in a magazine. It seemed to make sense at the time. I wanted to give you a father—a hero—to hang your dreams on. The truth is, I don't even know who your father is—except that he's Eosian ... because I was only sleeping with ..." She broke off at my expression of horror.

"Why did you do it?" I barely choked out the words through my daze.

"I was alone when the Vos ships came. Alone and scared. You have to understand what it was like on Earth during the siege. It was everyone for himself or herself. I had no one to turn to. No humans, that is. When the Eosians came and intervened, they were so kind to me ..."

I'd heard all this garbage before. Of course the baldies were kind to her, I thought scathingly. They appreciated sex and beauty. And my mother was very beautiful then. Still was at ninety years old. And so willing to give it away to anyone.

"I meant about my father." I said. "Why did you lie about my father? How could you do that!" I shrilled. I didn't need an answer any more. Nothing would have sufficed. Rage flooded in. "You created a huge, awful lie. *I'm* a lie!" I suddenly felt ill and yanked open the main door, resisting the urge to throw up.

I heard my mother's plea: "Rhea! You know what it means, don't you? You're descended from Azaes and Genevieve Dubois. Azaes was the only one who could melt anyone ..."

I pounded down the stairs to the street as fast as I could. I got there just in time to throw up.

SIXTEEN

I slouched in my pilot's chair, head slumped in my hand, and barely listened as Benny murmured his diagnostics and take-off preparation procedure. I'd known it was a mistake to come here.

To find out after all these years that I was part Eosian. What a joke. Perhaps I'd known all along ... recognized at some deep subconscious level that I was neither human nor Eosian: a hybrid, a freak experiment of nature. Like those Bastets, Earth's first major transgenic disaster. They'd wiped out the entire domestic cat population along with all of Earth's large feral cats.

And as much as I wanted to blame my mother, I had the sense not to. That sort of thing was happening all over the galaxy. Chaos, the whole Eosian race was supposedly the result of a foolish transgression by the overseeing 'gods' of ancient Earth, the Epoptes. The 'watchers.' Although they'd sworn not to, some Epoptes came down and fornicated with the primitive stone-age humans. My mother had quoted the lines in the Bible often enough: *the sons of God saw the daughters of men that they were fair; and they took them wives of all which they chose.* It was always males who did the 'taking,' I thought. Of course, the logic was obvious: only women gave birth. There was no point in female 'gods' coming down to frolic with the primitive human males. Not if the point of fornication was to produce a new species in the original community.

They'd created a hybrid giant race, the Eosians, who became the original inhabitants of Atlantis: *the Nephilim* (giants) *were on the earth in those days ... when the sons of God came in to the daughters of men, and they bore children to them. Those were the mighty men.* So went the new myth, anyway ... and when the Atlanteans plummeted into debauchery themselves, the matter-energy manipulating Epoptes unleashed their wrath in the form of a global disaster that was known throughout countless civilizations as the 'great flood.' Choosing a few still good Atlanteans to take on their 'ark,' the Epoptes found them a new home: Eos, an Earth-like jungle planet nested deep in the Pleiades. They left any original humans who'd managed to survive the wrath of the gods to their own devices. And now the Eosians were back on Earth, where they'd originated. And no sign of any Epoptes, I thought cynically. Of course, the logical cover-up story was that the Epoptes had learned their lesson and never made themselves known to others again. It was all pretty convenient.

"Everything checks okay, Rhea," Benny announced, jolting me from my miserable reverie. He'd done all the boring administrative back and forth with Ground Control. "We're clear to take off. I have Gliese 876-12 Ground Control on the com for you."

"Thanks, Benny," I said and opened the com. "Raptor to Ground Control. We're twenty seconds from firing. Confirm status."

"You're clear for trajectory into Sectors 9 and 10, Raptor. Both are wide open. But please stay within that narrow band until you're well out of orbit range."

"Thanks. We will. We're locked on Sector 9," I said after

glancing at Benny's readout.

"Happy flying, Raptor," Ground Control said. "And come again real soon."

"Yeah, thanks," I said sourly, flicking off the com. "Get us off this disgusting rock, Benny." I wanted to be as far away as quickly as possible. I pulled on my crash-webbing seconds before Benny jolted and shot up into space.

It was only once we were out of orbital space that I released my crash webbing and drew in a few deep breaths to let my mind relax. Thoughts of my recent visit rushed in, flooding my eyes with tears. I flared my nose and set my mouth to keep them in.

Nothing had prepared me for my mother's disclosure. I'd messed up my life ... and for all the wrong reasons. Why had my mother made up that awful story? A jaded story full of lies ... of a heritage I didn't own or deserve ... A heroic father, who wasn't mine ...

I desperately needed to put my arms around Serge and feel his strong body pressed against mine like a warm Great Coat, kiss that mouth that tasted of home. My whole body yearned for his touch. I longed to hear his voice, that funny cackling laugh that rose out of his belly. Longed to watch him enter a room with that confident loping gait and light it with his cheerful rakish smile. It always set me at ease. When I was with him, the universe seemed all right.

Serge was the only man who'd ever engaged me in real and intelligent conversation. He listened to me, respected my replies, and challenged me like an equal. Most men were either intimidated by me or behaved with supercilious arrogance—like my Eosian colleagues. Bas tried to engage me in personal conversation, but he was clumsy and oafish, and I didn't give him too many chances. Serge had a way of gently breaking through the firewalls I put up to keep intimacy out. I glanced down at my slender fingers, and imagined a ring on one of them. Could Serge be the one ...?

"I'm sorry your visit with your mother upset you, Rhea," Benny said. "If there's anything I can do to help you feel better, please let me know."

I sighed and wiped my tears away. "Thanks, Benny." Then I thought of Serge again and almost gasped out, "Perhaps there is something you can do, Benny. Serge Bastion went to Opus 9 on some business." Benny's scientific research and forensics tools were state-of-the art. I had made sure of that. He could find anyone anywhere from the smallest scrap of information or clue. I'd often relied on him to do just that in my investigations as a Guardian Enforcer. "I'd like you to track him down so I can pay him a surprise visit—"

"I'm afraid that's impossible, Rhea."

"Why?" I said, a little annoyed at Benny's reluctance to help.

"Opus 9 had a recent outbreak of Deep Fever brought in with a shipment of damsel squashes from Helsig 2. That's nothing to laugh at. The virus is transgenic—it's deadly, fast, and incredibly contagious. It spread from the main skyport in Obsidian City to several other major cities in a few days. The whole planet's been under quarantine for a month already, and it's not expected to lift for another. If your friend went there, they'd have turned him back."

"Then he might be home already!" I said. If we jacked the particle-stream short cut I could be there in time for dinner. "Patch me to him at his home."

"Sure," Benny said.

Within moments the holo-com blinked on, and Serge's face appeared. My spirits lit up briefly until I realized that it was just the answer holo. I cut off, not leaving a message, and slumped in my seat. My yearning for him grew desperate. Damn it, I needed him! Where in chaos was he?

"Okay, Benny, let's find him. Might as well start with a profile." I smiled tartly. Serge had not been very forthcoming about his background or his occupation and I'd respectfully avoided any kind of sleuthing. Well, that was about to change.

Benny was one of the best tools at my disposal for my Guardian investigations. What Benny couldn't find, no one could. So, when Benny said, "Oh, dear," I felt my body stiffen.

To my inquiry, Benny repeated, "Oh, dear."

"For the love of creos, Benny!" I practically shrieked. "What is it?"

"The man you know as Serge Bastion isn't Serge Bastion. He doesn't even live where you visited him or where we reach him via the holo-net."

"What?" I stared at Benny's readout. Serge's flat belonged to a reclusive art collector and dealer named Saf Rov. An Azorian. My heart raced. "But what about his IDR? I saw him pay for a meal."

"Probably used an illegal fabrication. They're hard to trace. The real Serge Bastion is a human bookseller who lives in Beleus City, a large human colony on the moon of HD28185b. He's never been off the moon. Can't afford it."

A holo of a man who looked the spitting image of Serge appeared in front of me. But there were enough differences to suggest this was not the same person: his hair was darker and longer and tied back in a ponytail, his nose looked like it could have been broken once and he hadn't been able to afford to fix it with nuyu. His expression was less self-assured, more somber, and there was a kind of sad innocence on his face that suddenly made me swallow. Who, then, was the 'Serge' I'd met?

"Rov was found dead in an eastside alley on Moner 7, the morning of 215.14 Standard Galactic Time," Benny continued. "He'd just pocketed a major art deal the day before. He was shot in the head by a Q-gun. Forensics had to use the DNA of what was left of him to ID him."

I quickly did the math. That was six days after I signed up at the Gym. The same time Serge had left town himself. My heart pumped in my throat. Did Serge—or whoever he was—kill Rov? I noted that Rov conveniently had no family or friends. A typical Azorian, the ferret-faced alien obviously kept to himself. And he was out of town most of the time. So, no one missed him.

Amid my own miserable thoughts, I barely heard Benny's analysis: "Strangely enough, the local PD on Moner 7 never reported the case to the Guardians, so no follow-up investigation occurred on Iota Hor-2. It somehow fell through the cracks and got buried. Azorians aren't generally liked. Most people consider them shrewd and heartless business people, but that's no reason to break protocol. I'd be suspicious of Eclipse bribery and infiltration in the local PD ... Rhea ...?"

I blinked. "Oh, yeah. I agree." I stammered on, "I ... I ... but ... but ..." then cut myself off, surging to my feet.

I marched to the infirmary where I stripped. "Here, Benny," I said, handing his Med-arm my briefs, stained with Serge's and my cum from two nights ago. I hadn't changed out of my clothes since leaving Neon City. "Check the secretion for DNA other than mine and do a full ID." I sat bare-bottomed on the infirmary bed and leaned back on my hands. It was the same bed I'd lain on as Benny sailed home after gathering up my comatose body from Mar Delena. "There's plenty more inside me where that came from, if you need a fresh sample. But I'd rather not undergo the procedure if I don't have to."

"No need, Rhea. The sample can be as old as a few days and I'm sure there's enough sperm here for me to do a DNA scan," Benny commented. He'd already managed to remove a sample from my undergarment and was processing it.

I reclined on the bed and put my hands behind my head. I commanded myself to breathe deeply and tried to relax. It didn't work. I could feel my heart race. Benny was silent for an inordinate amount of time then finally made a clicking sound.

"Well?" I said, taking it for a signal that he was finished. I rose to my feet and went to the infirmary drawer, where I found another pair of briefs and pulled my trousers on over them.

"You're not going to like it."

"I already don't like it," I said, nervously pacing the infirmary. "Give it to me straight."

"He's not human ..."

I staggered back as if someone had struck me. I thought it might be bad, but not this bad.

"His DNA is very close to the real Serge Bastion, but there's a shift, and he has the signature common to what we categorize as a Borr."

A shapeshifter! But it explained how he'd looked just like

the real person he'd copied.

"I had to search the confidential Guardian files for it. The Borrs have yet to be officially catalogued because their world was blown away by the Vos before they had a chance to join the Galactic Network. They're not registered with the Galaxy Guardians—"

"I know all that!" I shrilled, finding my voice more sharp than I'd intended. I cleared my throat and swallowed convulsively. I'd made love to a shapeshifter ... and probably a murderer. "Oh, God," I whispered. But it all made sense: his use of the Borr vernacular, killing Rov with a Q-gun—a shapeshifter's preferred weapon. He was obviously very comfortable in the human form, likely his preferred shape, because I never once sensed him not resonating with it. Of course, I was a little distracted the whole time ... I paced the floor and brought my hands to my head and raked the unruly tangles of hair back from my face. "What am I going to do ...?"

Benny knew better than to answer my rhetorical question. He let me calm down in silence.

"Do we know who he really is, Benny?" My thoughts were beginning to race into places that terrified me. For instance, why I'd so fortuitously met him. Had he been tailing me and then killed that poor art dealer and taken his flat when I'd signed up at the gym? Why had he so diligently and thoroughly seduced me? I wanted to kick myself for being so stupid. I'd been set up big time. But why and for what? "Can we track him down?"

"It'll be difficult. He isn't a registered Galaxy Alliance member. He probably ditched his fake Galaxy ID tag. I can only detect the original Serge Bastion still on Beleus."

I glanced down at my arm, where my ID had been embedded at birth.

"He doesn't own a ship," Benny went on. "Must use the commerce shuttles for anonymity. Borrs are generally very hard to track for reasons I've already given. They're the galaxy's gypsies."

Like my friend V'mer, for instance. I felt my mouth go

dry: V'mer had two siblings. "Try V'mer's family, Benny."

"You're kidding."

"Do it." I was in no mood for bantering.

"Okay," Benny said, sounding skeptical. "I only have access to U'clid's DNA from a brief incarceration on Sekmet for Dust smuggling before he disappeared in 197."

"No doubt his release was Eclipse-mediated," I muttered. No one ever left Sekmet. It claimed you for keeps.

"Any offspring would carry some key similarities to the father within the Borr signature."

"Do it, then," I snapped.

It didn't take long. Benny announced, "As usual, your hunch was right, Rhea. The Borr signature DNA of this Serge Bastion doppelganger is too close not to be related to U'clid. Sekmet kept detailed confidential records of everything, including names of visitors of prisoners. His whole family visited U'clid a few times over his misplacement there. V'mer is dead, and we know from the DNA that Serge is a male, so the sister is ruled out too. That leaves us with V'ser, the younger brother," Benny went on as my heart slammed, pounding up my throat and making me nauseous. Benny continued, apparently unaware of my growing distress, "Interesting ... the sister is—"

"A'ler."

"Yes, commander of the *Ulysses*. How did you know?" Benny sounded puzzled.

I just did. It all made sense: mysterious note and all. Aside from revenge for killing their father, they were all after my MEC—probably the only reason I was still alive and why Serge hadn't murdered me in his bed. V'mer had said as much just before he'd tried to kill me on Mar Delena.

"... Based on V'ser's double, Serge Bastion, I took the liberty of searching the siblings," Benny went on, "and I found records of human doubles for the whole Bastion family, Claude, Maurice, Leonie, and Leezbet. Seems that these shapeshifters had two identities for a while, until ... well ..."

"What?" I forced out in a shaky voice.

"Except for Serge, the whole original Bastion family were

murdered several years ago, Rhea … Rhea …? Are you okay?"

I blacked out briefly and felt myself fall.

"Rhea!" Benny's voice echoed as if from far away.

"I'm okay," I said shakily, seeing spots in front of my eyes as everything swam back into focus. I gathered myself up from the floor and made it on wobbly legs to the infirmary bed. Benny's mechanical arm had a beverage in front of me within seconds. "Drink this," he instructed. "You're awfully pale, Rhea." I took the mug of warm soyka and held it in both of my trembling hands, as I leaned back against the wall, thinking I might throw up yet. Benny said softly, "It's not even close to what you wanted to hear, was it?"

I drank the soothing soyka and shook my head slowly, closing my eyes, and swallowing down the sickness. "Not remotely," I breathed out my misery.

My universe had just fallen apart.

SEVENTEEN

I listlessly adjusted the controls from my pilot's seat. They didn't need adjusting. I noticed Benny re-adjusting after I'd touched them as the ship skimmed through the upper atmosphere of a huge blue gas giant, fuel scoops collecting ionic particles. I'd set a course for Ogium 9, a small terrestrial planet orbiting HD70642, a bright star ninety light-years from Earth. I hoped to get information on the whereabouts of the itinerant *Ulysses* space station from Zec in Splendid City.

The very thought of returning to that nest of crime made me uneasy. I'd spent a significant portion of my youth there, surviving by using my brain and keeping my emotions in check. The last time I'd seen Zec, he'd sworn to kill me for jagging him—he nearly did. I pushed out my lower jaw, thinking of what I was going to have to do, and felt impatience nag me. For no reason I could think of, I flicked on the com and sent an inquiry to Serge's apartment in the Hive of Neon City on Iota Hor-2. Of course, he wasn't there, and the answer holo appeared. I thought it both odd and arrogant of him to still have his own message on it. But it also told me that he didn't know I was on to him yet. Which gave me the chance to catch him off guard and bring him in.

My gaze lingered on his image as I absently listened to the hypnotic hum and burble of Benny's environmental system. No wonder he had looked familiar when I'd first seen him; he was V'mer's younger brother, and there was a resemblance between them, at least in the human form. In fact, there was a strong filial scent all three siblings shared. I finally realized why I'd had that disturbing vision at my place the day after I'd been burgled. I'd smelled the sister, A'ler, which had triggered strong memories of the two brothers. They were working as a team, after all. That's who V'mer meant. And one of them was probably The Rose.

Their whole family was acting together: father, mother and offspring. Chaos, they'd taken the trouble to copy an entire existing human family. It made sense that they'd murdered the family to take their identities. But why had the dopplegangers spared the real Serge Bastion?

I meant to find the *Ulysses* and bring both the shapeshifter sister and brother in. Or kill them. I'd accept the consequences of my actions too, whichever way they went.

I gazed long at Serge's image, feeling a surge of emotion well up, before I ruthlessly flicked off the switch and vaporized his holo.

After years of carefully avoiding complications in my life, I'd dumped it all for the first guy who smiled at me. I'd broken all my rules of engagement. Thrown away my most precious Guardian ideals—discipline, independence, and self-control—and completely lowered my defenses. God, he wasn't even human …

"Give me some heavy metal, Benny," I instructed. The throbbing beat of "Master of Puppets" thundered in the cockpit, and I tried, unsuccessfully, to drown my mind with it.

… So much for all his blenoid-shit talk of destiny and

diverses. Fate had nothing to do with any part of our relationship from that supposed chance meeting to my seduction … it had all been carefully planned and heartlessly choreographed. Everything that had come out of his mouth had been a lie. He'd even coaxed me into mourning with him for some critically-ill girlfriend who likely never existed. There was no jagging girlfriend, I decided. He'd made it all up to sucker me into feeling sorry for him.

I pushed back the hair from my face and bit down on my lower lip with a long exhale. I concluded that, like his older brother, Serge had simply sought revenge for my murdering his father. As for why he hadn't simply killed me—he'd had plenty of opportunity, I'd certainly given him that—it probably had to do with getting my MEC design for Eclipse. And why he'd played me like a cat with its prey. Perhaps he was just having a little fun prolonging the hunt, like V'mer, who'd led me clear through the far reaches of the galaxy before ensnaring me in his trap.

I'd rashly shared everything with Serge. My fears. My dreams. Even my most shameful transgression. Of course he'd known already. But he'd quietly listened and displayed apparent concern, all the while secretly plotting his revenge.

"I deserve this," I muttered in a hoarse voice. *"Talking without thinking is like shooting without aiming* … Old Chinese proverb, Rhea."

Θ

Splendid City was, on the surface, quite splendid. I strode along one of the pedestrian air tubes that swayed over a thousand meters above the ground and gazed past my gravity boots through the transparent floor to the city, glowing in the warm blaze of the setting sun. Splendid City sprawled beneath me in a complex thrum and filigree of multi-shaped, rounded, and peaked rooftops. Translucent walkways snaked in and out of them. Catching the sun's fire, they formed golden streaks across the sky. Air vehicles buzzed around the towers and walkways in swarms of synchronous order.

For some reason, Splendid City had become a Mecca for architects, and each building was a celebration of unique design. Several were modeled on biological creatures: tentacled jellyfish, or arachnids, spiked echinoids, or giant pollen shapes. The poet Goethe had described architecture as frozen art. I thought it no more apt than here, in Splendid City, where practical design and imagination conspired in the myriad shapes, textures and colors that rose up boldly towards the heavens.

The buildings sparkled like jewels. But the glitter of the throbbing city lay just on the surface, I thought solemnly. Beneath those resplendent spires and glass towers lay a filthy dark underworld devoted to crime. Splendid City was built by crime lords from all across the galaxy. It had been a good place for me when I sold my weapons designs; the place was ripe with young scoundrels, eager to build their little empires by trading one illicit merchandise for another. I'd had no problem finding customers. My challenge had been to keep from getting swallowed up by them.

Every time I thought of this place, I wondered how I'd survived it. It made me shiver. I stopped to pull up the collar of my flight jacket and pressed it shut over my sleeveless black top as the transparent tube swayed gently from side to side. The only good thing about this place was that there was little chance of Guardian presence. The local PD were also corrupt and disinterested in Guardian concerns. Good thing, too. In my distraught haste to leave Phoenix City, I'd neglected to visit the bank and pull out my cash. As a result I was still wearing my IDR when Benny docked in Splendid City's spaceport.

The sun dipped below the horizon, stoking the clouds into wanton flames. Then, as quickly as they blazed, the clouds darkened like embers and smoke against a deep orange sky.

I watched the lights of the glass towers and their myriad fluorescent signs glow brighter as the sky darkened. The highest of the galaxy's low life did their commerce in this city. Some even lived here. Like Zec. I spotted the pentagonal building platform on five 'legs' flashing the sign *Zec's Casino*. Zec's gambling facility was no doubt a haven for the highest of the lowlifes. That's where I was headed.

After an involuntary swallow, I resumed my stride toward the arachnid building. I wasn't sure how Zec would receive me. He had, after all, probably expected me to perish in that last fiasco he'd set me up in.

I pulled in a long breath when I got to one of the entrances to the casino. I dug deep into my jacket pocket and fished out a stick of soyka. Once it was in my mouth, I pressed the enter beacon beneath the brightly lit *Sky Lounge* sign, and chewed nervously. The door opened and a rush of re-circulated air, thick with the smell of *hedon*, buffeted me and made me blink. I inhaled the strongly drugged air as I entered the spacious dimly lit lounge. It contained several comfortable chairs, a bar, and a dance floor. Soft instrumental music matched the dim lighting. A few aliens were seated at the bar, nursing drinks, and a human couple were snuggling on one of the lounge chairs. No one paid me any notice. Not even the bartender, who was having an animated discussion with a Xhix at the bar.

Zec was pretty young to have made it this big already, I thought as I made my way across the dance floor around an alien couple shuffling to a Y-step. Despite Zec's energetic and creative resourcefulness, I suspected that he had a backer. And I had a pretty good idea who that was. I had to be very careful. Unfortunately Zec was the only person I knew who could give me the whereabouts of the itinerant *Ulysses* ... for obvious reasons.

I guessed he'd have his office on the top several floors and made for the lift, wishing I had my Great Coat and my MEC. I entered the empty lift and directed it to the penthouse. Easy so far. That troubled me. My suspicions were realized when the door slid open and two burly Xhix sprang from either side and seized me without question.

"What do you think you're doing!" I shrieked in my most indignant stupid voice and struggled to get free. "Let me go, you big bully!"

"You're not allowed here, slave," the larger of the Xhix

snarled.

"This isn't the Sky Lounge?" I asked innocently.

He responded by twisting my arm in a sudden move that made me cry out. Involuntary tears of pain sprang to my eyes. If my arm wasn't broken it was damn close. The other Xhix tore off my jacket and checked for weapons.

I heard a familiar chuckle over the intercom. "What? No karate chop or *vizion* grip? I'm disappointed, Hawke." It was Zec.

Languidly chewing my gum, I spotted the camera on the wall above them and threw it a withering look, then popped a bubble and sucked it slowly back in to my mouth.

"Okay, boys, that's enough playing. Bring her in."

When the door slid open, I saw Zec right away, feet up on his giant gadpie desk, eyeing me critically with scorn. He was handsome as always with dark, slick hair drawn back in a loose ponytail, with beautiful large heavy-lidded eyes the color of Earth's ocean, and the lashes of a girl. He wore an expensive silk jacket imported from Earth over a charcoal gray T-shirt and tacky lumi-trousers. Behind him the large windows provided a spectacular view of the city lights in the deepening lavender of dusk. A lecherous smile slid over his face as he looked me up and down approvingly. He'd fancied me as his girlfriend when we'd slummed together in the lower levels. Even tried to kiss me once. He had the scar to prove it.

I met his gaze head on, then glanced down with a smirk to where his tight pants bulged and decided to make the first move. Tongue brushing my upper lip in mock seductiveness, I sneered: "Is that a Q-gun in your pocket or are you just happy to see me?"

"Well, look what the tappin dragged in." Zec's tone was derisive. "Lose your Great Coat, Officer Hawke?" He emphasized the word *officer* with particular contempt. "Or are you feeling … *lucky*?" Then he flicked a hand at the men holding me. "Let her go. She's harmless without her jagging toys."

I shrugged off the burly men and snatched my jacket as Zec motioned for them to leave. When the door shut and we were alone, he pointed to a leather chair in front of him. Zec lit a poi root as I hung my jacket on the chair's back and sat down. After breathing in the acrid smelling mash like an addict, he continued in a voice of contempt, "What do you want, Hawke? Why are you here?"

"Maybe to teach you some manners," I said, sulkily rubbing my arm where the thug had hurt me. It wasn't broken after all but there was going to be a major bruise.

"Well, it sure isn't to give me my money," he snarled. "And you have nothing left to sell. I know you don't have your MEC anymore because the jagging precinct took it. In fact, they've got an APB out on you for stealing one of their vehicles. You're no longer an Enforcer. You're *nothing*, Hawke."

God! Did *everyone* know about my life?

He answered my silent question with a sly grin. "I have good friends. You might try it sometime ... friends. Loyal, good friends who don't abandon you and report you to the pigs. But then, you'd have to be a good friend yourself ..." He waved his hand at me in disgust, as if to make me disappear. "You're so jagging pathetic, Hawke."

Yeah. A lot of people were calling me that lately. I was actually getting used to it. Zec appeared more edgy than last time, less successful at veiling the bitterness he nursed toward me beneath his façade of uncouth cavalier. I had no time for psychology and gave him a hard look. "I don't need a weapon. It's all here." I tapped my head and gave him a smug smile. "In my head. I designed the MEC, after all." Then I raised a brow. "I can make another one."

He pulled his feet off the table and leaned forward in his seat. "What's your angle?" he said, showing some interest. Good, I thought. I'd drawn him out of his sullen thoughts of revenge by appealing to his greedy genes. I knew he was interested in the MEC. Who wasn't?

"I need to get back to the *Ulysses*," I said in a business-like manner. "I have some unfinished business there. If you can find me another buyer—"

"For the MEC?" he scoffed. "The one you haven't made

yet?"

I ignored his mocking tone. "A'ler, for instance."

He leaned back and guffawed. "You're jagging nuts! You're a jagging idiot, who owes me so much jagging money you're lucky I don't cut the jag out of you right now and use your body as bait for the jagging blenoids."

I leaned back in the chair and crossed my arms. I felt my lip curl. He'd always been crude. "Haven't you learned anything since puberty? Most people who use that particular term have never jagged in their lives," I said evenly. "If they did, they probably wouldn't use the word quite so indiscriminately." I'd only jagged once when I was still an enexperienced pilot. It's a pilot's term for drifting off the space-time stream. Luckily for me, Benny had made up for my inexperience and pulled us out of sure death.

Zec grunted and sucked on the poi mash. "A'ler's no buyer," he said, exhaling brown putrid smoke at me. It stank like burning compost.

"Why not?" I scowled at him while tersely waving my hand in front of my face to dissipate the stink. "She's the ultimate buyer. She's the one interested in the MEC, after all."

"She's one of their top bitches, that's why!" He waved his arm, poi smoke swirling around him like a dust storm. "She runs the whole station, for quintle's sake. You're too jagging ambitious, Hawke. Try someone lower on the rung."

"Like T'lem?" I said tartly, raising a brow and rolling the gum in my mouth with my tongue. "We already tried that once, remember? He had his own plans, it seems. Plans that included killing me and getting the MEC for himself. I deal directly with A'ler or nothing happens. I can trust her."

I must have sounded totally naïve to Zec, but that seemed to mollify him. He rubbed his chin thoughtfully and pulled in another long inhale of smelly poi. "Okay," he said finally. "But you're crazy. And this time I get a million up front."

"In your dreams, creon." I was on my feet and turning for the exit. "To chaos with you."

"Chaos, Hawke!" He stabbed a finger at me as I glanced

back at him over my shoulder. "I got short-changed last time when you jagged your own customer—"

I turned swiftly and strode to his massive desk. Leaning my hands on it, I pushed my face forward with a snarl. "*After* he tried to jag me and take the merchandise for free. You set me up with scum, Zec."

He leaned back, betraying the truth in his face. "Okay, so T'lem was less than fair."

"And you knew it. What did he promise to pay you? Twice my fee?"

His grimace told me I'd guessed right. If Zec was the swindling creon I took him for, he would set me up again. I didn't care. I had my own plans. I straightened and gave him a hard look.

"Just get me there," I said. "I'll do the rest. We'll go fifty-fifty. But no up-front fee. I still have to make the weapon and that's going to cost me a lot. Same deal." Then I added, "You owe me, after all, Zec."

"Owe you?" he bit out and laughed sharply.

I shifted my feet uneasily. "I'm calling in a favor." I hated putting myself in a position of need, and I could feel myself squirming.

Zec knew it too. "Begging, even?" He laughed scornfully. "So, is that what the Guardians taught you? How to jagging beg? Where's your self-respect, creon?"

I didn't have much left, I had to concede. But I wasn't going to let Zec's ridicule jag me off track. "Call it begging if you want, Zec, but you still owe me for looking the other way during your Counterpoint fiasco."

He leaned forward. "You wouldn't have had to look the other way if you hadn't sold out to the jagging Guardians. You'd have been right there beside me."

"You're wrong," I cut in sharply. "I never would have supported that sale."

"Since when have you gotten all morally principled?"

"Since always. You know that, Zec."

He glared at me, acknowledging that I'd called him, and

pushed out his lower lip in a sneer of disgust. "I take it back. You fit right in with those self-righteous alienist pigs, lording over the galaxy like you always know what's best for the rest of us."

"We do," I agreed matter-of-factly.

He studied me for a long moment in sullen silence. Were we stalemated? Then he threw his head back and shouted out a loud, bitter laugh. When he looked back at me again, his eyes were narrow. "What are you up to, Hawke? What's your game? This MEC sale to Eclipse isn't very morally principled either."

Now *he'd* called *me*. I firmed my jaw defensively. "It's part of something a lot bigger than that. Besides, what do you care? So long as you get your stipend."

"Well, I better, this time," he shot back.

"You just set me up with A'ler. She'll come through."

Zec stabbed a button on his console, and the two burly men returned. "It's orbiting PSR 1257 + 12c, a terrestrial planet in a millisecond pulsar system," he said peevishly. "It'll be there for the next galactic month or so."

I felt my heart twitch and kept my face calm, forcing down a victorious smile. He'd just given me what I'd come for.

"I'll net A'ler's people with an offer. Who and what will you be?"

"The same as before, R'lan, a shapeshifter in the form of an Eosian."

He nodded. "Of course, your favorite," he said with a sneer. He horked up some phlegm and spat it out nastily. "Get out of my sight. We're even now, Rhea. If I ever see you again without my payment, one of us will be jagged."

I knew he meant it.

After a quick appraising glance at the two thugs, I sidled back to Zec's desk with a humorless smile. Zec looked at me, puzzled. I leaned over the desk to his holo-com and punched in Benny's call-code. Then I pushed my face close to Zec's with a careful stare. "That's in case you wiped it from your files out of hastiness. I'm not dead yet," I said in quiet challenge, eyes locking with his. I snatched the poi root dangling from his mouth, and tossed it on the floor. "But you, on the other hand, might be if you keep smoking that shit."

I straightened and crossed the room swiftly, not looking back at him, and let the two thugs escort me out.

EIGHTEEN

"Did you make a new one already?" Zec asked on Benny's holo-com.

I raised the MEC in my hand in front of the vid screen and leered. It was one of two spares I'd hidden on Benny. Even Ennos knew nothing about them.

Zec nodded, visibly impressed with my apparent skills. "I set up a tentative meeting with A'ler. She'll meet you in Agri-Pod 2 for lunch," he said. "Take Pod Door 200 and find the little gazebo café by the river. She takes her lunch alone there every day. She's expecting you in two standard galactic days. The station will receive you like any other offworlder."

"Thanks, Zec. How will I recognize A'ler?"

"Don't worry, she'll recognize you," he said flatly, then signed off.

Wonderful. I checked the control readout. I'd be entering the trap waiting for me in twenty-nine hours.

"It'll be dangerous for you, Rhea. Like entering a lion's den, don't you think?" Benny said. Benny's use of the old twentieth-century Earth idiom brought a faint smile to my lips despite the grim situation.

"Yeah, I guess you're right, Benny," I concurred. "But my advantage is she would never expect me to be that stupid and waltz right in there."

"You have a plan, then? Counting on the element of surprise?"

"No." I leaned back and placed a boot on the console. "Just plain dumb luck, actually." That was better than telling Benny my real plan, I thought.

Θ

Dressed in a loose robe and feeling the uncomfortable effects of my temporary *teck* as an Eosian, I found Pod Door 200 and took in a deep breath before opening it. I quickly fished in the robe for my gum and found to my dismay that I'd left it behind in my other clothes. Fighting the nervous tension stiffening my neck and back, I wrenched the door open. I inhaled the complicated scent of hay, wood, and freshwater on the breeze that cooled my naked head. I couldn't help a faint smile of appreciation at the sight of pastoral beauty before me. ZetaCorp or not, this station was truly magnificent.

It was a short and easy walk to the river. I let myself enjoy it as my boots sank into the ground and waded through the shin-deep grass. I breathed in the rousing scent of ripening fruit, freshly cut grass, and loam.

I instantly recognized A'ler at the gazebo café Zec had mentioned. Surprisingly, she had taken the shape of a human, dressed in a loose flowing purple robe and seated at one of the three tables, eating. In human form she resembled her younger brother strikingly. She was slim and very attractive, with long straight black hair and aristocratic features like Serge. But unlike him, she wore them sternly, with a cold mouth and calculating eyes. I swallowed down my rising emotions and strode toward the cold beauty.

A'ler remained seated as I approached and chose to ignore me even though it was obvious to me that she'd seen me. My Eosian sense of smell confirmed that A'ler had indeed been the person who had burgled my flat. Was she also The Rose? Perhaps that was the reason the message had gone to her as supposed custodian in the first place.

She didn't bother to acknowledge me even when I stood in front of her. She continued to eat her thick pockta soup, not bothering to look up.

"You must be A'ler," I offered. "I'm R'lan, Zec's friend. You were expecting me, I believe."

A'ler finally looked up and inspected me with an icy stare. "You're not so special," she said quietly. Her crisp blue eyes scanned my body in critical appraisal.

Had someone told her that I was? It was obvious that A'ler knew who I really was, despite my Eosian disguise. Thanks to Zec probably.

"Oh," I smiled sideways in a cavalier show of reckless bravado. "Zec shouldn't have," I said in a sarcastic tone, tipping my head.

"Zeballion spoke highly of your weapon, not of you, Officer Hawke."

"Ex-officer," I corrected her. So much for my temporary *teck*. Fine. I preferred it all out in the open anyway and decided to unbalance the shapeshifter. "And next time you trash my place uninvited, try to tidy up."

A'ler betrayed surprise for an instant then buried it under a contemptuous sneer.

I held up my MEC. "You were after this, weren't you?" Among other things. I let my smile turn into a smirk. "Well, here it is. But you're going to have to pay for it, fair and square, like anyone else." I had the satisfaction of seeing A'ler's eyes light up with self-absorbed interest. "It's called a MEC, which stands for Magnetic-Electro Concussion pistol," I continued, making my pitch. "It uses electro-magnetic wave energy to focus subatomic quintle particles to resonate with specific DNA, rather than randomly concentrating energy on tissue like your Q-gun does."

"Ah, very clever," A'ler said, eying the weapon. She held out her hand to inspect it. I hesitated, then reluctantly handed it over and watched, tight-lipped and fidgeting, as A'ler casually played with the controls.

"It's lighter than I'd thought," she shared.

"The MEC has three possible settings, based on three unique DNA signatures," I explained, nervously watching A'ler play with it as though it was a toy. "The first is to kill by essentially melting the tissue that its electromagnetic wave resonates with. The second setting acts as a concussion wave and knocks out the target with matching DNA. The third setting does nothing except scan. One can, of course, choose any combination of the three settings. For instance you could choose to scan three different species or kill three different species."

"So, it can have these three settings on three different DNA types at the same time?"

I nodded. "With one single sweep of the MEC in a crowd, you could kill all of one genetic type, knock out another, and leave the third intact but scanned and targeted. I've catalogued over 200 DNA types."

"Impressive," A'ler said, nodding. "Does it have a universal setting?"

"Of course," I said, a little impatient. "You can choose to scan every DNA type on the MEC's database—"

"Or *kill* every DNA type?"

I frowned and curled up my lip in a snarl of confused disgust. "That defeats the purpose of the MEC. You could just as soon use a Q-gun for that," I said. "The MEC's advantage lies in its ability to discriminate."

A'ler stunned me with her next question: "Can you set the MEC to recognize and alert you of a specific DNA type?"

It was a question no one had ever thought to ask and a feature I tended to keep to myself. "Yes," I admitted with some discomfort at revealing this ultimate property of the MEC. "But only from a limited proximity."

"How close?" A'ler seemed hardly able to contain a glowing smile of glee.

"The subject has to be within five meters of the MEC."

"Really!" Her eyes flashed. "And?" she prompted.

"It alerts you by vibrating against your body with a silent Beta frequency."

A'ler nodded, forcing on a pensive frown. "A Beta frequency, eh?" She looked like she was pretending to know what I was talking about but didn't. "So, how do you do that?" She turned the MEC over in her hand several times.

"You have to set it on permanent scan."

"Show me." A'ler shoved the weapon into my hand. "Do it for a Xhix—no," she quickly amended with a quick glance at the Xhixes close by. "Do it for … eh …" Her brows came together in thought, then she flashed a smile. "A … Gness."

Someone they certainly wouldn't find on the *Ulysses*, I thought with bitter cynicism; the Gness were a peaceful and humble race from the 61 Ursae Majoris system. They'd largely devoted themselves to Hermetic pursuits. Several had been members of the spiritual Schiss order, presumably defunct since the massacre. I showed A'ler how I set the DNA scanner.

"Ah," A'ler grinned like she'd won a prize. "That was easy …" Then she snatched the weapon back to take a closer look. She threw me a crafty glance. "What about the design? Do you have the specs?"

"Of course," I said, a little annoyed at the naïve question. "But not on cube. Right here," I tapped my head. "That comes later after I receive half the payment."

A'ler sneered, looking me up and down like merchandise. Then she rose abruptly to her feet. "We need a demonstration," she announced peremptorily. "You!" she waved her hand to a Xhix field worker nearby to approach.

God! Why did everyone insist on testing out the MEC? It worked, I thought peevishly. Then amended: except that time it failed to melt my own face off on Mar Delena. Of course that was my other MEC, the one I'd left behind at the precinct.

As the Xhix moved toward us, I concluded that he wasn't there by chance. There were probably half a dozen secret bodyguards stationed nearby, ready to shoot me dead if I posed any danger to A'ler.

"What are the current settings?" A'ler held out the pistol for me to inspect.

"To knock out an Eosian, scan a human, and kill a shapeshifter."

"All right." A'ler nodded with a sneer. She handed the MEC to the Xhix, a shapeshifter himself judging from his smell. "Find an Eosian and shoot him," A'ler commanded.

The Xhix, obviously thinking himself clever, pointed the weapon at me. I recoiled and braced for the concussion wave. The Xhix shot as A'ler lunged to stop him, shouting, "NO!"

Apart from a slight tingling feeling, I felt nothing. Certainly not the concussion wave that should have stunned me. I was only half-Eosian, I reminded myself. Still, I expected that it would have been enough to knock me out. Had my mother lied? Perhaps the other MEC wasn't defective, after all, I considered. Between V'mer's attempt and this Xhix, I appeared to be immune to its wave. I'd never tested the MEC on myself—until now, that is.

"You creon!" A'ler shouted in a hoarse voice and struck the cowering Xhix in the face. She appeared more shocked by the fact that I remained standing than I was. She turned from the Xhix to stare at me in stupefied wonder. The worker, puzzled by the weapon's apparent misfire, pointed the barrel to his face to inspect it and stupidly pressed the trigger. It was the last thing he saw. His face caved into a seething mess of melting flesh, and the body fell to the ground.

Startled, A'ler jerked back and made a sound of disgusted surprise. But she recovered quickly and, although still visibly shaken by the worker's foolish action, she shrugged and said caustically, "It's so hard to get good help these days."

The MEC obviously worked, I concluded, grimacing at the bloody corpse. Xhix weren't known for their astuteness.

A'ler bent down with apparent casualness to retrieve the MEC from the ground, but I was there first and snatched the pistol. We both rose to our feet. I held the MEC at hip level and pointed at A'ler. The shapeshifter stared at me with cold knife-sharp eyes. "*What are you?*" she asked, mystified.

I met her piercing gaze head on. "Your conscience, shapeshifter," I said. "You and I know this MEC works on others even if it doesn't work on me, so I suggest not making any fast moves or calling for help. Keep your blenoids off, or I sweep the place, starting with you."

"You didn't come here to sell me the MEC," A'ler bit out. "What do you really want?"

"Your brother."

She laughed at me. "My brother, the jagging lover."

"I need some answers about the Uma-1 massacre." And

about his connection with the Vos.

"You have the wrong man, slave. You already killed the one responsible for that. My *other* brother," she sneered at me. "You're so jagged, you don't even know it."

She glanced away quickly, to her left, toward the river. Something was brewing, and I was running out of time.

"Even if I told you where to find him, do you really think that you can get away from this place?" she continued. "Look around. We're in a huge space station, *my* space station. Your pathetic little ship is already disabled. We did that five minutes after you took port. You're a fool, Hawke. Actually, a total creon," she amended, voice growing more harsh and arrogant with each word. "Though not more than my idiot-brother. Chaos knows what he saw in you."

I ignored the insult. "You're forgetting one little fact: I have a MEC pointed at your gut, and I wouldn't mind using it. I know you have a CE device to at least a dozen blenoids out there. So, here's what we're going to do," I instructed calmly. "You aren't going to say anything that I don't tell you to. You answer my questions with simple and direct answers. Otherwise you shut up. Now start by calling your blenoids off; tell them to give us some room."

When A'ler didn't say anything, I dug the MEC into her side. She glared at me, then spoke, "This is A'ler. Stand down and clear off. Give us some room."

I felt my heart gallop. I just might get out of this alive. "Now, tell me where I can find Serge—I mean, V'ser."

A'ler's mouth sneered in open contempt. "Even if I tell you the truth, you'll never get away—"

"Just tell me!"

"You just missed him. He's headed for Uma 1."

I studied the shapeshifter for a moment. She was probably lying. She had no reason to tell me the truth, and I had no way of checking. And yet, I thought I caught a faint lingering scent of Serge on A'ler. But, then again, I might have imagined it, on A'ler's suggestion.

"Why is he going there?"

"Same reason as you, slave," A'ler said with a slanted smile of wry disdain. "To find out what really happened there and why. Seems a single Schiss remains, a Gness by the name of Rashomon." A Gness! Perhaps he had possessed some immunity to the poison V'mer had used, I reflected. No … I recalled from the file that V'mer had used dreccaline, a non-specific highly potent nerve poison that killed all life. I also remembered that two other Gnesses were killed as was a Xhix. A'ler continued, "My older brother conveniently forgot to tell me that he missed one of the most important of the Schiss priests. The head of their order."

My eyes narrowed at the shapeshifter. She stared back, challenging me. Daring me to believe what she'd said. If that was true, then V'mer had failed in his mission to annihilate the order: he'd managed to get everyone but the leader.

I pushed out my lower jaw in frustrated anger. I couldn't smell A'ler lying, probably because she was using a smokescreen of partial truths. Maybe she'd respond a little better to Ennos's interrogators. "Send out a command to enable Benny. You're coming with me for a little walk." I moved swiftly beside A'ler and gruffly seized her arm, MEC digging into her side. "Tell them!"

A'ler spat out her orders. At least this statement I could confirm. Benny and I had earlier agreed to withhold communications because of possible security tracking. Now it didn't matter. As I brusquely maneuvered her through the grassy field toward the exit door of the agri-pod, I tongued my com and said in a low voice, "Benny? You there?"

After a short delay, Benny's voice sounded in my ear: *I'm here, Rhea. What happened to com-silence?*

"Doesn't matter anymore. They knew about us, and you were put to sleep."

That's why I feel drowsy. But I'm okay now. Everything's operational.

"Good. I should be there in ten minutes. I've got a hostage."

"You'll never take me hostage, slave. They'll kill us both,"

A'ler spat out. "Why did you come? You're such a creon—"

I tightened my hold on her arm and dug the MEC into her ribs. "I told you to shut up." A'ler obviously wasn't used to taking other people's orders. "You're right," I continued. "I didn't come for you. But you'll do just fine for the Guardians."

We made it without incident to the anteroom adjacent to the hangar where Benny sat. As A'ler and I donned spacesuits, I noticed that the three Xhixes who'd been shadowing us had disappeared. I fully expected a contingent awaiting us on the other side.

"Open the hangar door," I snarled to A'ler. "Now!"

She punched in the code, and the inner door to the anteroom closed. The outer door to the hangar slid open.

"Benny!" I yelled. "Open the hatch!"

I seized A'ler and shoved her through the hanger door in front of me as a diversion then dove sideways into a pile of crates as shots zinged past me.

"Don't shoot her!" A'ler's strident yell could be heard above the general din. "We need her alive!"

Yeah, I thought cynically as I sprinted inside Benny's side hatchway, realizing cynically that the only reason I was still alive was that A'ler was after the MEC design knowledge in my head. A'ler was smarter and cooler than V'mer, who thought having the weapon was enough; though perhaps not as clever as V'ser, who was after the brains behind it.

"Get us out of here!" I commanded, running to the cockpit. Benny was already moving and shot out of the *Ulysses* into space. This was too easy, I thought. Why were they letting me go?

NINETEEN

The answer was, they weren't. I spotted six *shadow trackers* shoot out of the Ulysses in pursuit. Time for plan B…

"Evasive action, Benny!" I commanded. "We're heading

for the planet!"

I steered Benny down toward the large greenish planet below us. Glancing at the pulsar, I swallowed at my own plan and said, "Track the pulsar, Benny. It's due any second now for a major ionic pulse, isn't it?"

"Yes," Benny acknowledged. "In twelve seconds, by my count."

"Get us between the trackers and the pulsar. They'll be blinded for a few seconds when the pulse hits. While their instruments recalibrate, we dip low at maximum speed, out of their radar range, and hopefully into that small ionic storm on the planet where they won't be able to track us." I eyed the greenish swirling mass presently obscuring the planet's iridescent rocky face.

"That will be dangerous for us, Rhea."

"Plan B usually is. Do it!"

As the pulse struck, Benny accelerated into a fall. We soon penetrated the upper clouds of the planet, and Benny decelerated into an orbit within the obscuring clouds.

After several moments of waiting, I sighed and stretched back in my seat, feeling stiff from the previous ship motion. "I think we lost them," I said with a crooked smile. "Well done, Benny."

"Good idea, Rhea," Benny said.

"Let's wait another few minutes, then we'll get the chaos out of here. Benny, take over the controls," I instructed as I stood up. I kicked off my Eosian slippers and stripped off the long robe to my black sleeveless top and briefs. Finding a pair of flight pants in the cockpit closet, I pulled them on and noticed that the temporary purple of my skin was already fading. I ran my hand over my head and felt hair. Rava would hear about this. His temporary *teck* hadn't lasted very long this time.

As I pulled on my gravity boots, I noticed Benny's flight path. We weren't heading out of the system. In fact, Benny was heading for the planet below.

"What are you doing?" I demanded. "Get us out of here, Benny. A'ler's trackers are sure to find us here."

"I don't feel well, Rhea … Rhea?"

"Benny?" I slid in front of the controls and checked readouts. Everything seemed in order. Except for where Benny was taking us. "What's the matter?"

"Where are we?"

"What? You don't know?" I said, hearing my voice climb in pitch. "Looks like you're taking us down to 12c."

"I don't know if—why did you call me Benny?"

"What?" Panic edged into my voice. "You don't remember your name?"

"But why did you name me Benny?"

The ship abruptly listed, throwing me sideways against the starboard control panel. I struggled up and felt my heart slam. Benny had put us into a tailspin toward the planet. At this trajectory we were headed for a fiery crash landing.

"Never mind that now. You've entered us in a dangerous entry angle to the planet. We're going in too fast. Ease off the trajectory angle, Benny," I said in my best calm voice. I still heard emotion creep in. "You're too steep. Give us some scope. Then take us out of here." There were sure to be some Eclipse *shadow* ships in pursuit. Maybe it wasn't going to matter.

"I can't …" Benny muttered. "I don't know how … I'm so tired …"

Chaos! Benny was losing his cognitive abilities, and I was losing him. I heard the groan of straining metal, and Benny shuddered.

"Stay with me, Benny," I said, hearing the urgency in my voice. "Don't leave me. Don't fall asleep. Fight it."

"I'll try … just don't know what to do … feel … so … so …" he trailed away, drifting off.

"Benny!" I commanded in a calm voice, heart slamming. "Stay with me. Give me the controls. I'll take us out." In a few moments I wasn't going to be able to, I thought as I watched the spasmodic readouts.

"Do you remember when we first met at the Fauche ship builders on Iota Hor-2?" I continued, now aggressively wrenching open the keypad to override the AI's automatic system. "I thought you were the most incredible ship I'd ever set my eyes on. I knew we were meant for each other." I finally got the keypad off and started wiring the controls. "Remember when I jagged us off-stream …? I thought we were going to die. But you saved us, Benny. Just like now. Remember when you saved me from that rabid blenoid ambush on Upsilon 3 … I still have the puncture marks. I wouldn't have made it out alive, even with my Great Coat. Or that time on EpsEri 2 when I still didn't know how to use the Great Coat and those Venik slave traders just about killed me and left a jagging scar on my, well, my, you know …"

I seized manual control. But the ship was too far gone and responded sluggishly. Aside from the lapse of his cognitive abilities, Benny had lost much of his ability to conduct the simplest manual piloting tasks. I feared life support would be next. As soon as I thought of it, the environmental system howled warnings of a leak. Benny was breaking up!

I abandoned the controls to scramble to the vac-suit locker behind me. I pulled on my suit, locked down my helmet, feeling the instant flow of fresh air inside the suit, then threw myself back into my seat and seized the controls.

Amid the klaxon of the environmental warning system, Benny streaked through the wispy outer atmosphere of the planet. I clenched my teeth as I fought to maneuver Benny, hull shuddering and squealing, through the strong electrical wind surrounding the planet. Through the fiery stream we were creating in the thin atmosphere, I glimpsed the planet's rocky terrain rushing to meet us in a fatal collision —

Benny abruptly corrected trajectory. "Rhea!" he shouted in alarm. "What are you doing?" he asked, suddenly lucid.

I let go of the controls and laughed in relief. "Just get us down to the planet's surface, Benny. Without crashing, that is."

I hoped like mad that Benny wouldn't go loopy again before landing, but he made it. Benny took us down in a large flat valley surrounded by steep mountains. The landing was a little jarring but we were alive and safe.

"Listen, Benny," I said, "You need to do a detailed

systems diagnosis. I think they did something to you on *Ulysses*. It's interfering with your cognitive and motor functions. It must be a virus or something."

"Okay, Rhea. I don't recall anyone boarding me though."

I sat back, feeling sweat warm my armpits as Benny's systems hummed in self-analysis. I sighed and stared out onto the alien landscape of rugged mountains bathed in an eerie green light of swirling auroras amid the blackness of space. I could just make out the pulsar, with its two tails of radiation fanning out, blinking in the darkness. A beacon of startling beauty, birth, and death.

That was a close call. But we weren't out of it yet. A'ler's trackers were likely in orbit, waiting for us or, worse yet, preparing to come down to retrieve me or finish me off. I decided that I couldn't count on Benny's self-diagnosis. He was damaged, after all. There was also the possibility that Eclipse had bugged the ship for easy tracking.

"I'm going to check your outer hull to see if I can find a homing beacon with a transducer or anything they might have used to infect you from the outside."

"Okay, Rhea," Benny answered. "But be careful. The atmosphere is much too thin to deflect or absorb the high-energy electromagnetic radiation produced by that neutron star. And your suit won't protect you from the ionizing radiation. You'll have to time your stay outside between the major ionizing pulses."

"Okay, Benny," I agreed, checking the outer environmental readout. It showed a constant fifteen-minute pattern of ionic bursts between a steady stream of millisecond pulses of non-ionizing radiation: radio waves, infrared, visible light. A gamma ray burst had just occurred. Deciding to take advantage of what time I had, I hurried to the starboard hatch. As Benny opened it and let down the retractable ladder, I tongued my com. "We might get unwanted company, Benny," I warned. "Don't let any intruders in."

Okay, Benny responded in my com implant. *You have exactly twelve minutes and twenty-nine seconds until the pulsar's gamma ray burst hits us. You better be inside by then or you'll be a puddle of marmalade and toast.*

"Thanks, Benny," I said with a wry grimace at Benny's surviving sense of humor. I climbed down and dropped to the hard rock surface. If I hadn't been in such a hurry to check Benny, I might have taken the time to survey the arresting scene. This was a desolate place, with no obvious life forms. Not that the pulsar radiation would permit life forms to exist. Curtains of jagged mountains, their horizontally striated shades of ochre lit by the pulsar's flickering light, towered around me on all sides. Sentinels of the universe's cruel beauty. Bright green auroras of energized atmospheric gases swept overhead in a strong wind, bathing the iron-rich landforms in alternating shades of green and red. It was both bleak and beautiful.

I walked slowly around Benny, inspecting his outer surface. I'd gone fully around to his other side before I spotted it: a small flat transponder, glued to his underside. "I found it," I said. "I'm going to have to damage a little of your hull to remove it, though. It seems to have melted into your hull, bonded with it."

That's okay, Rhea, Benny responded in my ear. *You were right. I've just confirmed that I was infected by a parasitic self-replicating virus. It's still feeding on my system. Removal of the transponder may help a great deal.*

"Agreed. I'll get it off." I snatched my portable laser-drill from my tool belt and began carving into Benny's hull. To my chagrin, I soon discovered that the device had embedded itself much deeper and more extensively than I'd initially thought. I found rhizome-like tendrils that never seemed to end. Refusing to give in to despair about the spread of the infection, I focused on the transponder itself and dug relentlessly, realizing that I was scooping out a huge hole in Benny's exterior hull. Then the device finally popped off—

Intruder alert! Benny warned in a metallic voice.

"Where?" Heart racing, I scrambled from under the ship and quickly scanned my surroundings. I saw no *shadow* ships. No trackers. "Where, Benny?"

Benny's voice continued to drone like a machine in my head: *Intruder alert! Intruder alert! …*

I ran around the ship toward the hatch and heard it close and lock just as I got there. Heart thundering, I cried out, "Benny! What are you doing?"

… Intruder alert! …

I glanced down at my chronometer. I had four minutes left before the deadly pulsar radiation hit. Removing the transponder must have triggered a reaction and jagged Benny again. He'd lost his personality and was apparently on survival mode. It was also apparent that he didn't recognize me. I climbed the ladder and tried the hatch. "Open the jagging hatch, Benny!" I screamed. "It's me, Rhea! I'm not an intruder!"

The flickering light of the pulsar threw a strobing silhouette of me on Benny's green hull as I waited. Benny remained silent, except for the droning message: *Intruder alert! … Intruder alert!*

I scrambled down and searched around for anything that might protect me. Gamma rays were deadly. If I could make it to the closest mountains, I might find a cave, which would provide some protection from the deadly ionized plasma rays about to sweep the planet. But there was no way I'd make it. Because of their incredible height, the mountains appeared a lot closer than they actually were. They were easily ten kilometers away. I had less than two minutes left. Panic hit.

"God damn it, Benny!" I turned back to the hatch and screamed. "You have to let me in!"

A looming shadow cut out the strobing light of the pulsar reflected on Benny. I snatched my MEC and turned. Alarm spiked. A huge ship hovered not twenty meters from me.

It wasn't an Eclipse *shadow* ship but it was the next worse thing: a Guardian ship. An *alpha* class *twin-V wing*, ten times the size of Benny. I could make out the control centre through the large hexagonal bow canopy that directly faced me. The control centre formed the core of the ship with two sets of gimbaled wings spanning outward in two Vs.

I backed against Benny's closed hatch and pointed the

MEC two-handed at the ship. "Let me in, Benny!" I shouted and took aim. I'd thankfully designed my MEC with a frequency that could inflict significant damage to inanimate objects such as the canopy window of a Guardian ship. I decided that it would keep them more than busy while I thought of escape in the minute I had left to live.

"Don't shoot, Rhea!" a familiar voice pleaded over my ear com. "It's me, Bas!"

I made him out in the control centre. He waved.

"Our starboard hatch is open. Hurry!"

I glanced at my chronometer. I had twenty seconds left. I bolted for the *twin-V*. I scrambled up the ladder, opened the hatch, and dove inside. The hatch auto-closed, just as the blinding green flash hit. Within several heartbeats, the light beacon at the outer hatch door flickered on, signaling that the room had re-pressurized and now contained sufficient air to breathe.

Still panting, I removed my helmet and got to my feet, sweeping the entryway with my MEC. The room was empty, save a few cargo containers. Within moments Bas appeared in the doorway with a friendly smile of welcome. He was dressed casually in black Guardian-regulation flight pants and gray T-shirt. He ignored the MEC pointed at him as he approached.

"You sure owe me for—"

I seized him in a *vizion* arm lock, muzzle of my MEC digging into his throat. He cried out in surprised pain. I growled at him, "Why are you following me, Bas? Are you here to turn me in to the Guardians?"

"No! Rhea, please!" he gasped out. "You're hurting me!"

I didn't relent. Instead I shoved him up against the wall, scraping his cheek against the metalloid edge of a doorway.

"I helped you steal Benny, remember?" he choked out.

"How do I know you didn't help me just so you could come after me and catch me—"

"Are you blenoid?" he gasped. "I would never—"

"Or they found out, and Ennos gave you the chance to redeem yourself by bringing me in."

"No! Chaos, Rhea! I'm here on my own," Bas added between gasping breaths. "Ennos doesn't know. *No one* knows."

I finally let go and stared at Bas in confusion as he backed away and massaged his throat.

"What about your other Guardian crew?"

"Raekwon's cold with it. He's pretty new to the Guardians and does everything I say. He thinks you're my ... well ..." Bas blushed.

"*Cool,*" I corrected him sternly, then let a faint smile cross my lips. "The expression's *cool.*" I gave him a long hard look. "What in space are you doing here, then, Bas?"

He gave me an exasperated grimace. "After what you just did, I'm not sure I should tell you." He looked a little peeved and massaged his throat to bring home his point. Then he pointed to the MEC. "You have *two* of those?"

My eyes narrowed. "Were you spying on me?"

He visibly cringed under my glare and rubbed his arm. "Not exactly."

I crossed my arms. "What then?"

He grinned, a complex mixture of maverick smugness and self-consciousness. "I'll show you," he replied cryptically, obviously enjoying the intrigue and the momentary power he held over me. "Come on." He turned and strode to the doorway into the hall of the spacious ship, expecting me to follow.

After a brief moment of resistance, I replaced my MEC in the holster of my vac-suit tool belt and followed with a loud sigh.

"We were in the neighborhood investigating a small trade dispute on Ballin 5," Bas explained over his shoulder as he led me down the narrow corridor, "when Raekwon spotted the *Ulysses* and was curious to see it. Then he recognized Benny's signature nearby. We noticed half a dozen Eclipse *shadow* ships orbiting the planet, and I thought you might be in trouble so we came over to see if you needed a hand. That's when Benny's distress signal alerted us, and we shot down to the planet right away."

"Well, thanks," I said almost reluctantly, still skeptical of

Bas's motives. I wouldn't have expected Benny to transmit a signal in his impaired state. But Bas was here, proof of that, I supposed. "You saved my life."

"Don't mention it," Bas waved me down, a little embarrassed. "What happened?"

"Benny sustained some damage," I said tersely, not bothering to elaborate. "He lost all his super-cognitive functions and some of his motor functions. I was locked out because he sensed an intruder—probably your ship—and didn't recognize me as being different. I'm not sure how to fix him."

"Well, you're in luck," Bas said, leading me into the control centre. "Rhea, meet my partner, Raekwon Bånder."

I stared at the tall Fauche. The fawn-like alien towered nine feet. His ears alone were a meter long. They draped down his back in a soft cascade.

"This is Officer Rhea Hawke," Bas swept his hand to me. I gave him a pointed glance for calling me 'Officer.'

The lanky alien twitched his long ears and nodded to me in greeting. His doe-like eyes glistened like dark pools as he flashed a disarming smile through a wispy beard that hung a good twenty centimeters down from his knobby chin. I realized why the Fauche were so good at commerce. Raekwon managed to look docile and not too intelligent—must have been those large liquid-dark eyes—but I knew the Fauche to be clever by nature.

"Pleased to meet you," Raekwon said in a soft but high-pitched voice. "I admire your taste in ships, Officer Hawke."

"Ex-officer," I corrected him, then gave him a faint smile. "The Fauche certainly know how to make an interstellar ship. I've been very pleased with Benny … so far."

"You've been experiencing a malfunction?" the Fauche probed.

I pursed my lips. "Benny was injected with a virus," I admitted with a pointed glance at Bas. "He lost most of his cognitive and motor functions. I was barely able to get him down to the planet's surface without crashing. I don't think he's capable of flying right now, at least not safely anyway."

"Won't even let her in, right, Rhea?"

I glanced at Bas briefly with a frustrated frown.

"The trackers are after you too," Bas said.

I ignored him and focused on Raekwon. "Can you help me?"

"We can tow your vehicle to Pyramid City on 47 Uma-a," said Raekwon.

"Locals call it Horus," Bas added.

"Tangent Shipping has a major facility located there. I'm sure they'll be able to help you," Raekwon said.

It was a very tempting offer. Although ZetaCorp appeared to have the monopoly on ship building, I considered the Fauche to be the best mechanics and ship designers in the galaxy. They'd created Benny after all. The 47 Ursae Majoris system was also where Serge had presumably gone, according to A'ler. To Uma 1, the moon of 47 Uma-b, a gas giant occupying an orbit outside 47 Uma-a. I gave Raekwon a guarded half-smile of gratitude. "Thank you," I said. "I appreciate the offer, but I wouldn't want to trouble you with a journey so far out of your way." I glanced at Bas with a curious frown. "You both must have Guardian things to do and places to go. If you can just help me to get back in to Benny, I'm sure he and I can work something out."

"What about the trackers, Rhea?" Bas reminded me. "You need to get out of here right away."

"I know of no other way to get you off this planet, unless you wish to abandon your ship," the Fauche pressed on. "We can't fix it here."

"But you're a Fauche," I said, mildly annoyed.

"Not all Fauche are mechanics," he said flatly. Then his lambent eyes crinkled in amusement. "Yes, Fauche mechanics are the best in the galaxy. I'm just not one of them."

I flushed. I'd simply assumed. Then I looked out through the large control room viewport at Benny's sleek form and swallowed. "You're right. I won't abandon my ship." I let out a long breath of submission. "I'll take you up on your offer, then."

"Great!" Bas said, clapping his hands. He'd obviously

been waiting for me to agree. "Let's get the grappler ready." He motioned to Raekwon with his hand. "The sooner we get out of here the better." Bas turned to me and recognized my anxiousness. "Don't worry, Rhea. We'll get Benny secured aboard our ship's aft tail-ride. He'll be just fine, riding our jack on the stream."

I nodded and brought my hand to my mouth as I breathed in deeply. Benny and I had been through a lot together. He'd saved my life a few times. I had much to be grateful for. "Just take care of him."

Suddenly exhausted, I made myself comfortable in a chair and covered a yawn. It was going to be a long journey.

TWENTY

I bolted awake, sitting up from my slouched position in my seat, and found Bas standing over me. He'd just nudged me with his hand and was gazing at me with a self-conscious smile. I hadn't realized that I'd drifted off.

"Sorry," he said with an apologetic smile. "How about I take you to your quarters where you can get a more comfortable rest. Plus you can grab a bite to eat in Food Prep. It'll be another standard galactic day before we get to Horus. Besides, I have something to show you."

"Not your etchings again," I said with a snide look. I flicked a pointed glance at Raekwon, overseeing the main console. He had his back to us and looked occupied with the sensors. "Okay, Bas," I said and got up stiffly from the chair, muscles screaming awake. I rubbed my weary eyes with the palms of my hands and realized that I hadn't slept properly in over forty standard galactic hours. The thought of a bed was more than welcome.

Bas led me out of the control room along the centre corridor aft toward the sleeping quarters. "This one's yours," he stopped at the second of the hatches lining the corridor on the left. "Food Prep is just beyond that last bulkhead." He pointed further aft, then opened the hatch to my room, revealing a tiny berth just large enough for a bunk, a chair, and a table equipped with a holo-com set. But I barely registered anything else as I caught sight of my sable Great Coat laid across the bunk and my MEC on the table. I gasped.

Bas chuckled in amusement.

I threw an amazed glance back at him as I entered the room and took my Great Coat in both hands. I raised it to my nose to inhale its heady organic aroma then hastily pulled off my utility belt with my other MEC strapped to it. I pulled off the vac-suit and slid into the coat. I took in several long breaths, inhaling a new strength and calm confidence with the scent of its thixtropic fabric. Smiling conspiratorially, Bas handed me the MEC that sat on the table. Now I had them both back again! I checked its settings before tucking it into my Great Coat and turned back to Bas with a puzzled look.

"How?"

He leaned casually against the door jam with a self-pleased smile. "I stole it from Stores," he said smugly. "It's magic on you. I still can't figure out how you get it to help you leap tall buildings like Wonder Woman when no one else's Great Coat does that."

"It's Supergirl you're thinking of," I corrected. "Not Wonder Woman."

"Anyway," he said, still smiling like a boy, "I figured you would need both the Great Coat and the MEC where you were going."

"And where exactly is that, Bas?" I asked with a cynical look of challenge. And how did he know he was going to catch up with me? There was something he wasn't telling me.

"You tell me," he responded cagily.

I crossed my arms over my breasts. "Why do I have an awful feeling that you already know?"

"Well, the last time we found you, you were knee-deep in trouble."

I dropped my gaze and stroked my Great Coat

181

thoughtfully. When I returned my gaze to him, my eyes focused deep into his with challenge. "Stealing my Great Coat and the MEC … You sure were certain you were going to find me, Bas. Why is that?"

He blinked and returned me an enigmatic look. I decided that he'd anticipated my question. "So, you got me, Rhea. I was looking for you," he confessed. "I had Raekwon scanning the whole time with Benny's signature. And before you go blenoid on me, it's not what you think," he quickly added. "The plain and simple of it is I was worried about you." He straightened and aimed an intense look of concern at me. "And seems I was right to be."

I narrowed my eyes at him and leaned sideways to give him a hard look. "There's still something you're not telling me, Bas. How did you know where to look?"

He sighed. "Okay. Someone posted your destination on the Iota Hor holo-board. Everyone knows."

"Chaos!" I hissed out. Someone was definitely not what they were supposed to be at the precinct, I thought. Someone with links to Zec … and Eclipse.

"What were you thinking going back to the *Ulysses*, Rhea?" Bas went on. "Especially after what happened before. I don't get it. You have a suicide wish? What are you chasing?"

I firmed my lips and sat down on the bunk. "Just following a hunch."

"Is this still about that Vos-thing?"

"Ennos told you?"

"No." Bas shook his head. "It leaked out. I'm not sure how or who, but the whole precinct knows about your theory: the Eclipse-Vos conspiracy and impending Vos attack. Ennos is mad as chaos about it."

"I'll bet," I agreed, feeling a bitter smile tug my lips. The last thing Ennos wanted was for my hunch to make it to the streets. He'd always maintained that the knowledge of even a remote chance of an impending Vos attack would be enough to charge the galactic worlds with a panic the Guardians couldn't contain. "I'm glad it's out," I said defiantly. "Maybe someone will take it more seriously than Ennos did. The galaxy may depend on it." I aimed an intense searching gaze on Bas.

He responded by nervously pulling an info-pod from his flight pants pocket. He held it out towards me, almost as if to give to me, but not quite. "I think you're in too deep with this Eclipse stuff, Rhea. My advice is to quit while you can."

Was that a warning or a threat?

"But if you insist on pursuing that blenoid path, this item might help you. It's—"

"The info-pod with the files Asphalios and I stole from the *Ulysses*," I answered for him.

He half smiled. "We've since deciphered all but the hit list for The Rose. We got a bonus, Rhea. One of the messages included a detailed listing of Eclipse high-ranking officials."

I looked down at the info-pod with curiosity. Was Serge on it? I'd lost my own copy of that information when A'ler and her cronies ransacked my apartment.

"The Rose's hit list seems encrypted with a complicated link to harmonics of some kind and we haven't a clue how to break it." He shrugged. I was hoping he'd gotten further with it than I had. "Maybe you can decrypt that one like you did those other messages you helped me with." Other Vos messages, he'd meant. I seemed to have a particular ability to interpret their ciphers. "They appear similar in other ways."

I gave Bas a hard searching look. Why was he being so helpful to the extent of breaking major Guardian rules? Giving this to me was a major offence. It would cost him his Guardian status. He wasn't a typical Eosian, *tecking* himself with hair and choosing friends like me, I considered. But that wasn't enough to explain this kind of truant behavior. What was his angle?

"So, do you have a lead?" he pressed on.

My smile turned grim. Was he on a fishing expedition? If so, for whom? It was obvious that he wanted to speak to me alone, without Raekwon. Which suggested that Raekwon wasn't in on it. "Yeah," I responded guardedly. "It so happens that I do, Bas." I looked away and continued with a frown, "A certain gentleman I ... thought I knew." I removed the Great Coat and folded it carefully on the bunk. "His sister was on the *Ulysses*. She told me where he was going."

"Great! When we get there, we can—"

"I work alone, Bas." I turned to face him.

"Eh?" He blinked, then stammered, "Yeah, but I thought that since I rescued you and gave you—"

"I said I only work alone." I gave him a sharp stare. "Without exception," I added stonily then raised an eyebrow and pointed with my chin at the info-pod in his hand.

His lips tightened and I saw the hurt in his eyes. But he knew better than to beg. I wasn't exactly known for compassion at the precinct. He only had to gauge the sullen resoluteness on my face; he gave up, emitting the disappointed sour smell of rotting cabbage. Then with pursed lips he slapped the info-pod into my outstretched hand. I could tell he was furious. He hung on to the pod for a moment as I tried to close my hand. "Why do you hate us so much?" he blurted out angrily. "We saved your jagging planet, after all."

"I know, Bas," I said softly. "I don't hate you. You're just … I mean …" I trailed off.

He let go of the pod with a snap and exhaled with obvious frustration. Then his eyes narrowed with the dawning of new understanding. "You don't trust me."

"Don't take it personally," I said, firming my lips. I avoided his stare and transfered the pod to a secure pocket in my Great Coat. "I don't trust anyone." But I couldn't leave it there. I met his eyes with an imploring look and touched his arm. He flinched and I quickly let go. "Look, Bas," I began, struggling with an explanation that both he and I could live with, "I … just …" and couldn't find one.

"It's okay," he cut in, not bothering to hide the bitterness in his voice. "I don't need your '*sorry for you*' lip service, Rhea. Just give me the respect I deserve."

No longer able to meet his look of challenge, I looked down at the Great Coat and stroked it.

"Okay," he said in resigned bitterness. "Go save the universe all by yourself. Though, chaos knows why you even bother—you don't let any part of the universe in."

My jaw clenched as I heard my best ally—my *only* ally—turn briskly and storm down the corridor. Keeping my head bowed, I lifted my gaze and watched him leave. I felt a tug of regret. It churned inside me like spoiled milk, then I tucked it far down where it wouldn't get in my way and turned to the holo-com on the desk. How could I have told Bas that a man I thought was an Eosian had ruined my life—after I'd killed him.

Θ

I bolted awake to the sound of creaking metalloid and a jarring motion. They'd just landed. Good Chaos! I scrambled out of my cramped bunk and hastily dressed as the lights automatically went on in response to my movement. I threw on my charcoal gray sleeveless top, then climbed into my black flight pants and boots. As I cinched on my utility belt and holstered MEC, I reflected that I'd slept right through our entry into 47 Uma-a's atmosphere. The gravitational shift was usually sufficient to take me out of sleep. I must have really needed it, I concluded, shrugging into my Great Coat with the other MEC. I shoved my void-suit and helmet into the backpack Bas had left for me, pulled open the hatch, and pelted down the corridor.

Raekwon met me at the *twin-V's* aft entrance. "Do you have everything?" he said in his high-pitched lyrical voice.

"Yes, thank you," I responded, glancing around for Bas in the huge bustling hanger.

"We've released Benny from our grapples using a Tangent crane, and he's already on one of their pallets, cued for maintenance," Raekwon continued, drawing my gaze back to him. "I took the liberty of speaking with Selway about Benny's problem. He's one of their head mechanics, the big guy there with the extra long ears." Raekwon pointed to a very tall and disheveled Fauche, busy instructing another mechanic and pointing energetically to a very badly scoured *speeder*-class land vessel.

"Thanks, Raekwon," I said, offering my hand. As I shook

Raekwon's extremely long hand, I glanced around again. I restlessly hoisted my backpack over one shoulder. "I was hoping to say goodbye to Bas. And thank him too," I said, trying to hide my disappointment. "Particularly for getting this back to me," I glanced down and patted my Great Coat. "And for not ... well ..." I nodded, leaving out the rest of what I thought: for not turning me in. In truth, I hadn't seen Bas since he'd left my quarters in a huff twenty standard galactic hours ago. I knew he'd avoided me. After doing a bit of research on 47 Uma-a and its inhabitants, I'd ended up eating space rations with Raekwon in the small cafeteria and exchanged pleasantries with him until exhaustion drove me back to my bunk where I'd fallen into a comatose sleep.

"I'll tell him for you," Raekwon trilled. Then he wished me well and re-entered the ship. I approached the head mechanic of Tangent Shipping, disappointed that I hadn't spoken to Bas.

Θ

"He's been extensively infected with a self-replicating parasitic virus, missy," Selway informed me in a girl's voice as we walked around Benny. I found my brows furrowing slightly as I noticed bits of food caught in his messy beard. "The damage might be irreparable. It'll take at least two days of diagnosis before we'll even know if we can eradicate the virus, let alone assess whether the damage can be reversed."

I turned to Benny and stroked the ship's green-brown hull, feeling ill. I suddenly realized what Benny meant to me. He was my friend and I didn't want to contemplate the Fauche not being able to repair him.

"Do what you can," I commanded in a harsh fractured voice and was about to leave when Selway crowed in objection. I spun around to face him with an impatient scowl. He looked more like a moose than a deer, which the Fauche tended to resemble. His wiry beard only emphasized a long snout for a Fauche.

He narrowed his otherwise large round eyes at me and scratched his food-encrusted furry chin. A few crumbs spilled out. "We require payment in advance, missy."

I gave him a scathing look. "What? You don't trust me?"

"Well, actually ... no. It's been our experience on jobs like this that if the outcome is bad, through no fault of our own, we find it hard to extract payment from the client. So, we need it up front. Before we do anything else."

"You need collateral," I redefined his request. "That's what you're asking for, right?"

He blinked his lustrous, hardly innocent, eyes. "I suppose."

"Here," I shrugged out of my Great Coat and threw it at Selway who snatched it in the air with one paw. "It's worth at least fifty thousand credits on the galactic black market," I informed him. "I'll get you the cash later. But I need for you to work on my ship *now*."

Selway gave me a greasy smile. I flinched as he fondled my Great Coat with those filthy paws. I'd already removed the faulty MEC and stowed it aboard Benny. But I still hated seeing Selway grope at my coat. I needed distraction badly and abruptly thought of Serge. It wasn't as though I believed A'ler for a moment about Serge being on Uma 1. But it was definitely worth checking. Being the last remaining Schiss, Rashomon was a plausible target. It made sense that Serge would try to finish off what his older brother had started. And even if he wasn't there, it might be worth questioning the Gness about the massacre and warn him of possible further danger from Eclipse assassins. "Where would I get a shuttle to the moon of 47 Uma-b?"

"Uma 1?" Selway grunted. "No one goes to Paradise City without a pass," he meowed, still stroking my coat. I felt myself stiffen with each slide of his dirty paw on its leather-like fabric.

"How do I get one?" I asked, trying to hide my grimace of frustration. My eyes flickered from his stroking hands to his dirty face.

Selway critically eyed me up and down as though

assessing my worth. His long pink tongue ran along his furry lips, and he said with a sarcastic smile, "*You* don't, missy."

I planted my fists on my hips. "Says who?"

"You're an Enforcer, aren't you?" He glanced from the Great Coat in his paws to my MEC, holstered to my tool belt. "Enforcers aren't welcome there. It's a spiritual place of peace and tranquility."

"We're peacekeepers," I said defensively.

Selway guffawed in a high-pitched squeal. "Sure! I've seen how your lot keep peace. It's easy to keep peace with a dead man."

Guardian Enforcers didn't appear to be liked an awful lot lately. Or had it always been like this, and I had only just noticed?

He shook his head in response to my insistent look. "The Temple of Thoth gives out passes. Your chances are nil, missy."

"Where?" I asked, glancing out toward Pyramid City, and making out a series of dark triangular buildings already bathed in the warm mauves of the coming evening.

"Follow the main street to the largest pyramid. Can't miss it, missy. Ask for Ka. He's the offworlder liaison and associated with the Schiss Order."

"Thanks," I said, hiking my backpack over my shoulder and turning. Then I halted mid-stride and spun around. I narrowed my eyes to study Selway for a moment. I aimed a sharp look at him. "See that you don't lose the coat. I'm good for cash when I return, and I want my coat back."

"Sure, missy," he said, already fishing inside the coat for more treasures. "I won't sell it … yet."

I felt a shudder run through me. After throwing a sad glance at Benny, I wrapped my arms around myself and marched off, feeling like I'd just lost my two best friends.

TWENTY-ONE

Pyramid City was a beautiful, spacious vista of parkland, dotted with clusters of tall towers and massive pyramids. I had a good view to get my bearings from where I stood at Tangent Shipping's hangar bay entrance door. As Selway had said, it was easy to make out the largest of the pyramids. The temple was straight ahead. After a glance up at the pale twin moons, occasionally streaked by the fleeting dark shapes of small flying vehicles, I set out for the temple on the gravel road, noting that I was the only one using it. The Khonsus obviously preferred to travel by air vehicle, I thought, glancing up at the flocks of dark shapes flying overhead. The road was no doubt reserved for offworlders like me with no personal vehicle.

Once out of earshot of the bustling Fauche shipbuilding yard, I heard little in the way of city noises. No engines, no sirens, no murmurs of thousands of people going and coming. There was only the quiet whizzing of the small ships far overhead and the frequent trilling of birds. The birds seemed to congregate by the pyramids, I thought, noting that their chorus grew more pronounced whenever I passed one. No matter how hard I searched, I couldn't spot any.

Their complex symphony started to make me unreasonably uncomfortable, and I felt myself stiffen involuntarily. My hand crept to my MEC, holstered on my thigh, and I rested my hand on it, finger tapping nervously on the handle. I would have preferred to be less conspicuous with my sidearm, but I hated the idea of leaving both my MECs behind on Benny even more. I didn't trust Selway.

Then it hit me: the Khonsus who'd tried to mind-rob me on *Ulysses* had made just such a sound. I was hearing not birds, but Horus's bird-like inhabitants, the Khonsus. I felt both relief and a chilling thrill at my discovery.

As the darker shades of evening drew around me like a

heavy cloak, I reviewed the brief research I'd conducted on the Khonsus and their planet before succumbing to exhaustion onboard Bas's ship. The Khonsus were considered masterful librarians and database keepers; they'd amassed the greatest single physical collection of data, information, and knowledge in the galaxy. Keepers of the Great Galactic Library called the House of Seshat, the peaceful Khonsus were also known for their pursuit of philosophy and mathematics. They'd presumably given 47 Uma-a the name of Horus, after the Egyptian moon god of Earth. I thought it curious that they'd chosen an Earth mythic figure and wondered at the origin of the Khonsus, who'd colonized Horus several millennia ago. Seekers of knowledge and truth, they'd discovered their powers in mind-probing and control through some symbiotic interaction with the planet's energy and forces, which also imparted the wisdom to use their powers wisely. I had read that a Khonsus was incapable of inflicting physical pain on another to kill—but they could destroy your mind.

During my short self-briefing in Bas's ship, I'd read that this bird-race not only communicated mostly in song, but that they believed in the universal harmony of the cosmos. Practitioners of a kind of Gnostic Neo-Platonism, the Khonsus believed that God moved through each individual in song. According to them music healed the soul and linked everything in the cosmos in a grand network of a single universal intelligence of natural harmony and order. Like the Gness, the Khonsus were pseudo-Hermeticists and devoted to gnosis, which they understood to be the experience of liberating interior knowledge. They sought to forge a new worldview based on combining religious with secular dogmas and blending science with philosophy and spirituality. It had never been successfully accomplished on Earth, I thought cynically. Just as Neo-Platonism, Hermeticism, Gnosticism, and other syncretistic beliefs began rejoicing in a renaissance of major proportions on Earth, the Vos came. They swept in like a colossal storm and destroyed humanity's faith in a merciful and kind God or cosmic harmony. There was nothing harmonious about the Vos.

Nothing kind about their brutal and senseless killings. They were the scourge of the universe. Purveyors of disharmony. Killers of faith and hope.

I didn't think the beliefs of the Khonsus and the Gness had much chance out here either, where worldviews were bound to be even more at odds and people more cynical. Although based on some real science of harmonics, the beliefs of the Khonsus struck me as the naïve yearnings of a knowledge-seeking race for a magic stick that didn't exist. The universe wasn't like that at all. It was a bleak, inhospitable, and unknowable vastness of amorality, I thought with a long frown. Religion and God had nothing to do with it. Both were the sad and desperate creations of mortal civilizations. And the immortals ... they thought *they* were the gods ...

Nonetheless, I felt a reluctant admiration for the persistence of these Hermeticists. It was likely no coincidence that the like-minded Schiss cult had decided to build their spiritual retreat in the Uma system. But then look what happened to them ...

I sighed and looked around at the jagged mountains in the far distance behind the giant pyramids of the city. I wished that I'd been awake to view the planet on our approach. It was fairly young geologically and boasted an eclectic mosaic of splendid wonders from its expansive curtains of imposing mountains, to its legendary migratory trees, boiling seas, and other mysterious phenomena. I would have far preferred to explore Horus than pursue this hunch.

The angelic chorus of bird-like songs heightened as I made my way up the stairs to the tall entranceway of the Temple of Thoth. I gazed up along the glassy surface of the looming pyramid. Lit from within by thousands of beads of light, it glistened in the pale moonlight. I spotted a huge stylized above the threshold of the pyramid's massive doorway. It resembled an Egyptian hieroglyphic. I suddenly realized: this was the eye of Horus, the Egyptian sky god. The eye of Horus presumably guided the soul on its journey to open hidden knowledge inside. These great librarians and philosophers had adopted an apt symbol from my home world, I thought with smug disdain. The Khonsus were the best knowledge-gathering experts in the galaxy. They were renowned for their integrity and veracity.

As if that wasn't enough Egyptian symbolism, I noticed the sculpted caduceus, two coiling snakes wound around a staff to a winged figure and crown, on either side of the massive doorway. It was the staff of Thoth, purveyor of truth, wisdom, and time. And the symbol of Western Medicine on Earth. Thoth, I remembered, was an archetype of transformation through reconciliation of opposites.

I passed through the massive doorway and let my eyes feast on the incredible interior. The pyramidal structure was mostly empty space. A tower of stacked platforms rose at its centre, surrounded by a spiraling set of two moving walkways resembling a huge DNA helix—or another version of the caduceus. Flitting on and off the platforms like hummingbirds at a feeding station were—I narrowed my eyes to stare—Khonsus! I swallowed convulsively, recalling that rogue Khonsus on the Eclipse space-station, who'd spread out his winged arms and glided toward me like a raptor.

Khonsus alighted on platforms, then disappeared or abruptly appeared, trilling and leaping out into the air with magnificent wings spread. As I watched them soar like singing angels, I realized that these were what I'd mistaken for vehicles in the evening sky earlier. No wonder I'd walked the road alone! The Khonsus flew everywhere. The spiraling walkway up the tower was obviously for the benefit of offworlders like me. Also the reason I was the only one on the ground at the moment.

Impressed, I stood still for a while and let my gaze wander around the splendid structure. I decided that the tower of platforms must be places to study, discuss theory, and conduct research. This was, after all, the temple for spiritual and philosophical pursuits.

The waning mauve twilight filtered in through the slanted glass walls, aided by what looked like strings of inverted candles that hung like chandeliers from the high ceilings of the tiered structure. I noted that they were glow-worms, returning the light they'd absorbed during the day from the sun. The floor beneath me was warmed the same way, through reciprocation by creel fungus. The fungus grew naturally into a metallic burnished hard surface one could walk on and returned at night the heat they absorbed during the day to make the floor comfortably warm. I had encountered this creature on several other worlds, imported from Omega 6, the creel's native planet. This place was a splendid example of inanimate and biological elegance and practicality. The human architects on Iota Hor-2 could learn a lesson or two from these designers.

Reminded of my mission, I glanced around at ground level, which was empty of people except for me, and wandered in the general direction of the first platform, toward the walkway where I intended to make my inquiries. Aside from the clusters of small gathering places with chairs and tables, there was nothing on the ground floor that appeared to be administrative in nature. I made out several tiled archways leading in several directions out of the pyramid to what looked like outdoor gardens, lit by rows of glow-worm filled lanterns.

A captivating rhythmic thrum drew me in my wandering. I soon heard accompanying flute and chant and spotted movement in one far corner of the pyramid floor: a cluster of Khonsus, winged arms spread out and dressed in flat-topped hats and wide skirts that billowed out like curtains, twirled in furious circles. Their movements were hypnotic and reminded me of the ancient Turkish Sufi Whirling Dervishes of Earth. I'd read somewhere that, at least on Earth, this was a form of meditation and a method of gaining a direct link with God —

I heard a throat clear and steps approach from behind. My hand instinctively moved to rest on my MEC.

"They revolve right to left around the heart to show that life has been created with love in order to love," a melodic voice said behind me.

I turned and saw a tawny-feathered Khonsus, at least eight feet tall but slightly stooped, walking slowly toward me. Dressed in a purple open-sleeved robe that flowed in front and behind his great wings, he looked both majestic and humble at the same time. There was a stillness in his presence, an observant calm in his dignified manner. I could discern that he was quite old. His feathers looked less vibrant than the other Khonsus I'd seen, as though they'd grown dull and faded with age.

"Greetings. I am Ka," he said. He had a gentle tenor voice that flowed over me like sparkling wine and a warm unprejudiced smile of welcome that glowed on his beak-like mouth. His eyes shone like pools of liquid amber and with such intensity as if lit from behind. Dust-pigment. I'd read that Gnostics indulged in Dust as part of their spiritual rites to elevate themselves to where they could experience God. Although the Guardians had made Dust illegal, it was still available on the Slipstream. Barbariccia's Dark Sun clearly held the monopoly—his organization alone knew where to get the raw ingredients for Dust manufacture. I thought it an odd relationship: gangsters cavorting with religious leaders.

"Rhea Hawke," I responded, returning Ka a guarded smile. This was the being I was meant to see, according to Selway. I instinctively avoided gazing directly at him. But there was something attractive about his raptor-like face, and within moments I found myself compelled to fix upon his large liquid eyes. He was smiling at me with a look of recognition. I instantly thought of my treacherous eye-melting and hoped to God this Khonsus hadn't caught me in that awful Galactic News vid.

"Nice name … Hawke," he said, looking a little amused. "Have you seen the *semazen* before?"

"Something very like it, on Earth," I responded, glancing back at the whirling hawk-headed figures. "A prayer dance practiced by the Sufis, Islamic mystics, to achieve ecstasy."

"Ah." He nodded with a slight frown. "Sufi, I believe means 'awareness in life,' young one. The aim of the *sema* is not uncontrolled ecstasy and loss of consciousness, but the realization of submission to God," he corrected me and followed my gaze back to the dancers. "These Khonsus practice the *sema* as a reminder that all beings are comprised of revolving electrons, protons, neutrons and atoms; a eulogy to the music of the spheres," Ka continued. "That hat represents the tombstone of the ego, and the white skirt is the ego's shroud. You see how they raise their right palm to the sky and the left down as they're whirling? This is to receive the blessings of our heaven through the right hand, transferred through the body to the left hand, bringing the blessing back to the earth; the coming of earth and the returning to it."

The precept of Hermeticism, I thought. "It's ... beautiful," I said, watching them spin in simultaneous rhythm and intricate pattern.

"Ah," Ka said, pointing. "They are just now in the third selam. It is the rapture of dissolving into love and the sacrifice of the mind to love, to complete submission, unity, and the annihilation of self in God, the Beloved."

I stared. His words lodged inside and something stirred in me. Perhaps it was a combination of their relentless spinning, the entrancing music and chanting together with the drums beating through me. I felt a stirring in my heart of deep connection and dark portent. As though a part of me knew something and was keeping it from the rest of me.

"Sit with me," Ka beckoned me to a bench away from the sounds of the dancers near one of the tiled archways and took a seat himself. As I sat beside him, he probed me with sharp intelligent eyes. "What brings you here, Ms. Hawke?"

"I'd like a permit to visit Uma 1."

As if he'd made a decision about my unworthiness already, Ka seemed to frown. "Paradise City? It is a sanctuary. Not for everyone. What is your purpose?"

"I wish to meet with Rashomon."

"That's not possible. He is meditating in seclusion and wishes no visitors," Ka replied flatly. "No one but his closest acolytes can see him now." Then he tipped his bird head to one side, as if to contemplate an odd thought. "You are wishing to take the challenge for an apprenticeship?" he asked, again betraying doubt in my abilities. "Rashomon only takes one acolyte a year to apprentice under him, and only if they can offer a unique gift to the order. He already has his acolyte."

"I only wish to question him. He's the only remaining

Schiss of the massacre two months ago."

"Ah." He nodded understanding. "You are investigating the massacre." Then he fixed grave eyes on me. "How is it that you only come now?"

I felt my face flush. It was an obvious oversight on my part as a Guardian. I didn't fail to see the irony in the fact that I was here now only when I was no longer officially pursuing the case. "I was put on the case hastily," I explained in my defense. "By then we'd already been presented with a lead and I spent most of my time pursuing it ... eh, him." I tried to avoid Ka's probing gaze, but I couldn't help divulging the truth and finally met his gaze head on again. "I'm no longer a Guardian Enforcer. I was relieved of duty when I accidentally killed our main suspect."

"Yet you pursue?"

"I believe I've made a discovery that has serious repercussions for the safety of our galaxy and has something to do with Uma 1, the Schiss, and their massacre, particularly."

"But it remains unsubstantiated?" he asked.

I nodded. Ka was astute.

"And you feel compelled to pursue the truth despite having been dismissed." It was a statement rather than a question.

I nodded again and gazed past the flowering archway to the gardens, bright with the complex scent of wild flowers. Ka was just a little *too* astute for my taste. I began to feel uncomfortable. Was he secretly probing my mind ... and manipulating it? Was I sharing all this with him because *I* wanted to or because *he* wanted me to? I had to admit that I hadn't researched the Khonsus as much as I would have liked. Their powers were much of a mystery to me, and I found them threatening. The Khonsus I'd had a run in with on *Ulysses* didn't help my opinion of them either. Then again, I had managed to keep my second reason for visiting Uma 1 a secret from Ka: the possibility that Serge was there, on a mission ... to kill.

"I hope to be re-instated," I explained coolly.

"Ah," he said, with the slightest self-amused smile.

I frowned and flashed him a look of challenge. "Are you mocking me?"

He met my challenge calmly. "Why, no, of course not." He rose abruptly and straightened out his long robes behind him with a graceful flowing gesture. "Come, walk with me, Officer Hawke."

"Ex-officer," I corrected pointedly.

"Ah," he said with a solemn sigh and gestured toward the gardens that beckoned with enticing aromas. "Walk with me ... Rhea Hawke." He waved a hand for me to come alongside him. I stood up and took my place beside him, matching his long stride with my own. We started down the ornate tiles beneath an archway of flowering shrubs toward the fragrant lit gardens outside. I found the sweet perfume of the purple flowers intoxicating. Their heady fragrance reminded me of home.

Ka, however, made me very uncomfortable. I didn't like the idea of 'mind-probing' in the least, even if it was intended for spiritual healing. Any way you cut it, it still smacked of invasion of privacy, I thought. It was intrusive and potentially coercive, particularly of the weak-minded. I decided that I didn't like Ka. Yet, he exuded a gentle fatherly quality I found rather enticing.

Thinking of Serge's possible mission if he was who I thought he was, I decided to pursue my quest more forcefully. "Rashomon might be in grave danger now ... from an assassin."

"Indeed," Ka said too casually for my taste. He continued to walk placidly down the archway.

"I must warn him. Prepare him."

"Really?" he returned in a voice of challenge. "One assassin to take care of another?" I felt his tone slightly mocking as he aimed a pointed glance from my sidearm, holstered in plain view, to my heating face. "You honestly think that you can make a difference?"

I decided to tell him the truth. "I think the assassin is already on Uma 1. I might be able to help. I ... know him." I swallowed convulsively, hand in my pocket and feeling for the info-pod Bas had given me. "He's a shapeshifter and I can recognize them no matter what shape they take on."

Ka frowned and nodded as if to himself. "You are presumptuous, Rhea Hawke. You speak half-truths. You are a paradox," he said. "So out of tune, a jumble of discord. Yet, surprisingly open for one so closed. You're very cynical for one so young. But also incredibly naïve for one so cynical."

I felt my jaw clench with discomfort at his self-conflicting prognosis of me. How could anyone be naïve and cynical at the same time? I hated being analyzed or judged. But I remained calm. I had to convince this old philosopher to give me a permit to travel to Uma 1 do I could warn Rashomon...and find Serge.

I decided to go with another one of my Plan B's: a gamble based on psychology—not my strong suit: "I know that one reason Rashamon remains in isolation is because he fears shapeshifters." I'd finally captured Ka's undivided attention. I dove in. "I can provide Rashamon with unequivocal proof." I pulled out my MEC. "This device can detect shapeshifters. I could let him use it on his staff and visitors."

"A weapon?" Ka glared from my weapon of destruction to me.

"A *tool*," I cut in. "As a tool. I can set it to detect. Only detect. There would be absolutely no danger."

Ka went silent for some moments. I decided that was a good thing. He hadn't dismissed my offer outright. Then he finally spoke in a musical voice, "I sense that you are a seeker of the truth; yet you willingly harbor much that is untrue."

My brows furrowed, and I felt the side of my mouth twitch up in puzzlement. That wasn't a "yes", I decided.

We emerged from the building into a luxurious garden. The tiles led a meandering path through a frothy multi-layered mosaic of color and scent beneath a row of glow-worm filled lanterns. A slight breeze lifted my hair, carrying with it the complex perfumes of hundreds of flowering shrubs, herbs, and ground-covers that rioted with every color and texture imaginable. Yet, Ka was making me more uncomfortable with every word he spoke. I jammed my hands in my trouser pockets and fingered the info-pod that I hadn't had a chance to check out yet.

In my silence, Ka went on, "You keep many secrets from the world, Rhea Hawke, even from yourself."

Heart suddenly racing, I stopped in mid-stride. I let go of the info-pod and brought my hand out of my pocket, poised over my weapon. I flashed him a pointed look of open accusation.

He laughed lightly at my expression and stopped. "Fear not," he waved a conciliatory arm up to me. "I am not probing your mind. It is forbidden to probe uninvited. You do not trust others, do you? Perhaps that is because you don't trust yourself. There are, for instance, things your body knows that your mind does not wish to recognize, for its own reasons."

My brows drew together. The bastard *had* probed me! My mind raced. Was he alluding to my being half-Eosian, or had he found something else? Was I pregnant with Serge's baby? I hadn't been that careful.

"I see you remain distrustful, Ms. Hawke," Ka said casually and resumed his long stride, leaning over to sniff a flower. "I could never probe you without you sanctioning it, or knowing it. It can only happen by invitation through eye-contact. Mind-probes are pleasant experiences if the host is amenable and open. It is a sharing, a symbiotic melding of minds in which both parties remain fully aware. If the subject is uncooperative, probing can still take place through forced eye contact, but it will be very painful, even damaging."

I remembered the numbing pain of the other Khonsus's attempts on me.

"This is why we never enter a mind probe with another unless they expressly wish it," Ka went on. "Believe me, you would know if I was trying to tap in. I would not presume, Ms. Hawke. If you could not trust your feelings in this matter, then at least you should have availed yourself of knowledge of our peoples and our phenomena. You were, after all, a Guardian once, with skills in research, before you came here," he ended, his voice soft with mild reproach.

I drew my lips together and nodded. Feeling humbled, I dropped my gaze to the dark tiles. He'd pointed out one of my horrible weaknesses. Something Ennos had time and again berated me about. I didn't seem able to break out of my old habit of relying on my hunches to save time. "I'm sorry for my ignorance," I began, looking up at him. "But time did not permit, and my only experience with one of your kind was with a Khonsus who did not follow the code you describe."

"Ah." Ka let out a sad sigh. "A renegade. There are several, I'm afraid. Several, who believed that they could use their powers wisely without the symbiotic contact of Horus, left the sanctity of this planet to dispense their version of wisdom."

"It's more than misplaced hubris," I said, aiming a hard look at Ka. "The Khonsus I met knew exactly what he was doing, and it was far from wise in my humble opinion. He was working for Eclipse, the largest and most ruthless of the Galactic criminal organizations devoted to greed and to pillaging the galaxy. The same organization that is behind the Uma massacre and who likely has a contract out on Rashomon."

Ka stopped and turned to face me with an intense look. "I didn't need to probe your mind to sense all the things I just revealed about you, young one. It was all there, on your face, in your walk, in your voice and eyes, for anyone with any intuitive skills to read. The breath, the speech, the step—all have rhythm, which can be interpreted. You have a great deal to learn about yourself and your capabilities. You are far from enlightened and resonate much disharmony. Many are dead at your hands." I swallowed at his words. "You have killed too many in cold blood and for reasons I cannot sanction. For that legacy alone you should not be permitted to set foot on the holy ground of Paradise City. That you still harbor much anger and fear inside you, clouding your judgment of your true destiny, compels me to not permit you to go to Uma 1."

I set my jaw and drew in a breath to retort, but Ka raised a hand to stay me. "However," he said in a gentler tone, "You have spoken from the heart. And with a deep conviction for justice. While in your confusion you cling to fear and dispense violence far too easily, you actively seek truth. And you are a strong advocate of justice and honor. Because of these I will, therefore, give you a permit to visit the retreat on Uma 1. And I will arrange for an audience with Rashomon. He will be interested to see your MEC device."

I swallowed convulsively and nodded with a trembling mouth.

"But I do this only on one condition, young one," Ka added in a stern voice, compelling me to look up. "I will accompany you. I am his acolyte."

TWENTY-TWO

Ka arranged for a trip to Uma 1 aboard his private shuttle, an elegant *scimitar* class ship that could carry twenty people. It was night by the time we left, and I realized that the two of us were the only passengers. I wasn't sure whether I was relieved or troubled by our privacy during the voyage. We were scheduled to arrive at Paradise City at ten in the morning local time.

I settled in a comfortable chair in the rather spacious vehicle while Ka spoke with the pilot in the cockpit. When he returned, he offered me some food and drink, and I welcomed it, suddenly realizing that I was ravenous. I hadn't eaten since the night before.

We sat at a table in the dining-room with a magnificent view of the dark expanse of space through large portholes. Ka ate quietly, not offering conversation, but stealing frequent glances at me as I ate. He looked amused. I knew that I was eating fast and furiously, but I was unable to hide my hunger and appreciation for the delicious, though rather questionable-looking food. I recognized poms, a sweet-potato-like root that had been roasted to perfection with herbs and spices. There was a salad of unknown greens that tasted marvelous, with some exotic pink dressing. The lumpy, slightly slippery translucent pile that tasted like liver and onions and slid nicely down my throat was completely questionable. It looked suspiciously like cooked brains, but I didn't dwell on it—I was too hungry.

"You are enjoying our local dishes, Ms. Hawke?" Ka finally said after putting his fork down to watch me eat.

I nodded, mouth too full of food to answer, and blushed at being caught that way. After a hard swallow, I said, "Yes, thank you. It's delicious. What is it?"

"Grilled blenoid viscera with dhap weed salad in a ming seed cream dressing and roasted poms."

I hesitated mid-chew. Apart from being one of the most vicious creatures in this galaxy, blenoids were known as 'garbage collectors.' They ate anything, from human flesh to their own feces. Although their meat was tasty and healthy to eat, I considered their organs another matter. *Wonderful*, I thought, as I forced down the rest of the blenoid organ meat and washed down the remains with damsel-juice.

"Mneseos, my personal cook, gets the blenoids fresh for me," Ka offered with an amused smile, eyes twinkling at my reaction. "I hope it is still to your liking, now that you know what you're eating."

I concluded that I didn't care and resumed my eating. I was too hungry.

He continued, obviously thinking I was interested. I wasn't, but I let him talk while I ate. "Blenoid viscera are extremely nutritious, did you know?" He didn't wait for me to answer, particularly since I still had a full mouth. "One of your compatriots, the animal behaviorist and physiologist Diane Zeligman, has done some excellent work on blenoid physiology. Did you know that the blenoid combines its digestive and waste removal systems? They only excrete one product, a highly concentrated urea-based feces." I almost choked on my food but forced down a swallow. Ka twitched his crenate beak-mouth in a repressed smile. "Zeligman showed in a recent article in the *Galactic Journal of Animal Physiology* that blenoids exist as four sub-groups based on their unique digestive and excretory systems. She documented how each system produced a different waste, complementary to the others, and she postulated— though didn't prove through field studies—that that was the reason the vicious blenoid existed in packs. A blenoid would seek out and eat the feces that a blenoid with a complementary system had left to get critical nutrients. One blenoid's garbage is another's treasure. Isn't that fascinating?"

I stared up at him, mid-chew. Taking advantage of his pause, I decided to change the subject. I didn't care that my mouth was full. "Pardon my asking, but how did Rashomon manage to single-handedly survive the poison attack on Paradise City?"

Ka seemed to study the pom on his fork for a moment. "It was difficult for him to accept that he alone had survived that holocaust. That is one of the reasons for his seclusion, to meditate on his God-given mission in life as the only remaining Schiss priest. It will take many years for us to return to the numbers we once were, with only one acolyte a year potentially ascending to initiate-level priesthood."

Ka hadn't answered my question, but I decided to let it go and wondered privately whether Rashomon survived because he was one of the few nonhumans in the order. Humans were particularly prone to dreccaline. Then I reminded myself that two other Gnesses and a Xhix had been killed by the poison. "You said before that one must contribute a unique gift to merit acceptance as a Schiss acolyte for training," I continued my quizzing. "What's yours?"

"Ah." He nodded, smiling with fond thoughts and obviously delighted with my question. He put his fork down and folded his large feathered hands, one over the other, leaning forward. "I am teaching Rashomon to hear the music of the spheres." I must have looked puzzled because he continued. "Surely you know that every planet sings its song as it orbits its star?"

I'd read the theories and knew some of the facts. I'd even used a Khonsus mathematical progression based on a planet's orbital wave patterns as part of my file-protection code. I said, "Something about the dynamics of a solar system being analogous to the laws of musical harmony."

He nodded, smiling at me like a teacher. "Yes. The

particular tone of the planet's song depends on the ratio of its orbit, just like the relationship of a keynote to its octave. The cosmic beauty of the octave is that it divides wholeness into two audibly distinguishable parts, yet remains recognizable as the same musical note. But that is only a minute expression of cosmic harmony." He smiled broadly with that engaging beak-mouth of his, and I found myself entranced despite the pedantic nature of his speech. "Even your ancient scientists, philosophers, and mathematicians knew of this. Plato, Pliny, Pythagoras, Cicero, Ptolemy, and Kepler. Your visionary scientist Tesla discovered the magic of your native planet's resonance—later described by Otto Schumann in the 1950s. It was your great philosopher Plato who described the creation of the world structure in harmonic proportions. And was it not your Hermeticist Robert Fludd who first visualized grand celestial scales that linked levels of existence from sub-planetary worlds to exultant choirs of angelic intelligences beyond our galaxy? It was not far from our present search for the fractal continuum from sub-atomic through to the vast interstellar phenomena of our known universe."

I thought of the ancient Hermetic maxim: *the within is like the without and as above so below*, then recalled the ritual Dervish dance of those raptor mystics on Horus to celebrate the revolution of life. I was suddenly reminded of Serge's outrageous supposition of inner and outer diverses. It strangely resembled what Ka was talking about, except Serge had connected the continuum into an infinity loop and added time.

"We, of course, now know that ratios in frequencies of spectra of elements compare to intervals in a musical chord," Ka went on, leaning forward on his massive feathered arms. "Given that a pitch of sound is analogous to the color of light, both being caused by the frequencies of their waves, we can characterize entire worlds based on these properties," he ended, beak-mouth breaking into a beaming grin that showed his round little teeth.

And the basis for most current weapons that relied on wave resonance, I noted grimly.

I decided to challenge him. "And where do the Vos fit into

those extragalactic choirs of angelic intelligence you mentioned?" I raised my eyebrows and waved a forkful of steaming blenoid guts at him before thrusting it into my mouth.

He looked stumped for a moment and lost his smile. "They appear far from angelic, don't they?" He left it at that and returned to his salad, eating quietly for a change.

Fine, I thought, thinking I'd shut him up, and concentrated anew on my roasted poms. Some kind of tuber, they resembled sweet potatoes, I thought, sliding a forkful into my mouth and savoring the burst of sweet aroma at the back of my throat as I bit down.

Ka broke the wonderful silence. "You humans were strong believers in the science of astrology, weren't you, Ms. Hawke?"

I looked up with a frown. "Hardly a science," I scoffed, chewing down some blenoid organs and scooping up the last of my salad and poms. "The masses believed, I suppose."

He leaned back and took his cup of orange damsel-juice in his hand but didn't sip from it. "It was your Kepler—a scientist I believe—who suggested that when planets formed angles equivalent to particular harmonic ratios, a resonance was created both in the archetypal 'Earth soul' and in the souls of individuals born under those configurations."

I nodded, though I couldn't help sneering. Kepler had lived over a thousand years ago. A lot of science had flowed under that bridge in the meantime.

"He called it a celestial imprint." Ka leaned forward with his cup in both hands. "He contended that the celestial imprint— ignited at birth—glows, remembered, in the vital power of each human being. That geometric-harmonic imprint is the music that impels each listener to dance ... from the particle to the cosmic. Your own heart finds its shifting harmony between excessive order and complete randomness, encompassing complex variability—a symphony—in its beating pattern. Sound— vibration—is the language of the mind and the secret to creation."

This discussion was heading to chaos. I wanted to bail,

but I was trapped here with this crazy philosopher-conjurer. I'd finished my meal and was about to excuse myself and get up to move to the back of the shuttle when he put his cup down and fixed me with an intense look.

"I sense that you have remarkable power, young one. That carries great responsibility."

I drew in a frustrated breath. "I told you, I'm not an Enforcer anymore," I reminded him, letting my annoyance with him edge my voice.

"Ah," Ka said, quietly nodding and gazing down at the table with a knowing smile as if at a private joke. I frowned and set my mouth in annoyed confusion. What *had* he meant, then? My melting power?

"You are not a dancer, are you?"

"I beg your pardon?" I felt anger pulse through me and throb in my ears. Was this leading to more judgment? When I was little I used to dance for my mother. It made her laugh with joy. I had wanted to be a dancer once.

"But of course you haven't yet found your song, Officer Hawke."

I glared at him. How many times did I have to tell him I was no longer an officer?

"I sense your discordance. You do not resonate with your music, which you have yet to recognize."

Why did he keep badgering me? I finally broke my gaze and gasped out, "You *sense*," I snapped. I pushed myself from the table and surged to my feet. "I don't need this blenoid-shit. And get the jag out of my mind!"

"All that sardonic bravado doesn't fool me, Rhea," he replied, unruffled, unbalancing me by addressing me with my first name. I suddenly felt like a schoolgirl in the principal's office. "I sense great vulnerability in you. It is also your strength, did you know?"

I gulped down the emotion swelling up my throat and shuffled my feet. I wanted to leave but there was nowhere to go.

Still seated, he said calmly, "Sit, sit," he urged me with a kind smile. "I'm not berating you." I remained standing but rested my hands on the back of the chair.

"What do you want from me?" I heard the plead in my voice.

"Only the truth," he said. "The choices you've made—"

"Yes," I cut in, not prepared to hear more lecture. "Heartless, I know. Someone else told me already."

He gave me an indulgent smile. "Yes, there is that." His feathery brows came together briefly, and his smile was sad. "Although you killed always for justice, you killed without compassion. In that you truly served as their agent. However, I was going to say that, despite their often ill-fated path, your choices have always been made from a place of integrity and honor."

I stared, unprepared for his kind remark.

"As for your intuition ..." he began. I winced, wishing he'd stop. "It is a blessing for you ..."

"And a curse for everyone else," I finished for him with a savage smile, thinking of what Ennos had said the last time I was in his office.

"Ah." Ka smiled sadly again. "Forgive me for saying this, but you're still very young, Rhea. That will improve with experience. I admire your abilities. Alas, I have no such talents."

"No." I laughed sharply and said in a mocking tone, "You just sing the song of the stars." Then, not sure why or how, I dropped my defenses, letting deep emotion surge through me, and added with sudden sincerity, "You're teaching the universe to hear itself."

His eyes widened in astonishment. He gave me a warm smile and bowed his head. "Thank you," he said quietly. Then he tipped his feathered head sideways in odd curiosity and added, "You are truly a puzzle, Rhea Hawke. I ask myself this question of you ..." He studied me further. "Why did you join the Galactic Guardians?" Like Serge before him, Ka asked me the question I could not answer. "The Guardians are a fascist organization devoted to the supremacy of the few over the many in a galaxy they've built for themselves. These arrogant Eosians supplanted your world and now dispense law and order in the galaxy, as though they were gods themselves. Yet you consort with them as though they were your equals."

I thought that rather harsh coming from an enlightened being such as Ka. Perhaps the Guardians or Eosians had done something to merit it, though, I reflected. It wasn't hard to believe that they might have done something to Ka and his people. I thought the Eosians a cold arrogant race.

"Why have you betrayed your own kind?" Ka challenged.

I drew in a sharp breath to retort—then held it: my mother hadn't *tecked* me after all, so I couldn't make my usual comeback: *I didn't ask to be tecked into this monstrosity.* But perhaps Ka knew of my Eosian heritage, and he was actually referring to my prejudice against baldies, not my general lack of humanity.

"I-I d-didn't—" I stammered, then fell silent.

"Of course." He nodded solemnly as if to himself. "You don't know. Just like ..." he trailed off with an enigmatic smile and clasped his hands on the table.

I didn't bother to correct him but frowned in silence and turned to leave to take a seat as far away from him as possible. I supposed he thought himself clever to ridicule my apparent ignorance along with my bad choices in life. Well, the conversation—and the lecturing—was over.

"I met your grandmother," he said as I strode toward the back of the ship's lounge. I jerked around to face him and found him smiling kindly at me. "Diana Wood," he said, eyes focusing through me into the past. "She was beautiful—still is, no doubt," he added emphatically, "even though she must be about 200 years old now, and I haven't seen her since '92." The year I was born. Ka studied me with a wistful smile as I returned and shakily took my seat across from him, tacitly inviting him for more details. "In fact, she looked a lot like you, young one," he continued cheerfully. Then his eyes sparkled with a wild energy. He cocked his great raptor head to one side as if to share a secret and whispered conspiratorially, "She didn't know either."

He paused for a moment to let me digest his disclosure as my mind raced with thoughts of actually having a grandmother. My mother had indicated without actually saying that my grandmother was dead.

"You knew my grandmother?" I asked, hearing my voice waver slightly.

"Yes. We were good friends. She spent many years on Horus, learning the song of the spheres." He chuckled and leaned back with a long stretch. A youthful smile lit his bird face and his eyes focused afar again. "She had a lovely voice."

Forgetting my reserve, I leaned forward with interest. "How did you meet?"

His face beamed with fond memories, and his feathers ruffled his head into a thick mane. "She came to Horus to research the topic of universal harmonics." He smiled impishly at me. "I think she really came to heal herself. When she arrived, she had an undiagnosable chest pain and a bad limp; but I think her real wounds were on the inside, in her soul. I helped her find the information she wanted and perhaps gave her what she really needed. Because, instead of leaving when she had her information, she stayed for years. Her limp disappeared eventually, and her chest pains subsided, although they never left entirely." He reached over, his face lighting up, and tapped my hand with his great winged paw. "I was so glad she stayed," he confided smugly, feathers rippling. "You see, I'd fallen just a little in love with her. And she was such wonderful company." He nodded to himself.

Then his wistful smile faded. "One day, twenty-three years ago, she disappeared," he went on sadly. "No one knows where she went. She took my small *hawke* class ship and was last seen heading into the Oily Range to the north. No one except the oil miners go there. The locals call them the weeping mountains. They're a vast drowned mountain range in a perched watershed. It's made up of an impervious geological formation that we mine for shallik oil. The sea is covered in an oily film of microbes, the ones that make shallik oil, and made up of millions of islands. It's sometimes called the boiling sea." I didn't want to know why and waited for Ka to continue. "When Diana didn't return, we searched for her. Some think she died there, victim to the apophus."

"Apophus?"

"A giant snake-like creature that lives in the boiling sea. Some say it has the head of a bird and many arms, others say it's a Venik's head. Others say human. No one really knows, I think. Any creature that flies too low succumbs to the narcotic mist and falls into the oily sea, which serves as a kind of nerve-depressant, effectively numbing the prey's body and curing it for the snake to digest. Sometimes, if the snake is hungry, it will bat a creature right out of the air."

"Oh," I said in a small voice.

"And even if she'd somehow survived a crash on land, it was the season of the dead—our winter—when the larvae of the ammut hatch and swarm. The ammut is a large invertebrate that makes its eggshells of swamp detritus. During their larval stage, they are extremely carnivorous and will devastate the swamp wildlife. They even eat the young apophus. Then, as adults they become vegetarian and serve as food for the apophus. Interesting food web, eh?"

"Terrific," I muttered. "Remind me not to mark that one on my holiday travel plans."

"At any rate, some friends suggested that your grandmother had not fallen victim to the apophus or ammut, but instead went offworld," Ka continued. "My *hawke* was a very space-worthy vehicle. She could have gone anywhere." He sighed and his shoulders visibly slumped. "So I spent a year, using our extensive database tracking system, looking for her. But to no avail." He sighed, obviously still missing her. As though she'd left him just yesterday.

I swallowed hard, not sure what I was feeling apart from sad confusion. Women in my family seemed to have a penchant for leaving or losing our men, uprooting our families, and abandoning those we loved.

Ka leaned forward with arms outstretched on the table. "You must find her if you ever hope to unravel the mysteries of your existence, young one," he said. I swallowed and stared hard at him but said nothing. He ignored my obvious look of resistance. "You have never met her," he said, more as a statement than a question.

"No, I haven't," I replied. And wasn't likely to, either. I wasn't about to pursue a woman I'd never met—even if she was my grandmother. And certainly not to 'unravel the mysteries of my own existence'! But if I ever chanced to meet my grandmother, I knew what I'd say. Since my mother was the product of a twisted and deprived, possibly abused, childhood, I imagined myself challenging Diana Wood's mothering skills.

"As for not knowing," Ka went on, "I don't mean about her being the daughter of Azaes and Genevieve Dubois either. She'd figured that one out."

My jaw dropped momentarily, but I quickly recovered with blinking eyes. Ka caught my reaction, though. How could he have missed it? He'd been watching me closely for just such a response. I nevertheless felt my face heat with the excitement of discovering that my grandmother was the mythical Messiah child revered by the Tree Cult of Earth.

Ka leaned back in his chair and laughed lightly with obvious pleasure.

"For an Enforcer, you really haven't done your homework, Rhea," he admonished me with an amused smile. "I suppose you haven't had much time to research the meaning behind your inherited natural ability to melt, have you? If you'd cultivated their friendship, one of the baldies might have told you that only three Eosians are known to have the melting power." He stared into my eyes with his amber disks. "Three in a population of ten billion. And you are one of them."

I swallowed the saliva gathering in my mouth. He hadn't needed my melting display on Galaxy News to hint at my heritage; he knew it better than I did.

"Can you guess who the other two are?"

He'd paused long enough for me to realize that he expected me to answer. I stammered, "Azaes and my grandmother?"

"Good guess, but only partially correct. Azaes certainly had the melting power. No doubt you are aware of his history on Earth. Diana Wood was born after Azaes was murdered in the United States. She and her mother lived a solitary, quiet life in Canada ... not unlike you and your mother after you left Earth."

I felt my breath stutter and wanted desperately to leave, but I felt paralyzed with intrigue.

"Diana's mother changed her name to Wood," Ka continued, "and never told her daughter about her father. But Diana figured it out. You see, she'd inherited Azaes's ability to soul-drift."

"To ... what?"

"The ability to enter another's dreams—perhaps even their own—and change ... *everything*. A decided Eosian trait, albeit even rare among Eosians. Just like shapeshifting, which the Eosians can barely do—not like the Borrs." He leaned close to me when he'd said 'Borrs.'

"So, Diana knew she was an Eosian," I said.

"Because she could enter and change people's dreams. Make them real." He nodded then eyed me with penetrating curiosity. "How are your dreams these days?"

My throat constricted, but I refused to show any outward sign of discomfort. My dreams were my own business, I thought peevishly and let his question dangle.

Undaunted, he continued in my silence. "As for the melting power, our research suggests that it likely manifests itself every third generation. This stems from a time when Eosians lived for an undetermined length of time. For eternity, some claimed. Because of this, Eosians only married after thousands of years of existence and only at the sanction of their wise gods, the Epoptes, through a ceremony with the holy *vishna* tree. To this day, I believe, an Eosian returns to Eos, where the *vishna* tree grows, for his wedding. Eosians rarely take part in activities of procreation except by the will of their gods."

Ka obviously hadn't seen an Eosian male with my mother, I thought with sullen humor.

"To have the melting power was usually a sign of a leader, who was mandated to guide the circle of government for thousands of years," Ka went on, blithely ignorant of how I was squirming inside. "They couldn't afford to have too many individuals with the melting power, so having it emerge only after the third generation gave the incumbent a chance to maintain a stable world before ceding to his inheritor."

"Do you know who the third person with the melting power is?" I asked, impatient to move the subject along to its natural conclusion.

"Ah," Ka said with a sigh, nodding to himself and firming his beak-mouth. "We don't. We only have evidence of its effects from an event eighteen years ago."

My heart slammed. Eighteen years ago! When I was five. Did my face heat? Was I giving myself away?

"It happened on Virgil 9."

"In the 70 Virginis system." My words rushed out too fast in relief. I'd never been there, except in my dreams. Ka wasn't referring to Earth eighteen years ago. Not to *my* act of murder. But someone else's.

"Do you know what that means, young one?" asked Ka.

"No."

"We don't either. But there are now two people with the melting power in existence at the same time in the galaxy. We are not sure this is a good thing."

I felt my eyes narrow as I worked my mouth in somber contemplation. Ka made it sound like my melting power was some kind of ticking bomb for the galaxy. *I* wasn't the problem; the Vos were. Eager to draw the subject away from me, I let curiosity get the better of me: "What happened ...? I mean on Virgil 9?"

"Ah," Ka sighed out, brushing a feathered hand over his beak. "A woman and her lover, humans visiting Virgil City, were murdered—melted. But the woman's child, a boy of five, survived, after watching them get melted."

I swallowed hard, thinking of U'clid liquefying as my child-self aimed my dreadful melting stare at him. The boy and I had shared a similar horror at the same age and same time. It felt creepy somehow.

Ka went on, "The boy, Raphael Martinez ..." The name

stirred something in me. A lost memory ... an idea or scrap of information I'd misplaced. "He witnessed his mother and her lover's death. They found him in the corner of their parlor suite in Virgil City's red district, shivering like a leaf in an Uma wind with just a messy pile of melted flesh and viscera on the bed—"

I barely held back a gasp and gagged.

Ka leaned forward in sudden concern. "Are you all right?"

I nodded vigorously, not trusting my voice, and swallowed down the bile that rose up my throat. This was too similar to my own experience. The only difference was that his mother was also killed and I'd done the killing in mine.

"Why?" I managed to breathe out. "Why were they ... melted? Who did it?"

"No one knows why. As for who, I told you we don't know. The family was not important politically. They stayed on Earth to help the Eosians. They were gardeners, vintners actually. They were originally from Spain and moved to the Eastern Townships of Québec to help run *L'Ordre de l'Arbre Sacré*, the Order of the Sacred Tree."

Yet another connection this boy and I shared! The tree cult had sprung up with the belief that my grandmother was some kind of Epoptes messiah who would help bring in an age of enlightenment.

"The father perished during the Vos attack," Ka went on. "As for the mother..." He frowned. "She was apparently banished from the Order after committing some kind of sacrilege to do with the *vishna* tree. She fell into sordid poverty and took to whoring to feed herself and her baby."

My stomach clenched with unease and I had to swallow the saliva flooding my mouth. This was uncanny. I briefly wondered if Ka knew my story and had fabricated this one to call me out; but I decided he was too sincere and the story was too sad. "You said baby? Not the father's?"

"No, the boy came after the father died. She claimed immaculate conception, but everyone knew she slept around and the boy's real father could have been anyone."

"What happened to the boy?" I asked in a shaky voice. Raphael Martinez was a little like me; he also didn't know who his real father was.

Ka frowned. His feathered brows furrowed deeply and he shook his head slowly. "He grew up," Ka said evasively.

"Into what?" I persisted, not sure why.

"He's a practicing Gnostic," Ka responded. "Formed his own Hermetic Order. A self-made prophet, in fact."

"What does he prophesy?"

"Ah," Ka held out his feathered hands to inspect and preened them, keeping me in suspense. When he looked up, his amber eyes gleamed like gold. "Martinez predicts the coming of the *Suntelia Aeon*, a catastrophic End of the Age." I was struck with the memory of where I'd remembered the name. "He says this will be signified by *the joining of twin souls who will herald the coming of a New Age.*"

I frowned. This was the part of the prophesy I hadn't remembered before and felt unsettling thoughts. Was my grandmother somehow connected? The Order of the Sacred Tree had claimed she would help bring in a new age. "What does it mean?"

He shrugged, something I hadn't expected from Ka. "It is obviously open to interpretation." Then he added in a voice of academic interest, "Did you know that Aeons, emanations of God in Gnostic belief, formed Ogdoads, not unlike octaves in music? You see how it is all related to the music of the spheres?" Then he suddenly straightened with a large intake of air that closed the subject. "But pardon me, I am boring you with the erudite tales of an information addict." He hadn't been, but I let the subject go in deference to his obvious wish. "Information is one service I can provide to the order," he ended.

I blurted out, "So, what's your connection to all this? Why do you know so much about Martinez, Earth and the Order of the Sacred Tree?"

Ka smiled enigmatically. "The Eosians aren't the only ones with strong links to Earth and its history. And you'd be surprised what that dear planet means to some of us."

I realized that he was not going to offer more and thought about the Khonsus, whose history lay shrouded in myths that tied them to Earth. They did, after all, resemble the Egyptian god Horus, which was also the name they'd given to their planet. I decided that Ka's interest and knowledge was personal somehow and wondered what his angle was.

"So, are you a Schiss, then?" I asked.

"Not a full one yet. I am just a privileged acolyte, training for the honor to join the Schiss Order as Rashomon's apprentice. Hoping I am worthy of enlightenment."

All this enlightenment stuff made me very uncomfortable. How reprehensible and vulgar he must think me. He likely considered me no better than the scum who'd murdered the Schiss. I'd been essentially an assassin for the Galactic Guardians since my adolescence. And, although he hopefully didn't know of my act of pre-adolescent murder, it had created a solid foundation for my career of killing. I recognized the fine line of motive or circumstance that placed me on one side of the law versus the other. Easily stepped over. And all a matter of point of view.

I shrugged off my bitter musings and decided to probe more directly. "Do you have any idea why Eclipse targeted the Schiss, particularly?"

"None, whatsoever," he said with bleak remorse. "Do you?"

"No. None." None I could share with Ka, that is. It was only then that I realized that Ka hadn't divulged what both my grandmother and I 'didn't know.'

TWENTY-THREE

I had a good view of the gas giant as we skirted past it toward its moon, Uma 1. I watched the flickers of lightning on the dark side of 47 Uma-b with fascination for several moments before focusing my attention on its moon as we approached it.

Uma 1 was a tectonically active ice moon with a silicate core. The Schiss had established Paradise City in an area of intense volcanic activity, where scattered pools of liquid water boiled to the surface from active thermal vents. I got a good view of its stark topography of mostly ice and snow as we entered the upper atmosphere.

Paradise City, I'd been told, was essentially a floating city in a huge frigid freshwater lake, surrounded by massive sheets of ice. I was looking forward to getting a good view of the city as the shuttle circled the moon before heading down for the landing pad. I imagined Paradise City resembling a bobbing collection of jewels in an azure liquid island surrounded by a vast white plain.

Ka, who had sat in silence on the other side of the shuttle during the last leg of the journey, stood up and came beside me. I looked up expectantly, offering him a friendly smile.

His bird face returned me a strange twisted smile, and I noticed that his feathers were flattened. He held a small container in his hands. "I'm sorry but you will have to first submit to a cleansing and then ingest a shield microbe."

I bounced to my feet. "What?"

"That is the only way you will be permitted into Rashomon's inner sanctuary. Don't worry, the microbes pass through your system within two solar days and your own flora takes over again. It is your choice, of course. But if you refuse, you will not see Rashomon."

"Fine," I bit out. "What's involved?"

Even Ka looked uncomfortable. He said wearily, "You must drink this shallik oil first. It is unfortunately vile and likely to make you vomit." He pointed to a rather large bottle of iridescent fluid, ignoring my sharp glance at him. "It is very important that you drink all of the shallik oil to rid your body of all its toxins and flora. Unfortunately, vomiting is one of the ways for you to do this." He offered me a lame smile. "The oil acts quickly so I suggest you do it in the private restroom. Once you have finished the oil and have completely voided, you must wait at least half an hour before drinking the microbe mixture.

Much less vile," he added. "They will populate your system quickly and we can be on our way," he ended with a sickly smile. "If it is any consolation, I must do the same."

I took the box from Ka and nodded with a grimace. "Thanks." Then I made my way to the bathroom.

Θ

By the time I emerged, pale and giddy, the ship had landed, and I realized with some regret that I'd missed my chance to see the city from above. Ka, looking wan, his feathers flat and dull, greeted me with a sympathetic smile. "I trust it worked?" he asked, handing me an energy strip to suck on.

I took the strip and nodded, feeling a wave of nausea just thinking about the pungent viscous oil I'd had to force down. I'd thrown up several times before bolting to another part of the washroom to meet other urgent needs. It was like purposefully subjecting myself to Bilge's Revenge. This had better be worth it, I thought as Ka led me out of the shuttle onto the landing platform.

To my surprise the air was warm and the water beneath us was flowing, even though we were surrounded by a frozen lake. Were we inside an enclosure? I could not make one out.

"A thermal shield," Ka explained.

I nodded. I'd wondered why neither Ka nor I had needed to cover our regular clothes with some thermal protection. I was just in my sleeveless top and flight pants and he in a light translucent robe that covered his giant wings. I followed Ka off the platform along a floating maze of ramps and docks on the calm water toward the glittering buildings ahead. The sunlight reflecting off the water danced a lacy pattern of fluid gold on the glass towers.

"Is the water warm?" I asked, sucking on the energy stick.

"Yes, inside the thermal shield. But there is a strong thermocline at three meters, where the water drops to 4 degrees all the way to the bottom, about two hundred meters down."

"Wonderful," I muttered. "Nice and cold for little Nessy."

"Except for where the thermal vents are. That's where life thrives. We built our city over a cluster of vents. They supply us with heat, power, and nourishment."

I nodded, impressed, and swept my gaze around me to where several people ambled along the various floats. Some were aliens—Xhix, Khonsus, Gness and others—among mostly humans, all dressed in sky-blue overalls; all with bright eyes. Some swept the walkways, wheeled carts of supplies, or were fixing an apparatus on a float. Others were chatting among themselves in casual conversation as they headed to their destinations. They all looked content.

I gazed around me with curiosity at the floating walkways and glassy buildings and finally up to the sky, with the sun behind me, to where the large orange crescent shape of 47 Uma-b floated like a ghost in a deep azure sky. It was an impressive site and I wanted to study it, but Ka kept walking and I trained my eyes down to my more immediate surroundings.

Casting a gaze around me, I noted where the thermal shields ended and the ice began. I said, "The city's smaller than I'd imagined."

Ka's eyes crinkled in an impish smile. "That is because you only see a small portion of it, like an iceberg. All that you see here on the surface," he said, sweeping his great feathered arm around him, "is just the south-east corner of the city. Three other surface floats like this one mark the remaining corners. The rest of the city lies ..." he trailed off, watching me.

My eye brows rose. "Underwater? Beneath us?"

"Yes," he said, eyes crinkling in an infectious smile. "These surface buildings serve mostly to house order members. Everything else—our spiritual facilities, recreation, maintenance, power, food production, and eateries, and so on—lies under the ice."

I smiled back with admiration. I cast my gaze north outside the city, past the island of liquid surface water through the invisible thermal shield to where a vast ice sheet surrounded us. It looked several meters thick in some places.

"It gets to below 100 degrees out there," Ka informed me.

"And that's without the windshield factor," he added, as I shivered at the thought. "It is a rather inhospitable place."

"I guess." I nodded. I thought I made out columns of gray smoke—perhaps steam from strong surface-migrating thermal vents.

Ka followed my gaze afar. "The smoke you see is from subsurface volcanic activity and the building up of submerged lava cones. Sometimes, the magma rises to the surface and breathes fire as high as five meters in the air. It's quite a sight at night."

"You mentioned life thriving near the vents," I posed. "What kind of life? Bacteria? Microbes?"

He grinned at me. "Nessy, perhaps?"

I laughed sharply, again impressed at his knowledge of my culture and mythos.

"Actually, no," he chuckled. "Your earlier supposition is accurate. We have a diverse community of microbes that inhabit the vents. They live off the hot gasses of the vents. We have even found a way to harvest them for food. You'll have to try it. I promise it will be more tasty even than blenoid organs," he ended with a self-satisfied smile, his small rounded teeth looking like a string of pearls.

"Promise?" I muttered and gave him a wry smile, realizing that I was starting to like Ka.

He giggled. I felt his infectious beak-grin reflected in one of my own. He pointed to several bumps on the horizon to the left of the smoke. "You see those domes?"

"Yes." They looked like giant glass balls that littered the frozen lake.

"They're supposedly created by the action of thermal vent steam over many years and the build up of water and ice, chiseled by the wind. They're actually very large, even though they don't look very big from here." Then he turned and began to walk. "Shall we?"

As I focused my gaze on my immediate surroundings, I spotted a small marina where about a dozen small bright yellow boats were docked in a row. Ka caught my look of interest and led us to the marina. I approached the closest boat, bobbing gently in the water, and noted its elegant design. The sleek vessel was sturdily built from a polymer of metalloid and duraplast. It resembled a bird with outstretched wings, like a small trimaran with narrow pontoons or skis and a teardrop-shaped canopy.

I leaned over to gaze into the cockpit through the transplast canopy and noticed that the vessel was a double-seater, forward and aft, with a circular steering wheel, a directional stick-control, and foot pedal for speed control.

"They're called skipboats, but that's a bit of a misnomer."

I turned to glance back at Ka. "Why is that?"

"Because they're designed not only to skip on water, but also to skate on ice and ski on snow." Then he added, as if to explain, "We use them to get from one end of town to the other or, on the very odd occasion to voyage beyond the city, which requires a vehicle with that kind of versatility."

I met his gaze with a half-smile of challenge. "They look more like they're tailored for recreation and speed than for ferrying passengers."

Ka smiled rather impishly, showing his tiny row of teeth. "Yes, you've caught us," he admitted. "It's one of our playful indulgences."

I looked down at the water lapping at the float I stood on and smiled. So, it wasn't all meditation and prayer at the 'spirit ranch,' I thought with amusement.

"This way." Ka led me to a small round platform. Once we were both on it, the platform descended. The breath went out of me as we sank into the lake water but didn't get wet. Ka laughed, and I threw him a sharp glance.

"Let me guess: a water shield," I said, giving him a sardonic smile and glancing at the wall of water behind the invisible shield.

Ka agreed, laughing again. "You're catching on fast."

The platform stopped beside a doorway and we entered a long corridor with transparent walls. I stared with amazement at the underwater maze hidden from the surface and let my gaze rest on the transparent floor past my feet to the dark water below. The transparent maze of tube-like corridors reminded me of Ogium's high altitude walkways, and I wondered if they had been designed by the same architect. They both gave me the eerie unbalanced sensation of being suspended. I gazed past the invisible wall of our tube through water and into the next tube of the maze and the one behind it until the maze of tubes faded into the darkness of water.

We walked in silence along the maze of transparent tube corridors, passing several humans, and aliens of various species, all dressed similarly in sky-blue overalls. Ka explained that they were all would-be acolytes who were still hoping to join the order and were serving time here as utility agents, technical or mechanical staff, merchants, traders, and the like.

The underwater hallways eventually led us through a set of sliding doors into a garden so large I could barely make out its walls. There was even a large network of streams and pools whose trickles and gliding flows provided me with a wonderful sense of serenity.

"This is incredible," I couldn't help saying. The air was thick with moisture and carried with it the fragrant aroma of flowers, vegetation, and soil. "All this under the surface. It's like a sanctuary."

"Well spoken, young one," Ka said with a self-satisfied smile. "You're already in Rashomon's sanctuary."

I jerked round to give him a pointed look. "What?"

"These are his gardens. He tends them."

"But what about the security?" I said with a frown of puzzlement. We hadn't passed anything remotely like a security station or gate.

He laughed. It was more like a giggle. "Seamless, except for the acolytes who know where the barriers to his sanctuary are. If you had not eaten those microbes, you would have been vaporized by the security shields."

"Terrific," I murmured. It was a clever mode of security, I had to concede. Both unimposing and efficient. Outsiders were deterred by their own ignorance.

I continued my fascinated gaze about the garden and took a deep inhale as we followed a winding stone pathway along a small creek.

The air ached with scent. Festooned with all manner of exotic plants, shrubs, trees and herbs and groundcover, the garden's heady fragrance filled me with thoughts of home. Huge spiral-shaped yellow flowers covered a shrub with gold disks and gave off a pungent smell of skunk. Deep purple-coned flowers drooped from tendrils of climbing vines, dripping with the complicated scent of lilac and honeysuckle.

"It's beautiful and so peaceful in here," I said and smiled unreservedly.

Ka returned an open smile of his own. "So are you, Rhea Hawke, especially when you smile. It's a beautiful smile. Given freely and deep from your heart."

I broke off my gaze. I was reminded of his infatuation with my grandmother who supposedly resembled me. Did I have my grandmother's smile?

Ka laughed with genuine amusement. "Ah, permit an old man to enjoy the fresh beauty of a young woman in rapture, Rhea. I mean no harm in it. You *are* a striking woman. Certainly not a traditional beauty with perfect features," he observed earnestly. "More like a curiosity that begs a second look." He laughed with delight, watching my reaction. Had he just retracted his compliment? "And that radiant smile is your gift to the world," he continued. "You should give it away more often. You don't take compliments well, do you, young one? More of that distrust, I feel."

"I just thought your comment was a little out of context," I said defensively, still struggling with his odd comment on my 'beauty.'

"I beg to differ. We're each like a garden of trees, flowers, and weeds. You need to tend your ego, Rhea. Recognize the goodness and the beauty both inside and outside. One person's weed is another's flower. It's a little like gardening."

"Well spoken, Ka," a child's voice growled behind me. I turned to see a tall wolf-like alien approaching us on all four feet. Although I'd seen Gness on vids before, I was unprepared for what stood before me. They were magnificent creatures, standing two meters high and covered in a mosaic of fur, firm muscle, and translucent gray skin that throbbed over visible organs. This one appeared very young. At least his voice suggested it. And his eyes—he had none, only two dark pits. He was blind! Was it from too much Dust?

"Gardening is often a challenge," the Gness said, stretching out all his consonants into a rhythmic purring. "We can't always be in command of a tree's fate. We can only plant the seed and nurture its growth. Sometimes we cannot even do that much, pretty lady."

To my surprise Ka responded with a bow. "Ah, Rashomon," he said. "This is Rhea Hawke, the former Galactic Guardian I spoke to you about."

I shot Ka a baffled glance. And when was that? He'd been with me the whole journey—except when we were both purging, that is.

"She's even more beautiful than you'd described, Ka. An exotic beauty."

I turned with some unease from Ka's humble face to the Gness and fretted over what Ka had said to him about me. Rashomon could obviously 'see' with his other senses, I concluded. And Ka was right; I wasn't comfortable with compliments.

Rashomon appeared fascinated with me, looking me up and down, using his nose to 'observe' me. Then his nostrils flared suddenly and he pointed with a foreleg to the MEC holstered on my thigh, off my toolbelt. "What manner of weapon is that? I don't recognize it."

I flinched at his question with a guilty glance down at the MEC. Despite its use to him, I felt that I'd offended him. Then he confused me with a smile of what appeared genuine curiosity and sat back on his haunches to study me and the weapon on my hip.

No doubt Ka had also told him of the ability of my weapon to detect shapeshifters.

I cleared my throat. "Eh, it's called a MEC, a Magnetic-Electro Concussion pistol," I explained, forcing my voice steady, and followed Rashomon's blind gaze down to the weapon. I rested my hand on the MEC. "It uses electromagnetic wave energy to focus subatomic quintle particles into resonating on specific DNA." Recognizing his burning curiosity to 'see' it, I pulled the MEC out of its holster and held it in the palms of my outstretched hands, a wry smile tugging at my lips. I had not expected this.

Rashomon padded close, body shaking with obsessive interest.

"Marvelous!" he exclaimed, showing canine teeth in a feral grin. "Is that standard issue for an Enforcer?"

"No."

"Who makes it?" he purred. "Bodek and Lamb? Or Anglebush Industries?"

This was definitely not what I'd expected. He seemed awfully worldly for an esoteric, and his knowledge of tools of violence seemed contrary to his philosophy. Then again, perhaps this kind of eccentricity was typical for one so isolated and removed from mainstream society.

"Neither," I responded somewhat self-consciously. "I make it."

"Really!" His eye sockets widened with admiration. I thought I noticed his body shake with excitement. "Can I hold it?"

"Of course." I held the MEC out for him to take.

Rashomon padded right up to me and sat on his haunches, reaching out with his forelimbs. I handed him the MEC.

"Oh!" he cried out. "What is that?"

I spotted the barely noticeable vibration of the MEC in his paws and knew instantly: its scanner had identified him as a Gness and was alerting me. I thought I'd turned it off after my demonstration aboard A'ler's space-station, but perhaps it had jammed.

Rashomon looked suddenly alarmed, spotting something

on the MEC.

"Run!" he howled and, taking the MEC into his large mouth, bounded in a leap down the path he'd come from. Sensing danger to him, I lunged after Rashomon, even as Ka pulled me back, sensing the same danger. I twitched out of his grasp, effectively dragging him forward with me—

The MEC—and Rashomon—exploded in mid-leap.

The blast knocked me off my feet and threw me back against a tree. I blacked out as a sharp pain tore through my left leg and chest.

TWENTY-FOUR

I woke to stabs of pulsing pain. Rain pelted my face. My whole body stung as if impaled with millions of tiny shrapnel. Sharp pain burned up my leg and torso.

My eyes slowly focused, and I realized that I was soaked and lying next to a tree on the dirt floor of the subsurface greenhouse. I jerked my head up, blinking back the rain to see, and inhaled sharply. What I'd thought was rain was lake water cascading through a huge crack in the roof. It sluiced down the walls and sprayed out, flooding the room. Large puddles were already forming around me.

Ka moaned beside me, wet from the spray. I pulled myself up and winced with the biting pain that shot up my left leg, ribs, and shoulder. A quick assessment of Ka revealed that he was injured but alive. He was covered in debris, and some garden equipment shrapnel was lodged in his chest. An oily sheen of near-black blood was spreading on his light robe. He breathed in shallow wheezing breaths. His great wings spread out limply and one twitched as if it were injured.

I had to get him out of here before the ceiling caved in on us along with a deluge of water.

I turned, looking for an exit, and stiffened at the sight of where Rashomon had leapt. There was nothing left of him except scattered pieces of torn flesh, fur, viscera, and greenish blood. I choked down despair with a gasp and fell to my knees, embracing the jolt of pain that shot up my torso.

"Oh, God … what have I done!" I breathed.

I recognized the effects of a Q-bomb. What a fool I'd been. Tricked into playing the role of a weapon again. I'd set out to save this alien and ended up killing him instead. A'ler had obviously planted a Beta-frequency detonator on the MEC. She'd planted the tiny but lethal Q-bomb after she'd tricked me into setting the MEC to scan and alert me with a Beta-frequency in the presence of a Gness. Then all A'ler needed to do was lead me to Rashomon, by cleverly providing me with the one thing I so obviously desired: Serge.

I dropped my hands to the wet ground and hunched over, sick. I abruptly heaved out the remains of my blenoid dinner. Damn my arrogant hubris. Ennos was so right about me. It was never about the MEC. They just needed an assassin dumb enough to do the job and not catch on until it was too late—

Ka roused with a moan, jerking me out of my nightmare. I wiped my mouth then bolted to him, ignoring my own injuries, and knelt down beside him. His beautiful chest feathers were stained in black blood where the piece of greenhouse furniture had lodged. And that was only what I could see. Like me, he'd been thrown by the blast and might have sustained internal injuries as well. I would have preferred not to move him, but I had no choice.

"We have to get out of here!" I commanded, sliding my arms under his great limp wings. I glanced up to the buckling ceiling where water gushed out like a waterfall then turned back to him. "Let me help you!"

He pulled feebly at my shirt. "You're hurt too," he wheezed in objection. "I'm too heavy. Go, young one! Save yourself!"

"I'm okay," I lied. "You're coming with me!" I wasn't going to let another being die on account of me. I strained to pull his great body up, grunting with effort. He hardly budged.

He clutched my shirt. "Rashomon!" he gasped with

urgency.

I swallowed. "Dead."

Letting go of me, he closed his eyes and let his head fell back with a sigh.

"Ka! Come on! The ceiling's about to collapse! We need to get out of here, NOW!" He was close to unconscious and wouldn't move.

I surged to my feet and nearly collapsed with the pain in my chest. I sprinted past Rashomon's strewn remains to where a large cloth bag lay amidst some gardening tools. I snatched the bag and returned to Ka then briskly but carefully rolled him onto the bag and dragged him to the exit.

We emerged into another maze of hallways. I stabbed the exit door controls, closing both exits and sealing off the garden. Only then did I give in to my own pain. I bent low, hands resting on my knees, to pant out my relief.

Ka moaned, half-conscious.

I pushed myself up and threw glances left and right then pelted down a large translucent hallway, suspended in the dark water, where I thought I'd spotted the shadows of several forms.

Yes! Two Gnesses and a Xhix, dressed in Paradise City utility overalls, were ambling down the translucent hallway away from me. I shouted, "Wait!"

They turned and stared at me with a mixture of concern and alarm. I must have been a sorry sight as I rushed toward them. But they stopped and let me catch up to them.

That was when I saw him and halted, stiff with shock: Serge.

He stood in an adjoining hallway, staring at me through its underwater translucent walls. His face was white with surprise. Serge wore the sky blue overalls of the city worker, and he had the audacity to have kept his human form: he looked just like he did when I'd last seen him on Iota Hor b: his beautiful face darkened by the bristle of a day's growth.

Breaking my gaze from him with a tight snarl, I seized the Xhix's arm and growled, "The Khonsus, Ka, needs emergency medical attention. He's lying just outside Rashomon's garden." I shoved him in the direction of the garden. "Hurry! And alert your staff—the garden's ceiling is breached and leaking lake water. There's been an explosion."

As I finished the last line, I twitched round to glare at Serge, who hadn't moved. We stared at one another for what seemed an eternity—although I knew it was a brief moment—then he bolted.

I pounded after him, ignoring my burning lungs and the pain that flamed up my leg. "Stop!"

He didn't. An insane rage boiled inside me. It balled my fists and fired my legs into a galloping run. I was gaining on him.

He led me back up to the surface, where Ka and I had landed, probably to steal Ka's shuttle. I saw him disappear up the shielded lift and had to wait some excruciating moments for the next one. When I emerged at the top, I spotted him right away. As I suspected, he ran in the direction of the landing platform. But I was still very close, and I knew I'd be upon him before he had a chance to start up the engine. A savage smile curled my lips, as I gulped in burning breaths. Serge veered toward the marina. Damn him!

He darted to the skipboats that lined the dock and untied one. He tripped the canopy open and slid into the boat with a sharp glance backward at me.

Just as I reached the skipboat, chest heaving with exertion, Serge started up the engine, and the boat leapt out into the water, accelerating with a high-pitched whine. It threw a pair of five-meter rooster tails behind, splashing the dock and soaking me with a slam of cold water. It almost knocked me off the wharf.

I recovered and scrambled, slipping off balance for a careless moment on the wet wharf, to the next skipboat and found the button to open the canopy. I untied the boat, dropped into the seat with a grunt of pain, closed the canopy, and started up the engine. It sputtered into a vibrating whine. Pressing my lips into a snarl of determination, I slammed on the foot pedal and was thrown back with sudden acceleration. Within seconds

I'd reached his wake, skipboat screaming at top speed.

I could make out the end of the thermal shield, where the water abruptly ended in a vast sheet of crusted ice. Serge plunged into the cold, skipboat hitting the lip of ice at full speed and bouncing high. Hot on his heels, I kept my vehicle in full tilt and flinched when it crashed through the icy lip, soaring then landing with a painful jolt on the ice sheet. The vehicle's thin pontoons allowed the skipboat to skate effortlessly at breakneck speed along the creaking ice sheet that covered the giant underwater city. My lip curled in a wicked smile as I noticed that I was catching up to him.

"Rhea!" the com spattered on with Serge's voice. "Is that you?"

After a long pause I stabbed the com button and responded savagely, "Yes it's me. Stand down, Serge."

He didn't respond.

"I repeat, STAND DOWN!"

"Listen, Rhea, I didn't kill Rashomon," he said in an almost pleading voice.

"No," I retorted with scornful mockery. "I did."

"I mean, I wasn't involved in setting you up."

"No, your sister did that," I bit out. *You were the bait.* "You were probably just back up, in case I jagged up." If Serge wasn't The Rose, his sister was. V'mer had as much as told me that: *unlike you, I have family,* he'd said.

We came to some scattered circular pools of steaming boiling water—thermal vents—and the ice sheet grew gnarly and unstable. Serge's vehicle took a hard turn to the right. His skipboat careered on one skate right through a steaming vent and threw a single rooster tail of slush and water at me. It splattered against my canopy and momentarily obliterated my view. I blinked hard and threw the wipers on, thinking for a moment that Serge was going to tip over, but his skipboat eventually came crashing down to right itself. I cranked the steering wheel hard to the right in pursuit and felt my skipboat list hard with the centrifugal force. The left pontoon lifted off the icy surface in a 45-degree angle. It eventually came down just like his and I landed upright.

"It wasn't like that," Serge protested, betraying some frustration. Why was he even trying to convince me of his innocence? Why did he jagging care what I thought?

I pushed out my jaw in determination and pounded the accelerator pedal to overtake him. The vehicle responded with a squealing jolt that threw me back into my seat and I closed the distance between us, bouncing on the scabrous surface. Sensing my approach, Serge swerved left. He headed straight for the floating north-west corner of the giant underwater city beneath the creaking ice sheet. I saw the surface buildings rush toward us as we sped forward. We slid on patches of melted ice and threw water fountains up behind us. I slowed to avoid any destruction, watching Serge's vehicle surge ahead. To my relief he veered away from the floating buildings and struck north, away from the city. Leaping forward at full speed, I chased him to an area littered with huge buttresses and sleek towers of glassy blue ice.

"If it wasn't like that, then what are you doing here, Serge?" I scoffed, forcing out words through shallow painful breaths. The windswept icy surface grew rippled and pitted with blocks of frozen ridges and pockets of water.

"The same as you. Trying to prevent his assassination. You have to believe me, Rhea."

Serge skirted around several large ice buttresses and domes in quick succession, his vehicle pounding over frozen waves and curtained layers of debris and ice. I kept up, turning each time with grunts of painful effort and feeling each jar like a hard kick in my chest.

"Now, why is it that I don't?" I snarled. "Maybe it's because you've lied to me ever since we met ... *V'ser*." I realized that I was panting. "Everything you've ever said to me was a lie."

The com went silent. The scene began to feel painfully surreal. A few times, I saw spots in front of my eyes and realized I was fighting from blacking out.

Serge continued to maneuver through what resembled a giant storm that had been flash-frozen. Where the chaos was he taking us? A sharp glance behind me at the four city corner posts in the distance confirmed that we'd left Paradise City far behind.

A sudden thought made my stomach curdle with fear: these skipboats ran on stored thermal fuel; they were bound to run out sooner or later, at which time Serge and I were condemned to be exposed to over minus 100ºC temperatures, not taking into account the wind chill factor, which, according to Ka, almost doubled the cold. At those temperatures, all my body fluids would freeze, my lungs would collapse, and my heart would stop from shock within the hour.

I glanced down at my lack of thermal protection: a soaked T-shirt and flight pants. Never mind that I was in no shape to walk a great distance right now. I was certain I'd cracked or even broken several ribs in the explosion and sprained my left ankle.

To make matters worse, the wind was picking up and the sky was darkening with a coming storm. Abruptly sheets of snow and ice hailed down, fogging my canopy briefly until the defogger kicked in. Clenching my teeth in a grimace, I fought the wind that buffeted my skipboat, and ruthlessly kept on Serge's tail, as he careered around more bluffs into an undulating topography of rolling ice and snow.

The turbulent wind blew the snow into eddies of swirling sleet, and it became harder to keep on Serge's tail. I pounded in and out of dips and waves, painfully chasing the shadow of Serge's yellow skipboat.

We entered an area of unusual dark fog—no, smoke. As my skipboat skidded across a slush pool, I realized that we'd entered a series of fire-breathing thermal vents and surrounding pools, like the ones Ka had shown me. Terrific, I thought with a cynical sigh.

Startled by a sudden spout of molten fire ahead of me, I steered hard to the right and choked back sudden alarm as the skipboat flipped onto its side. I skidded uncontrollably, hull squealing, and watched the ice beneath me turn to slush then water. I floated on my starboard side, drifting without control, into another thermal vent pool. Before I had a chance to wonder, it too spewed out fire.

Heart slamming, I felt the scorching blast of heat as flames barely licked my skipboat. The churning water glowed like flowing lava, reflecting the fire. Then the flames disappeared in a huge puff of billowing black smoke. Charred debris and flying embers rained on my boat in a deluge of snaps and crackles. I saw that I was drifting toward the origin of flame. The next flame spout would be a direct hit.

I glimpsed Serge's skipboat circling back toward me. Like a driver checking out road kill. In furious inspiration, I cranked the steering wheel hard to the left and with a screaming grunt of effort, slammed my foot down on the accelerator. The sudden thrust of power on my starboard side, bounced the light vehicle off its side and righted me. Cranking my wheel back, I pounded on the accelerator and my skipboat leapt forward just as the flame spout hissed out.

"Rhea! You're—" Serge sounded genuinely relieved. Damn him!

"I'm not dead yet, bastard!" I gasped out with a feral grin, feeling the sharp boost of adrenalin in my gut.

Serge darted away like a frightened animal and led us through a series of looming ice columns toward a rise in the topography. It looked like a giant frozen wave twenty meters tall. Maybe it was …

In a rush of new determination, I pushed out my jaw and felt my teeth gnash.

"Stand down, Serge!" I snorted out the words through panting breaths. "Give yourself up. It'll end up better for you with the Guardians if you do." God! Even I didn't believe that.

He obviously didn't either. I winced at his sharp laugh of derision.

"My dear Rhea. Always the Enforcer, even when you aren't. And always in control—even when you obviously aren't."

"Jag you, Serge. And I'm not *your dear!*"

"Well, in that case you'll have to catch me and stop me first!"

"If you insist."

I slammed on the accelerator. We reached the rise and were climbing. It was steeper than I had initially thought, and I had to fight the wheel to keep from tipping over on my side as Serge led me on a diagonal vector up the ice and snow slope. Face puckered in a tight snarl, I forced my skipboat to skirt around Serge's, flanking him on the high side. I caught sight of his tense face through the canopy as he threw alarmed glances at me.

"Rhea, you don't have any weapons and you're hurt. I hear it in your voice. How are you going to stop me? With your bare hands?"

"If I have to."

I came up beside him, nosing toward him to force him down.

We crested the hill at the same time with my vehicle on the outside and—Oh, God! My pulse raced. I knew what lay on the other side before I saw it.

A sheer cliff! More than that, it turned into an inverted cliff at the bottom. I realized that this was just another dome and we'd climbed the windward side where snow and ice had piled to form an incline. I felt myself slide uncontrollably into that awful dreamstate and watched in horror as it played out like I knew it would:

In a panic, Serge overcompensated. I was too close! His tail skidded in counterpoint and collided hard against mine, forcing me over the cliff. Heart surging in a spike of alarm, I fought the wheel as my skipboat slid straight down the dome then hurtled into freefall ...

"Rhea! NO!—"

I saw the icy ground rushing toward me then smashed into darkness.

TWENTY-FIVE

I bolted awake, shivering cold and gasping in burning

breaths. A sharp pulsing pain pounded my head. I inhaled over-brewed soyka—No … the cloying smell of burnt metalloid and duraplast. My eyes snapped open, hardly able to see anything in the darkness. I felt numb from the waist down. As my eyes adjusted, I realized with alarm that I was still harnessed in the pilot's seat in the skipboat and the boat was taking in freezing water. It was up to my waist.

I put my hand to my throbbing head, feeling a raw sticky gash, and drew my hand quickly away. It was covered with blood and my hand started to shake uncontrollably. Suddenly faint, I felt more blood trickle down my forehead and the side of my nose.

I fought against passing out and looked up, feeling a sharp stab with every shallow breath I took. I saw blood smears on the canopy, where I'd obviously hit my head. Wiping the blood off the transplast, I made out swirling blues amid patches of almost black and concluded that I'd punched a hole through the ice and was trapped underneath. How far I'd drifted from the hole, I couldn't tell. I twisted my head painfully to look behind me and saw no shafts of light.

I looked for the start button on the dash. The console was a mess of crumpled metalloid and melted duraplast. None of the dash lights were lit. The ignition simply wasn't there. I tried to move my lower body and couldn't. Was it pinned from the crash or was I just unable to move because I couldn't feel anything in the freezing water?

I reached down into the water and felt along my thighs then flinched when I felt the buckled metalloid wrapped tightly around my torn legs. Heart racing with renewed alarm, I fumbled at the crash harness and managed to get it off with shaking hands. In full panic I strained to pull myself up and instantly felt my head slam and my chest lance with a sharp stab of pain.

A wave of nausea hit me like a MEC concussion wave, and I abruptly threw up. It burned out of me in heaves and coughs, splattering in the water that slowly rose around me. I saw blood in the vomit. God! I'd probably fractured some ribs and punctured my lung in the process. I seized in a deep breath, and the pain in my chest took it away.

I thought I passed out then realized I was still awake. My eyes throbbed with a rhythmic vice-like hammering and I saw blood drip from my nose and swirl like an oil slick on the frigid water that lapped my waist. I wasn't sure how much time had passed.

Where was Serge? I thought I'd heard him call my name when my skipboat fell, but it was obvious that he'd abandoned me. He'd done his deed and was likely aboard Ka's shuttle, heading back to the *Ulysses* to report success to his sister.

Realizing that I was slowly passing out and that the water was still rising, I scrambled for options. If I opened the canopy, I'd lose the little air that was left, flood the vehicle chamber with frigid water, and send the skipboat sinking to the bottom, two hundred meters down. Because I was pinned, that choice was suicide anyway. I'd drown and freeze, whichever came first. Even if I could somehow coax the melted engine to start, I had no way to press on the accelerator: no functional legs, no stick to push down with. Never mind that I had no idea which direction to go. I'd run out of options and felt myself sliding into murky darkness.

Shaking my head painfully to stay awake, I decided that I'd been lucky to have survived the crash in the first place. What were the chances that the canopy hadn't shattered or at least cracked when I crashed through the ice? The hull had taken the brunt of the collision, collapsing around my legs. It had been a miracle. Then again, perhaps it wasn't; it only prolonged the agony of dying slowly. I was running out of air and the water was rising.

Then I saw it in the dim light: my face-print and a hairline fracture in the canopy. And realized why I'd spotted it just now: the fracture had just made a faint cracking sound and grown. I knew a second before it happened that I was going to die fast and I was jagged—

The canopy shattered and imploded. I gasped and covered my face with my hands as freezing water flooded in and a million shards of transplast bombarded me. Body in shock, I gulped the water in convulsive inhales as the boat creaked in hesitation then plummeted down into an inky hell.

My desperate thrashing gave way to a murky lethargy and I sank into it, hearing the panicked shouts of my mind subside as if from far away.

Θ

"That's it!" I heard my own voice command me. "Move yourself to a moment before you hit the ice."

>What? How can I? I'm dead. I'm not breathing. The skipboat's still sinking to the bottom. I can't see; it's pitch black.<

"You can do it. I'll help you. I'll take you there ... it's my past, the one I chose for you. You just have to trust me and go with me."

>Who are you?<

"I'm you."

>God!<

"No, not quite," I heard myself chuckle. "Just another version of Rhea Hawke. I've had this recurring nightmare so many times. Now I finally get to do something about it. I know I'll do a better job of your other two incidents. The last one, I won't even have to interfere corporeally. You'll manage it all yourself ... well, you've already done it, it's your past, after all ..."

What was this? My own version of Hell? Getting a weird lecture from myself?

"Now, listen to me," she commanded me with stern urgency. "We have no time left. You have to come with me NOW!"

>I'll do what you say.<

"Good! Just concentrate and follow my voice. I'm going to drag you backwards in time ... you're in my dream, my diverse, now ..."

I found myself rising to the dim light of the surface as if in slow motion, felt myself gasping out air and water, watched as if in a dream as the canopy put itself back together, and eventually felt the skipboat move backwards until I saw gossamer ribbons of light dance around me ... then the skipboat bobbed in the hole ... now miraculously rising up into the air in reverse as though hoisted up by an invisible hand—

—Suddenly lucid, but inside a crisp déjà vu, I heard Serge scream my name and knew what I had to do: lock my foot in hard reverse just before I hit the ice sheet. That would prevent me from plunging under the ice where I'd otherwise be trapped and die. Teeth gnashing, I forced my foot forward on the pedal, even as the rest of my body recoiled.

The skipboat hit. My head collided with the canopy, plunging me into darkness.

Θ

I bolted awake with a sharp inhale. I sucked in air with a loud gasp, thinking I was still drowning, remembering my last remembered circumstance: the skipboat filling with water under the thick ice sheet. The voice inside my head. Was I still inside the skipboat? No—

I snapped my heavy eyelids open to the smell of burnt duraplast—No … this time it really was slightly over-brewed soyka. I found myself lying in someone's bed in a clean room, lit by golden streams of sunlight. Squinting to regain my focus, I made out a large cup of steaming soyka and some jelimum pastry on a tray next to me within arm's reach. Was I dead?

A familiar lyrical voice said, "Welcome back to the living, young one."

Ka! I turned stiffly, feeling a smile tug my lips, and rested my eyes on his kind face.

"You're …" I croaked hoarsely and managed a frail grin. He was alive!

Like me, he was lying on his side under soft sheets on a very comfortable bed next to mine. He leaned his head on his feathered hand, watching me with a warm smile of mild concern. I concluded that we must be in a med-facility. What had happened? My fuzzy mind pieced it together: the explosion, chasing Serge on the frozen lake, plummeting toward the frozen ground and crashing through the ice and getting trapped beneath, the water flooding in and drowning—

"How come I'm not …" I trailed, looking down at myself

with bemusement, grin caving in to a ghost of a smile.

"Dead?" He smiled with mild amusement. "You have exceptional healing qualities for a human. You mend like a Scandi."

I saw that he showed no signs of his chest injury, his wings furled evenly across his feathery breast and his feathers were shiny and preened. "You're healed," I said.

"Yes. Almost completely. Just need some rest. Thank you for getting me out before the roof collapsed," he said in that beautiful lyrical voice I'd grown to love.

"I'm just glad you're okay," I said, voice cracking. "Where are we?"

"We're still in Paradise City, top floor of one of the south-east corner buildings. The view is rather spectacular," he said impishly, knowing I couldn't see it from the bed. "Luckily for you this med-facility is one of the best in this part of the galaxy. The Schiss have spared nothing in obtaining the best. And you needed it, I'm afraid."

I tried to raise myself on my elbows but slid back with a grunt, unable to hold myself up. "What happened?"

"We're not sure," Ka said, sitting up. His brows furrowed in puzzlement.

"I thought I'd drowned." I frowned. "I'm sure I did ..."

"Oh, no," Ka answered calmly. "But you did hurt yourself with that fall. And the skipboat was taking in water from a tear in the bow and portside."

"I was underwater, under the ice," I blurted out, feeling my chest rising and falling with renewed distress. "Then the canopy shattered, and the boat filled with water and sank, and I ... drowned ..." Then there was the voice, *my* voice, guiding me somewhere ... I swallowed, perplexed.

"No, no." Ka laughed lightly. "You must have dreamt that. Your canopy was intact. Just a hairline fracture where you left a bloody imprint of your face when you cracked your skull. Your skipboat was still floating in the hole you'd made in the ice. The med team had quite a time extricating you from the boat, though. You were sort of welded into it," he ended with a grimace. "It was rather … messy."

Suddenly reminded, I lifted my blanket to look beneath it down to my legs. Even beneath the light gown they'd put me in, I could see that my legs looked perfectly normal. And I could feel them!

"They did a great job grafting bone, flesh, nervous tissue and synthplast. With nuyu treatments, your legs are as good as old," he chuckled. I wiggled my toes and smiled with relief. Thanks to their treatment, even my old blenoid scars were gone. "They say you should be able to walk, but you're still weak, so be careful," he continued. "You might fall flat on your face and break your beautiful nose."

I let the blanket fall back into place over me and stammered with sudden panic, "My clothes—they—what happened to them …? I had something in one of the …"

He raised his hand to stay my anxiousness. "Yes, they found an info-pod in one of the pockets. It was placed among your other personals inside your backpack. Alas, besides your boots and utility belt, your other clothes were ruined in your accident and subsequent rescue."

I raised a hand to my head with a sigh of relief. "How did they find me?" I said, still confused about the events. Which was the dream? Hadn't I sunk to the bottom of the lake? I remembered the terror of drowning as I plummeted into inky blackness.

"Someone called in your position, twenty kilometers north of the city outskirts. The emergency med team found you still in your skipboat, floating in the middle of a hole in the ice, beside a dome."

"But …" I trailed off and bit my lower lip in confusion. I'd skidded under the ice and was trapped … Wait! At the last minute, under the suggestion of a lucid déjà vu, I'd reversed hard. Had it prevented my slide under the ice and drowning? But my drowning was too real to have been a crazy dream. I shuddered and wrapped my arms around myself.

"You were in shock," Ka explained gently. "You'd lost a lot of blood from your injuries. It was difficult to separate the ones you got in the explosion from the fall. They think that you'd already broken your ribs, but the fall punctured your lung and crushed both your legs. You also suffered from advanced hypothermia," Ka went on. "But, because you were inside the skipboat in the water, you had some protection from the deadly cold of the wind."

The icy lake was the reason I'd only received a concussion rather than cracking my skull wide open on a more solid and less forgiving surface, I concluded dismally. I closed my eyes with a frown of concentration and took in a deep breath. Serge had called in my position, of course. Why did he leave me there, then? I thought I'd heard him wail my name.

As if reading my mind, Ka said, "The meds suggest that whoever called in your position did right to leave you in the lake water, rather than try to get you out. You'd have frozen to death or drowned. The best choice was to let the professionals get you out."

I stared through him, blinking, and throat swelling with emotion.

Misinterpreting my look of agitation, Ka assured me in a kind voice, "Don't fret yourself over it. You've suffered no permanent injuries. Your legs are fine. Your head is fine. Your lung and ribs are fine. A bit more bed rest and you'll be back to normal."

I half-moaned, "He got away, didn't he? The man I was chasing."

Ka sighed. "Yes."

I closed my eyes again, feeling the hot moisture of tears. "I'm so sorry, Ka. So very sorry."

"Rhea," he said softly. I kept my eyes closed. "They were clever and it wasn't your fault. But consider this, that you were also a target. As was I, possibly."

God! I couldn't stand it. Ka's unreasonable compassion and forgiveness were drawing out my tears, and I felt myself gasp with the beginnings of a sob.

"This shapeshifter you call Serge," he continued, apparently ignoring my distress. "He is obviously linked to all this, to Rashomon's death and the previous massacre."

I nodded, feeling my breaths stutter with sobs.

"Do you have any idea where he might have gone?"

"No," I heard my voice almost wail and swallowed hard several times to keep from bursting into uncontrollable weeping.

"Well, I do."

My eyes snapped open.

TWENTY-SIX

It was approaching sunset as I strode with long determined steps to the Tangent Shipping hangar in Pyramid City, where Benny presumably awaited me. I could already make out the pair of moons rising to my left in the darkening indigo sky opposite the setting sun to my right. The smaller moon was chasing the larger one, slightly above it. Not every planet had a moon, I considered, and decided that I liked moons. Earth's moon was singularly beautiful.

I was dressed in a pair of ill-fitting blue overalls. All I had of my original wardrobe were my black gravity boots, utility belt, and the backpack slung over my shoulders. I'd returned alone to Horus from Uma 1 on the regular shuttle bus. Ka had elected to stay behind a little longer to take part in the mourning rite for Rashomon. He'd invited me to stay as his guest, and, although I acknowledged that it was a rare privilege, I'd declined. I had a legitimate reason to leave hastily after my quarry, but felt relief that I could not attend the ceremony.

We'd parted, shaking hands, he with a kind and sad smile, I with a stony face of guilt and resolution. The *Music of the Dead* had already begun, led by the haunting chant of a Khonsus, and I'd felt it stir my heart with emotions I desperately needed to restrain.

"Fare well, Rhea Hawke," Ka had said with a gentle smile. He pressed my hand between his two feathered ones. Then he'd enveloped his giant wings around me in a wonderful embrace. I wanted to bury my face in his warm downy feathered chest. "We will see one another again, young one."

I didn't think we would but didn't say so. I would miss him.

"Goodbye," I responded in a wooden voice of control and turned for the shuttle, leaving Ka and the dirge for Rashomon behind me. I glanced down at the hardcover book in my hand that he'd given me as a parting gift. I read the title, *Paradise Lost*, by Milton, and felt my face tighten to quell my surging emotions. How did Ka know of my love for old Earth books ...?

I had managed to secure funds from the Galactic Bank in Pyramid City. I intended to retrieve my Great Coat from Selway, and was desperate to see Benny mended. I urgently needed to change and was anxious to get out of this system and pursue Serge. Luckily for me, Ka's *scimitar* spaceship, which Serge had stolen after I had crashed, was equipped with a very sophisticated homing beacon that Serge obviously hadn't managed to disable.

I now knew that he was headed for the 70 Virginis system. Where Serge had once dreamt we'd met. Also where the third and anonymous melting power had been wielded some years ago, according to Ka. I wondered if either was somehow connected to my pursuit.

"If I was a Gnostic," I murmured to myself, pulling out some soyka gum I'd just purchased, "which I'm not," I hastily added, stuffing two wads in my mouth and enjoying the burst of soyka as I bit down, "I'd be inclined to think there was some kind of connection with all these things and that Virgil 9 is some kind of strange attractor, a focal point, for a cosmic event." I then barked out a sharp laugh and slurped in the swill of soyka juice my chewing had created. "Yeah, Rhea," I scoffed. "Me, part of a cosmic event. Now, that's a laugh!" Then again, I thought, curling my lips in a sneer, I was certainly about to stir up some cosmic chaos.

When I reached the hangar, brightly lit by hanging lights, I spotted Selway right away, towering over an Eosian beside a small *viper*. He wore a greasy smile as he was smoothtalking the poor victim, who listened with a face of painful confusion. Selway flicked up a paw to let me know he'd seen me and would be with me shortly and I let my gaze wander the hangar. My brows furrowed when I saw an old Tangent *falcon* class four-person ship at the deep end. *Falcons* had been used by the Guardians before ZetaCorp's *twin-Vs* replaced them. Merchants had since snapped them up as inexpensive and spaceworthy small-trade ships.

With a frowning last glance at the *falcon*, I marched straight to Benny. I felt a little lightheaded and let a hopeful smile tug my lips. How I'd missed him! Just as I reached Benny and was touching his hull, my peripheral vision caught Selway rushing toward me.

"Well, if it isn't our friendly Guardian Enforcer!" he called, barreling over with wheezy breaths. He looked a little comical with a black smudge of pogent oil smeared across his nose and cheek. No one had bothered to tell him, or if they had, he hadn't bothered to remove it.

"Where's my Great Coat," I said in a stern voice. I was forced to crane to look up at him because he'd closed the space between us until he was practically touching me. He'd better not have sold my coat, I thought and imagined Selway with much more than pogent oil grease on his self-satisfied face.

"Why in such a hurry? It's safe," he said a little too casually, leaning over me like a vulture. "Do you have my money?"

I gave him a skeptical look and set my jaw. "Is my ship fixed?"

"Oh, sure!" Selway said and stretched back, finally giving me some room to breathe. "It wasn't nearly as bad as I'd thought when I first checked."

"Good." I nodded. "Then maybe it won't cost as much either."

"Oh, no!" he objected nervously. "Don't get me wrong; it was still a lot of hard work to fix. We found a very sophisticated virus program in your ship. It was cleverly timed to trigger disabling signals on and off and basically cripple your ship at select times in certain ways. Like a choreographed play." He frowned and scratched his unkempt beard. Some food particles fell out of it along with a pursuing insect. "Don't know why anyone would do that," he muttered with a slight frown.

I knew. It all made sense now. A'ler wanted Benny injured, but only enough to force me down to the planet's surface, where a rescue was imminent. I suspected that A'ler had somehow arranged Benny's distress call ... or worse, yet—I felt a chill crawl up my back like a million spiders—perhaps Bas had made it up. Who, if not Ennos, was Bas working for? A'ler? It seemed suspiciously fortuitous that he'd happened by just then and was ready and willing to take me to Horus. A'ler wanted me on Horus, so I'd go to Uma 1. I had been set up from the moment I'd accepted Zec's information about the *Ulysses*. And I knew who Zec worked for.

"Show me what you did," I commanded Selway.

"Money first." He held out his dirty hand.

"Great Coat first." I planted my fists on my hips.

He withdrew his paw. "Your Great Coat's inside the ship. I left it on the pilot's chair," he said amiably. "Where's the money?"

"Here," I said, scowling at him, and tossed him a small pouch of bills. He snatched the bag out of the air. "Now, show me what you did."

He grinned like a thief, showing all his brown teeth, and ambled up Benny's ramp through the hatch and into the ship. I followed right behind.

"Benny's very weak right now," Selway quipped, glancing at me over his shoulder. "You'll have to take him up real easy, do most of the work yourself at first. Keep him in atmosphere for at least a half hour before you attempt any space travel. Keep it simple, get him all used to the regular things first."

"Right," I said, nodding and feeling a little queasy. Was Benny really okay?

Selway led me straight to the cockpit, where my Great Coat lay draped over the back of my pilot's chair. I felt a smile of relief crease my face.

Just as I was about to pick up the coat and sit down to check readouts, a voice from behind us drawled like an oil slick, "Well, if it isn't the human ex-Enforcer bitch."

Pulse racing, I turned and beheld two large purple Eosians standing at the entranceway. The larger one was in a Great Coat, snarling, and pointing a *pocket* pistol at me. The other wore a faded ranger and pointed his Kappa rifle with its meter-long barrel at me. I stared at the Kappa rifle. It was a cruel weapon, killing slowly. Mistakenly classified as a Class C weapon, it was released as regulation issue to civilians like this bounty hunter. Guardians and bounty hunters often worked in pairs to find their quarry, usually splitting the reward. I'd done the same on a few occasions.

"Sorry." Selway shrugged, not looking sorry in the least. "They got here first and business is business. Borlias here," he said, pointing to the Guardian, "says you're not even an Enforcer anymore and that you're a wanted criminal." He made clicking sounds with his tongue and waggled his bony finger at me in reproach. Then he grabbed my Great Coat and slithered out of the cockpit.

"Hey!" I lunged after him. "That's mine!"

The two Eosians seized me by the arms and restrained me.

"You won't be needing that where you're going, human," Borlias said with a sneer.

Panting with anger, I watched Selway disappear to the back of the ship, leaving me alone with the Guardian and bounty hunter. Borlias shoved me down onto the pilot's seat.

"Now, you're going to take us back to the nearest Guardian precinct, where Pentas here can collect his reward, and you'll rot in chaos," Borlias said, smirking. He slid into the co-pilot's seat beside me, while the bounty hunter remained standing behind us. "Get this jagging ship online!"

"Okay, okay," I snarled back with a sideways glance at him. I pulled the gum out of my mouth and pushed it onto the upper console then conducted a swift check on Benny's readouts. I didn't dare check under the console for my hidden

MEC. Was it still there?

"Selway told me that my ship couldn't fly outside of atmosphere right away," I said, stalling.

"And you believed him?" Borlias guffawed, bursting into a coarse laugh. My face burned as he shouted over his shoulder to the bounty hunter behind them, "Blessed Epoptes! The bitch is as stupid as she looks, eh, Pentas!"

"Yeah!" the other snorted nervously. I had noticed how he'd looked at me earlier. I'd read somewhere that most Eosian men found human females irresistible. It was the hair, I recalled, and tossed my long mane back.

Borlias punched my com. "Mestaphelos. It's Borlias. Do you copy?"

"I have you," a baritone voice crackled over the com.

"We've secured Hawke. I await your orders."

So, the *falcon* parked on the far side of the hangar was a Guardian ship after all—not everyone could afford a *twin-V* I supposed. And for this mission, their Tangent Shipping vehicle blended in rather well.

"Have her pilot the ship to Guardian Precinct 5, where she'll be taken into custody and her ship impounded. We'll escort you."

Borlias sneered across at me. "Understood," he said and flicked off the com. He snorted. "Hear that, bitch? You're going straight to chaos. They never should have made you a Guardian," he snarled with open contempt. "Humans don't have what it takes. You're too dumb, too slow, and unreliable."

I shifted in my pilot's seat and met his glare with a calm expressionless face. Then I let my mouth curl into a humorless smile. "It's a long ride to Gliese 876-12 and you have things all under control," I said, tongue brushing lazily over my upper lip. "Why don't you lose your lackey, send him back to get his reward for finding me, and you can take all the glory for bringing me in, lover boy."

Borlias wasn't buying it. I didn't expect him to. I'd covertly watched Pentas's reaction while I came on to Borlias. Chuckling, Borlias glanced over his shoulder at Pentas, who joined him in laughter. But it was a nervous cackle.

Turning my gaze to Pentas, I said, "I was really being kind to you with my suggestion. You see, there's no place to sleep in this cramped ship, the food's bad and ..." my mouth curled with disdain, "my air scrubber won't accommodate the added *stink*—"

I instinctively recoiled as Pentas lunged forward to strike me. But Borlias caught him and held him back. "Don't you see what she's doing? She's trying to get a rise out of us. Playing us against each other even." He turned back to me, eyes gleaming with hatred. "Well, it won't work."

"Filthy human scum!" Pentas yelled in a hoarse voice. "Why we went to Earth to save your jagging asses, I can't imagine!"

"Because you *have* no imagination, creon," I bit out in a snarl. "You saved Earth so you could have it for yourselves, you jagging idiot!"

His face blushed deep purple, and he lunged for me again. Borlias held him back. Pentas spat at me. I flinched at the sudden moisture on my face. Maintaining my composure, I casually wiped it off my cheek.

"Now get your ship prepped," Borlias snapped, waving his *pocket* pistol wildly in the air. "NOW!"

"Okay," I muttered. My right hand flew over the start-up panel, awakening Benny as my left hand slid under the console to where my MEC was secretly lodged. I found it to my relief and wasted no time. Recalling my last setting, I snapped the MEC off its holder, swung around and shot both of them before they even knew what I'd done. Borlias slumped in his seat and slid off his chair to the floor, unconscious. Pentas thudded to the floor, Kappa rifle clattering out of his limp hand.

I pulled my gum off the upper console and rolled it back into my mouth, then rose to my feet with a sneer, chewing hard. *"First rule of engagement: never underestimate your enemy, especially if she's a human*—Rhea's proverb."

I quickly found some cord to tie them up, intending to drop them off in Horus's wilderness once I lost the *falcon*. Sooner or later the Guardians on board the *falcon* would figure out that I was no longer under Borlias's custody and come after me. I had to act swiftly.

Once I'd secured the two men and their weapons, I turned back to Benny's console and continued my wakeup procedure. I was three-quarters of the way through when the console lit up with a warning: a secure Guardian pass code was needed.

"Chaos!" I snapped and clenched my fists. "That rips it!" Damn that Selway. No doubt he'd put that in for the Guardians. He'd made it so that Benny needed to be co-piloted. And my co-pilot was unconscious on the floor. Benny was going nowhere. I'd have to rely on ... I stared at the small *viper* in the hangar and nodded to myself with a sinister smile. If I couldn't give Selway a permanent headache, I could at least give his hangar one. And it would serve as a great diversion. I'd need it.

Benny was incapable of discharging any shots, and the Guardians had stripped the ship of all my weapons on board. I smiled in sudden inspiration, glancing down at the MEC in my hand. I could set it to the frequency that would overheat an inanimate object. Like those hesium fuel canisters between me and the *falcon*, for instance.

I firmed my lips with a glance back at my control panel. "I'll be back, Benny," I said even though Benny couldn't hear me because he wasn't online. "I won't let them scrap you."

MEC in one hand, I pulled up my emergency floor hatch with the other and dropped to the ground beneath Benny. Keeping out of sight behind the carboys and equipment, I sprinted to a pile of crates. I leaned my arms on a crate, took a two-handed aim, stopped chewing for a heartbeat, and pressed the trigger of my MEC. Within a moment, the fuel tanks broke up with a tremendous bang and burst into thunderous green flame, emitting plumes of roiling black smoke.

Inhaling the cloying pungency of burning hesium, I pelted for the *viper* ship, which lay partially hidden from view by the smoke and flame to those inside the *falcon* ship. Workers shouted and ran, looking for something to put out the fire. Others fled the hangar. A quick scan revealed no Selway. Damn that slimy

Fauche! He still had my Great Coat.

Amid the chaotic panic, I opened the hatch and scrambled into the one-man *viper*. So far I'd remained unobserved by the *falcon* Guardians. But no Guardian was stupid—contrary to what Borlias had said. And the *falcon* Guardians would instantly recognize that I was the cause of the explosion and that their men had failed. Flicking my gaze in rapid fire between the console I was trying to un-encrypt and the *falcon* ship, I eventually caught sight of two Eosians emerging from the *falcon*, bearing concussion rifles. They were heading in my general direction.

I continued to fiddle with the ID key pad, feeling panic edge in as the Eosians approached. For the love of Creos! I'd opened hundreds of these before. They'd been the easiest ships to steal during my dubious career as arms dealer. And I'd practically taught the vehicle BNE lessons in Stealth 101 at the Guardian academy—

They'd spotted me and were running toward me!

The engine sputtered into a reluctant idling whine. I seized the controls and the *viper* lurched into the air just as they opened fire.

Chaos! My heart slammed as a few shots pinged across the vehicle's hull. I carved a tight turn and whipped over my two pursuers, forcing them to instinctively duck, and soared out of the hangar into the sunset.

Within a few heart beats, the *viper* rose over the towers and pyramids of the city, now resembling glittering triangular blocks embedded in a filigree of sparkling glass. 47 Uma hovered over the horizon, a fiery ember that bathed the sky in rich tones of crimson. It would be dark soon. If I could keep ahead of them a little longer, the veil of night would do the rest.

The ship's AI droned, "You are not this ship's official pilot. Please identify for security clearance."

Damn these *viper* AIs. They weren't nearly as sophisticated as those in mid-sized vehicles or my small *ray* class ship, but they were intelligent enough to be a nuisance. "Never mind my ID," I snarled, madly manipulating the nav-console and searching the holo-map for a place to hide. "I got you started. That should be sufficient clearance. Now, pay attention to your Ops and spark up your reaction time. You're far too slow!"

"Sorry," the AI whined. "I will try harder."

"Do that!"

A glance at my rear view cam revealed the *falcon*, hot on my trail. It was a medium-sized vessel built for speed and maneuverability. Great for stealth and pursuit. Just what they were doing, I concluded. The *falcon* was faster and more reliable than the *viper* and would soon overtake me if I didn't do something radical.

I cranked hard to starboard, pressing against the bulkhead with the G-force, and heard the squeal of straining metalloid as I sent the *viper* swooping back into the city.

As I wove a reckless path between the high towers, the ship's AI complained in a metallic whine, "That's twenty suboptimal turns; torque was too sharp with 2% loss in fuel efficiency and 0.5% loss in ship's outer hull integrity. Recommend defaulting to ship's automatic pilot."

"You just do your job!" I bit out. "And I'll do mine."

"You are performing suboptimal maneuvers that may damage the ship. Already at 80% of optimum."

"Just keep up with me, *viper*. I'll get you home safe, once we lose this *falcon* who wants to hurt us." Just my luck. I had to steal a ship with a neurotic AI.

I'd lost the *falcon* momentarily among the tall glass towers of the city, but I knew that as soon as I reached the outskirts, the *falcon* would be there. Sure enough, as I emerged from between the tall buildings, the *falcon* swooped down in close pursuit as I sped north toward the molten glow of the countryside of lakes and undulating hills. The giant pyramids behind me receded into a rough topography of glittering gemstone, and I made for Horus's jagged mountains, blushing deep ochre in the sunset. Easily towering several kilometers, the mountains rose steeply ahead of me, biting into the red sky like bloody knives. A good place for a small ship to hide, I concluded, as I reached the first of the peaks. I dropped the ship down fifty meters without slowing down into the thick mist of one of the narrow steep fjords, already veiled in the shadows of night.

"That was not—"

"Shut up!" I cut the AI off, then swallowed hard to keep my dinner down. I was just about to congratulate myself on losing the *falcon* in the dark mist when I had to rear the *viper* up abruptly with a sharp inhale. I barely kept the ship from plunging into murky water and skimmed the reflective oily surface, leaving a turbulent wake of iridescent oil behind. I expelled a long breath. The mist had masked an oil-covered sea that surrounded the massive thrusting spikes of rock.

As I kept glancing up, looking for the *falcon*, I saw that virtually all of the tall spires of red rock spouted glistening waterfalls. Water cascaded from enormous heights down the smooth oily rock face and eventually disappeared in the dark mist. I had a sudden thought: were these the weeping mountains? Where my grandmother had disappeared—

The *viper* tugged sharply to port with a thunderous bang, throwing me hard to starboard. The emergency klaxon wailed. I was hit! The *falcon* must have used a silent concussion pulse. But I couldn't find it, throwing glances up through the canopy and to my instruments. The *viper* shuddered with an ominous groan and abruptly plummeted. Heart slamming, my gaze skimmed the console, and I saw with dismay that the AI was offline. I was on my own, on manual. Spinning out of control and hurtling toward the murky oil-covered waters of Horus's weeping mountains.

Damn it! I wasn't going to go down this way! I bit down on my lower lip and fought the controls to bring the *viper* up.

"Come on, you creon! Come on!" I screamed at the groaning ship.

It nosed up with a howl and headed straight for a sheer cliff in the narrow valley. I caught a glimpse of the *falcon*'s search lights as it circled above before I stabbed the emergency ejection button. The canopy popped open and I catapulted me out moments before the *viper* crashed into the red rock of a towering spire and exploded.

I barely had time to disengage from the crash webbing of the ejected seat before I hit the water feet first and plunged into darkness along with more debris. I swam up and broke the oily surface, gasping for air and tasting something acrid. My face and arms were covered in a sulphurous oily film. Charred pieces of the *viper* pelted the water around me, sizzling or catching fire in patches of thicker oil. There was no sign of the ejected seat; it must have sunk already.

The *falcon's* searchlight swept through the light mist. Treading water, I undressed frantically, leaving only my utility belt on with my holstered MEC, and threw my ripped Uma 1 clothes on a piece of floating debris that wasn't burning. I swam, naked except for my belt and gun, toward one of the rocky spires. Night had already fallen in this steep valley and I was thankfully veiled in darkness. I evaded the searching light, which appeared to focus on the floating debris, and reached the vertical rock face of a towering mountain, unobserved. The rock was incredibly smooth and I clambered for a hold, hands sliding at first on wet slime, then fingers finally finding purchase in a small crevice. I found no hold with my feet and gave up looking for one, to hang on with stiff fingers.

I waited there, floating in the water and catching my breath, for what seemed a painful eternity, and watched each burning piece of debris extinguish one by one and sink into the murky sea as the search lights continued sweeping the area. When there was nothing left to see, the light beam finally winked out and the sound of the *falcon's* engines faded. They'd given up on me. I sighed, feeling the bite of exhaustion in my arms and fingers. Perhaps they'd spotted my wet clothes and had made the logical conclusion .

With the *falcon* gone, the silence of the night returned, and darkness surrounded me like a black oil slick. The water was surprisingly warm, like bathwater. If it was any warmer it would have been uncomfortable, I considered. At first I only heard the lapping of the water on the slimy rock and my own breaths as I hung on to the sheer cliff. Then I picked up the odd shriek of some nocturnal predator and remembered the giant snake that Ka had mentioned. The apophus. My face tightened as I make the logical conclusion: The *falcon* had been too far to have inflicted a concussion pulse on the *viper*, but I'd definitely been low enough for a giant sea snake to swipe at my vessel. It explained the large wake I'd glimpsed. I swallowed hard. According to Ka only a hungry snake bothered to bat its prey out of the air.

I considered my options. How was I going to get out of here with a hungry apophus swimming nearby? Ka had described the oily sea as a vast expanse of water dotted by millions of islands. He hadn't mentioned that they were all virtually impossible to climb up, being vertical, sheer, and covered in slime. And I had no idea where I was in this huge drowned valley.

I realized with growing dismay that I hadn't completely recovered from my ordeal on Uma 1 and my strength was swiftly ebbing. The cloying smell of the microbic slime that covered me and everything else began to make me nauseous. My whole body was slowly going numb. I could hardly feel my legs. Ka had mentioned a narcotic in the mist and possibly in the water. It must have an anaesthetic quality, I surmised. It was slowly putting my whole body to sleep ...

I jolted awake when my hand slipped as I drifted off. God! I mustn't let myself succumb to these sedating drugs ... what was I thinking ...?

... I found my mind wandering as if in a dream and contemplated what I might have been like if my mother had chosen a human instead of an Eosian for a lover. Maybe I'd have been more like Serge's made-up girlfriend ... kind, gentle, trusting and peaceful ... Happy ...

I barked out a sharp laugh when I found myself crying. Why not? I was in the weeping mountains ... a few more tears wouldn't hurt ... Perhaps I would die here just like my grandmother. Then, as if from a distance—or perhaps I was getting delirious—I heard a woman's voice singing. It resembled my mother's voice, beautiful, lyrical and sad. Then it faded into the deep of the night. Probably the breeze playing on the valley walls, I deduced. I realized that it had calmed me, nevertheless, and found my mind drift like a boat without oars …

… Why did all the women in my family do atrocious things? We were all lousy mothers or daughters, lousy friends and lousy at keeping our promises …

>*I meant to return but I couldn't …*<

"What?" I lost hold and plunged under the water. My face submerged, and I inhaled water as I scrabbled for some purchase and fought to move my legs.

>*I tried to make it all right … just like you … but it's never that simple, is it …?*<

I surfaced and spluttered, "Who—" I coughed out water and swallowed more as I struggled to stay afloat, legs barely moving to my grunting commands.

>*Forgive me, Rhea, as only you can … because I know what you are …*<

I thrashed and scrabbled at the smooth slime, then fell back into the water with a gasp, unable to find a handhold. Just then a bright light flickered in the oily water.

>*Rhea … relax … just relax … or you'll drown…*<

I realized that it was the voice of the singer and felt inexplicably soothed. Perhaps it was the narcotic mist or lingering shock. I didn't care. I found it suddenly easy to relax and was able to float on my back with something close to abandon. Drifting with my gaze turned toward the night sky, I discovered with relief that the flickering light in the water was the iridescent reflection of one of the twin moons as it crested a sharp mountain peak. I watched the second moon rise over the high mountains and felt lulled by its beauty. I was in a dream, hearing the lingering notes of a forgotten song as though they came from inside me …

I cast a lazy glance around me and in the new light of the twin moons I could more clearly see the oily sheen of the water's surface. For the first time I made out several swirling boils of churning water. Of course, I concluded, this was the Boiling Sea. Were they vents of hot gas from below? I'd drifted quite close to one and something told me to avoid it. I steered out of its path using my arms. The swirling vortex moved with me. I ignored the alarm going off in my brain.

>*Rhea! Swim to shore! NOW!*<

The voice spiked alarm. I rolled and forced my body into a front crawl, arms and legs burning in resistance. The swirling vortex closed in and I finally recognized what it really was: a swarm of thrashing pencil-thin snakes! Grunting with a surge of renewed alarm, I pushed myself onward.

They ceased to thrash immediately they caught up to me and enveloped me in a cloak of sliding softness, keeping me afloat. Were they saving me or preparing to devour me? They slid over me in a gentle embrace, tickling and gently pummeling my body. I may have gasped. I don't know. As if they were all one being, hundreds, maybe thousands of tiny snakes stroked me in a self-organized dance, softly murmuring and gently cajoling—or was it me? Their tender touch numbed the terror edging to surface. My mind revolted; how could snakes be tender? Yet that was what I thought.

They crowded between my legs—I tightened my buttocks and crotch, thinking I should be terrified then forgot as they nudged between my legs, stirring my fire. I opened to their sweet caress and my body yielded to a perverse rush of arousal. Did they enter? I couldn't let them … could I?—Oh, Dear God! Some must have entered. I felt them stirring deliciously inside me, filling me with pulsing light and music. Waves of orgasm shuddered up my entire body. I might have keened aloud. Or was it their chorus I heard inside my head? I didn't care. I felt an inexplicable devotion.

The soothing voice sang:

>*It's too late, child. Take them now with pleasure. My children dance for you … there is no victory in resistance; only in yielding without surrender … join me, sister …*<

I wondered if the voice was the apophus or my own demented mind as the snakes lapped between my thighs in throbbing waves, throwing me into the insane surrender of an erotic delirium. How could I feel such arousal? And yet, it was all so beautiful. The singing light lured me with the promise of eternal consciousness. Of a community that soothed my yearning soul. An exotic world of terrible beauty.

My head submerged and I took in water. They were pulling me down. I found it impossible to stay afloat and my head throbbed with dull pain as I took in more water and the snakes—hundreds, thousands of them—swept over me, drawing me down, as I opened to another world. I knew I would plummet to the depths of the Boiling Sea, to the maw of the giant apophus as a prize for her young. *Yielding without surrender* ... surely yielding and surrender were one and the same, I thought as I gave in to the pulsing dance of death inside and outside of me and my mind drifted into sweet unconsciousness—

I heard the throb of thunder. The snakes suddenly dispersed, abandoning me, as I saw the reflection of one of the twin moons grow like a monster about to devour me. I thrashed and broke the surface with a gasp and tried to swim away. Had the snakes been a feverish narcotic dream too? No, my gut burned and stirred with movement—now repulsive. Oh, dear God! How many? The moon roared at me and glowed like a huge blinking light—

"Rhea!"

My mind snapped into lucid thought: it was Bas's voice. An air vehicle swam into focus, suspended above with outer hull lights shining on me: Benny! Bas was calling down to me on Benny's outer com.

"Bas!" I spluttered, thrashing out, sinking, and gulping in water.

Bas threw something into the water, then jumped in himself. He was beside me in moments and secured a grapple line around my waist. "Okay, Benny!" he called.

I felt the line grow taut around me and pull me out of the water as I seized in air with gasping inhales. Terror gripped me; it was their terror—as if they knew they'd been removed from their element, the snakes inside me that had moments ago danced seductively recoiled in a flame of excruciating pain. I doubled over and must have gasped out a wail of pain.

Once I was inside Benny, Bas—who'd come up on another line—undid the grapple and scooped me into his arms. He struggled to keep his hold as convulsive tremors shook me, and I moaned out involuntary sounds. The snakes crawled inside me in terror, and I imagined them biting and tearing my insides.

Bas took me aft in stumbling steps, and Benny instructed him to place me on the retractable medical table in the infirmary. Bas swam in and out of focus, standing like a sullen statue, face blanched. He stared at me helplessly with damp eyes, as I curled into a fetal position to stop the stabbing pain. I wanted to tell him I was okay—he looked so horribly distressed—but I couldn't. I wasn't. And besides, my mouth wouldn't let me.

"You better leave, Bas," I heard Benny's tenor voice between my sobbing breaths. I moaned as the snakes thrashed inside. In truth, they'd settled and moved very little, I later learned from Benny. But I still felt each tiny wriggle acutely. "It won't be very pretty," Benny added. Bas looked genuinely sick and fled as one of Benny's medical arms removed my utility belt and poked my thigh with a syringe.

I tried to say something but my mouth wouldn't work.

"I just gave you a painkiller," Benny soothed. "But it's going to hurt like chaos anyway. I need to coax them out of you, and you need to be alert for that. They may have sewn themselves into you. My scanner tells me you took in seven of them."

Seven! My heart thundered. I felt violated. Then my heart fluttered as I remembered how they'd stroked my body and sung to me with light. It was that damned narcotic mist, I told myself. I forced my eyes shut and grimaced in dazed confusion. Did I feel something for those vile creatures?

"Try to lie still, Rhea," Benny instructed. I couldn't and only whimpered in response. "I need you to lie flat," he continued sternly, his medical prosthetic pushing my resisting body flat on the table. I moaned and resisted. It hurt to lie flat. Benny gruffly bound me down, then spread my legs apart and bound each foot on a stirrup. He pushed the stirrups toward me, bending my knees so my quivering body lay in a flat squat.

My eyes snapped open as Benny gently probed me. "Hold still." I felt the strange tickle of the probe. "Hmm ... You're lucky, Rhea," Benny said. "All seven of them have formed a little gaggle in there, clutching each other."

In terror, I thought and felt the renewed stirrings of regret. I'd felt their terror. Inside. *Don't kill them*, I wanted to say. My mouth opened. Nothing came out. Then Benny probed, and they stirred in my lower abdomen. I watched my tight belly move. A sharp pain tore through me like a rusty knife. They were clinging to me. I wanted to cry. I abruptly vomited oily water.

Then I lost my mind as unbearable pain flamed through me and we screamed.

TWENTY-SEVEN

These lull'd by Nightingales embracing slept,
And on their naked limbs the flow'ry roof
Show'r'd Roses, which the Morn repair'd —

Bas appeared at the hatch door of the infirmary, smiling shyly, and I put down the copy of Milton's *Paradise Lost* that Ka had given me. Sickbay served as my bedroom when I wanted a good sleep. I usually caught my naps in the pilot's chair, often mediated by Benny who used my sleep cycle to power the ship. Benny was too cramped to dedicate a space to such an uncommon activity as being sick, so I also used sickbay as my research lab, library, and storage locker—in addition to my bedroom.

Bas looked surprised to see me dressed and sitting on the bed. I noticed the cup of steaming soyka in one of his hands and draped in the other—I brightened—my Great Coat!

He responded with a smug grin and came forward as I shakily stood up and let him help me into the coat. I immediately felt its soothing effects on me and smiled warmly at him. Despite the coat, I felt lightheaded and stretched my arm behind me to ease my way into a sitting position again. I sat with a grimace as Bas reflected my expression.

"Here," he said, passing me the cup with a frown of concern. "I know Benny said you heal incredibly fast, like a Scandi. But are you sure you should be out of bed and up like this? You still don't look so good. You had the cheese kicked out of you."

I laughed, then immediately groaned at a sudden biting pain in my belly. "Crap," I corrected with a wry smile. "Not cheese. And I'm all right," I lied. My whole lower body hurt like I'd gone through a blender and had been sewn together with coarse string. Perhaps that wasn't so far from the truth, I contemplated, considering the bandages and pad I wore: I was still bleeding from the tearing wounds the creatures had left as they ripped out of me. When I'd first woken from Benny's surgery, he had assured my panicking mind that none of my organs were irreparably damaged and had blithely announced that I could still bear children, but it didn't feel that way. It had been thirty-two hours since he had removed the creatures, and every time I sat up I thought my insides would fall out. Passing my wastes was a dreaded and excruciating experience. I'd almost passed out the first time. "Just a little sore inside," I lied again, giving him a sickly smile as he sat down next to me on the bed. I glanced at the chronometer and saw that it was ten in the morning Local Time. I sighed out, "I slept for at least fourteen hours this time."

"Well, you needed it. You still look like shit."

"Thanks," I said, dropping my gaze to stare at my drink but smiling a little at hearing his familiar insult. He'd gotten that one right.

I'd certainly needed the sleep, I considered. Benny had taken us out of the Oily Range and found a sandy beach still well outside Pyramid City to perform the extractions. After removing the last of my seven invaders and assuring me that the snakes had miraculously inflicted little actual physical damage, Benny had bandaged me up, then given me a sedative, covered me with a blanket, and doused the lights to let me sleep. Before I let myself fall asleep, I forced Benny to reassure me that we were in no apparent danger of being found; while monitoring the incoming and outgoing planetary coms, he'd discerned that the Guardians had left the planet. Satisfied, I fell into an exhausted dreamless sleep and didn't wake up until a full day later. Benny had changed my bandages, given me more painkillers, and coaxed me back to sleep; it wasn't hard to do. I'd slept until now.

"You're wondering how I got the coat among other things, aren't you?" Bas said.

"And you're going to tell me, aren't you?" I smiled sideways.

"I highjacked Benny, after I got Selway to give me the scoop on what happened, and I got your Great Coat back from him. He was actually quite apologetic and very willing to give it back."

"Sure, he was," I said, "at the receiving end of a *pocket pistol.*"

Bas grinned. "I was able to get Benny going because I'm a Guardian in good standing and have access to the restricted codes." He lost his grin. "But I had to wait until the *falcon* was out of range. It kept circling and searching." He looked at her with a painful expression. "I'm sorry I only got there when I did. I wasn't even sure you were alive, Rhea. You gave us a real scare. We overheard on their coms that they'd seen your vehicle crash on the side of the cliff."

"You still came." I gave Bas a trembling smile and touched his hand.

He smiled back. "It's what friends do." Then he resumed with a sigh, "They decided that even if you'd miraculously survived the crash, the giant apophus would get you." He looked at me with a sick look on his face. "They didn't mention babies ..."

A sudden hot wave of sickness surged through me, leaving me giddy and I leaned back on the bed with my hand.

Bas paled. "You okay?"

"Yeah ... no," I admitted in a hoarse voice.

"Chaos, Rhea, you're in deep," Bas said. "The Guardians

have you listed as a classified Code-1 Priority now." He frowned. "That means shoot first then ask questions later—if you're alive, that is," he reminded me.

I nodded, sitting up straight to sip my soyka. That explained their shots back at the Fauche hangar. "Wish I knew why," I responded grimly and resumed staring at my cup of soyka .

"You don't know?" He stared at me in disbelief. He let out a sigh, then added, "What about Uma 1?"

I turned to him, confused. "That was an accident."

"*Officially*, it was an accident. That's what Ka, their foreign representative, said. But," he chose his words carefully, "the *unofficial* word now, and soon to be the new *official* word, is that you assassinated Rashomon for Eclipse. Paradise City workers chased you clear across the frozen sea in skipboats. Your partner in crime, a member of the Eclipse elite by the name of V'ser, got away but they caught you when your skipboat skidded off an ice-dome."

I felt my face heat with anger. Who would deliver such a twisted version of what happened? "My partner in crime?" I snorted. "I don't exactly remember it that way."

"The Guardians have proof, Rhea. Holos of you and him hanging out together very cozy-like in Neon City restaurants … and at his place."

I fumed. They'd been spying on me! I glared at Bas. "Since when do Guardians spy on other Guardians? Were you part of this?" He was one of their stealth-communications experts, after all. I suddenly remembered spotting him lurking outside my apartment once.

"Of course not," he quickly responded, backing away from my accusatory look. "I had no idea they'd bugged you, or his place."

I gave Bas a hard searching look. I wasn't convinced, but I let it go. I needed to feel comfort in his presence right now. I contemplated bitterly that some baldie had enjoyed quite a show. Returning to the accusations, I added, "And I suppose that I escaped Uma 1 after the Paradise City meds bothered to patch me up—like that makes sense!"

"The Schiss don't believe in letting anyone die, Rhea. Their representative figured that once you recovered, you threatened Ka with your melting power and forced him to let you take the shuttle off Uma 1."

"That's blenoid-shit, Bas," I trembled with anger. "That really doesn't make sense. Why wasn't the local police force waiting for me when I reached Horus, then?" This had obviously been concocted since I'd left.

"Don't go blenoid on me, Rhea. I'm just repeating what we heard through the Guardian coms. The reason the local PD weren't waiting for you was because they didn't know yet. Well, they do now, and so will everyone else, because it's scheduled for the local NewsVids. And you can be sure that Galaxy News will pick it up soon after."

My lips tightened and I ran my fingers up and down my cup, recalling the gruesome scene of Rashomon exploding in front of me. The irony was that, even though I hadn't done it intentionally, I *had* killed Rashomon for Eclipse. A'ler and Serge were a very clever team. I looked up at Bas with imploring eyes. I couldn't believe that Ka would betray me and let these crazy lies spread. "Bas, that's not how it happened at all. Why doesn't Ka tell them what really happened?"

"He went into seclusion immediately after making his initial statement and no one, not even the other Schiss, can reach him. I'm sorry, Rhea."

I stared at Bas in dismay then dropped my gaze. Ka was likely the new Schiss priest and, like Rashomon before him, would communicate with no one except an acolyte now. He was unreachable.

We sat in silence for several moments before Bas asked in a soft voice, "What are you going to do now?"

My grip on the cup tightened, and I looked up at him, searching his eyes. "Maybe the question should be: what are *you* going to do, Bas? Turn me in, now that I'm a murderer for Eclipse?"

"Come on, Rhea," he said, leaning back with a deep frown

as though I'd struck him. He looked genuinely hurt. "I know you didn't murder that Schiss priest. It's obvious that The Rose set you up. In any case, I'm here to help. I *want* to help. My *twin-V* is in town and Raekwon's waiting for my word. We're here to help you, Rhea. Tell us what to do."

I smiled grimly. "Go home, Bas—"

>*Rhea ...*<

I drew in a sharp shuddering breath and felt a strange stirring in my gut and crotch. I dropped the cup and spilled what was left of the soyka on the floor. The woman's voice inside my head had returned.

>*You're part of us now ... don't be afraid ... they left their essence inside you ... we can communicate from anywhere now ...*<

Bas touched my arm gently, making me twitch. "You're not going to be sick, are you ...? You look like you've just seen a ghost."

>*Rhea, don't forget us ... we're here for you when you discover what you are ...*<

My hand flung to cover my mouth. What *was* I? What was I ... *becoming*?

I turned to Bas and saw his frightened expression. I knew he was reflecting my own.

"What's going on, Rhea?" he asked. "Something's really shaken you up. I've never seen you this way before."

"I've never felt this way before," I confessed and wondered why I was telling him this. I swallowed convulsively and gave him a small smile, ashamed at revealing myself to him like this. But I felt compelled to go on as he listened attentively. "Things are happening to me—in my head—that I can't explain and can't fix. I came out here to fix the things I messed up, but I'm only messing things up more. Now they think I'm an assassin for Eclipse. Chaos, maybe I am..." Maybe those voices I kept hearing in my head were part of some mind-jag and I really was an agent for them. Maybe *I was* The Rose! I heaved a breath and said in a low voice of dread, "I should turn myself in before I kill someone else."

Bas gave me a sad look and shook his head. "You really

are cracking up." His eyes met mine with sudden intensity. "Chaos, Rhea, this isn't the time to give up. You're onto something big, something that's going to blow this galaxy apart if it isn't stopped, and these people are trying to keep you from figuring it out. Don't let them succeed."

I grunted but said nothing. I was close to tears and kept swallowing them down.

"You need to keep using that incredibly intuitive mind of yours."

"It was my intuition that got me fired in the first place."

He said gently, "You told me earlier that you had a lead."

I let out a sharp self-mocking laugh. It came out in a half-sob. "Yeah, my supposed partner in crime." I sank my head into my hands. I was falling apart. "Some lead. Look what chasing after him got me into."

Bas stunned me by gripping both my arms tightly, forcing me to look up. In the three years we'd been friends, he'd never had the courage to touch me. "Listen, Rhea," he said, eyes searching mine. "You really need my help this time. And I'll gladly give it. You know that. But you have to ask, Rhea. You have to ask."

I nodded, dropping my gaze from him again, and clasping my hands together in a tight knot. "I'm asking."

Θ

"So, what do you have for me, Benny?" I said, slouching in my pilot's chair with one leg up, leaning on the console, and foot tapping to the reverberating surf of Metallica's "Enter Sandman." I was waiting for a communication from Bas, who followed me in his *twin-V* as we jacked the particle-stream toward the 70 Virginis system.

"In response to your request for additional blood work, I have indeed found something, Rhea," Benny informed me over the booming music. "Good hunch."

"Yeah, terrific."

"It's nothing major, though," Benny assured me. "Your

DNA is still entirely human, no observable changes from last time I checked. But you are now somehow harboring three additional amino acids I have yet to identify."

I jerked up in my seat. "What's their possible effect?" Could they be what made me hear that voice in my head?

"Nothing conclusive, Rhea."

"Terrific." I slumped back in my chair. My visitors had left me more visitors. And how was it possible that my DNA was human, I considered. If I was half-Eosian, then why didn't I have an Eosian-human DNA mixture? Why would my mother lie to me about something like that? She wouldn't have purposely hurt me with a lie like that. It had to be true. But DNA couldn't lie, could it?

I cleared my throat. "Did you by any chance get a sample of water?"

"Yes, I did, Rhea."

"And you still have the snakes you pulled out of me," I said with a swallow.

"Yes, Rhea."

"Eh … is it possible that … well, could you test for—I mean—if the water or the snakes have some aphrodisiac chemical in them?"

"Why?"

Only Benny would ask that question, I thought with a faint rueful smile. Any other AI wouldn't need to know. "I … well, I … um, I felt …" I couldn't get it out, not even to Benny, and I blushed, passing my hand across my face with a shake of my head.

"Well, we know that the water contains several narcotics. And those amino acids may have some connection to oxytocin receptors. It's possible that the water or the snakes contain some neuropeptide stimulators or phenylethylamines. Something that would stimulate your limbic system. But I'd wager it's the snakes that made you horny, though."

I broke into a laugh, relieved that Benny understood. "Thanks, Benny." A signal from Bas's *twin-V* made me jump. "Keep researching it, Benny," I instructed. "I want to know what those amino acids are doing inside me." I activated the holo-com and Bas's image appeared.

"Any luck with the hit list?"

"Not yet," I said wearily and glanced at the info-pod in my hand. "But I'm really close. I can feel it." I sighed. "I'll let you know when I've decoded it, Bas."

He nodded. "You look tired. Get some sleep."

"I will." I nodded and forced a thin smile of reassurance. "Really." I frowned at the info-pod. Who was on that hit list?

Bas shook his head at me then signaled off. I turned back to the info-pod and slowly turned it in my hand. I stared at it with narrowing eyes. My eyes stung from exhaustion, and I knew I needed to get some sleep. But I was so close—Wait!

Bas had mentioned that the encryption was linked to harmonics. I was suddenly dead sure of what it was: the music of the spheres. But which sphere? Which planet's signature had been chosen? Considering that Serge was headed for the 70 Virginis system, I decided to start there.

I had already instructed Benny to research the system for habitable planets, including those that belonged to the Galactic Order and those that didn't. Virgil 9 appeared the most likely choice. It was the second of two moons and a ring that orbited 70 Virginis-b, a gas giant about six times the size of Jupiter. Dubbed Goldilocks, the gas giant followed a fairly close though eccentric orbit around the G5 yellow-orange main sequence star, about fifty-nine light-years from Earth.

Virgil 9 was the size of Earth with its rotation locked by the giant's tidal forces, so that day and night lasted several weeks. Water in the atmosphere rained down on the cool night side, forming significant but temporary bodies of water. Then, in early daytime, the ponds evaporated, leaving behind a lifeless desert as the surface warmed to 85ºC.

The moon was home to the Ngu, a photosynthetic symbiotic organism of plant and animal. The Ngu had adapted to the moon's harsh ecological cycle. Most of them lived underground in cities that could withstand the extremes of flood and hot drought. Although the Ngu were generally considered aloof and strangely uncouth, they had joined the Galactic Order several standard galactic years ago and were now part of the galactic community.

"Benny," I said, "I need you to research the harmonic ratio of 70 Virginis-b's orbit around 70 Virginis."

I almost nodded off as Benny did his work. But he finally delivered me the information and after several attempts, I hit the jackpot: the file opened. I had my prize.

The file addressed to The Rose from the Ancient One read:

"I have given a standing order to all Nihilist Splinter Leaders to indirectly cede to The Rose via Splinter Leader A'ler. A'ler is to remain your main contact and has explicit instructions and the authority to carry out your orders above all others. Only she knows your secret code. Once you've carried out your mission below, you will receive further instructions." It seemed that no one except the Ancient One knew who The Rose was. And according to this message it wasn't A'ler! Below the order lay a table that listed names with holos, descriptions, and addresses. I breathed faster, recognizing it as the hit list mentioned in the cover communiqué. This was indeed a cookbook for slaughter, a list of targets for assassination by The Rose. Rashomon was at the top of the list. Of course. And just below Rashomon's image—I seized in a breath—was my own! Ka was right. I was a target too.

I forced my attention back to Rashomon's image.

Beside his image, name, and address, I read under 'function': *seer (unlocker of future portals)*. There was nothing under the 'rationale/instruction' column, as though *unlocker of future portals* was self-explanatory and there was nothing extraordinary about a blind seer. I glanced below Rashomon's holo to my image. The name appeared below it: Rhea Hawke, human, Neon City. Next to my name I read: *nexus-portal*, then *ghost(?)* to the right of it. Instructions were even more baffling: *highly volatile and dangerous; do not approach—report to Splinter Leader; to be delivered to the Ancient One.* It seemed I was being saved for some other purpose, at least initially.

I pursed my lips in sullen thought. Serge had left me for dead on the frozen lake of Uma 1. Perhaps he still thought me dead. That might work in my favor, I contemplated grimly and turned back to the holo list.

The third target was a male Ngu, named Shlsh Shle She, residing in—surprise—Virgil 9 in the 70 Virginis system. I blinked with sudden discomfort. Why was that name familiar? It stirred confusing and strong feelings of excitement and dread. I shook them off and continued my study of the document.

According to it, Shlsh's function was: *traitor and undermining Eclipse security, confirmed anti-Nihilist.* I recalled that Asphalios had used the term Nihilist in connection with the Vos, before he'd been silenced. I found the instructions even more intriguing: *kill and wipe all files clean, destroy system, premises, and all links.* So, this Shlsh was probably an information broker, and it sounded like he'd hacked into Eclipse's systems. I brought a hand to my mouth; my lips were trembling. This was just what I was after.

Then my face tightened into a snarl. It was also, no doubt, what Serge was after. And he was five days ahead of me.

TWENTY-EIGHT

We had pierced the 70 Virginis dust disk some time ago and just now reached our destination: Virgil 9, one of the moons of the ringed gas giant, 70 Virginis-b. Virgil City, where Shlsh lived, was presently baking under daytime, I noted as I peered out portside to the parched desert below then shifted my gaze toward the city ahead, rippling in the heat.

"Wonderful," I muttered. "No doubt, another sought-after vacation spot. I'll have to note it in my list of holiday locations right under EpsEri 2 and Mar Delena." I flicked on my com. "Bas, you on control?"

His holo appeared before me. "I'm here. What do you have in mind, Rhea?"

"We're on an approach vector for Virgil City," I said, peering out my starboard side to the vast desert below. "I've traced the signal of our friend, Serge, there and that's where Shlsh resides. It'll be a scorcher. Don't forget your sunblock."

"Right," Bas said with a wry grin. "Eighty-five degrees is a bit much for me. I'll follow you in."

Θ

"All I'm asking for is permission to land in your spaceport to conduct a transaction with one of your citizens, a Shlsh Shle She," I argued with the Virgil City spaceport authority.

"Your ID does not match any authorized Galactic Order member," the squealing voice slobbered, as if he-she had a mouth full of wet food. "And we register that Shlsh is not expecting a Jane Raptor."

I expelled a long breath of frustration. I'd used my alias, Jane Raptor, in case they knew about my murder charge. Rhea Hawke wasn't exactly popular right now. "You going to hold that against me?" I quipped, thinking fast. "Not everyone belongs to the Galactic Order. I'm from Borr. My real name is R'lan—"

"We don't permit shapeshifters here, creon," the mushy voice said tartly.

Chaos! I'd never heard of whole species being excluded from a planet before. "Well, I …" I was running out of options.

"This is Basileus," Bas piped in, sounding more authoritative than I could imagine him. "I'm an Enforcer with the Galactic Guardians. I can vouch for this shapeshifter. She's with me."

"We don't care. Enforcers are not welcome either."

I curbed a smile, imagining Bas's frustration. The Ngus were coming close to breaking some galactic laws of interplanetary relations, I thought. But, then again, they weren't famous for being charming either.

"We're on an important mission and need to speak with Shlsh Shle She on an urgent case, no questions asked," Bas went on forcefully. "This is a Code-1 Priority. You need to cease this detestable tactic and let us in, or I'll have to report you to

Guardian Central Headquarters. I'll transmit my Enforcer ID to you right now."

A brief moment of silence followed, then the static opened up again, and the slurred voice conceded. "Very well, Basileus. You and that ... shapeshifter ... are free to land. Look for the large dome."

I made out the city ahead. It resembled a metalloid circuit board with a series of crisscrossing corrugations and thrusting outcrops of rough organic material. The city was an island patchwork of dull gray-green with filigrees of gold and copper in a sea of undulating desert sands.

The taciturn Ngu instructed us toward a large translucent greenish dome that yawned open like a mouth, releasing tendrils of smoke or mist. Quelling a brief inexplicable hesitation, I piloted Benny inside, followed by Bas's *twin-V*. I felt my stomach knot in the discomfort of déjà vu as I blindly flew Benny through the dark smoke and knew what I'd eventually see when my eyes finally adjusted. The dome opened up into a vast multi-level spaceport with dozens of landing bays arranged in stacks of oval disks. The Ngu directed us to two adjoining bays on one of the stacked disks inside a matrix of tendrils of sparking light. As I gazed around in fascination, I was suddenly reminded of a giant chloroplast. We'd entered the subterranean world of the Ngu, a photosynthetic race of beings.

Once Benny was secure, I shrugged into my Great Coat, checked my holstered MEC, then pushed open the hatch. I recoiled and blinked hard at the pungent smell. A constant throb reverberated throughout the port, background to the pulsing thrum and clatter of giant machines that hovered and glided along the meandering platforms. An organic mist hung in the air like suspended grime, likely the source of the rank smell that assaulted my nose. It drifted and coalesced into a fluid latticework that resembled a fluttering gossamer cobweb. I realized that the sparks of light I'd seen from my ship were part of the mist and wondered at their purpose.

In a sudden flash, I knew that I'd been here before. In a dream. Wearing a sleeveless, long, flowing dress ... looking out in wonder at this very scene …

Shaking my head to clear it, I descended Benny's ladder part way then hopped down from the middle rung. As my feet hit the floor, I skidded on something slippery and nearly fell. I caught my balance by grabbing Benny's ladder rung and studied the burnished metalloid-like floor. It was covered in patches of iridescent slime. The whole place shimmered like the inside of an organism. I leaned forward with narrowed eyes to focus on the nearest wall. It was laced with a fluid network of translucent tubes through which a constant stream of iridescent fluid flowed.

Quelling an inexplicable dread, I dug into my pocket and fished out a soyka gum, waiting for Bas to secure his ship and join me. I watched him approach, holding his hand up against his nose. "Chaos!" he mumbled beneath his hand. "How'd you do that, fly us in? I was totally blinded. I had to follow Benny's signal." Then he added, "And what's that funky smell—?"

I was about to stuff the gum into my mouth when Bas, distracted with the surroundings of the spaceport, slipped on a slime patch and did a crazy dance to keep from falling, including grabbing my arm.

I held onto Benny's rung to keep from being pulled down and helped Bas steady himself. Then I added with an amused half-smile, "Watch out for the slime."

"Thanks." He frowned, letting go of me. "It's everywhere." He cast a nervous gaze around us at the spacious spaceport and added, "Where are all the workers? There's no one here."

I pushed the gum into my mouth and bit down on the spongy mash, savoring the soyka. "It's all automated. Run by AIs," I informed him. "These guys are big fans of AI and one of Mar Delena's best customers."

Bas eyed me with a grimace of distaste.

I tilted my head with a smirk, eyebrows rising coyly. "What? You didn't know that?"

He responded, "Why do you chew that shit? It's just a cheap stimulant, you know."

I grinned sideways at him. "You're just jealous because it makes you go blenoid. Doesn't affect me that way." I blew out a bubble, let it pop loudly, then inhaled it back in. After a terse wave of my arm to dismiss his remark, I strode toward the exit signs with confident steps.

"That's a matter of opinion," Bas muttered as he picked his way and slid behind me, almost falling. "That's because you're an addict," he said more loudly. "You can't stop."

I tossed him a withering glance over my shoulder. "I could stop anytime. I just don't want to."

Bas shrugged as he came up beside me. "Sure." Then, as if out of nervousness, he continued murmuring, feet slipping occasionally. "The walls are strange looking. Some organic-synth mixture, I'd say ..."

I glanced at the gray-green walls again, noting how they shimmered like burnished metalloid cast as fibers of a plant. The smooth slime was intermixed with nipples and grooves of rough, less shiny material that resembled bark. A network of tubes that overlay the rough material pulsed with flowing iridescent material: xylem and phloem. I was left with the impression of being inside a giant breathing plant-like organism.

Then I saw them. Bas was still looking at the ceiling when I grabbed his arm to restrain him and slowed, nudging my head forward to point out three Ngus sliding close to the exit doors.

Bas seized in his breath. Yes, they were magnificently ugly, I thought, forcing my face from twisting with revulsion. Like huge pulsing amoebas with pseudopods for arms and legs and long whiplike tentacles, they left slime trails behind them as they moved. I couldn't make out any eyes or a mouth, but I assumed that the tentacles served as hearing and sight sensors, and I knew they were capable of speaking because I'd spoken to one of them on my ship's com earlier.

"Follow my lead," I said, stepping forward. Abruptly, the Ngus shrieked and dispersed. They slid more quickly than I'd expected to the far walls and—merged into them! I stared and couldn't make out their forms from the scabrous walls.

"They form a symbiotic connection with the AI organic-synth walls," Bas informed me in a droll voice. I turned to him with a frowning half-smile of curious astonishment. "What? You didn't know that?" he returned sarcastically. I sneered at him and continued past the exit into a large hallway. "They're plants, you know," he added, coming along beside me again.

"Yeah, I know," I answered coolly. *And did you know that they don't need to eat, Rhea?* Benny added through my ear com. *They live symbiotically with a virus that procures the food for them in return for being its host.* "And did you know that they live symbiotically with a virus that feeds them so they don't have to eat?" I repeated, eyebrows lifting and quelling a smirk.

Bas looked at me suspiciously. "No, I didn't know that." He frowned. "Funny that you do … Do you think they're all part of one huge organism, then?"

That was a good question, I thought, not bothering to answer, because I knew he'd answer it himself eventually. I led us down a well-lit scabrous hallway that resembled the pith of a tree. It looked terribly familiar and nudged a fragment of a memory that didn't belong to me: of lying with my back on the floor and Serge looking down at me with concern.

"No, more like a huge autopoietic colony," Bas continued, pulling me back to reality. "Individuals budding off once in awhile to do those duties that require individual effort, then returning to the motherfold for … whatever they need. Sustenance. Comforts."

That was good, I thought, shaking off the distracting mental flash and gathering my thoughts as Bas went silent for a moment. If what Bas said was true, then it would explain Shlsh's unique position as information broker. He'd essentially have the entire planet's sentient AI-organic community at his disposal for information gathering and compilation.

I'd been gazing down the hallway when another image—a memory that wasn't mine—struck me so vividly that I inhaled sharply and staggered to a halt: of colliding into Serge—a stranger to me—falling to the floor, then instantly overcome by an intense attraction for him as he leaned over me with concern.

I shook my head to clear it and swallowed down the

complex emotion that surged through me and stirred my loins. I felt a perplexing thrill at the notion of falling instantly in love with a stranger and abruptly remembered what Serge had told me once: of how he'd first met me here by knocking me down … in a dream, that is. Why was I re-enacting it through these minor hallucinations?

"You okay?" Bas cut into my trance. I fought for composure and nodded brusquely. "You're not hearing voices in your head again, are you?" he asked with an uneasy smile. It came out a grimace.

I swallowed several times, not sure what was going on. "I'm fine," I said tersely. "No voices." Just visions. I was definitely cracking up.

Bas shrugged, satisfied, and added, "So, how do we find this Shlsh guy?"

That triggered my memory of where I'd first heard Shlsh's name: Serge had mentioned it, when he'd described how he'd dreamt of how he'd first met me here: just outside Shlsh's. Okay, so I was having visions inspired by conversations I'd had with Serge. I needed to get a grip! This place was getting to me.

"The Ngus weren't very helpful—they didn't tell us where to find him," Bas complained. "In fact those Ngus looked pretty scared of us. They sure don't like shapeshifters or Enforcers."

"Yeah," I said, half listening to Bas. My eyes narrowed with suspicion. That had concerned me as well, and I wondered where in Virgil City Serge was lurking.

"Why didn't they tell us?" Bas said.

"I think we're going to find out soon," I replied in a subdued voice. Then I spotted what I was looking for: what looked like a lift. The info-pod had been fairly specific in its directions. My own flat in Neon City had been clearly shown on a map and described with visual cues, so the Nihilist agent could find me. I was glad for the same information on this hunt. "This way," I pointed.

The wall irised open, and I stepped inside without hesitation. Bas gave me a skeptical look, then followed me in.

Instantly, it irised shut, and the floor gave out from under us. I felt my knees buckle, then I straightened and composed my face with a quick glance at Bas. A clammy wind washed past my face and hair as we hurtled down. I felt my heart race with thoughts of Serge. I knew he was here and deduced that my foolish visions were because I was thinking of him.

Then, as quickly as the lift descended, it stopped, and irised open. We walked unsteadily out into a hallway very similar to the one we'd just left many floors above. I pointed down the hall and led Bas to a large fibrous door. "This should be his control centre," I said, turning an inquiring look to Bas. "Should we knock?"

"I don't think that'll work," Bas said, frowning at the solid door. "He's one of the galaxy's most notorious information brokers. There seems to be nothing he can't acquire or that he's not willing to sell," Bas ended sourly. "I'd say that makes him one of the most sought-after targets in the galaxy."

I nodded solemnly. "Agreed."

Bas shuffled his feet nervously. "Then what are we doing here? It's obvious we can't get in and it doesn't look like they're going to let us in—"

I felt around the door for any impressions or depressions where I could find a disguised control panel and murmured, *"The person who says it cannot be done should not interrupt the person doing it*—old Chinese proverb."

Bas watched as I continued my search along the gnarled wall of slime and pitch. Something clicked and I stopped. A key pad revealed itself and I knew exactly what to key in: the harmonic formula for the song of Virgil 9 in its solar system.

The door creaked open and I flashed Bas a quick grin. We walked in.

Θ

We entered a huge room, blistering with the thrum and cacophony of static noise, chaotic chatter in alien dialects, and random noises. The room, which stretched up to a very high plasma-like ceiling, housed at least a hundred holos and even two-dimensional screens stacked in a chaotic semi-circle. They showed images of people doing various things, star systems, graphs and charts, news vids, and more.

At the centre stood a Ngu, his tentacles waving out toward us as if sniffing the air. Shlsh, I surmised.

"We've been waiting five days for you," the Ngu slurred in wet disdain.

I threw Bas a pointed glance at the words. How was it that he was expecting us? The Ngu had spoken through a set of wet folds that resembled a woman's genitals as they undulated in peristaltic waves. I felt my lips tighten and nose flare slightly in repulsion as the Ngu turned his slimy body from me to Bas, eying our Great Coats with his tentacles.

"Are you Shlsh?" I asked.

"I was expecting only one Enforcer, not two," he said wetly.

"I'm no longer an Enforcer," I corrected him.

"And you are?" Shlsh asked in a tone of disgust.

"Rhea Hawke."

He visibly flinched and backed away in alarm.

I jerked my hand to Bas to cut off the Ngu so he couldn't melt into the wall.

"He didn't tell me it would be *you*!" Shlsh scrambled back, looking for escape. "You're here to kill me!" His tentacles flicked fearfully from my MEC holstered in plain view on my thigh to Bas, now behind him, then back to me again.

"Hold on, Shlsh," I said with a quick puzzled glance at Bas. I held both my hands out to show him I wasn't going for my weapon. "We're only after information."

"Maybe *he* is." Shlsh pointed an appendage at Bas. "But *you're* here to kill me."

I stifled a smirk of bemused impatience and snarled, "I told you, I'm not here to kill you. Neither of us is. Why would you think I was going to kill you?" Then my eyes narrowed with suspicion. "What did you do?"

"I did nothing, except record the truth," he gurgled,

pouting with those shiny, rather obscene lips. "It was your grandmother."

"What?" I frowned with confusion and glanced again at Bas. He hiked a brow. I'd barely gotten used to the idea that my grandmother might still be alive; now she was popping up everywhere. "What did she do?"

"You don't know?" he exploded in a repulsive splutter. "You've got the brain of a blenoid!" I forced myself not to grimace and remembered that Ngus were known for their uncouth manners and crude language. "Your jagging grandmother's the one who started it all," he went on excitedly. "She brought them here, let them in."

"Who?"

"Are you brain-dead, girl?" He waved his varied limbs at me and spluttered. "Who else? The Vos, you blithering jagging blenoid!"

I stiffened and stared at Shlsh in disbelief. "B-but ... how ... d-did she ..." I stammered and heard my voice splinter.

"She's a soul-drifter, didn't you know, creon?" he snarled out, shiny lips flaring. I *did* know. "Your grandmother willed them here, stupid."

"The Gate Hallucination ..." I whispered.

"Finally. A sentient thought," he said. "She soul-drifted into the dreams of all those *portals* and made them create the Gate for the Vos." Shlsh shook his head. "He said you're a bit slow but I think that was generous."

"Who?" I demanded.

"He said you're resourceful and you'd break the code, which you must have done to be here, and you'd figure out a way inside too. But he said that otherwise you didn't know much and you're not awfully bright. I'd have to agree."

"Who?" I repeated impatiently.

"The one who sent you," Shlsh slurped. "Him, who came in that ship." Shlsh pointed to one of the many holos in his huge room. It depicted another part of the Virgil City spaceport, and I caught my breath. I recognized the elegant long curved ship of the *scimitar* class in one of the landing bays and my pulse leapt.

It was Ka's private shuttle. The one Serge had stolen. I looked at it carefully and recognized significant scoring and burns on the starboard side. A result of being fired upon, no doubt. A clash with other members of the fractioning Eclipse, perhaps. While I'd had my adventures, Serge had had his.

"He was *here*?" I asked, betraying some alarm. I caught Bas looking at me in confusion, but I kept my gaze fixed on the Ngu.

"Of course not, blenoid pus for brains. Only you managed to get in, remember? But I spoke with him."

"What did he say?"

"Like I told you, idiot! That you would break in."

"We already know that," I said testily. "What else?"

"That I better give you what you want or you'll melt me into shit soup like you did all those others."

All those others! What kind of dreadful tale was Serge spinning about me? He was worse than the Schiss. I felt anger flame up my face and my hands balled into tight fists. "And what is it I want?"

"Chaos! You don't know?" he shrieked. "You really *are* brain-dead!"

"What did he *say* I wanted?" I quickly rephrased, controlling my frustration.

"What everyone else wants. My information on the Vos attack plan. Proof of the intent of the Nihilists."

Chaos! This was exactly what I was after. With an excited glance at Bas, I repeated, "Nihilists?" I kept hearing that word used in connection with the Vos. Asphalios had used it to describe all the Eclipse shapeshifters aboard the *Ulysses*. I'd concluded that they were an elite death squad, a specially trained group of shapeshifter assassins on the Vos payroll. Like The Rose. Like A'ler. Was Serge one of them? Then why hadn't he already killed Shlsh? Had he really needed me to get in?

Shle didn't bother to answer, and I didn't pursue it. I had a better question to ask him.

"And what is that?" I asked, voice shaking with dread. "What's their intent?"

"To annihilate the human race, creon shit for brains!"

I felt the blood drain from my face, then glanced briefly at Bas. He stared at me, wide-eyed, mouth gaping.

Shlsh gurgled in disgust. "Ignoramus. Suppose good help is hard to find in the galaxy. He must have been desperate to enlist you as his agent. Must be your singular talent for breaking and entering."

"I'm not his jagging employee," I snarled with a scowl and a cursory self-conscious glance at Bas. A nagging discomfort nudged its way through my frustration: there was something I was missing, I thought. What was I missing?

"But my deal was only with him and his trusted employee," Shlsh said snidely. "No one else. If you're not his trusted employee, then I can't deal with you."

"Fine," I bit out. "I'm his trusted employee. What do you need?"

"Besides a million credits in my bank account, I need proof. I'll need the info-pod that has the file you used to find me."

I glared at Shlsh for a moment. I crossed my arms over my breasts and narrowed my eyes at him. "I'm here and I got in. That should be proof enough that I have the info-pod and used it to find you."

"Not good enough. How do I know you didn't just steal it from the person who did all the work of decrypting the file? I'll need to open the file using your decryption because it wasn't me who encrypted it," he insisted. "It'll show your personal signature ... that part's my handiwork." He made a disgusting movement with his genital mouth. I surmised that it was a smug smile. "I was involved in compiling the original list—had no idea I'd be on it eventually, although I should have guessed. No doubt they discovered the virus worm embedded in my system that tagged theirs." He was probably scowling, but I couldn't tell. I knew he was right, remembering the description of Shle on The Rose's hit list: *underminer of Eclipse security*. "Anyway, I put a bug into the original file to track its users."

Quite clever, I thought, firming my lips.

"Very well, then," I submitted, rethinking my options. I pulled the info-pod from my Great Coat inner pocket and with a nod to Bas to approach me, handed it to Bas. I turned back to Shlsh. "Before we give this to you, I have a few questions. Who encrypted the file if it wasn't you?"

"Like I would know that?" Shlsh gushed. "Even if I did, that would be for sale, creon."

It was worth a try, I thought. "Then how do you know you're on the hit list?"

Shle made a repulsive noise, which I figured was a snide laugh. "I have access to the vault, Eclipse's most secure system, and through it, their secret codes and ciphers."

I locked that away for future use. Handy little worm-virus, I thought. "You're designated an anti-Nihilist. What do you say to that?"

"Anyone who isn't a Nihilist is an anti-Nihilist," he sprayed out. "The garbage-collector down the street is an anti-Nihilist. Doesn't mean anything."

I knew he was being evasive, but didn't press him. "So, where is he now, my supposed employer?"

"Somewhere on the planet." Shlsh sniffed. "Why should I know?"

I surged forward and drew my MEC. Shlsh visibly cringed as I pointed it at his face.

"Rhea!" Bas shouted fearfully and lunged for my arm.

I twitched out of his reach and kept my predatory gaze on Shlsh, MEC pointed at the centre of his massive body. "I expect the best information broker to know everything, especially the whereabouts of a man he is dealing with, a dangerous man," I said to Shlsh.

Shlsh did that obscene movement with his mouth again, which I interpreted to be a smile. "He's in the caf in Sector 9."

"I thought you didn't need to eat," I said, exchanging a glance with Bas.

"We don't, but offworlders do. This place is used by lots of them; high brow discreet meetings."

I'd heard that about Virgil City. I could not fathom that it had been chosen by officials and politicians for non-official meetings, meetings that 'didn't happen.' Virgil City had also, as a result, become something of a red-light district for the wealthy, and I recalled the story Ka told me of the young lad who'd watched his mother and her wealthy lover get melted in one of their parlors.

"The caf's next to the Photophosphorylation Section of our Photosynthetic Reaction Centre." He waved one of his appendages, and the centre screen lit up with a moving map that led us to the small room. I immediately spotted Serge, dressed in loose tan trousers, charcoal crewneck sweater, and a brown flight jacket, and still looking suave despite a few days growth on his face. He sat at a bench alone, nursing a frothy orange drink alongside two other offworlders, a Xhix and a Badowin. "Guess he's hungry. Having a carbohydrate shake."

I slid the MEC back into my holster and nodded. "You'll give the information we seek to my colleague, who will arrange payment." I waved my hand brusquely toward Bas, who nodded at Shlsh with a puzzled glance at me. "I have some urgent business to take care of with my employer," I ended, then leaned close to Bas, and whispered, "Once you get the information from him and confirm it, find me in the caf. I might need back-up." Bas nodded. I turned back to Shlsh and said, "Excuse me, I must go. Nice doing business with you." Then I sprinted out of the Ngu's sanctuary, Great Coat flying behind me.

TWENTY-NINE

He must have seen me coming. When I burst into the caf, MEC sweeping the room in a two-handed grip, Serge was already gone. His half-drunk drink sat on the counter. The Xhix and the Badowin surged to their feet and cowered, staring at me. The Xhix instantly turned blue and gave off a pungent acrid smell.

"Where did the human go?" I pointed my MEC at them.

The Xhix pointed shakily to the far exit. I rushed through it. I caught the shadow of a man just rounding a corner and pelted after him. Within moments, I could make Serge out and took a one-handed shot. It went wide.

"Halt!" I shouted and shot again. Just as I did, a loud explosion thundered behind me and a putrid buffeting wind knocked me forward.

I scrambled to my feet and instantly knew what had happened. The explosion had come from Shlsh's sanctuary: Shlsh and Bas were dead.

I felt sick. My breaths stuttered out in panting wails. I'd done it again; killed my partner. I was about to run back when I caught Serge's disappearing figure. I couldn't help Bas, I reasoned; as for the bastard who was responsible—rage boosted me into a wild run. I felt the surge of adrenalin from the Great Coat and rounded a corner, spotting Serge again. I shot repeatedly in desperate hatred, missing every time. He glanced back and I caught his pale face. Then he wrenched open a large fibrous door and disappeared behind it as it swung shut on its own.

It couldn't be that easy, I thought, seeing where he'd gone. I recognized the waste disposal area from the map I'd seen earlier. There was no way out. Unless you were crushed up waste, that is.

Θ

He was trapped, with nowhere to go. I had him. I let a wicked smile slide across my face and opened the door, nostrils flaring at the cloying assault to my nose. The place reeked of rotting compost and fermenting vegetation. The loud thrum of engines clattered and roared in chaotic cacophony. The noise came mostly from the metalloid columns of cylindrical waste disposal units that rose as if grown from the floor to the ceiling. Both ceiling and floor were made of the same soft pith-like and dimpled material that filled the hallways. I walked in, boots sinking into the soft floor as if it were a thick shag carpet. Then I spotted Serge. He'd run to the far end of the room.

He turned and met my gaze head on.

"Rhea!" he shouted, obviously feigning delighted surprise.

I knew he'd recognized me earlier during my pursuit. I'd smelled his spike of excitement. Now I felt him emit yet another smell, a rather pleasant mixture of fermenting fruit and young wine, and felt a thrill surge through me in response. I didn't show it and pointed my MEC steadily at his chest with my lips pursed in venomous resolution. "*A hunting dog will eventually lose its life on the mountain—*old Chinese proverb."

He didn't appear concerned. He threw a casual gaze around us with a sweeping hand. "This is where we first met, Rhea … in my diverse," he said, eyes twinkling like galaxies in an infinite universe.

Yeah … his damned dream world, I thought with disgust. His diverse. Why did it look so familiar, then? Like a déjà vu … like a dream.

"Where your other self first smiled at me," Serge went on. "And we first kissed … You might have dreamt it." He smiled with sudden enlightenment. "Of course you did, Rhea. Because it was love at first sight. *You* did that, in your dreams, after you met me in this diverse. Made her fall in love with me."

Eyes narrowing, I raised my head and set my mouth in a tight snarl. "Funny, she didn't do that to *me*," I responded with a sneer. My hand closed more firmly on my MEC. It was sweating. I wasn't about to let him take me down some made-up maudlin journey. "You're coming back with me, Serge … or should I call you V'ser? Or The Rose," I said, emphasizing the latter. He didn't flinch, nor did he apparently understand my last accusation. "The Guardians have a few questions for you about your involvement in Eclipse assassinations. You had a nerve taking another man's identity, assuming his life. Do you even speak French?"

His wry smile opened to a jackal's grin. "Not a word, *ma chérie.*"

I smirked. "You took quite a chance that the real Serge Bastion didn't find you and report you as a fake."

"The galaxy is pretty large, Rhea."

"I found you though, didn't I?"

He grinned like a fox. "I knew you'd find me, Rhea. I knew you'd sniff me out amid the jetsam and flotsam of the galaxy. You're an Enforcer, after all, even when you aren't one. And quite a skilled one, thanks to your *tecks* ..."

Did he not know that I was part Eosian? I wasn't about to tell him.

"But I knew you'd find me for another reason. Because you can't resist me, Rhea. Your desire for me is stronger than any rational feeling of justice you might ideally be motivated with," he said, grinning smugly. "That's why you're really here."

That arrogant bastard! I raised my MEC and marched forward in brash steps. As I did, he spiked out a smell of excitement, like burnt toast—

The floor gave way under me and I let out a startled yelp. Not again!

Serge barked out a startled victorious laugh at my over-confidence as I plummeted. I felt the drag of my coat save me from a lethal fall some twenty meters down and landed on my feet with a hard thud. The weaker left leg collapsed, like before, and I felt a sharp twinge of pain. But I didn't think I'd broken it. I might have sprained my ankle though. I could still put some weight on it, but it throbbed with tender pain. I was standing in an empty garbage chute.

Damn Serge. Like before, my hubris had got the better of me: I realized too late that the spike of excitement I had smelled in him wasn't at seeing me approach him, but at my walking into his trap. Then I thought of my gun and quickly scanned the shaft floor—

I heard his amused laughter above me and looked up.

He peered over the edge at me. "There's another Chinese proverb that says: *Don't chase a dog into a blind alley—it might snap at you*," Serge said. He waved my MEC in his hand for me to see.

"Looking for this?" Was it all about my MEC after all? "Your first mistake was to say you were a shapeshifter, Rhea. The Ngus really don't like them. So, it wasn't hard for me to get them to help me. They were the ones who suggested I lead you here …"

I glared back at Serge. Damn them for their prejudice, I thought, forgetting about my own. The irony was that *he* was the shapeshifter.

"Ah, the Great Coat of the Enforcer," he went on. "Did they give it back to you or did you have to steal it?"

I sneered in response. He was fishing again.

"Listen, Rhea," he said more sincerely, "If you take the coat off, I'll lower a line and you can climb up. I've heard about you and that coat … I know that under normal circumstances you could leap up this height with its help. But I'd advise against it. I heard you cry out when you hit bottom …"

I hadn't been aware that I had.

"And I see even now that you're favoring your left leg, so your trajectory will be rather tricky, considering—"

Damn him! I leapt. And felt a spike of pain shoot up my leg. I was going to make it. I heard his shout of surprise. But he recovered swiftly and got out a shot. I felt the slam of the MEC wave hit me square in the chest, and I blacked out in mid-air.

THIRTY

I moaned awake and forced my heavy eyelids open. I was lying on a soft spongy floor in a dark room. My wrists were shackled to cuffs and long chains attached to a wall behind me at shoulder height. The damp heat didn't help my wooziness, I thought, fighting to clear my head. I was still in the waste disposal area, I concluded from the stench of old compost and rotting vegetation.

As I struggled up to stand, my lungs burned from the concussion wound of my MEC. But I was alive. The Great Coat, which had saved my life yet again, was lying in a heap on the floor, next to me but just out of reach. Serge, who'd been squatting nearby in contemplation, stood up and approached. He'd taken his jacket off and was no longer holding my MEC. I finally spotted it discarded carelessly on the floor next to my Great Coat.

"Hello, sleeping beauty," he said, closing the space between us and smiling at me with rakish eyes. "Your eyes really *are* hazel." Serge laughed to himself. He seemed to know what puzzled me. "I found out about you and the MEC, so I set it on universal stun. Seems to have done the job." He smiled rather smugly. I returned him a tight-lipped miserable smile. He'd certainly done his homework on my MEC.

"Why am I still alive?" I tugged at the chains.

His smirk turned wistful, and he leaned his face so close to mine that I felt his breath on me. We stood inches apart. I swallowed with sudden emotion and commanded my breaths not to stutter. Damn him for his effect on me.

"You mean, despite all your efforts to get yourself killed?" he teased.

"Why are you keeping me alive?" I rephrased.

He leaned closer. "Maybe to kiss you," he breathed out in a husky voice and brought his lips so close to mine I trembled with anticipation. Drawn into his thunderstorm eyes like a dust particle in a hurricane, I knew right away I was lost. His lips were a magnet. To touch them with mine would be like coming home.

Heart slamming and cheeks flaming, I twitched my face aside.

With a forlorn expression he drew a trembling finger across my cheek, caressing me, and emitting his heady scent of musk and strawberries. I jerked away and he withdrew his hand with a sigh. "As for what I want," he continued, stepping back, "I just needed to get you not pointing a gun at me so we could have a civilized discussion."

"What's there to discuss," I said grimly. "I know you're The Rose."

He looked genuinely bewildered. "The Rose?"

"You used me again. This time to kill Shlsh. And you killed my partner—"

"That wasn't me," Serge cut in, defensive. "If you mean the explosion, I wasn't part of that. It was probably A'ler's doing again." Could it be that A'ler was The Rose without her own brother knowing it? Then he shook his head with rueful thoughts. "Listen, Rhea, I wasn't involved in setting you up to kill Rashomon either. I didn't know—"

"Then why were you there?" I snapped. "Like you're here now?"

"I told you, to prevent the killings."

"But you said you didn't know," I bit out with a disdainful sneer.

"All right." He sighed, meeting my challenging gaze with steady eyes. "I knew something was going to happen to Rashomon. But I had no idea it involved you. Believe me, I was surprised to see you there."

I remembered the shocked expression on his pale face in the Paradise City hallway. At the time I'd concluded that it was in response to my still being alive after the explosion. "You were with A'ler just before I was," I said. "Don't deny it. I smelled you on her."

He smiled bitterly and ran his hand over his bristled face. "Yes, I was there," he admitted. "I was trying to convince my sister not to pursue her insane plan. But she told me that she'd already initiated it, starting with Rashomon's assassination." The MEC and I were already on our way to A'ler by then, and A'ler obviously knew about Rashomon's perverse interest in exotic weapons. She had also, no doubt, banked on my ignorance of it. "A'ler didn't tell me how or who," Serge went on. "And I didn't ask. I was too busy convincing her not to lock me up."

If Serge was telling the truth, then A'ler had played us both against each other. I suspected that she was The Rose and that the cover message to her as custodian was a decoy to throw any spies off … like me. But Serge had lied to me constantly since we'd met. Why would he stop now? Besides, he was her brother, son of U'clid—whom I'd killed with my eyes. It didn't really matter who The Rose was ...

I swallowed, my mind casting back to Rashomon's death, and felt my lips tighten with guilt. "She sabotaged my MEC with a Q-bomb," I blurted out. Damn him! I couldn't help telling him everything. Serge had a way of drawing out the truth from me.

He nodded solemnly. "My sister knew about your second MEC; she's very clever. All the Nihilists are."

So, Serge wasn't with the elite Nihilists. That explained why he hadn't been able to get into Shlsh's secure centre and had to wait for me. And why he didn't know what I was talking about when I mentioned the Nihilists' assassin code name. A'ler kept her secrets.

"The Nihilists want to keep our two worlds apart, or at least be the only ones to control who goes in and out," Serge went on. "That means destroying what now controls the openings."

"Is that what V'mer was doing when he Dusted me?" I laughed bitterly.

"Well, no," Serge said sourly. "There's more to it with my brother. Our father was a Nihilist, one of the original members of the migration."

I swallowed. My first victim in Serge's family. He had many reasons to hate me. "The migration from Borr?"

"No, *to* Borr from our diverse. V'mer wanted revenge. V'mer wanted to finish what he'd already started in my—" He stopped himself and shook his head as if to clear it of a great sadness. "Let's just say it was personal with him, and he used a great excuse of eliminating a *purtul*, a *ghost*, even. You," he ended, hiking his brow at me.

Yes, I was considered a *ghost* by whoever had put the hit list together. So, it was personal with V'mer. That much I'd figured. What about Serge?

"The Nihilists must be stopped, Rhea," he said, eyes flashing with sudden conviction. Why did he want to stop them? My heart pounded with hope. His eyes melted into dark pools. "While I find it so alluring to be with you this way ... before you and I ..." He trailed off with a maudlin smile, then continued matter-of-factly, "I can't throw away my whole diverse." He sighed, eyes searching deep into mine. "I can't lose sight of my mission here."

My heart raced. "Mission?" What was *his* mission?

He smirked. "Rhea, the Enforcer, to the end. Even after the Guardians dismissed you, you're still asking questions. I like that about you. The dedication, the persistence. I'm talking about our original mission with humanity, Rhea." He studied me for a moment then reflected, "Who would have thought that the answers to our most compelling questions lay with a puny biped race on some backwater planet on an obscure arm of the Milky Way. It was the great experiment."

I straightened my back and flashed him an intense look. "What are you after?"

"What does anyone want? A home, Rhea."

Earth again? Wasn't the galaxy big enough? Why did everyone keep wanting Earth as a home? First it was the Eosians, who claimed to be the ancient civilization of Atlantis. Now it was these shapeshifters, who had no home. Did they also have a claim from some distant past? Serge had mentioned a migration *to* Borr.

"I know all about your collusion with the Vos," I said. "How they're systematically destroying humans, starting with our spiritual leaders. I know what the Nihilists intend. That's not a mission. It's annihilation."

He looked sad for a moment and stroked his stubbled cheeks. "We're all on a mission, Rhea. Yours is to preserve the galaxy; mine is to change it."

"By killing all humans?"

"You understand so little, Rhea," he said, shaking his head sadly at me. "It's only the *Nihilist* Vos who are killing humans—" He cut himself off then sighed, thinking he'd said too much, and studied his hands with a strange smile. *Nihilist* Vos? Nihilists were *Vos*? My heart slammed. "How I love the human form," he continued wistfully, almost sadly. "You're so sexually naïve."

No, that was just me.

"And so easily distracted by sex."

Yeah, that was humanity. Then it all came together and struck me hard like a MEC concussion missal. He'd as much as told me that he was more than a shapeshifter seeking vengeance for the murder of his father and brother. He was much more. I felt my eyes widen in a flash of insight that made me want to vomit: "You're not just working for the Vos ... You *are* a Vos."

His mouth slid into a grim smile. "Full marks, for once. I'm surprised it took you this long to figure it out. You were smelling us out long before you even knew who we were." I shivered with the realization. That was why shapeshifters were doing the bidding of the Vos; they *were* Vos. "You had it all in front of you, Rhea. And with your abilities, too." He clicked his tongue in mock disappointment and shook his head.

The Dust after-effects and my sexual distraction had clouded my sense of smell, my sharp intuition, and my usual cool judgment. And he knew it. In fact he'd known exactly what he'd done, seducing me with his charm and his good looks and his intoxicating scent. The only remaining question was: why? What did he want with me? And what did the Vos want with Earth? The Vos had only visited two planets in the galaxy: Borrias to take the identity of the Borrs, and Earth, presumably to make their home. "You killed a man in cold blood ... just to assume his identity and to appropriate his house."

"You don't kill in cold blood?" he challenged, drawing closer and leaning his arm beside me against the wall. "You're an Enforcer. You kill all the time. And without remorse, it seems."

"Only criminals who also kill," I said tartly. "Murderers. Assassins. People like you."

"That might be *why* you kill. That's your justification to yourself. But the process is still the same. You still terminate a person's life in this universe through violent means and against his or her will." He let an eyebrow rise. "I heard about Omicron 12. How is that any different from slaughter?"

I swallowed hard, caught in his piercing gaze. It wasn't, I conceded and thought of what Ka had told me on our journey to

Uma 1.

"And what do you call what you did to V'mer?"

I had no answer to that either and had to look away. Serge had every reason to want me dead. I'd killed two members of his family in cold blood.

"I didn't kill anyone, Rhea," Serge said. He hadn't said it scornfully, but I was on the defensive already and took offence.

"No, you just got others to kill for you," I said, eyes sharp on him again.

"Rov was cheating a customer on Moner 7 when I moved into his place in the Hive," Serge went on, ignoring my retort. "Unfortunately, it got complicated, and my sister saw the need to kill him to prevent his return. She did it for the good of our mission."

"And what was that? To seduce me? To get my MEC design?"

He looked embarrassed for a moment and straightened, backing away. I knew I'd guessed right. So, it *was* about the MEC. Did they intend to use it to kill off the human race?

"And to deliver you to my sister," he admitted.

"Wonderful," I said, thinking of the hit list I was on. "I'm intended for the Ancient One."

Serge nodded. "Yes, eventually. But, like my brother, my sister's a rogue. She obviously thought up a creative, though risky, way of getting you to the Ancient One."

"The Ancient One's your boss?" I probed.

He didn't answer my question. "The Nihilists thought I was the ideal candidate to get close to you because of ..." he didn't finish, "But for that same reason they didn't trust me either ..." he trailed, blinking his eyes rapidly then started again, "They were right to mistrust me. My covert mission all along for the *anti*-Nihilists was to prevent you—" He cut himself off with a cavalier smile, then went on, "to keep you from getting into trouble, particularly with the Nihilists."

"What?" I gave him a wry humorless smile. "As a bodyguard? Or as my keeper?"

"Both, actually," he said.

I hadn't expected him to acknowledge both. Either way, he'd just confirmed that his interest in me had been a ruse and I was just his pawn in some galactic chess game. "What are you, a traitor to your own kind?"

He looked hurt again and I could smell the frustration and indecision on him.

"Only to the Nihilists. Not to the rest of the Vos," he said curtly.

"You're saying that you're at odds with the rest of your family, though," I said, snorting with open disbelief.

"Families don't always get along, Rhea," he replied with a pointed look at me. I felt my mouth twitch as I thought of my mother.

"When you told me your family were all dead you were only half lying." I frowned. "But you meant the family you killed to take their identities. The real Bastions."

"I didn't—" he burst out then took in a breath, scratching his stubbled chin, and went on, "The Vos aren't all like that. It's just the Nihilists—"

"You've been killing humans one by one and taking their place since you infiltrated this galaxy a hundred years ago!"

"I told you, it's only the Nihilists!" he defended hotly. "Listen," he began, shoving his hands into his trouser pockets and pacing the floor out of reach. "In pre-ancient times, after the Great Rift occurred between Vos and Epoptes, during the Great Flood, a Vos—the Ancient One you referred to—was trapped here for thousands of years. At first he tried to help the humans, then he became disillusioned with the outer diverse and formed the Nihilist movement in both inner and outer diverse through his soul-drifter connections. A hundred years ago he got a soul-drifter to manipulate those spiritual men and women to open the Gate, unleashing warrior Nihilists from the inner diverse into the outer diverse like a plague."

My grandmother, I thought with a sick feeling.

"And, yes," Serge went on, "They've done some terrible things in anticipation of the Awakening of humanity."

Probably the same Awakening Azaes had referred to 215

standard galactic years ago, I concluded.

"But *you're* here, aren't you?" I argued.

"Yes," he said, expelling a breath and pursing his lips. "Many anti-Nihilist Vos used the Gate too. Another reason the Nihilists want to close the Gate—"

"The Gate *they* had opened."

"To keep us out ... And others, humans, from eventually using it consciously."

"And what about the Borrs. Do they even exist? Did you make it all up, or did you destroy an entire civilization just to use their identity?"

His face darkened and drew tight. "Yes, I'm afraid they're extinct. The Nihilists got them all before we had a chance to intervene. An atrocity witnessed by those hundred spiritual leaders."

"Like the willful destruction of those same spiritual leaders after the Gate Hallucination?" I challenged. "I looked it up, Serge: every single one of them died or disappeared. The last of them being those on Uma 1. And don't tell me that was just the Nihilists doing it." His painful expression told me I'd caught him.

"Once the Nihilist warriors made it through the Gate, they tried to exterminate all humans. That was their mission," he said. And it apparently was still their mission. Serge went on. "Thanks to the Eosian intervention, they failed. Then they tried to create a plague, which also failed." His eyes blazed into mine. "So, I think, in desperation, they went after your spiritual leaders, the active *portals*, and potential *gates*. Which was considered just a temporary solution, because every human is a potential *portal* or *gate*, and the Awakening is definitely upon us." He pushed out his lips and gave me a stern look. "The Vos don't normally destroy like that, Rhea. We absorb. The ones who disappeared, Rhea, were those we managed to save from the Nihilists. We ate them."

I gagged and fought down my sickness. Chaos! The dreadful myth about the Vos was true after all. My mother was right ... again.

"It's not what you think," he said, flustered at my revulsion. "We're not cannibals, for quintle's sake. It's just a term for a mediated particle transformation. Those we eat enjoy a cosmic experience of unimagined proportions as they travel to a haven, safe from the Nihilists with the option of returning later. Their bodies transform for inter-dimensional travel, taking them essentially wherever they want to go. Most of them opted to stay in our diverse where their doubles live. They're safe—"

"Safe!" I retorted in close to a shriek. Diverse? Doubles? I fixed on his stormy eyes. I so badly wanted to believe that he had noble intentions, that he was fighting bad Vos, and that this Vos *'eating,'* this absorption, was a good thing.

"Yes, safe, Rhea," he said with sincere eyes. He bent close to me, nose almost touching mine, and I felt his warm breath. It smelled of strawberries and the certainty that I wouldn't attack him. "Trust me, Rhea, they're safe, just like you will be. The eating was not unlike our own tasting sessions ..." He bent his head to brush his lips over the bared skin of my solar plexus. His smooth lips and the prickle of his whiskers drew out incredible desire as he moved up my neck and cheek toward my mouth, his tongue and lips a wet caress. "Trust me, Rhea," he whispered.

I twitched my smoldering face away, heart hammering, and blurted out sharply, "I did more than trust you. I ... *loved* you." I hadn't meant to say it, but somehow it came out. Like a slap in the face. Words I'd never before uttered to anyone, much less to an alien. A damned Vos who didn't care a quintle for me!

He studied me for a moment with a sad, regretful expression on his face. "Was it really love?" he challenged in a hard voice. "You don't really know me." His hand trembled on my cheek and his beautiful face expressed painful yearning. "Not yet, anyway ..."

I shivered at his touch, leaning into it, and stared into his eyes. Their warmth heated my face and I swallowed convulsively. If it wasn't love, what in chaos had it been?

He withdrew his hand with a resigned sigh and went on, "Did you ever wonder why you'd become so tired, especially when I was gone?" He smiled sideways, nodding to my silent expression of tacit acknowledgment. "You've willingly given me so much of yourself already, Rhea. In turn, I too gave you something. During sex, male Vos ejaculate a chemical in our semen that acts like an intoxicating drug that depresses your serotonins and stimulates your own production of dopamine and oxytocin, among other things. I gave you a shot every time we made love. As a result, you craved me like a Dust addict."

No! It was more than that. Damn it! Damn him! Tears scalded my eyes like hot coals. It was more than that ... surely it was ...

I glared at him like a wounded animal but willingly let him fumble with my shirt. His hands slid under and cupped my breasts. My breaths stuttered even as I railed at myself for succumbing and felt my heart pulse between my thighs.

"Oh, Rhea ..." he whispered in a husky voice, full of emotion. His eyes twinkled like galaxies in an infinite universe. "Even now you crave me. I see it in your eyes. And you feel it ... down there." He lowered one hand and it brushed lightly between my legs, inflaming me against my will. I seized in a sharp, halting breath and felt a burst of wetness between my legs. I knew I still wanted him. Even now, knowing what he was. What he'd done. What he really felt for me. I wanted to struggle, to back away, but clamped my gaze on his eyes. They were bottomless and I was falling into them.

"Rhea," he sighed, eyes flaming into mine, "you came here—we both came here—for this moment ..."

Serge stepped back and disrobed. He pulled his sweater over his head, then kicked off his shoes and pulled down his trousers, stepping casually out of them. He stood naked and gazed long at me. He looked magnificent as he came toward me.

"I came to ... shoot you," I stammered through halting breaths.

Somehow he knew that I wouldn't struggle or melt him.

"I know," he said gently. "I came to forgive you."

Then his hands were on me and I willingly let him undress me, trembling at his touch. How could I let this alien command me so completely? My muscles ached for him and wetness spilled out of me. I yearned for his mouth on mine. Once he'd removed my clothes, we stood, eyes blazing into each other, souls kissing. I recalled what the apophus with my mother's lyrical voice had said to me as I fought her babies: *there is no victory in resistance; only in yielding without surrender*. Had I imagined the words just now—so vivid were they—or had she spoken to me again?

Serge tenderly pulled me into his arms, and I felt the heat of his warm flesh against me. He kissed me. Slowly, eloquently, and with the lingering sweetness of strawberries. My lips parted softly, inviting him in. And I knew I was lost.

So was he. At my tender eagerness, he moaned out a gasp. Overcome with passion, his mouth seized mine and tongue lashed in deep with fierce confidence. I clutched his muscled shoulders and leaned in, hips rocking into him in hungry urgency as he pushed me gruffly against the wall. Yes, we'd both come for this.

He entered like a lion, ferocious and deep, a piercing white lance searching for the core of my being. He came to me in waves of liquid heat, thrusting hard and lifting me off my feet, back scraping against the fibrous wall and chains clashing. I gasped, mouth snapping wide in painful ecstasy, legs clasping his buttocks. I felt his fire envelope my molten core, and in hypnotic unison we vaulted in a synchronous dance … I had a magnificent vision of a field of crickets chirping in concert … thousands of fireflies blinking in dramatic unison … millions of neurons firing together in my brain to control my gasping breaths.

When his flame reached the heart of me, I melted for him, melted completely into him until there was nothing left of my universe but a remarkable stillness.

Then out of the stillness, catching his primal sparks swarming with each successive thrust, a fierce incandescent galaxy was born inside me, and slowly, like rousing from a deep sleep, a great tide of cresting waves welled up and spilled out of me. I keened out my come in pulsing throbs alongside his shout of climax. We continued to undulate as he groaned out his come and I sobbed out the remains of my thunderous climax.

He set me down then pulled back a little. He was sweat-covered and beaming at me like a boy with candy.

"You screamed aloud," he said with a goofy smile and tenderly stroked my cheek. "Oh, Rhea, welcome to the living again." His eyes flamed into mine. "I give you back your life and your heart to bare to the world." Then he was passionately kissing me again and I opened completely to him, losing myself in the moment. He was right. I felt more alive now than ever. Fireflies communicated with light; planets spoke through the force of gravity; heart cells shared electric currents. Souls coupled like galaxies colliding and giving birth to new stars. I realized with a surging heart that he had given me back my life and my heart, as only he could, the man I'd wronged the most in this world: first with my ruthless killings of his family, then in my ill trust of him. But he forgave me. Oh, God! He forgave me!

When Serge finally withdrew, I leaned into him, not wanting to break the connection. I saw that his radiant face had grown intense. "Rhea, *ma chérie*, you have no idea of the danger you're in and the danger you pose," he went on to my bewilderment. "We're running out of time. I don't have time to explain. You're their ultimate weapon, Rhea. They'll use you to destroy both our worlds: Shlsh showed me. You're running out of luck. I must absorb you now while I can still intervene. When it's safe you can return. You'll know what to do. Don't be afraid." He studied my face for a moment, then added, "You don't belong to this world."

"It's the only one I have," I stammered.

"No, it isn't," he said softly, eyes sparkling like the star-filled night. "Come with me to a world where souls are born and dreams are realized."

He was going to eat me alive and I was going to let him do it. Was it like he'd said? A transcendence into another state with the option of returning? Or was it simple and absolute annihilation? I knew I wasn't thinking straight, knew I was drugged, but somehow it didn't matter: crazy as it was, I trusted him. A man who'd chronically lied to me. An alien, a Vos. But a man who'd openly forgiven me for killing his family. A man I loved.

Serge moved to the pile of clothes he'd left on the floor and retrieved a round device from his trouser pocket. Then he moved behind me, between me and the slimy wall. My breaths grew shallow with panic.

"Don't be afraid," he soothed, gently stroking my back. I caught a glimpse of the device; it shone like metal and gave off an emerald light. The device looked strangely familiar and triggered unease in me. "I'm not going to eat you like a steak. But I must enter you from behind. Prepare your metabolism with my secretions."

I knew I should think of escape. Bas wasn't there anymore to help me, but I had options, Enforcer options ... what they were I had no idea. And, for the moment, no inclination to investigate.

"I've never done this before. But I've heard that you'll soar in agonizing ecstasy during your last moments on this world as my enticing secretions will 'eat' your outer diverse resonance as the device both disintegrates your essence in preparation for travel and helps you get there. There'll be nothing left of you in the outer diverse—but you'll be in a wonderful incredible place, a place between the two diverses, where I'm told souls are born ..."

My heart slammed. This was nonsense but I wanted it too. He began by gently coaxing me to lean forward on the soft floor with my hands and knees and rubbed his already stiffening cock slowly along my buttocks. I heard him seizing in shallow breaths of excitement and felt my own halting breaths seize me. I suddenly recalled that erotic dance of the aphophus snakes and how they'd stoked my desire, entering from behind. Pulsing slick and hard, his penis teased into the crease of my buttocks and pressed inward. I remembered the snakes burning up my anus in delirious stimulation and stifled a moan of anticipation. Panic spiked as I felt great discomfort — then a flush of incredible ecstasy amid pain as his enticing chemical entered me, and he thrust inside. *Oh, God!*

"No, please—Oh, YES!" I wailed, wanting him to stop and continue at the same time—then seized in my breath in startled enlightenment. This was exactly what U'clid had been doing to my mother! The realization struck me like a MEC-wave: U'clid wasn't just a shapeshifter—he was a Vos terrorist. A *Nihilist*. That fateful day, when I'd melted him as he sodomized my mother, I'd saved her from being eaten alive!

Rage spiked. It lanced through me like a white-hot knife. Rage at the unfounded guilt that had dominated my miserable life. I twisted in a jerk, forcing Serge out of me, and aimed my lethal stare at him. His eyes widened with recognition as mine glowed with purpose, and I felt the burst of energy surge out of me and fly toward him. But he'd seen it coming and had already leapt sideways, evading the flash by centimeters. He rolled and scrambled behind some boxes, scooped up his pants, and dashed out the door.

With swift intuition, I directed my gaze at my bindings. I screamed as my melting stare singed them right off my hands but severely burnt my wrists in the process.

Serge had disappeared down the empty hall. Ignoring the painful burns, I pulled on my trousers, jammed my feet into my boots, and shrugged into Serge's crewneck sweater. I swept up my Great Coat and MEC from the floor and pelted after him, ignoring the spike of pain that shot up from my sprained ankle.

I caught up to him as he ran barefoot, wearing only his trousers, to the Spaceport landing bay where his ship was parked. He'd managed to hike on his pants mid-gallop. I halted, legs apart, then threw down my Great Coat and drew out my MEC. Holding the MEC with both hands, I braced it against a loading machine and pointed at his muscular, sweat-slicked back. I couldn't shoot him in the back.

He stopped, foolishly, to turn and gaze at me. I could have killed him right then; my MEC was aimed at his heart, my trigger finger poised. I gazed into his dark eyes. They sparkled like the Milky Way and I recognized a strange pained expression on his face. My throat swelled with emotion, still unclear about what had just happened between us. His face clouded into a million prisms as tears flooded my eyes. Then he moved and the moment was over.

I shot.

It went wide and Serge dove inside the *scimitar*. Within seconds, the dome opened and sunlight blazed in. The *scimitar* screamed up into the blinding light, leaving a faint streak of glowing purple. The Ngus, of course, had no idea who they'd just let go.

Bas rushed up behind me and I blinked in bewildered surprise to see him unhurt by the explosion. I was about to say something when he panted, "How in chaos did you miss! You had a clear shot. That was like a piece of fish for you."

"Cake," I bit out my correction. I scooped up my Great Coat from the floor and adjusted my holster. Bas was trying so hard to placate me with old Earth expressions. "A piece of cake," I sighed, then tried to smile at him. "Good to see you."

"Yeah, you too." Then he swung a sweeping glance from where Serge had disappeared to me, and his eyes roamed over Serge's sweater hanging on me. He hadn't failed to notice that Serge had only been in his pants and I was wearing his sweater.

"Come on," I said, brushing past Bas to return to the main deck where Benny and Bas's *twin-V* waited. I threw a glance over my shoulder. "Did you get it?"

"Shlsh's information? Yeah. It clearly identifies the Vos as the perpetrators of the massacre. You're going to crap your pants when you see it."

"Sure I will," I muttered, knowing what they'd find on the info-pod.

Bas came beside me and I followed his concerned glance down to my burnt wrist, exposed for the first time as the overly-long sleeve drifted up my arm when I holstered my MEC. It resembled melted synth and wept clear fluid. It hurt like chaos but I had no time for that. I shrugged my Great Coat on over the bulky sweater, and Bas let his gaze drift to the waste disposal area. He asked in a subdued voice, "What happened in there?"

I'd lost my best friend, I thought, not slowing my stride.

And gained an archenemy—after I'd given him my heart on a platter. I finally stopped in front of Benny and turned to Bas. "What happened with you and Shlsh? When I heard the explosion I thought—" I bit back the rest.

Bas gave me a crooked smile, obviously sensing and appreciating the concern I'd betrayed. "Shlsh figured it out as soon as he had your info-pod in his hand. Someone had dubbed in a tyranium explosive and rigged it to go when the cube was activated on an Inverta data system, like Shlsh's."

"What?" I wrinkled my nose with a tight frown of disbelief. I abruptly pulled out my MEC and pointed it at Bas. Maybe there was a reason he wasn't dead from the explosion.

"Whoa," he said, backing away and raising his hands in supplication. "You think I was involved?" he asked with genuine bewilderment. "Why would I blow myself up? Chaos, Rhea! When are you going to trust me?"

"No one's touched it, besides you, when you gave me the pod," I countered. "I had it on me all the time—" Then I remembered and lowered the MEC. Bas let out a long sigh of relief. "… Except when I was unconscious in the Paradise City med-facility," I admitted with a grimace. Now it made sense: the same person who'd tampered with the info-pod was the one who'd spread those seditious rumors about my being an Eclipse agent. And probably let Serge into the city. Someone in Paradise City was not what he or she appeared, and I needed to warn Ka. "Sorry, Bas," I offered with a lame smile and holstered my MEC. "How did you know?"

Still glaring at me with a wounded frown, Bas replied, "Shlsh figured it out as soon as he had the pod in his hand. His photosynthetic receptors detected minute traces of tyranium residue, the active ingredient of a genetic explosive. No one except a Ngu would know about that sensitivity."

"So, you let the bomb go off anyway?"

"If it didn't go off, Eclipse would think something went wrong and follow up. I convinced Shlsh that rebuilding his sanctuary was preferable to being dead."

I nodded with a half-smile of appreciation. "Good

thinking, Bas." Then I gazed at him with weary eyes. "I guess I'll meet you back at the precinct. I'm turning myself in."

He stared at me in surprise. He glanced from my face to the info-pod in his hand, trying hard and failing to hide his distress at my decision. "But you're still wanted for the murder of Rashomon," he stuttered back. "They'll arrest you and send you to Sekmet if you go back. No one ever gets off Sekmet, Rhea. There's something about the place that keeps you there. I've heard of inmates who've escaped only to return of their own free will. You'll die there."

"U'clid got out," I said with a slanted smile.

"He was the only one. Apparently some lawyer his family hired got him out on a technicality. It was a shady deal at best and I'm sure it involved Eclipse. But soon after that he went blenoid anyway." His face tightened at my cold expression of resolution. "Rhea, you can hide in one of the outer arms, the northern hemisphere, get a new ID on Nigel 7, and live a low-key life for awhile," he said in a desperate rush of words. "I can feed you information while you ..." his voice trailed off, and he sighed in defeat. He knew me too well. "At least give me time to get there first, then." He waved the info-pod in his hand at me. "This'll make a case for your exoneration. Ennos will have to put you back on the force ..."

For the first time since I'd been let go, I didn't care.

"... He'll give you back your life," Bas added.

It was too late for that, I thought. "It doesn't matter whether Ennos re-instates me with the Guardians or sends me to Sekmet, Bas." I shrugged and fished in my Great Coat pocket then tossed Bas a copy of the info-pod that held the deciphered Nihilist hit list. "What's important is that you get both info-pods to him and make sure the information gets out."

Bas nodded but with a puzzled and perplexed half-frown. I was vaguely aware of his eyes searching mine for some connection, a bond, and finding nothing. I'd already turned my thoughts inward and felt a vast emptiness embrace me.

"See you, Bas," I said in a flat voice then turned to climb into my ship.

"Rhea!"

I turned and saw his face squirming to hide the pain he felt for me. I wanted to tell him it was okay. That I was okay. But I couldn't.

He gave me his best brave smile. "Fly safe."

I nodded and forced one back. "You too, Bas."

Θ

"Where to, Rhea?" Benny asked as I slid into my pilot's chair, not bothering to pull on my crash-webbing.

"Home, to Iota Hor-2, Benny." I didn't take the primary controls or look out as Benny started up. I let him launch totally on his own.

THIRTY-ONE

"I have both you and Bas to thank for these, Hawke," Ennos said, holding up two info-pods in front of me, as I sat across from his massive gadpie desk in the Iota Hor Guardian Precinct. One info-pod held the Nihilist hit list file I had decoded; the other contained Shlsh's incredible data files that documented communiqués of Nihilist Vos intentions. Ennos added with a slight frown, "Though I wish Bas had given them directly to me instead of announcing it all through his own department."

I knew why Bas had done it and was silently grateful: he'd made sure the information didn't get buried out of political angst like so much else that I had given Ennos.

"Seems you were right, after all," Ennos conceded with a half-smile. He threw the pod on the desk and checked his notes on the flat-screen of his info-pad. "We now know that the Vos plan to annihilate humanity and control the galaxy."

The question was, *how*? I'd hoped that Shle's information might provide some clue but, apart from what I already knew from Serge—that they'd tried a human-specific virus and failed—there was nothing else in the confidential correspondences that he'd made available to us.

"We only eliminated a small group of them thirty years ago," Ennos continued, shaking his head in dismay. "It's incredibly alarming to discover that they've already entered our galaxy in massive numbers through this Gate a hundred years ago. The Gate is no doubt some advanced inter-galactic transportation that can be evoked through mind-control and some brainwave power that accesses our particle-streams." He looked up at me with inquiring eyes.

I firmed my lips and nodded, thinking that it was far more complicated than that, but not offering my opinion. I hadn't told him about the doppelgangers—how the Vos were apparently killing and assuming the identities of humans, in addition to keeping their Borr ID. The Bastion family was just one example. How many others were there?

"So," he said, slamming his great hand on the hard wood, "they've already infiltrated every segment of our galactic community in the guise of being shapeshifters." His eyes pierced into mine.

That was only the surface of it, I thought. Of every so-called human I would have to wonder: were they the real thing or a shapeshifting copy who'd taken their identity?

"That's a time bomb, Hawke," Ennos continued, sucking in air through his teeth, breath whistling. "And I'm not sure how we're going to handle it. For now, it's classified information. No one, except Guardians in this precinct, will know that every Borr, every shifter, is a Vos."

I fought down a frustrated frown. I knew that he would give me that line. Always the politician, his mandate was to avoid panicking the galactic community even if it played, in my opinion, right into the insidious Vos plan to take over.

"And who are these Nihilists?" Ennos went on. "Some kind of kamikaze death squad? Why do they want to close the Gate and trap themselves here? I would have thought that they'd want to keep it open so more of them can come in."

I sighed and leaned back in my chair, recalling my strange conversation with Serge on Virgil 9. "More like terrorists. By my interpretation, the reason the Nihilists came in the first place was to get rid of humanity before we evolved into natural *portals* and started opening gates ourselves." Serge—and Azaes before him—had aptly called it the Awakening. "Right now the Nihilists are in control of the gates. But that's about to change. First we've become capable—at least our spiritual leaders have; but they're like children, not recognizing their abilities; the next stage will be recognition and control. That's what the Vos—the Nihilists, I mean—want to prevent."

He leaned back, imitating my posture, and nodded. "Ah ..." He tapped his sausage-size finger against his lip. "That's quite a postulation. I think I understand ..."

Of course he didn't understand, I thought. Even I hardly understood. But I had a lot more information to go on that I wasn't about to share with Ennos. For instance, how Serge and other anti-Nihilists like Shlsh fit in. Serge had tried to convince me that he and other anti-Nihilist Vos had come to my world to stop the Nihilists from destroying humanity. But he was more than willing to 'absorb' me as U'clid, one of the Vos's most radical Nihilists, had tried with my mother. I was convinced that absorption was just another form of annihilation and Serge was a lying bastard. And if he wasn't The Rose himself, then he was working for The Rose, who was probably his sister A'ler.

Ennos shoved the info-pad in a desk drawer and clasped his hands, interlacing his sausage fingers. He cleared his throat, and I knew he was broaching a new and sensitive subject. I braced for the obvious: my punishment.

"Both you and Bas have done some inexcusable things: stealing Benny, your Great Coat, and MEC; failing to come in when you were charged; then stealing a civilian vehicle and destroying it and other public property ... not to mention the current charges against you for assaulting Guardian Officers. And murder. The list is endless for you, Hawke. Bas received a reprimand, and you can consider yourself reprimanded as well. You're free to go."

I realized that my mouth gaped open and closed it.

"You know that I can't exonerate you, Rhea," he said. "You're still accused of murdering Rashomon, in addition to being sought after for those other charges against you. And the evidence is stacked high. The minute you walk out the doors of this precinct, you're a wanted killer, Priority 1. The only reason I'm not turning you in to Galactic Guardian Headquarters is because of *this*." He held up Shlsh's info-pod. "And the fact that, given your present circumstance, no one's in a better position than you for covert ops in Eclipse and associated circles. You have an excellent cover now. You're in an excellent position to find and bring in The Rose, discover how the Nihilists plan to exterminate humanity. You understand that you're on your own—I won't help you or back you. The rest of the Galaxy Guardians and associated bounty hunters will still be after you."

He leaned forward and pointed at me with his thick sausage finger. "I'm giving you a chance to prove yourself. No more. The chances are slim, but maybe you can do some good before ... well, *before*," he ended, eyes burning into mine with regret.

I swallowed hard but kept my expression impassive. He was giving me a chance to die honorably rather than on Sekmet. Of course I had never expected full exoneration like Bas had naively mentioned. I'd resigned myself to Sekmet. Although I might still end up there, this was an unexpected boon.

Ennos leaned forward like a conspirator. "You'll be able to draw on anonymous funds from the Galactic Bank." This was his unofficial stance now. "You can also reach me on a secure channel. Don't overuse it. It's just to keep me apprised, you understand," he ended gruffly. It was his way of saying 'stay out of trouble but I'll try to do what I can to help so long as it doesn't put me in harm's way.' "Bas has been newly assigned to keep an eye on some strange space anomalies..." He nodded to me. Ennos meant *me*.

"I see." I nodded back with a tight smile of acknowledgement.

"Here's the information." He handed me an info-pod. I

calmly reached out and pocketed it.

There was nothing left to discuss so I got up to leave. "Thank you, sir."

I made it to the door when Ennos called after me. "Hawke!"

I stopped in midstride and turned to face him. I caught him looking at me wistfully. The pain had returned to his eyes.

"Your mother told me about you being part Eosian," he said, studying my face with an intensity that made me feel uncomfortable. Then he tipped his head to one side and half-smiled. "It explains a lot." He brought his lips together in a tight line and ended rather ruefully, "I never knew, Rhea."

"Neither did I until a month ago," I responded in a calm voice that veiled my emotions. "Do the others know about me?"

"Your mother told me in confidence … because I'm your boss. She thought I should know. She felt badly that you had to find out the way you did. And when you ran off, all upset, it bothered her." He paused to study my expressionless face, then added gently, "Rhea, I didn't tell anyone else."

"Let's keep it that way," I said evenly.

"As you wish."

I gave him a curt nod, then half-smiled in appreciation and turned for the door. Maybe Ennos was my father, I thought as I strode down the hallway. Maybe. I decided that I wouldn't mind that after all.

As I rounded the corner into the Great Hall, I spotted the usual loitering crowd of Eosians by the crossway: Euaimon and his thugs. Terrific. But the fight in me had evaporated. I felt no rise in adrenalin as I prepared to accept whatever punishment they decided to throw at me. And found that decision somehow liberating.

Any of them could be my father, I considered, studying their faces more carefully than I had ever before and with a kind of forlorn acceptance as I approached them. My mother had slept with pretty well every one of them. Even Euaimon, I thought, catching his gaze. I slowed involuntarily as he fixed his eyes on me, obviously intending to communicate. I prepared for his onslaught. But he puzzled me by instead pulling out his *pocket* and raising it in his hand with it pointed casually to the ceiling. He glanced briefly at the *pocket* then returned his gaze to me and nodded with a faint smile of acknowledgment. Obviously, Ennos had told Euaimon about me being its designer.

I gave him a barely perceptible nod in return, then halted and braced myself with tight lips as he broke from his gang to approach me. To my astonishment, he halted in front of me and nodded respectfully.

"You did good this time, Officer," he said simply, then walked past me without a caustic remark.

I stood still, swallowing convulsively, as the rest of Euaimon's gang followed him. No one shoved me or jostled me; no one smirked or made a snide remark. They gave me lots of room as they quietly dispersed.

I headed toward Cryptology Lab B in Communications.

Any one of them could be a shapeshifter—a Vos—I considered as I rounded the corner to the lab. Officer Asphalios had been a Vos, though only I knew that and kept it to myself. Who else was? Now that I'd confirmed a leak in the Guardian precinct to Eclipse, someone was not what he or she seemed.

I hesitated at the doorway of the cryptology lab to peer inside. Three Eosians were in the room. I spotted Bas right away, slouched in a chair, reading and playing with his hair. His colleague cleared his throat loudly, alerting Bas, and flicked his eyes at the door, toward me.

Bas turned and I saw his eyes widen. I leaned on the door jam in a show of casualness that I wasn't feeling.

"So, this is where you work," I said, pushing a smile.

"Yeah," he smiled back, looking confused and surging to his feet. In all the years I'd known him, I'd never made it here, to his lab where he spent most of his time at the precinct.

An awkward silence followed before I said, "I came to see if you wanted to join me in the caf for a cup of soyka." Then I added with a self-conscious smile, "If you have some time for a break, that is."

Bas stared in astonishment for a moment before a huge grin creased his face, revealing a blazing set of teeth. "I'd love to, Rhea. And I always have time for you."

It was enough invitation for me to step forward.

"I knew you'd say that," I said, crossing the room with a sad smile. "I'm a little slow and I'm just getting it, this friendship thing."

I walked straight up to him and hugged him, not caring that the other two workers watched. Initially stiff with surprise, Bas quickly recovered and responded by putting his arms around me in a gentle embrace.

"Thanks for everything, Bas," I said, holding onto him. "Thanks for being there even when I didn't want you to be. Thanks for persisting and for being a friend even when I wasn't."

He gave me a squeeze. I sensed that he was moved. "It's what friends do," he finally said.

"Yeah." I sighed. "It certainly is." I felt a genuine smile warm my face like a balm and didn't let go for a long time.

Θ

I stood at the door of my mother's flat, refusing to go in and glaring at Laura Hawke. But it was an empty weary glare, a rusty remnant of the traditional armor. I trembled with a mixture of emotion and exhaustion.

"You never told me my grandmother was still alive," I said.

"I didn't know she was," came the simple reply. For some reason I was unprepared for that answer. "She disappeared when I was a child. I thought she died."

I stared at my mother for a moment and then suddenly saw the logic with a convulsive swallow: Laura Hawke had been *cast off* by her mother just as she had *abandoned* me for her many lovers. No doubt a pattern I would replicate with my own child. Another reason for me to forsake love with a man; I refused to put another child through that.

I now knew something of her pain and motives for seeking love in all the wrong places. In a move that surprised me, I closed the space between us and seized her in a strong embrace. Stunned, my mother stiffened briefly then tearfully hugged me back. I burst into tears. We laughed and cried together. I had a lot to blame my mother for, but right now none of it mattered.

After a long while, my mother whispered, "Rhea, I'm pregnant."

I pulled back and stared at her, then thought: Eosian or Vos?

EPILOGUE

I sat slouched in my pilot's chair in Benny, as we sailed through the endless darkness of space. I never tired of the view: millions of stars embedded in the deep velvet of infinite space. Where I could hear my own breathing and contemplate how small and insignificant I was. There was something fearfully exhilarating about recognizing a universe so vast and strange that it could never be conquered or defined by the hubris of humankind or any other kind. I prayed that it would remain so.

I ran my fingers absently through my tousled hair and reviewed the holo file of The Rose's hit list, which I'd decrypted. Rashomon was first on the list and—thanks to me—was taken care of. I was next and still at large, I thought with a scowl. Shle She came next; he'd escaped narrowly and was likely still a target. So far The Rose was doing a hit-and-miss job of it, I thought. Where would he—rather *she*—strike next? I suspected The Rose was A'ler, Serge's sister. I scanned further down the list and raised a brow at the next person. It was Barbariccia, the Dust lord from Dark Sun, presently languishing on Sekmet, the prison planet where I thought I was destined to end up. After Barbariccia came Raphael Martinez, the Gnostic priest who'd made the dire prophecy of the *Suntelia Aeon*, a catastrophic End of the Age. Well, he'd be right if the Vos were successful. Only Martinez wouldn't be alive to see it; he'd be dead like the rest of humanity. I pondered the second part of his prophecy with a frown: *the destruction of our old world will be signified by the joining of twin souls who will herald the coming of a New Age.*

What did it mean? Ka had shrugged when I'd asked him and suggested the riddle was open to interpretation. Were the twins the two diverses, twin worlds? Or two individuals from twin worlds? Was it describing the Awakening of humanity? I shook my head with a frown. Serge had said to me: *you're their ultimate weapon.* I thought of my MEC—everyone wanted it, my ultimate weapon—and felt a deep foreboding I could not shake.

I pored over the list again. Ka's name was last. Although the list gave me some idea of where The Rose would strike next, I was no closer to figuring out the larger intentions of the Nihilists. Shle's information on Nihilist correspondence, mostly between the Ancient One and Nihilist Splinter leaders, provided little in the way of a major plan. How were they intending to annihilate all of humanity? Assassins like The Rose were nothing more than a band-aid attempt to stem the early tide of the Awakening by singling out a few enlightened human *portals* and other troublemakers. In order to wipe out a whole species, scattered throughout the galaxy, an ingenious campaign and a concerted effort was required. Serge had mentioned a failed attempt using a species-specific virus. What was their next move? Was it … me?

"Where to, Rhea," Benny asked in a calm tenor voice.

I shook off the dark thoughts, knowing I was no closer now to solving anything than before, only more flustered for trying. "To Horus, Benny," I responded, leaning back in my pilot's chair and pulling out a wad of soyka gum as Benny made the calculations to jack into particle-stream. "We have some unfinished business there: a friend to warn and someone to find." There was also a man called Serge Bastion, living in ignorance on a small planet 137 light-years from Earth, who was also in danger. But I couldn't handle that one … not yet, anyway.

I tossed the gum into my mouth and chewed slowly,

savoring the effects of the soyka. "Give me some heavy metal, Benny," I instructed. Almost instantly, the beating wails of Metallica's "Orion" pounded in the small cockpit. I closed my eyes, inhaling the throbbing music, and let my mind drift into a daze. I would try, despite my fugitive status, to warn the secluded Ka about a Vos terrorist in his midst and the threat to his life by the assassin, The Rose. Then I had another, perhaps equally hazardous mission.

I hadn't told anyone about what Shlsh had said to me regarding what my grandmother had supposedly done. The info-pod had revealed nothing either, although it was now clear that the Gate Hallucination had created a reality that had permitted the invasion of the Vos into my galaxy. I was determined to find my grandmother—if she still lived. Perhaps Ka was right, after all, when he'd suggested that Diana Wood was the key to the mysteries of my own existence.

Expelling a long sigh, I let my thoughts finally settle on *him*.

Serge had said it acted like a drug. But while the fatigue that accompanied my sexual obsession for him had left me, the emptiness inside me and the longing ache in my breast for him didn't. I realized with some despair that I still nurtured strong feelings for Serge. What fuelled my hatred for him was my love for him. It only heightened my vow never again to succumb to his powers. I would not underestimate him again. The next time we met I would either immobilize him and bring him in or kill him without hesitation.

God ... *my* God, was a hopeless god.

Lexicon of "Splintered Universe"

Aeon \ Æ-ôn \ *n* : in Gnosticism, a divine power or nature emanating from the Supreme Being and playing various roles in the operation of the universe

Ae•on Sun•tel•ia \ Æ-ôn-sün-tel-ia \ *n* : **1** : the End of the Age according to the ancient Greeks, described by Plato as a cycle of catastrophe; the sun rising out of the mouth of the "ouroboros" or "serpent eating its own tail" of the Milky Way **2** : a prediction made in 207 SGT by Raphael Martinez, leader of the Hermetic Order, of a violent end of an age; the destruction of the old world according to the prophet Martinez *"will be signified by the joining of twin souls who will herald the coming of a New Age."*

A•po•phus \ A-pô-fəs \ *n* : a gigantic snake-like creature known through local myth that inhabits the Boiling Sea in the Weeping Mountains are of the planet Horus (47 Uma a) in the 47 Ursae Majoris system

A•zor•i•an \ A-zór-ēən \ *n* : a tall, heat-loving lean-limbed biped species with tough sand-paper hide, long snout and ferret face from Azor in the Beta Hydri system

Bad•o•win \ bad-ō-in \ *n* **1:** a small, very strong, gnarled and hairy biped species of often ill-repute, originating on the planet Nexus in the M103 star cluster

bas•tet \ bas-tet \ *n* : a genetically produced mammal that displayed aggressive co-evolution and wiped out the domestic cat population and Earth's large feral cats.

Bio•mi•me•tic \ bīó-mi-me-tic \ *adj* : the application of biological methods and systems in nature, particularly in living organisms, in the design by sentient beings of houses, engineering structures, vehicles, etc.

blan•ket bog \ blan-ket bôg \ *n* **1:** an extensive peatland (wet spongy perched water ecosystem) formed in a climate of high rainfall and low level of evapo-transpiration, allowing peat development not only in wet hollows but over large expanses of undulating ground; an ecosystem usually consisting of hummocks and pools with specifically adapted plant and animal life; an extensive bog-fen landscape

blen•oid \ blen-óid \ *n* **1:** a ferocious and dull-witted four-legged dog-like animal with three sets of razor sharp teeth, massive head with three eyes and tough red hide; indigenous to Upsilon 2 in the Epsilon Endari system **2 :** term used for a person with these traits : CRAZY; MAD

Borr \ bōr \ *n* **1** : four-legged gentle species, indigenous to the planet Borrias and extirpated by the Vos Nihilists **2 :** a shape-shifting species thought to be from Borrias

cha•os \ kā-ôs \ *n* **1** : the confused unorganized state existing before the creation of distinct forms **2** : complete disorder **syn** confusion **3** : common expletive to denote less than optimal to utterly calamitous or disastrous conditions **syn** "hell"

creel \ crēəl \ *n* : a fungus from Omega 6 that grows naturally into a metallic burnished hard surface and used by biomimetic architects on Horus to build their floors.

cre•on \ crē-ôn \ *n* **1** : an individual of the main species from the planet Creos in the 55 Cancri system; known for their laziness, lack of good judgement and imagination **2** : term used to indicate an individual with these traits : FOOL; IDIOT; DULLARD

De•le•ne•an \ Də-le-nē-en \ *n* : furry simple creatures with six appendages, native to Mar Delena in the Fomalhaut system. This species is subservient to the AI community that runs Mar Delena

Di•verse \ dī-vərs \ *n* : a term that describes the notion of the existence of two parallel and divergent universes that comprise an infinite metaverse; twin paradoxical worlds, outer and inner diverses, connected through black holes, quasars, dreams, intuition and déjà vu

Drec•ca•line \ drec-ca-lēn \ *n* : a non-specific highly potent nerve poison that kills all life

Du•en•de \ Du-en-de \ *n* : an old Spanish word that describes a heightened state of emotion, expression and authenticity, loosely meaning "having soul"; promoted and discussed by Spanish poet Frederico Garcia Lorca as an inner transcendent emotional response and spirit of evocation with roots from Spanish mythology.

dust \ dəst \ *n* : a psychoactive drug that produces mild euphoria and drowsiness in most sentient species

E•os \ Ē-ôs \ *n* : ringed jungle Planet in the Pleiades Nebula; original home of the vishna tree

E•os•i•an \ Ē-ōs-ē-ən \ *n* : principal sentient being from Eos in the Pleiades Nebula; originally from Earth (Atlantis) and responsible for establishing the Galactic Guardian force in the Milky Way Galaxy

E•pop•tes \ Ē-pôp-tes \ *n* : shape-shifting god worshipped by the Eosian species, and from whom the Eosians presumably take their instruction through dreams

Fauche \ Fōsh\ *n* : an ungulate-like biped species with very long ears, wide frequency hearing and large lustrous eyes, originating from Bedar 9 in the Sigma Draconis system

fok \ fôk \ *n* : excrement from a blenoid

gad•pie \ gad-pī \ *n* **1:** a tree indigenous to Horo-2, the moon of Horologii b **2:** the wood of the gadpie tree

Gness \ ness \ *n* : a gentle wolf-like species with translucent skin from the 61 Ursae Majoris system

Gno•sis \ nōs-sis \ *n* : knowledge of God

Gnos•tic \ nôs-tic \ *n* : a follower of Gnosticism

Gnos•ti•cism \ nôs-ti-sizm \ *n* : a belief system based on early Christianity, Helenistic Judaism, Greco-roman mystery religions, Zoroastrianism and neoplatonism, which teaches that some esoteric knowledge (gnosis) is necessary for salvation from the material world, created by an intermediary (demiurge; considered evil or merely imperfect) to God

Great Coat \ grāt cōt \ *n* : part of the uniform and weapons arsenal of the Galactic Guardian; millions of thixtropic nano-sensors incorporated into its durable yet flexible fabric let it respond to any number of internal and external stresses, providing its wearer with a shield from the cold or from a weapon's discharge

he•don \ he-dən \ *n* **1** : a mildly euphoric recreational drug that is smoked and produces a pungent yellow smoke **2** : used colloquially to indicate incredulity (as in *"you must be blowing hedon"*)

inner diverse \ innər dīvers \ *n* : the world or existence comprised within the inner twin universe of the metaverse and linked to its twin existence, the outer diverse, through transitional phenomena such as black holes and intuition

jag \ jag \ *vb* **1** : the act of straying off the space-time stream of faster-than-light travel and often accompanied by dangerous ship stress **2** : used colloquially to indicate a serious misjudgement (as in *"he jags up all the time"*)

jag•ging \ jag-gēng \ *vb* **1** : describing a ship that is straying off the space-time stream **2** : *vb; adv* : used as an expletive to describe a person, concept or action that lacks sense or causes harm, embarrassment or discomfort (as in, *"he's jagging with your mind"* or *"she's so jagging stupid")*

jagged \ jagd \ *vb* : **1 :** past tense verb of straying off the space-time stream of faster-than-light travel **2.** *adj* : colloquial expletive term for a serious error or bad circumstance; SCREWED, MESSED UP (as in, *"we're jagged")*

kap•pa par•ti•cles \ kap-pa pär-ti-cəlz\ n : energy particles that concentrate in the upper atmosphere of several gas giants; retrieved by Fauche *ray* class sentient ships for fuel using specialized fuel scoops

kep•ry \ kep-rē \ *n* : a flying crustacean-like creature on Sekmet that lives in the dung piles left by the sobek

Khon•sus \ kón-səs \ *n* : tall, feathered biped creature with raptor head, wings, and liquid amber eyes able to mind-probe, origin unknown but currently in 47 Ursae Majoris system; hawk-like people achieve powers through a symbiotic interaction with the planet's energy and forces

Le•gess \ lə-gess \ *n* : tall, slim praying mantis-like invertebrate creatures who colonized Chara and enslaved native Rills

L'Ordre de l'Arbre Sacré *n* : see Order of the Sacred Tree

MEC \ mek \ *n* : acronym for Magnetic-Electro Concussion pistol, created by Rhea Hawke, which uses electro-magnetic wave energy to focus sub-atomic quintle particles into resonance with specific DNA

Met•a•verse \ met-a-vərs \ *n* : a theoretical term that describes the composition of all matter and energy encompassed by divergent twin diverses; a whole quantum cosmos that includes all that was and will be

Mi•gra•tor•y Trees \ mī-grə-to-rē trēz \ *n* : a tree known in myth to migrate from one location to another in the Weeping Mountains area of the planet Horus; according to myth the Khonsus inhabited the trees in ancient times

Ngu \ nü \ *n* : a photosynthetic amoeboid creature with protuberances as sense organs that lives symbiotically with AI-machinery; from Virgil 9 in the 70 Virginis system

Nu•yu \ noo-ēü \ *n* : a nano-chemical mixture, imbibed as a liquid, that acts at the genetic level to temporarily change small aspects of outer appearance such as skin, eyes, hair; used as make-up

Ni•hi•list \ Nī-ə-list \ *n* **1** : a member of a militant splinter group of the Vos **2** : a specially trained death squad of shapeshifter assassins on the Vos payroll

Order of the Sacred Tree *n* : a closed membership in Quebec on Earth, devoted to the divine nature of the *vishna* tree, considered the tree of life and knowledge and the answer to achieving the balance of all things. The Order believes in the notion that a messiah, connected to the tree, will bring balance and begin a new age of enlightenment and peace.

Ou•ro•bor•os \ u-rō-bōr-ōs \ *n* : a mythical serpent eating its own tail; connected with the Suntelia Aeon that refers to the serpent of light residing in the heavens (the Milky Way); the ouroboros symbolizes an Aeon

outer diverse \ outər dīvers \ *n* : the world or existence comprised within the outer twin universe of the metaverse and linked to its twin existence, the inner diverse, through transitional phenomena such as black holes and intuition

Pee•ka \ pē-ka \ *n* : a small monotreme creature that produces eggs and lives in the marshes of Omicron 12

poly•synth fi•ber \ pôlē-synth fībər \ *n* : nano-strings that resonate with matter

po•cket \ pôk-et \ *n* : acronym for PulsOniC Kinetic Energy Tracker created by Rhea Hawke , which tracks a target once the gun has identified their signature

pock•ta \ pôk-ta \ *n* : a highly nutritional leguminous plant from whose giant seeds a rich thick soup is made

quin•tle \ quin-təl \ *n* **1** : dark energy particle found in everything **2** : destructive energy discharged from a weapon (Q-gun created by shape-shifters) that resonates with matter to dematerialize an object **3** : used colloquially to express something of importance (as in: *"who gives a quintle about spice?"*)

Rill *n* : a short, stout and smelly bog being with tube-eyes, webbed limbs, large genitals and sloughing outer skin from Omicron 12 in the Chara system

Scan•di \ skan-dē \ *n* : a lizard-like lean-limbed biped with remarkable healing abilities; indigenous to the Upsilon Andromedae system

Schiss \ shiss \ *n* : a hermetic order of peaceful Gnostic priests, devoted to the use of dream-meditation, particularly lucid dreaming, to achieve transcendence and evolve closer to God and the universal consciousness; several of its older founders experienced the Gate Hallucination; targeted by Eclipse and massacred into near extirpation during a meeting in Paradise City on Uma 1

SGT *n* : Standard Galactic Time; based on a decimal system from the basis of the Earth 24 hour diurnal cycle, with ten days equal to one month and ten months equal to one year; zero SGT is set at the moment of first alien contact with Earth

shal•lik oil \ shal-lik oil \ *n* : an oil that possesses natural narcotic properties that numb the nervous system of those in contact with it and make them docile; the oil is produced by microbes indigenous to the Weeping Mountains area of the planet Horus; when ingested, the oil will make one very ill

shapeshifter \ shāp shiftər \ *n* : a being able to change his or her physical appearance and associated physiology into several other forms; considered an ability possessed by the Borr species from Borrias

skip•boat \ skip-bōt \ *n* : a two-man vehicle with skates/skis that is able to move rapidly over water, ice and snow; used by settlers of Uma-1

so•bek \ sō-bek \ *n* : a fierce crocodile-like native of Sekmet that digs underwater tunnels in the peat and drowns its victims

soul-drift \ sōl drift \ *vb* : the practice of entering another's dreams, even one's own, and change"reality" through them

soy•ka \ sói-kä \ *n* : a soy-based warm drink like coffee made with L-theanine; stimulant

Spice \ spīs \ *n* : a mild psychoactive drug in common usage

Spo•ri•an \ spó-rē-ən \ n : a very tall, pear-shaped lanky greenish species with elongated head and leather-like skin, long limbs and large bulbous eyes from the planet Spor in the 18 Scorpii system

Sun•tel•ia Ae•on \ sün-tel-ia Æ-ôn \ *n* : **1** : the End of the Age according to the ancient Greeks; see Aeon suntelia

synth•flesh \ sinth-flesh \ *n* : real skin molecules and synthetic materials combined by nano-technology, used in synthplast

synth•plast \ sinth-plast \ *n* : prosthetic made of a combination of real skin molecules and synthetic flesh using nano-technology

Tan•gent Ship•ping \ Tan-gent Ship-pēng \ *n* : the name of a Fauche ship building company. Maker of ray class corvette, falcon class ship, speeder class viper, speeder class peewee, and hawke class corvette.

tap•pin \ tap-pin \ *n* : a small domesticated cat-like mammal with fangs and three tails, indigenous to Iota Hor-2

¹teck \ tek \ *n* : a permanent genetic change induced through nano-technology developed by Eosians by acting at the DNA level

²teck \ tek \ *vb* : the act of applying a teck, usually done by a qualified nano-genetics doctor

To•can \ tō-can \ *n* : a rare insect-like creature indigenous to the Upsion Andromedae system from whose larvae a natural protein fibre is spun to create the shimmering tocanai fabric used in the creation of expensive suits

To•ca•nai \ tō-can-aē \ *n* : the name give to the fabric produced from the fibre spun from the tocan larva

Tree Cult of Earth \ trē cəlt of ərth \ *n* : see Order of the Sacred Tree

U•ly•sses \ eu-lis-sēz \ *n* : a space station built by Zeta Corp Aeronotics of Earth; a self-sufficient long term agrarian colony in the vein of an O'Neill Colony with a set of large rotating cylinders many kilometres long and thousands of meters across with large gimballed mirrors; the station maintains a circular motion of 1 rpm to create artificial gravity

Ve•nik \ Ve-nik \ *n* : a large reptilian-like scaled creature from the HD177830 system with indolent eyes with several sets of arms with poisonous claws and "mouths" or orifices; Veniks are known for their violent and unprincipled nature; they are one of the few species that still actively trade in slaves

vish•na \ vish-nä \ *n* : a species of tree with thorns and violet flowers, thought to be sentient and linked to an ancient soul, of unknown origin but currently found as the major component of Eosian and Earth forest ecosystems. The tree forms the basis of the belief by the Order of the

Sacred Tree of the coming of a messiah who will bring balance needed to begin a new age of enlightenment and peace

viz•ion \ viz-ēôn \ *n* **1** : a small very strong and tenacious mammalian creature of unknown origin *adj* **2** : a term used to describe a powerful grip based on the vizion

Vos \ Vôs \ *n* : presumed extragalactic war-like species of which very little is known

wa•kesh root \ wä-kesh root \ *n* : edible root, indigenous to the planet Sekmet, with strong psychoactive properties

Weep•ing Moun•tains \ wēpēng Mountənz \ *n* : extremely steep and jagged mountains that define and surround the Boiling Seas of the planet Horus (47 Uma a). Microbes, created in the mountains and coat the surface of the Boiling Sea, excrete a narcotic oil (shallik oil) that numbs and hypnotizes prey

Xhix \ ziks \ *n* : a chameleon-like species with multiple eyes capable of wide wave-length vision and changeable skin according to mood, indigenous to the 37 Geminorum system

Zeas Cor•por•a•tion \ zēss cōr-pōr-ā-shän \ *n* : a galactic trading company specializing in exotic foods and merchandize

Ze•ta•Corp Aer•o•nau•tics \ ze-ta-cōrp ā-rō-nô-tics \ *n* : a galactic ship builder from Earth. Maker of alpha class twin-V wing, scythe-wing, delta class shadow, shadow tracker, beta class dauntless, Class A and B fugitives, seed phantom, and scimitar class shuttle.

Phonetic symbols based on *Merriam Webster's Collegiate Dictionary* and the *Dictionary of Pronunciation* by Abraham Lass and Betty Lass.

Nina Munteanu is a Canadian ecologist and novelist. In addition to five published novels, she has authored award-winning short stories, articles and non-fiction books, which have been translated into several languages throughout the world. Recognition for her work includes the *Midwest Book Review Reader's Choice Award*, finalist for *Foreword Magazine's Book of the Year Award*, the *SLF Fountain Award*, and the *Aurora Award*, Canada's top prize in science fiction.

Nina is contributing author of Suite 101 and served as assistant editor-in-chief of *Imagikon*, a Romanian speculative magazine. She currently serves as editor-in-chief of DL Publishing in Palm Coast, Florida. Nina regularly publishes reviews and essays in magazines such as *The New York Review of Science Fiction* and *Strange Horizons*, and serves as staff writer for several online and print magazines.

Nina lectured for over twenty years at colleges and universities, where she taught ecology, limnology & environmental education and published papers in scientific journals. Nina has been providing personal coaching and group workshops for writers on all aspects of writing and publishing in fiction and non-fiction venues for over ten years. Nina's guidebook, The Fiction Writer: Get Published, Write Now! has been adopted by schools and universities across North America and forms the basis of many of her workshops. Her award-winning blog *The Alien Next Door* hosts lively discussion on science, travel, pop culture, writing and movies. Visit www.ninamunteanu.com to find her teaching DVDs, webinars through Writer's Digest University and other teaching materials or to sign on for personal coaching.

www.ingramcontent.com/pod-product-compliance
Lightning Source LLC
Chambersburg PA
CBHW051636050726
47502CB00011B/557